D0728222

COLLECTING THE PIECES

COLLECTING THE PIECES

L.A. FIORE

This is a work of fiction. Names, characters, organizations, places, events, and incidents are either products of the author's imagination or are used fictitiously.

ISBN-13: 978-1537352435
ISBN-10: 1537352431

Cover Model: Franggy Yanez
Cover design by Hang Le
Editing by Editor in Heels, Trish Bacher
eBook formatting by Lisa DeSpain
Typeset graphics, title page art and paperback formatting by Melissa Stevens, The Illustrated Author, www.theillustratedauthor.net

For all those we have loved and lost

The Luckiest...Ben Folds
Stay...Rihanna
Kiss Me...Ed Sheeran
Make You Feel My Love...Adele
Take Me to Church...Hozier
Say You Love Me...Jessie Ware
Photograph...Ed Sheeran
Yours...Ella Henderson
How Long Will I Love You...Ellie Goulding
Wasted Time...Keith Urban
I'm Not The Only One...Sam Smith
Behind Blue Eyes...Who
American Boys...Halestorm
Say Something...A Great Big World
Everybody Hurts...R.E.M
The Promise...When in Rome
Animal...Neon Trees
Hot Dog...Limp Bizkit
She Talks to Angels...The Black Crowes

For some, love is like a fairytale that sweeps you off your feet and instantly turns your sorrows into joy. It's a lifetime of clear skies and smooth roads, where your dreams come true and your heart sighs. For others, love is a reckless ride—a sliding into home plate and taking that hit from the careening ball. It hurts, it cuts, and yet you go back for more because it makes you feel alive…it brings you back to life. Regardless of what love you find, the simple act of loving has the power to fix the broken, to lift the fallen and to light the dark. A gift of the heart, lost on some and taken for granted by others, but for those of us lucky enough to appreciate the beauty of it, it's the glue that takes all the pieces of ourselves and makes us whole.

then

Sometimes we find a love that we've wished for, a love that is beautiful and pure that heals our hurts and fills the emptiness.

~Sidney Ellis

chapter one

sidney

1997 · Invisible

I was left on the steps of a hospital as a baby. My birth mother, and possibly father, couldn't get away from me fast enough because they hadn't left a note explaining why they were abandoning me, nor a blanket, not even a teddy bear. In fact, they were in so much of a hurry to see the last of me that they hadn't even bothered with giving me a name. I was baby girl number three until one of the nurses named me—a person who'd cared for me for two days before never seeing me again. Sidney Ellis. At least I liked my name.

I lived in a group home in Trenton, New Jersey for the first ten years of my life. It always happened that I was either the youngest of the group or the oldest. Unlike little orphan Annie, I didn't get a family out of the strangers. To me, they were all just strangers. The people who worked in the home tried to remember birthdays, but there were just enough kids that more often than not a birthday would come and go without so much as a 'happy birthday'. And holidays? The powers that be claimed there was too much diversity among the children, which was really just their excuse to get out of celebrating any of them.

When I turned ten, I was fostered to a family and for the first time I allowed myself to imagine a family of my own. While I lay in bed, I secretly wished for a mom who would run her hand down my hair in affection. I saw that at school once from a mother dropping off her daughter and it was the loveliest thing I'd ever seen. So simple, but it was like that mom couldn't get enough of the wonder of her daughter. I wanted that. I wanted a dad who would play catch and teach me to ride a bike. And a brother or sister who just liked my company. I made all those wishes and held them in the very deepest part of me.

I was ten, but I felt a lot older. Growing up the way I did, I guess I matured faster than kids my own age. I wasn't worried about clothes and what clique of kids to hang with. I didn't agonize over if I'd get invited to the popular kid's birthday party or if my soccer team would win the championship trophy. For me, it was more where would I end up? Who would ever want me? Who would ever love me? And at ten, those questions were finally going to be answered.

The day I met my new family, Mrs. Crane, the woman who ran the group home where I lived, had found me a new outfit—a pretty yellow dress with little pink flowers all over it. I was a bit old for the dress, but she'd gone to the trouble to find it. My feet hurt in the white sandals; they weren't my size, but I made do.

A man and woman waited with Mrs. Crane when I entered her office and I felt terrible because, on first impression, they didn't look like the family of my imagination. The lady had been pretty once, her hair was long and blond and her eyes were blue, but she looked tired and unhappy, as if the world had beaten her down. The man was tall and had a stomach like Santa Claus. His hair was black but he was losing it in spots. His face held no expression, as if what was happening in that room held very little interest for him.

"Sidney, this is Mr. and Mrs. Miller."

The meeting veered further from my imagination because they

didn't immediately walk to me, smiling and reaching out a hand or offering a hug. They stayed rooted to their spots across the room and looked at me about as passionately as someone might study a tomato. Disappointment burned in my gut, but I remembered my manners. "Hi."

"Are you ready?" The lady asked.

I think I knew then that my wishes had fallen on deaf ears, but what was done was done. "Yes."

"Very well. Let's be on our way."

The man walked from the room without even saying a word with the lady following after him. Mrs. Crane, the person who had been the closest to a mother, really the only family I'd ever known, simply said, "Be happy, Sidney." And then I was forgotten, her heels clicking on the tile floor as she retreated down the hall. I stood in her office, dressed in clothes more appropriate for someone much younger than me, and felt totally and completely invisible.

The Millers were farther down the hall by the time I walked from Mrs. Crane's office, still walking toward the exit. Not once did they look back to see if I was coming. Defiance kicked in. I wanted to drag my feet, wanted to turn and walk the other way, wanted to run from the building and keep running until I found a place where I wasn't so alone. Instead, I hurried to catch up to them.

My new house was a small, pretty house on a street with other small, pretty houses in Princeton, New Jersey. As soon as I crossed the threshold, Mrs. Miller said, "Your room is the first door on the left." I waited for her to lead me upstairs, to show me around, to ease me into the life-changing transition, but she turned from me and followed after Mr. Miller.

It was a tiny room, just big enough to fit a bed, dresser and a desk. There were two windows, one that looked out to the front yard and one that faced the backyard and the woods that butted up against their property. The closet was filled with clothes; most of them looked worn, but they were for me. Based on what I'd seen so far of the Millers, I suspected the clothes were there because they were required—a mandatory checklist that had to be completed prior to me moving in—since it didn't seem likely they would have thought of it on their own.

I went in search of the Millers as hope stirred that they had only been uncomfortable earlier with the formality of the group home and Mrs. Crane, but now that they were home they would welcome me for real. The idea was one I liked so much my excitement nearly had me running down the stairs. It was a small house so it didn't take me long to find them. They didn't look like people waiting to welcome me; I had the sense they had already forgotten I was there. They had changed their clothes into sweats and both were lounging in the living room with a bottle of beer. A big bowl of chips sat on the table in front of them and the sound of the game on the television filled the small room. I stood there not sure what to do because though they knew I was there, neither acknowledged me.

Mrs. Miller finally looked over as she brought the bottle to her lips. She took a long drink then said, "There are frozen dinners in the freezer and soda in the fridge. Keep it down so we can hear the game." The words had barely passed her lips before her attention moved back to the television.

I walked back to my room and resisted the urge to slam the door behind me. I tried to keep the tears from falling as I settled on the edge of the bed, but they welled up and over my lids anyway. A knock at my door startled me.

"Sorry for just coming in, but you have to be hungry." It was a boy; he was older than me and he carried a tray with frozen dinners and soda. "Sidney, right?"

"Yeah."

"I'm Connor. Are you hungry?"

My stomach answered for me. He smiled and placed the tray on the dresser before handing me one of the dinners. He took the other and sat with me on my bed. "Not what you were expecting, huh?"

I didn't answer; I just stared down at the macaroni and cheese in the little black plastic tray.

"I know you're scared, but it does get better." He moved so he could see my downcast eyes. "It really does get better."

"Are they like that all the time?"

"Yeah, we're a paycheck." He sounded mad when he said that.

"A paycheck?"

"They get money from the state to foster us. We're a paycheck. Most foster parents aren't like that, but the Millers are in it for the money. But it could be worse. They don't yell and they don't make demands. There's always frozen dinners and soda. I'll show you around the kitchen tomorrow after school. You'll get used to it, trust me."

And I did. I didn't get the mom and dad I had hoped for, but I did get the brother, and he was even better than the one I imagined.

"Sidney, hand me that wrench." Connor's oil-covered hand shot out from under the car. He was turning sixteen, was getting his license soon and had bought himself a car. I think calling the hunk of metal he was currently working on a car was a leap, but he was in love. It had cost him a thousand dollars—all those hours at the Circle Market stocking shelves had paid off. The Millers had agreed to add him to their insurance policy, but only if he paid the difference the addition of him added. They gave nothing without getting something back.

It had been two years since I had come to live here and even with the Millers being completely uninvolved in my life, those two years were still the best I'd ever had.

Connor slid out from under the car. His overalls were stained from the various fluids leaking from what I believed, based on his swearing, were important components of the car. He was convinced he could get his baby purring, his words. I had my doubts, but when he climbed in and keyed the engine, it turned over with only the smallest billow of smoke coming out of the tail pipe.

His face split into the widest of grins. "Success."

"I can't believe you got this hunk of...I mean car working."

"Careful, Sidney, or I won't take you to the beach."

"The beach? Seriously, we're going to beach?" I had never been, but I so wanted to ride the waves.

"Yeah, first trip in the car after I get my license. We'll spend the whole day in the water and we'll stuff our faces with funnel cakes. We can even build sand castles if you want."

"I'd like that."

"With a car, we're only limited by our imaginations. The world just got a little bit bigger for us, Sidney. And one day, this place will just be a bad memory."

"It hasn't been all bad. I got you."

He turned from me, not because he didn't feel the same, but because he did and had trouble sometimes showing it. He shut off the engine and glanced back at me. "It's the same for me."

"I know."

"All right, it's time to wash my baby. You in?"

"Yep. I'll get the bucket and sponge."

I hadn't gone far when he added, "Thanks for helping. This wouldn't have been anywhere near as fun without you."

My heart felt so full it should have cracked through my ribs. I smiled then said, "You might feel differently when you're soaked to the bone."

"Bring it on, little sis, I don't sweat you."

Yep, he was even better than the brother of my imagination.

2002 · Butterflies

I spent an unusual amount of time getting ready for school because not only was it my birthday, but I was starting high school. A freshman. Nervousness had me brushing my hair again even though I'd already brushed it until my scalp hurt. Looking in the mirror, I studied my features but they looked as they always did. Nothing spectacular. My hair was brown, hints of gold in the brown, but still brown—the same color as my eyes.

In the five years that I'd been living with the Millers, it was all much of the same with them. Two more disconnected and uninterested people never existed. Sometimes I wanted people to know just how horrible they were as foster parents, because neglect was still abuse, but I had Connor and fear of them separating us kept me silent, because what had changed was me. I was no longer the lonely and empty girl I had been, and all because one person showed me kindness and love. Connor was my family and that was enough to start the healing. It wasn't the same for him. In the last three years I had started noticing a change in him. He loved me, I knew that, but it was like he hated himself. We had similar backgrounds and knowing I wasn't enough to help him find his way hurt. Watching him turn that anger into reckless behavior hurt more. And the fact that no one but me saw the change in Connor, that he was still invisible, gutted. My hope was that Connor would find that person that would heal his hurt. It was something I wished for every night.

I often walked in the woods behind the Miller's house and that was where I discovered what I wanted to do with my life. I'd found several stray cats and they reminded me of me—discarded and unwanted. Unlike me, I wanted to find them loving homes, so I worked with the vet in town, Dr. Livingston, and we had for all but two. Those two I'd named Tigger and Stuart and fed them everyday with food provided to me by Dr. Livingston. His office became like a second home, not that I really had a first one, and I absorbed every part of what he did like a sponge. We'd talked about me becoming a vet, even knowing it required lots of schooling, which cost tons of money, but he said I had the passion for it so the rest could be figured out. When it was time, he offered to help me with applying for schools.

"We've got to go, Sidney." Connor called from the hall. He was driving me to school today, though I wouldn't count on a ride every morning because Connor's attendance at school was iffy at best. But getting a ride for my first day of high school was definitely cool.

"Coming."

Grabbing my backpack, I ran from my room and flew down the stairs. Climbing into the passenger seat, Connor already had the car idling. My eyes met his and he grinned as he handed me a donut with a candle in it. "Happy birthday, Sid."

The Millers might not recognize birthdays, but Connor and I did. "Thank you."

"Are you ready for high school?"

"No."

"You'll be fine. And if not, I'll be there."

The high school was massive; a single-level brick building that sprawled out for as far as the eye could see. The parking lot was filled as kids walked in groups toward the entrance, though no one seemed in any great hurry.

As soon as Connor climbed from the car, his focus moved behind us and instantly he changed. His usual laid back easiness turned guarded. "There's someone I need to talk to. I'll catch you after school."

And off he went before I had a chance to respond. Curious about whom he needed to see, I didn't move and watched as Connor approached some guy at the back of the lot. He was leaning against a fancy silver car and had several other kids huddled around him. He looked too old for high school and was in serious need of a shower. He greeted Connor like a close friend, though I'd never seen him before. Not that Connor's friends made a habit of coming to the house.

Turning from Connor, I headed for the door and had just reached it when a sporty, black car drove past. Tracking the car, it parked as about a dozen kids moved toward it. When the driver climbed out, he was greeted like a celebrity. He was a distance from me, but there was no denying the boy was hot. Short, spiky brown hair and a body that was honed to perfection. There were girls inching closer to him, all trying to gain his attention over the others who were doing the same. And the guy, he took it all in stride. I'd expect arrogance, or at the least cockiness, and maybe he was, but his body language told a different story. He looked a bit uncomfortable with all the attention and yet resigned to it. I wondered who he was, but then the bell sounded and I turned and hurried inside. I didn't want to be late for my first day.

I was late for my first day, detained by a broken locker. Once I spied that my locker was not in working order, I headed to homeroom and was immediately sent to the office where a maintenance guy waited for me. Homeroom was almost over by the time he finished fixing the lock and as I unloaded my books and checked my schedule, the sound of voices came from farther down the hall. Glancing at the approaching people, I recognized one immediately. It was the sexy guy from the parking lot. He was with another guy, both pretty buff for high school kids, which clued me in that they were likely jocks. Up close, I had to change my opinion of him. He wasn't merely hot; he was beautiful. He probably had every girl in the school chasing after him because after just one look, he fascinated me—a condition felt by countless others before me I was sure.

He approached, seemingly lost in conversation, but as he grew closer his focus shifted to me. I held my breath, but I wasn't sure if I did so because I was afraid to lose his attention or draw more of it. And as he stared, the intensity of those dark brown eyes caused goosebumps to break out over my skin. A slight smile touched his lips before his gaze moved down my body in a leisurely study, as if he had all the time in the world. He walked past and yet his head turned to keep me in his sights. And me, I just stared back. My portrayal of a dimwit was cut short when he winked at me. Yep, he winked and in response my heart dropped into my stomach. He disappeared around the corner while I worked on remembering how to breathe. My body felt funny, like I didn't have any control over it. Like I'd been on a roller coaster and my equilibrium was off. Grabbing my books, I closed up my locker and started down the hall just as the bell rang. The hall immediately filled with bodies, but I didn't see any of them. I had wished that someone would see me; never in my wildest dreams would I have dared to wish for it to be someone like him.

Sitting in biology class, I studied the Bunsen burner while dreading who would be assigned as my lab partner. There were a few cute guys in my class, not like the guy from the hall, but cute enough to make me feel self-conscious. I tended to get klutzy when I felt self-conscious. I'd make a fool of myself if I were teamed up with one of them. Being cool was not something I did well. I heard the teacher call my name and waited in dread before he called Rylee Doughty. A girl, a bit taller than me with wild blond hair and grass-green eyes, sashayed over. She had the biggest smile on her face as she settled on the stool to my left.

"Hey. Sidney right?"

"Yeah. Hi."

"Man, I'm glad I was teamed up with you. I'd be all thumbs if I got one of them," she said as she tilted her head in the direction of the cute boys in the football jerseys.

I couldn't help the chuckle because talk about uncanny. "I was thinking the same thing."

"Hard not to with half of the junior varsity football team in our class. Now we can be cute from afar."

I suspected the boys would have really liked being partnered with her. Most of them were already staring at her, hitting each other in the arms and grinning.

"The teacher broke a few hearts when he assigned you to me." Her head jerked in my direction. Her eyes assessing before she broke out into laughter.

"You're funny."

I hadn't been teasing, but I didn't correct her.

"So, tell me about yourself, Sidney? Brothers, particularly older and really cute?"

"I have one brother, Connor."

"Connor Reid?"

"Yeah."

"But your last name is Ellis."

"We're foster kids."

"Ah. So you live under the same roof as Connor Reid. What's that like?"

"I've known him since I was ten, so much like a typical brother/sister relationship I would imagine."

"So you haven't spied on him in the shower?"

Oh my God, I'd rather go blind. "No, that's gross."

"Connor Reid is not gross."

"Connor, my brother, seeing naked. Yeah, definitely gross."

"I'm thinking we should have sleepovers at your house…often."

I laughed even suspecting that Rylee wasn't trying to be funny, but thinking of Connor in any way other than brotherly was foreign to me. I wasn't surprised to discover he had a fan club though, because I could appreciate that he was very cute even being my brother.

"And you, any hot brothers I should know about?"

"I'm an only child and extremely spoiled."

I couldn't tell if she was teasing or being serious.

She added, "I really am spoiled, but I try not to be too pricey. My parents are older, they dote over me."

She said that as if it explained things. She even sounded a little embarrassed by it, but the idea of doting parents appealed to me coming from a home where things were quite the opposite. She seemed to pick up on what I didn't say when she asked, "Not great at home, huh?"

"Doting is just not something Connor or I have experience with."

"I'm sorry."

I shrugged since how else could I reply?

"I think this is going to be a good year," she said.

After that moment in the hall with the hot boy and now meeting her, I was beginning to think the same very thing.

I strolled outside after the final bell had rung. It hadn't been so terrible for a first day. I had gotten lost twice, but based on the size of the school I didn't think that was so bad. One of the kids I had asked directions from had tried to send me upstairs, but I hadn't fallen for that. Many of my fellow freshmen had from the stories I'd heard in class all day.

When I reached the parking space where Connor had parked, it was empty. I looked around for his car, but the lot was mostly cleared out and his beat-up white Pontiac wasn't there. He'd said he'd see me after school, but he must have forgotten. I didn't know my bus number, which meant I was walking home.

I headed out of the parking lot thinking about all the homework I had. It was our first day and yet every teacher assigned homework. High school was definitely different from middle school.

Music came from down the street followed shortly by the sight of a sleek, black car pulling up alongside me. It was *him*. And in response, my knees literally went weak. Who knew that knees could really do that?

The window rolled down as he leaned over the passenger seat. "Do you need a ride?"

A ride? What's a ride? *He* was asking me if I wanted a ride. In what universe would that happen? The rule of not getting into a car with a stranger popped into my head. Did he count as a stranger? And should I take into account that I really wanted to get into his car? He grinned causing a dimple to peek out on one side of his face. "I'm harmless."

Surprised that he read my hesitation so accurately I asked, "I'm that easy to read?"

"Yeah. You're a freshman?"

"You can tell?"

He smiled now, not showing teeth but enough that I discovered he had twin dimples. "A little. You're Connor Reid's little sister."

He knew who I was? How did he know who I was? Then I realized I didn't really care how he knew who I was, only that he did know who I was. "Yeah, Sidney."

"I'm Jake Stephens. Your house is pretty far, let me give you a ride."

My house was far, but that wasn't why I agreed. I just wanted to be near him, wanted to share that small space with him, wanted to breathe in the air he exhaled. Holy crap, I didn't know I had latent stalker tendencies, but if I were to take up stalking I couldn't have picked a better object of obsession. "Ah…yeah, okay. Thanks."

Leaning farther over, he opened the door. I climbed in. He waited for me to buckle up before he pulled from the curb.

"How was your first day of high school?"

"It was okay, better than I was expecting."

"Did anyone try to send you to the second floor?"

"Yes."

"Every year. You'd think it would get old, but it doesn't."

"Have you ever sent freshmen to the second floor?"

Humor-filled, chocolate brown eyes turned to me. "Of course."

I felt lightheaded, but God he was hot. "Are you a senior?"

That earned me his face; the grin that tugged at his mouth was the icing. "No, I'm a junior."

I hadn't noticed the car had stopped and didn't realize we'd reached my house until Jake turned in his seat so he was more fully facing me. I didn't want to get out of his car; I could spend the next year or two just staring at him, but staring wasn't at all cool. I reached for the door. "Thank you for the ride."

"Any time."

If only he meant it, I would so take him up on that offer. I managed to climb from the car and stay upright. Hunching down, I peeked into the window. "See ya later."

"Definitely."

How I walked down the path to my front door without face planting, I didn't know. As soon as the door closed at my back, I leaned up against it and worked to slow my heartbeat but I was smiling like an idiot.

Connor returned home an hour later and came right to my room. "I'm sorry."

"It's okay. I got a ride home."

"Yeah? From who?"

"Jake Stephens."

"Jake? Really? I'll have to thank him."

I wanted to ask him about Jake, wanted to pry from Connor's head every bit of knowledge he had on the boy, but remembering the crowd of girls that had flocked to him that morning kept me from doing so. Reading more into the ride would be foolish, so instead I asked, "So what happened to you?"

Connor dropped on my bed and linked his fingers behind his head. "I had to see a friend about something and I honestly forgot you were at school. It won't happen again."

"It's okay. I probably would have forgotten you too."

He tossed my pillow at me. "Liar."

That night when I dreamed, I dreamt of Jake Stephens. It was, hands down, the best dream I'd ever had.

Rylee and I were eating lunch outside at the tables set up just behind the cafeteria. She was catching me up on her first fourteen years, like going into detail about her various clothes and hair styles. She was a riot, just one of those people that seemed to be perpetually happy. I envied her a bit.

"I did the purple hair. My parents were not thrilled with that, so I switched it to green."

I almost choked on my sandwich. "They had a problem with purple hair but not green hair. Are you kidding?"

"No. Green they said was more organic."

"How old are your parents?"

She laughed out loud; the fact that she caught on to my subtle humor had a grin pulling at my mouth.

My attention was pulled from Rylee when I caught sight of Jake Stephens walking from the building. Butterflies went off in my stomach—a feeling of anticipation that was very heady. My crush was silly, but I didn't have any control over how I responded to him. And honestly, I liked it. I liked that my heart skipped a beat and my hands grew damp and a chill worked down my body from my head straight down to my toes. I'd never experienced that, such a visceral reaction to another person. Watching him move was like art in motion—confident and a sexy kind of grace. He wasn't someone who cowered, he knew who he was and didn't shy away from it. How I wanted him to walk over to me and say hi. To acknowledge, even in the smallest measure, that yesterday meant something to him too. And as I wished for the impossible, those eyes shifted and landed on me as if he knew I was there. His focus didn't waver as he studied me and then he smiled; the familiarity in that smile settled very comfortably in my chest.

"You know Jake Stephens?"

Reluctantly I pulled my gaze from Jake to Rylee. "I met him yesterday. He gave me a ride home."

"Jake Stephens gave you a ride home? The captain and quarterback of the football team and homecoming king gave you a ride home?"

He was the quarterback; that explained his very fine body. "Yes. Do you know him?"

"Of him, but he's never given me a ride home." She wiggled her brows and leaned her shoulder into mine.

"It was just a ride. Connor forgot me. Jake knew how far my house was."

"Just a ride, that's a pity." She was seriously a clown.

"What do you know about him?"

"Why? Are you interested?" Her eyes lit up as she scooted closer.

"I think anyone with a pulse would be interested."

"That's true enough. Let's see. His dad is some big shot on Wall Street and his mom is a caterer, but to like famous people. He had a girlfriend, but I think they broke up at the end of last year. He's nice, but not superficially nice like some of the other bozos on the football team. He doesn't pretend a conscience to get into your pants. He's just a genuinely nice guy."

I caught a glimpse of that yesterday. Turning my focus across the courtyard, Jake was sitting at a table with his back to me and he was talking to the guy next to him. And even feeling that stir in my gut the sight of him caused, my excitement faded. He was out of my league, no question about that, but it was the slim possibility, however remote, that he could walk up to me and ask me out that caused the butterflies in my stomach. But hearing about his family had that slim, and extremely remote, possibility turning into a nonexistent one. There was no way a boy like that would ever date a girl like me. As if to prove that point, the most beautiful girl approached his table—supermodel beautiful—with her posse of friends following in her wake like ladies in waiting from back in the day. She stopped at Jake's table, her face breaking out into a big smile as her hungry gaze zeroed in on him.

"I'm guessing that's the girlfriend."

Rylee's normally upbeat tone turned somber. "Yeah, that's her. I guess maybe they didn't break up."

Those butterflies, yeah, they flew away.

Nuisance

I heard they aren't together. She's still interested, but he isn't."

Jake's relationship status really didn't matter. I'd have better luck scoring a date with Brad Pitt.

"Did you hear me?" Rylee asked as she nudged me with her elbow.

"I did."

She turned from sunning herself, her eyes narrowing on me. "What's going on with you? The other day you had little blue birds flying around your head when speaking of Jake and now…nothing."

"Reality's a bitch."

"What does that mean?"

"I was in a bubble, but that bubble burst."

"Because of her?"

"No, just knowing more about where he comcs from and where I do, the expression from the wrong side of the tracks certainly applies to me."

"Because you're a foster kid?"

I wasn't going to answer her, had spent my life keeping it inside. Who was there to complain to? Connor? He was living it too. But Rylee really looked interested and the idea of venting what I'd been carrying around for so long was very appealing. "You really want to hear this?"

"Yeah."

"It isn't so much that I'm a foster kid, but the fact that my foster parents aren't really parents. I was ten when I came to live with them. On my first day, as soon as they got me home they curled up in front of the television. That was my homecoming and in the years that have followed if they've said a hundred words to me that would seem high."

Rylee looked horrified and pissed. "Are you kidding?"

"No. I've never celebrated my birthday, never experienced Thanksgiving or Christmas morning. I don't know my birth parents. I was dropped on the steps of a hospital. The nurses were the ones who gave me my name. So in light of all of that, my crushing on Jake is ridiculous."

"Being neglected isn't a reflection on you."

"In a perfect world that would be true, but the world is far from perfect."

In a rare show of emotion, Rylee reached for my hand and squeezed it; her eyes were bright with tears. "I'm sorry, Sidney. The Millers didn't do right by you or Connor."

"Silver lining, I got Connor."

Her expression changed slightly as her lips curved up into a smile. "And what a fine silver lining he is."

There was no way I was getting to class on time. My art teacher held me up after class to review my project, but I'd forgotten that my next class was on the other side of the school. I wasn't running, but I was walking really fast and it was because I was walking really fast that I tripped over my own feet. It happened in slow motion. My books went sailing out of my arms, my hands frantically grabbing for them even as my body followed the books. I landed hard, my hands and knees breaking my fall, and damn did that hurt. After a quick inventory to confirm I hadn't broken anything, humiliation kicked in because I'd just fallen flat on my face in a hall filled with students. My hope that no one noticed was immediately dashed when laughter echoed down the corridor. If that wasn't bad enough, I couldn't flee because my binders and books were scattered across the tile floor. I kept my head down to keep anyone from seeing my face, which I was sure was as red as an apple.

I reached for my science book at the same time someone else's hand wrapped around it. Jerking my head up, my breath caught seeing Jake Stephens.

"That was a pretty hard hit. Are you okay?"

My hands and knees were killing me and my ego had taken a catastrophic hit, but I didn't say as much to him. "Yeah, I'm okay." I reached for my book. "Thanks for..." I was too humiliated to finish the thought.

"Sure."

He stood at the same time he reached his hand down to me. For a minute, I just stared at his hand and even knowing better, those damn butterflies started flapping around. As soon as I put my hand in his, heat sparked to life where our skin touched—a heat that seared right up my arm.

"What class do you have now?" He asked as we stood before he released my hand, which had the heat fading at the loss of his touch.

"Science."

"You're not going to make that before the bell rings."

"I know."

"I'll take you to the nurse. You can get a note from her."

"That's okay, I'll risk it."

"Come on. It's only the second week of school. You don't want to earn a reputation for being tardy so early in your high school career."

He said that in the most exaggerated way that my lips cracked into a smile. "If you walk me to the nurse, you're going to be late for class too."

"I'll get the nurse to write me a commendation on my chivalry."

I couldn't believe I wanted to laugh during what was the most embarrassing moment of my life. "I'll be sure to embellish on your good deed. Maybe they'll erect a statue in your honor in the courtyard."

"Now you're talking."

We hadn't taken many steps when Jake's head dipped, his eyes studying my face. "You're in pain."

"Maybe a little."

"How hard did you hit?"

"Hard enough."

"I'd carry you to the nurse, but I suspect you would expire from embarrassment if I did."

"You would be right about that."

"Is that me or just guys in general?"

Doubly so for him because even dying of embarrassment, I would die a very happy girl. "I think I should save my Scarlett O'Hara moment until I've been here for at least a month."

The sight of those dimples did strange and magical things to my insides. "Good thinking."

We reached the nurse's office and Jake held the door for me. "See you later, Scarlett."

He flashed me a smile before he strolled down the hall. It wasn't until I was sitting in science class later that I realized he never got his pass from the nurse.

The following day at school as I swapped out my books at my locker my thoughts were on Jake. I didn't understand why I had his attention, but I loved that I had his attention. Just thinking about him made my heart race. Never had I been eager to get to school and now I hated when the school day was over. Just the idea that I'd see him, even if it was just a glance in the hall, filled me with the headiest sense of anticipation. As if my thoughts conjured him, I shut my locker, turned and almost walked right into him. And what a sight he made, leaning against the lockers with his hands in the front pockets of his jeans.

His lips curved up before he said, "Hi."

I hadn't noticed in the two previous encounters I had had with him, but his eyes weren't just brown, there were flecks of green in them. I was staring; really I was looking in wonder probably a lot like how Harry Potter looked when seeing Hogwarts for the first time, but Jake was at my locker smiling at me. There was a good chance I might throw up. His smile grew wider and I realized I hadn't said anything. I did not dazzle him with my wit when I replied, "Hey, you didn't get a pass from the nurse yesterday. What did your teacher say?"

He leaned closer and lowered his voice as if what he had to say was private and for my ears only. "Nothing."

I was feeling a bit lightheaded being that close to him, so it took a minute for his answer to sink in. There was a sparkle of mischievousness burning in those brown eyes. "Nothing?"

"It was study hall and Mr. Lawson is always ten minutes late. Does that lose me some chivalry points?"

"I'm not sure."

He laughed and the sound just washed over me. "Honest, I like that. So what class do you have now?"

"English."

"I'll walk with you."

"Study hall again?"

"No."

"So you're risking being late for your class so you can walk me to mine. Why?"

He didn't say anything at first, just sort of looked at me with an intensity I really liked. "I can't stop thinking about you."

He did NOT just say that. As much as I wanted to jump up and down in joy, I instead tried for humor just in case I was reading more into it. "You can't stop thinking about my graceful face-plant?"

He leaned even closer, so close that if I moved just an inch my lips would be on his. "I hate to tell you this, but your face-plant wasn't at all graceful."

Lack of blood to my brain had it taking a few seconds longer to process his words. Tease.

He didn't wait for me to accept his invitation, taking my lack of answer as a yes, and started down the hall. "Have you always lived in the area?"

His question came as a reality slap, the unpleasant reminder of how so very different we were, but why not enjoy his attention while I had it. "I've lived here since I was ten."

"So how the hell did I never see you in school before this?"

That was easy. I was utterly forgettable. It was only this past summer that my body started taking on the shape of a woman and even still, I looked more like a board. I wasn't about to say that though, so I stayed quiet.

"You're gorgeous and we were in middle school together. I don't understand how I never saw you."

Gorgeous? Did he just say I was gorgeous? My jaw might have dropped, but really gorgeous?

"I don't plan on making that mistake a second time. If you don't want my attention, say it now because I plan on making a nuisance of myself."

The urge to look around to see who had put him up to this was strong. Or maybe I was daydreaming.

"What about your girlfriend?"

He looked sincerely confused. "Who? Allison? I broke it off with her last year." He moved into me, his big body crowding mine and I so didn't have a problem with that. "How'd you know about Allison? Have you been asking around about me, Sidney?"

I chalked up what happened next as a result of having him in my personal space. My mouth opened and the truth came pouring out. "Yeah."

A sound came from the back of his throat, the single sexiest sound I'd ever heard. "Tell me now to back off or I'm taking your silence as an all clear."

I'd never had anything I could call my own and here was this incredible guy asking if he could spend time with me. And I knew we were like night and day—came from such different worlds—but for the first time in my life, I let myself believe in the dream. "I'd like to see you being a nuisance."

"And there's my green light. Sweet."

I sat alone at lunch trying and failing to not obsess over the conversation with Jake from yesterday. He wanted to be a nuisance, oh my God, I so wanted him to be a nuisance. Rylee wasn't at lunch because the drama club was holding their first meeting. She tried to get me to join, but not only did I have zero acting talent, but crowds terrified me. Connor had the same lunch period; we had seen each other in line. I had hoped we could eat together, but he joined his friends at a table on the other side of the courtyard. I was a freshman and he was a senior, but it still hurt that he didn't include me.

Someone settled on the bench next to me. His body brushed up against mine and I knew it was Jake from the way my body responded.

"Can I join you?"

Like he had to ask and still I teased, "Don't people usually ask that before they sit down?"

"Just making it harder for you to say no."

"Why do you think I'd say no?"

"I can't quite read you, so I'm not taking any chances. There's a bonfire tonight at Carpenter's Field. Are you going?"

A bonfire. That sounded like fun. "This is the first I'm hearing of it."

"It's tradition. The Carpenter's have a bonfire the second weekend of school."

"Where's Carpenter Field?"

"The other side of town."

It sounded like fun, but I had no way to get there. And with how flighty Connor had been acting, he'd likely drop me off and forget about me. Walking twenty miles home held no appeal.

"Probably not."

"Why not?"

"I don't have a way to get there and I can't really count on Connor to remember to pick me up."

"Come with me."

Every part of me liked this plan, but I didn't like crowds. I was awkward and a freshman and he was a very popular guy. I didn't see good things coming out of that perfect storm of trouble.

"I'm not really great in crowds."

"We'll avoid them."

"I don't imagine you have much luck avoiding crowds."

Dipping his chin, he studied me for a second or two. "Why do you say that?"

"I saw you the first day of school and the crowd that circled your car when you parked."

"You were checking me out?"

Oh yes I was and drooling. "I was checking out your car."

"My car, okay we'll go with the car."

I should be embarrassed, him calling my bluff, but I wasn't. And how I could be so calm in his presence baffled me.

"Please come with me. And before you ask why, this is me being a nuisance. If you don't like crowds, we'll avoid them. But I want to see you tonight. Say yes."

How the hell did I say no to that? "Okay."

"I'll pick you up at six." He reached for his pizza and I sat transfixed as he brought it to his lips, so when he spoke again it took a minute for his words to penetrate my hazy brain. "You feel it too, don't you, Sidney?"

There was something in the way he asked that question. With a seriousness I hadn't yet experienced with him, so I answered honestly. "Yes."

Jake arrived exactly at six, and a half an hour later we were settled in chairs that were close to the bonfire but not right by the logs that were setup as benches. It was dark, people would have trouble seeing us if they didn't know we were there. I felt bad forcing him to be in the shadows and as much as I really didn't like crowds, I'd suffer through them for him.

"We can move closer if you want. I feel badly that you're not with your friends."

"You'd move closer for me?"

"Yes."

"Thanks, but I'm very happy right here. So what do you think of the bonfire?"

"It's beautiful. He does this every year?"

"Yeah, his way of kicking off the football season."

"Are you hoping to get a scholarship for football?"

"No. I like playing and I'm decent, but I don't think scholarship level good."

"From what I've heard, you might be wrong about that. Kids talk, teachers talk. Is it weird having people discuss you when you're not even around?"

"It's not really me, it's the player, the position. People love their football. It all comes with the territory. I don't mind it, maybe more so because it isn't what I want to do with my life. It's just a hobby that I happen to really enjoy." He then lowered his head and shook it slightly.

Why he did that, I hadn't a clue and even afraid of the answer I asked, "What's wrong?"

His head lifted, his eyes finding mine; the change in him confused me until he said, "We've only just met and yet it feels like we've known each other so much longer. How's that possible?"

I understood. I should be a blubbering fool around him, but for some reason he didn't make me feel self-conscious or nervous. It was easy, comfortable and we hardly knew each other. "I don't know. I'm usually tongue-tied and awkward around people, I don't feel that way around you."

"Good. Now tell me about Sidney Ellis."

I hesitated sharing my life with him, but it was my life. "As you've probably already figured out, Connor and I are foster kids. I moved in with the Millers when I was ten."

Tenderness moved over his face, his voice softly probing when he asked, "Did your parents…"

"Die? No, I never knew them. I spent the first ten years in a group home before the Millers decided to foster me."

"And how's that been?"

"Do you know the Millers?"

"A little."

"They're not very active parents."

"Meaning?" There was an edge of anger in his voice.

"They do their thing, we do ours. We're under the same roof, but that's where the family bond ends."

"That's fucked up."

"I'm used to it."

He touched my cheek, a delicate swipe of his thumb. "Maybe, doesn't change the fact that it's fucked up."

Sidney · Belonging

Connor sat out back smoking. I pulled up a chair and settled next to him. His head turned in my direction, his eyes going from me to his cigarette.

"I know. It's a terrible habit."

"So why are you doing it?"

He shrugged, his focus shifting to the woods behind our house. "I fed your cats."

"Thanks."

"I can't wait to get out of here."

"Me too. Does that make us bad people?"

His head snapped to me. "Why would that make us bad people?"

"They took us in."

"And are getting paid to do so. They didn't do this out of the kindness of their hearts, Sidney. We wouldn't be here if they weren't getting paid."

He wasn't wrong.

He shifted a bit, turning more fully in my direction. "I heard a rumor that you and Jake Stephens are together."

My face went beet red. I felt the blood pooling at my cheeks. "Yeah."

"He's a good guy."

"He seems it."

"What are your plans after you graduate?"

"I want to go into veterinary medicine."

"Yeah? I think that's great."

"I love animals, love watching Dr. Livingston work and how at ease he is with his patients. What about you?"

"I want to be anywhere but here."

"Have you given any more thought to college?"

"I'm not really college material. I'm barely passing high school."

"That's nonsense. You're barely passing high school because you're hardly there."

He looked at me from the corner of his eye as his lips formed a crooked grin. "That's true."

"I saw you the other week outside the Circle Market. You were drinking. Is that smart, to do that out in the open?"

"It's a little alcohol, Sid, nothing to worry about."

I *was* worried because Connor wanted away from here but he wasn't doing anything to make that happen. "I love you, Connor. I want to see you happy."

His arm came around my shoulders. "I am happy."

But that was said with very little conviction.

The sound of the front door slamming closed had us both jerking. "Speak of the devil," Connor muttered.

I stood. "I need to start my homework before I make dinner."

"Why is it you have to make dinner? Why the hell can't she fucking boil some water?"

"They're perfectly happy with their frozen dinners, but I don't have their iron stomachs. I don't mind, I'm teaching myself to cook."

"It's still wrong." He dropped his arm around my shoulders again. "Four more years until you graduate and then you're free. Just remember that."

"You only have a year."

"And I'm counting the days."

Connor was gone when I came downstairs the following morning and that kind of hurt that he hadn't waited for me, especially after our talk yesterday. Since I wouldn't be getting a ride, I hurried out to the bus stop.

I arrived at school and found Jake standing at my locker. My feet just stopped as I stared. He hadn't seen me yet, he was talking to someone, but the sight of him at my locker was one I really liked. Especially replaying his words, which I'd been doing all weekend, about wanting to make a nuisance out of himself. His head turned and our eyes met; he left his spot to join me.

"Morning."

"Hi."

He took my backpack, his fingers running down my arm as he removed the strap, and honestly the heat stirred by that simple touch burned in a really good way. "Did you have a good weekend?"

I had spent my weekend daydreaming about him, but I wasn't about to be that candid. "I spent it doing homework."

"I spent it thinking about you."

And though he was smiling, he looked to be waiting, watching my reaction very closely. I gave him what he wanted, the truth. "I thought about you too."

"Do you have any idea how badly I want to kiss you?"

"Probably as much as I want you to kiss me."

His voice sounded a bit gruff when he asked, "What class are we walking to first?"

"Biology."

"At least it's not chemistry, we've got enough of that going on."

He wiggled his brows, lightening the mood before he added, "Dissection. You'll start with an earthworm and graduate to frogs." He cocked his head, a grin pulling at the side of his mouth. "I have a feeling that doesn't gross you out at all."

"It doesn't. I'm fascinated with biology."

"Another layer to Sidney Ellis. I'll see you to homeroom and then I'll be back to walk you to class."

"Your homeroom is two hallways over."

"I'll just have to move quickly."

I swapped out my books and shut my locker before joining him. "I don't want you to get in trouble for being late all the time."

"My teachers love me. I'll be fine. Can I join you and Rylee for lunch?"

"Like you need to ask."

"So is high school all you thought it would be?"

"I'm surprised by how much homework is assigned, but yeah, it's way better than I thought."

He moved closer, his shoulder touching mine. "Am I a part of that?"

"What? Being better?"

"Yeah."

"You know that you are."

He reached for my hand, something so simple and yet my breath caught. It was a first for me, having my hand held. His big, calloused hand enveloped mine and it felt so perfectly right. Doubt wiggled in because I still didn't understand his interest in me, but I didn't want to question it. I just wanted to ride the wave.

He asked, "Is this okay?"

"Yeah, it's okay."

"I'm sensing a but."

I tried to dismiss his comment; he wouldn't let me.

"Sidney?"

"I just don't understand why you're with me."

He pulled me over to the lockers, his expression both incredulous and a little pissed. "Did you really just ask me that?"

Holding that intense stare was difficult, so I looked down at our hands. "Yeah."

He touched my chin to lift my gaze back to his. "Am I moving too fast?"

It wasn't the speed in which we were moving that I feared, but of him coming to his senses. Being dazzled by him only to be forgotten shortly after. Talk about setting yourself up for a nasty fall.

"No. I just don't understand why me."

"Do you want to be with me?"

"Yes."

"Then don't overthink it." He touched my cheek as his lips pulled up on the one side. "You're overthinking it. Okay, honestly, it's those big brown eyes that look wounded sometimes, a sadness that has no business clouding your expression. I want to remove that look, want to see you smiling and happy. That first day, I felt you like a punch to the gut. I want to explore this, us, because I've never felt that before."

His words moved me deeply and knocked me off-balance, so I responded with humor—a nervous response. "You probably say that to all the girls."

"Never, Sidney. I've never felt like this before. There's a game on Friday. I have to play, but I'd really like knowing you were in the stands. Will you come?"

"Yes."

"I'll pick you up, say around five?"

"A date?"

"Yeah, the first of many."

Friday arrived and as I dressed I went back and forth between excited and nervous. Connor had already left and the Millers weren't home, at least I was alone while I freaked out. The sound of the bell kicked off the butterflies in my stomach as I hurried down the stairs. I caught myself and slowed my approach, took a few deep breaths before pulling the door open.

Jake was dressed in jeans and a tee. There was a smile on his face, one that grew wider when his eyes moved down my body in a very thorough perusal. He looked past me as his smile dimmed a bit.

"Are your foster parents home?"

"No."

"Connor?"

"He already left for the game."

He had a thought on that, but whatever he was thinking he didn't share. Instead he reached for my hand. "Are you ready?"

"Yes."

We reached the stadium and parked before Jake turned in his seat. "I need to head to the locker room to change, but I've saved a spot for you and Rylee upfront. I instructed the student manager to show Rylee to your seats if he should see her. I'll show you before I join up with the team."

"I'm sure I can find it. You don't need to see me to my seat."

"Are you sure?"

"Yeah. Are you nervous?"

"To play? No. I've been doing this for so long it's like second nature."

"I've never watched a football game."

"Really?"

"Does it hurt when you get tackled?"

Cocky was how he looked now. "I rarely get sacked, but when I do the adrenaline is pumping so I don't feel much during the game. My muscles protest after I've cooled down. Come on."

I had no idea what sacked meant, but I'd ask Rylee. Jake climbed from the car and came around to my side and reached for my hand. "I want to get you settled."

"You don't have to."

"I know."

My tummy twisted and my arm tingled from the heat stirred by our joined hands.

"After the game, we can grab a bite to eat," he said as he led me into the stadium.

"You're going to feed me too?"

Wicked was how he looked in reply. We reached the bleachers; Rylee was already there. "Hey, Sidney."

"So after the game, I'll feed you."

"Sounds like a plan."

He didn't seem to want to go, his hand tightened on mine for a minute before he released it. "Don't leave."

"I won't."

"See you later."

"Good luck!"

He looked back at me from over his shoulder and winked before he jogged from the bleachers.

"Holy shit. He is so into you," Rylee squealed.

Dropping down next to her, I couldn't contain the smile since I loved hearing that, especially since I was just as into him.

"You're going out after the game too?"

"Yeah."

"Boy moves fast. I like it."

"He makes me lightheaded."

"Wait until he kisses you. You are so lucky."

I wasn't sure I'd live through him kissing me if I felt as I did just from holding his hand, and what a way to go.

The team entered the field, Jake leading them to the roar of the crowd. He reached the sidelines and searched for me in the stands. As soon as our eyes met, he smiled.

"You just made every girl in this stadium jealous," Rylee muttered next to me.

And I didn't care because that smile, I'd wrapped it up and stored it away so I could replay it whenever I wanted.

I watched the game, the first time I ever did. It was addicting and even being new to the sport I could tell that Jake was an exceptionally good quarterback. The team won, the cheering people were on their feet in the stands. Jake moved from the field and climbed through the railing, taking the steps two at a time, to reach me. Right in front of the entire stadium, he pulled me to my feet and kissed me. It was just a brushing of our lips at first, but then I heard him growl deep in his throat before he opened his mouth, his tongue darting out to push past my lips. And even as the crowd roared louder, I just melted into him because nothing had ever felt so right.

He pulled his mouth from mine; his heart pounded and his breathing was erratic. "I need a shower. I'll be fast."

"Okay."

"Wait for me."

"I'll wait."

His lips brushed along my jaw ending at my ear. "I want to kiss you again."

"I really want that too."

"Wait here. Don't move."

"My feet are rooted."

He touched my chin, rubbing his thumb along my lower lip. "I'll be right back."

"I'll be here."

He grinned and then ran back down the bleachers.

"Was that as hot as it looked?" Rylee asked.

"Hotter."

"I need a cold shower. I was here for the beginning," Rylee said.

"What?"

"Some people you just know are going to make it, that they are meant to be. You two, you're meant to be and I was here for the beginning."

After the game, Jake and I had burgers at a popular hot spot. I had trouble eating because I couldn't stop staring across the table. I was on a date with Jake Stephens and what really left me breathless was how perfectly right it felt.

"Aren't you hungry?" Jake asked.

"I'm fine. It was a good game, at least it looked good to me."

"Yeah, we were pretty tight tonight."

Heat burned up my neck thinking about after the game and the kiss he laid on me in front of the entire stadium.

"That was my first kiss." I couldn't believe I blurted it out like that. Mortified, I lowered my head.

He touched my chin and lifted my gaze. "Seriously?"

"Yeah. It was…incredible."

His expression surprised me. He looked upset. "I didn't know. I wouldn't have done it in front of all those people. I'm sorry, Sid."

"Why? It's already stored as my favorite memory ever."

"Your first kiss should have been private and more memorable."

"More memorable? You kissed me in front of a stadium full of people. It was memorable, believe me."

"You're not mad?"

"That the hottest guy in school, who just won the opening season game, kissed me in front of all those people? No."

He leaned closer, his face washed with humor. "So I can make that a tradition, kissing you in the stands after we win."

"You won't get any arguments from me."

"Sweet."

We were jarred from the moment when someone slammed up against the window. It was Connor and he looked drunk.

"Oh God," I whispered just as Jake moved from the booth.

"Wait here."

"I should help."

"He's drunk, Sid, please stay here."

"Okay."

Jake stepped outside. Connor walked over to him, really stumbled toward him. It wasn't a long conversation; Jake helped get Connor in the car. Connor's girlfriend, who looked to be sober, climbed behind the wheel. Jake waited until they were on their way before he returned to me.

"Drunk?"

"And high," Jake said as he settled in the booth.

"I'm worried about him."

"We'll keep our eyes on him. He's a senior and it could be nothing more than sowing his oats."

"Maybe, but I think he's getting worse."

"If he does, we'll get him help."

"You would help me?"

"Absolutely. He's important to you and you are important to me."

I lost my heart to him in that moment.

"Let's finish up here because I really want to kiss you again."

"This is Tigger and this is Stuart." It had been two days since my first kiss and still my lips tingled from the memory of it. I felt the need to share all I could with Jake. I wanted him entwined in every part of my life, but I didn't have much going on in my life. I did have my cats though.

"How long have you been caring for them?"

"A couple years."

"They seem very comfortable around you."

"I'd like to believe we have a bond, but I am the one who feeds them so it could be as simple as that."

"I don't think so. Why don't you bring them inside?"

"The Millers would never allow that."

"The Millers? Why do you call them that?"

"It's what they want us to call them, that or Kathleen and Gary."

Jake started to laugh, thinking I was joking, until he realized I was serious and then his expression turned dark. "You're not kidding."

"I wish I were."

"Unbelievable."

"Anyway, I just wanted you to meet the two other men in my life."

He yanked me to him, pressing my body to his. It was my very favorite place to be. His fingers were moving up and down my spine in the softest caress. "I like your friends."

"I like you."

He clearly liked that answer because he kissed me, long and hard.

"How would you feel if they came to stay with me?" He asked, but I didn't answer right away since my brain was still on that kiss.

"Sid?"

"Are you serious?"

"Yeah."

"Your parents would be okay with that?"

"They love animals."

"I…that would be incredible." With the magnitude of what he was offering, taking in Tigger and Stuart and giving them a home, I threw my arms around his neck and this time it was me who kissed him long and hard.

A First

Jake's house was huge; the Millers home would fit in their garage. Of course the Stephens' garage was big enough for six cars. Jake pulled up the drive as I fiddled with my dress. It was Thanksgiving and Jake had invited me and Connor to share it with his family. Connor had backed out at the last minute, said he had to work. I had wanted him to experience Thanksgiving, a first for both of us, and was really disappointed that he bailed.

Jake parked, his focus shifting to me. "You're upset about Connor."

"I think this would have been good for him, to see there's more than what we grew up with."

"Maybe he'll join us next year."

The idea that we'd still be together next year was one I really liked. "Maybe."

"Are you nervous?"

"To meet your parents? A little."

"They're going to love you."

I wasn't so sure about that, but I smiled big and pretty when he came around to my side of the car and helped me from it. Taking my hand, he led us inside. My breath caught because his house was amazing. The foyer was done in black and white tiles. A round table that looked like an antique sat under a crystal chandelier and the vase of freshly cut flowers sitting atop that table was exquisite. The stairs were huge, starting on the left of the foyer and curving up the wall to the second floor.

"How do you not get lost in here?"

Jake laughed, but I wasn't kidding. I'd need a map.

Jake's parents appeared from one of the hallways off the foyer. His dad was tall; Jake got his build from him. Even in his forties, the man was in great shape. His brown hair was cut short with a dusting of gray. His mom was almost as tall as her husband. Her long brown hair looked like sable, wavy and full down to her shoulders. Her brown eyes had hints of green, picked up by the green wrap dress she wore.

"Sidney. How nice to finally meet you." Mrs. Stephens greeted as she reached for my hand.

"Thank you for inviting me."

"It's our pleasure. Let's move to the kitchen because we're still prepping the dishes."

A home cooked meal not made by me, what a novelty. "Can I help?"

"Absolutely. The more hands the better." Mr. Stephens said.

Their kitchen was massive. Granite countertops, stainless steel appliances, a huge butcher block kitchen island, and a pot rack over it loaded with copper pots. "Wow."

Jake's hand found my waist as he pulled me closer. "Sidney likes to cook."

And I did. At first it was out of necessity and now I just enjoyed it.

"Wonderful. She can take my spot since I haven't a clue what

I'm doing." Mr. Stephens said, but it was directed at his wife. Obviously an inside joke. "How about I get us something to drink? What would you like, Sidney? We have iced tea, soda, coffee, sparkling water."

"Iced tea, please."

"Jake, how about you help me."

Jake followed his dad to another room that looked like a pantry of some kind as Mrs. Stephens stepped up next to me. "I'm sorry your brother couldn't make it."

"I'm sorry for the last minute cancellation."

"No worries. I have most of this under control, but I haven't finished with the bread. Would you like to help?"

"You bake your own bread?"

"Yes. I'm guessing you've never tried."

"No, but I'd love to learn."

"The aprons are in the closet by the refrigerator. Why don't you put one on, I would hate for your pretty dress to get covered in flour, and I'll teach you."

I had never had a grown-up talk to me like she did. Like I mattered. Like I was good enough to be here. I felt the tears burning the back of my eyes and my voice grew hoarse when I said, "Thank you, Mrs. Stephens."

She seemed to understand because her face grew soft as tenderness looked back at me. "You are so welcome, sweetheart."

"Your first Thanksgiving. What did you think?"

"I'll never eat again, but I loved every second of it. Thank you."

"My parents really like you." Jake said as he pulled me into his lap while we sat in his car outside my house.

"I really like them too."

"Christmas is next. What do you want for Christmas?"

"Nothing."

Jake had been brushing his lips over my shoulder, but hearing my reply he stopped. "You don't want anything?"

"I'd like for Connor to join us, but other than that no."

"Because you're not used to getting gifts?" Anger had his words sounding clipped.

"No, because I have you. I don't need anything else."

His hold on me tightened. "And you do have me, Sidney, totally and completely."

I was in my room doing homework, but I struggled with my focus since my thoughts kept veering to Jake. Five months we'd been together and every day was better than the last. I wasn't sure how I had gotten so lucky to find him, but I thanked the stars for him every night.

Flashing lights from outside reflected against my wall. I stepped to the window to see as two cops escorted Connor up the front path. The way he staggered, he was clearly under the influence. Mr. Miller knew a few of the local cops, they'd gone to school together; this was likely them doing a favor for him since, based on how he looked, Connor should have been arrested for underage drinking or drugs. Maybe this was a good thing. The Millers were home, the cops were here, maybe they'd finally get off their asses and parent Connor.

I heard Connor on the stairs before he slammed the door to his bedroom. The cops left a few minutes later followed by Mr. Miller stomping up the stairs after Connor.

"What the fuck! Where did you get the drugs?"

"Like you care."

"Pack your shit and get out."

No! How could he? At the first sign of trouble he kicked Connor out instead of trying to help him. The Millers were terrible foster parents, but this behavior bordered on criminal.

"That's fucking fine with me."

"I want you out tonight." I waited until Mr. Miller went back downstairs before I walked to Connor's room. He was packing up his stuff when I entered. His head snapped to me, fury behind his gaze until he saw who it was.

"Sidney."

"You can't leave."

"Believe me, I'm okay with this."

"But this is your home."

"This was never a home, for either of us."

"You're high and drunk all the time. They should be helping you and instead they kick you out. Where will you go?"

"I'll crash at my friend's place."

"The same friend you've been getting high with?"

Anger rolled over his face. "It's my life, Sidney."

"What kind of life is that? I hate seeing you like this."

He seemed rooted to the spot on the floor; his focus on the bag he packed. "The truth is I'm miserable here. I don't want to leave you, but I want out. And if I know you'll be okay by yourself, I'll be okay."

"Jake's parents can talk to the Millers."

Anger flashed across his face. "No. I don't need your boyfriend's parents getting involved."

"They're good people, Connor. I'd love for you to meet them."

"That's your thing, Sid, not mine."

"What is your thing? Seriously, Connor, what are you doing? You're barely getting the grades to graduate. You don't want to go to college. You aren't looking for a job that pays better and you spend your time drunk or high. What's your plan?"

"Whatever the fuck I want. It's my life, Sidney, to live as I choose."

"But you aren't living it."

"Sure I am."

"Partying is not living."

"The hell it's not. I'm having fun."

"And if I were to ask the Stephenses to talk with you—"

"I would be really fucking pissed and since you're the one thing in my life I love, I'd hate for that wall to go up."

"And as your sister who loves you, my only option is to sit back and watch you ruin your life."

"I'm hardly ruining it. It's a phase. I'll move past it eventually."

"I hope so."

"I know so. So you'll be okay here alone?"

"I'll be fine. I'm rarely here anyway."

"Yeah, off with Jake. I like him for you. He's a good guy."

"I'm going to miss you."

He walked to me and pulled me close. "I'm going to miss you too."

Jake and his dad were at a game so Mrs. Stephens had suggested she and I go to the mall for a day of shopping and lunch. It was another first for me and even being nervous and a bit uncomfortable, I also felt a lightness in my chest I had never experienced before. Guilt lingered there too, knowing that I had the Stephenses and Connor had no one. Not that he was helping with that because it had been over a month since he'd been kicked out, but he wasn't taking my calls.

When Jake learned about Connor, he'd been livid; he had wanted to go to his parents, but I explained Connor's reaction to my suggestion of doing just that. I hoped that Connor was finding happy and was moving away from all the partying.

Mrs. Stephens and I were in Neiman Marcus; she was going through a rack of party dresses because they were hosting a garden party. Spring was in the air.

"What do you think of this?" She held up the prettiest, pale pink dress with spaghetti straps, fitted at the waist before ending at the ankles in a full skirt.

"It's beautiful."

"Why don't you try it on?"

"Me?"

"This color against your skin tone would be exquisite." Lowering the dress, she studied me. "Unless you don't like it."

"I do. I love it, but I thought we were looking for something for you."

Her voice grew soft. "I've never had someone to shop with. I love Jake, but shopping for girls is so much more fun. It's a first for me, Sidney, being able to spend the day looking at girlie things, having lunch, maybe getting our nails done."

My chest grew tight and my eyes burned because despite her words, I knew this day was about more than that. She was sharing with me something most girls shared with their moms. And knowing she cared, that she wanted to give me a piece of normal, she went from being just Jake's mom in that moment to an actual mom to me.

Feeling too overwhelmed to say much I reached for the dress. "Where's the dressing room?"

Understanding filled her expression of just how much this day meant to me, and then she said, "We'll check out shoes next."

It was my sweet sixteen. School would be starting in a few days. Jake's senior year. I was in my room staring at the pink roses Rylee had sent me. The fact that she remembered it was my birthday, when it had been discussed once in a conversation we had last year, touched me. And the roses, I had never before received flowers, and these were gorgeous. I cried when I called to thank her, but she understood. Unlike in years past, Connor was not around to celebrate my birthday. I missed him, didn't see him nearly enough. We talked occasionally, but not as often as I'd like. I hated that he was alone and despite his words, I knew it hurt him to be kicked out of the only home he had ever known. The friend he was staying with was a bit wild and I had heard through the grapevine that Connor was doing as he'd said, partying hard. I just hoped he eventually partied himself out and grew up.

The knock at the door had me jumping up since I thought it was Connor. Instead it was Jake standing on the front stoop.

"Turn around." He said in way of greeting.

"Why?"

"Just do it."

As soon as I turned my back to him, he covered my eyes with a silk cloth. "What are you doing?"

"It's a surprise."

He led me from my house into his car.

"Jake?"

"It's a short ride."

We climbed from the car. "Not long now."

When we reached our destination, he removed the blindfold. We were in his parent's kitchen and sitting on the island was a birthday cake and next to it was a brightly wrapped present. Happiness so profound had tears running down my face.

"Happy birthday."

"How did you know?"

"I have my ways. Why didn't you tell me?"

"I don't usually celebrate my birthday."

His jaw clenched and his easy demeanor turned hard, but he shook it off and moved toward me. "Sweet sixteen," he said as he pulled me into his arms and kissed me.

"We should have cake." Though based on the gruffness of his voice cake was the last thing he wanted. And boy did I understand that.

"Right, cake. Good idea."

His fingers threaded through my hair as he pulled my mouth to his. "I should clarify. I'll settle for cake."

He took a lighter from his pocket, lit the candles and sang happy birthday to me. And then we had cake, delicious cake, but what I loved most about the moment was sharing my first birthday cake with Jake.

"Open your present."

My fingers shook a bit, but this was another first for me. I unwrapped the box and inside was Jake's football jersey. I had asked for one, told him I wanted to wear his name on my back. He remembered. "I love it."

"My parents are making dinner for you tonight."

"You're spoiling me, which will make it so hard next year when you're gone."

"Yeah about that. I'm not leaving you."

"Of course you are, but if it works out I'll join you when I graduate."

"Not going without you. I'm deferring my enrollment."

"And your parents?"

"They'd like for me to matriculate in the fall, but they understand why I don't want to. I've laid out my plan for them, they see how serious I am and how much thought I've put into it."

"I'm not going to lie. The idea of you staying here, that I get more time with you, I love that."

"Good." But he said that in relief as if I would have an objection to him wanting to stay with me. How had I gotten so lucky? "I want the day with you," he said.

"You can have all of my days."

"Thank you for dinner. It was delicious." Mrs. Stephens had made my favorite meal for my birthday dinner—chicken meatballs and spaghetti with sautéed broccoli. And after, she brought out a vanilla cake with raspberry filling and buttercream icing.

"We have a gift for you," she said, right before she disappeared only to return with a silver wrapped box with a big, white bow. "It's just something little."

Emotions flooded me; never had I had a day like this—one where I wasn't the one on the outside looking in, where I was wanted and loved. My eyes stung with tears as my shaking hands reached for the present.

"Thank you. You didn't have to get me anything, just being here is present enough."

"You only turn sixteen once." Mr. Stephens said.

Unwrapping the present, I lifted the lid and resting on top of tissue paper was a long, black box. And inside that box was the most beautiful gold watch.

"Look at the back," Mrs. Stephens said softly.

Turning the delicate watch over, the inscription had the tears I battled falling.

Happy sweet 16th Sidney
With all our love

I just sat there staring at the gift feeling overwhelmed with how easily they had all accepted me and more incredibly, loved me. Jake stood, hunching down next to me.

"Sid?" He wiped the tears from my cheeks. "You okay?"

Looking into those brown eyes, I knew this boy was the one I was meant to spend my life with. And how had I, Sidney Ellis, found not only the boy of my dreams, but a family of my very own?

"I love you," I whispered.

Tenderness and possession moved over his face.

My eyes turned to Mrs. Stephens' bright gaze. "Thank you for giving me a family."

She wiped at her eyes. Her shaky smile was beautiful because there was so much said in that smile. "There's something else in there."

Moving the tissue paper, there was a picture of Jake and me in a silver frame, a picture from his junior prom.

"We have one too. It's on the mantle."

The Stephens' mantle was filled with pictures of the family, just the family. Her adding a picture of me to the mantle meant that they really did think of me as family. And somehow that was even more profound than the watch. The wealth of emotions burning through me made speaking too hard, so instead I just held the picture to my heart and let my happy tears fall.

2006 · Shattered

Jake and I had both been accepted into Cornell and were starting our freshman year shortly, but before we did there was the small matter of getting married. My knees shook and my hands were so damp I feared I might drop the small bouquet of white roses I held. When I came to live with the Millers, Connor's love had begun the healing in me, but Jake had healed me. All the lonely and empty places were gone. He wasn't just the boy I loved; he was my family. I never thought I'd have this, have someone I could call mine. Never thought I was good enough for it, but Jake proved me wrong and I have never been so happy to be wrong.

"You look beautiful. Are you nervous?" Rylee asked as we waited in the corridor of town hall. She was my maid of honor. It was silly, but I hadn't wanted to drive over with Jake. I didn't want him to see me until it was our turn with the Justice of the Peace. Connor drove Rylee and me, but he disappeared shortly after we arrived. Whatever he was doing, he better hurry because we were up soon. My dress was a white lace sheath with spaghetti straps that I paired with strappy silver sandals. Rylee helped with pulling my hair up into a fancy knot. My wedding ensemble was simple and yet I never felt more beautiful.

"I'm excited, not nervous. I'm marrying Jake. Part of me can't believe it and another part of me knew this moment was coming from the very first time I saw him."

"I knew it. I told you, I was there for the beginning. You guys have it. What that *it* is I couldn't put into words, but you have it in spades."

And we did and just thinking of him had tears of profound happiness prickling my eyes.

"Don't cry. You'll smear your makeup." She studied me, her head tilting as her eyes narrowed. "They're happy tears, right?"

"Yes."

"You need to dry your eyes and fix your makeup. I'll take your roses. You take my purse. Your makeup bag is in there."

"What would I do without you?"

"You'd look like a zombie on your wedding day."

"Thank you, Rylee. I'm so glad you're here."

We shared a moment, her eyes turning a bit bright, before she said, "Don't make me cry too. Hurry, you're up in ten minutes."

Connor came strolling down the hall as Rylee called to him. "There you are! I was about to send out a search party."

"Relax," he said, but he was grinning. I could smell alcohol on his breath and I wanted to smack him for getting tipsy on my wedding day. It had been almost four years and he was still partying, showing no signs of stopping. I had thought he'd been getting high and drunk out of bitterness and anger, but I was beginning to think his actions stemmed from something much simpler. He liked it. And even for all my fretting and worrying, there wasn't a damn thing I could do about it but watch as Connor self-destructed. And as much as I wanted to scream at him to snap out of it, my wedding day wasn't the day for that.

"You look beautiful, Sid, except for the raccoon thing you've got going on with your eyes."

And even when he disappointed me, I still loved him. "Oh...I'll be right back."

Five minutes later, I rejoined Rylee and Connor and just in time because Jake and his parents were coming down the hall. I took in every detail of him because I wanted to remember always the sight of him in that moment. He looked beautiful, dressed in a simple black suit, white shirt and tie. The smile on his face was nearly as big as my own.

I pulled my focus from Jake to Mr. and Mrs. Stephens who had asked me to call them Lauren and Jasper, or mom and dad if I was so inclined. Even with how they had taken me in, loved me like their own, I had thought they would object to us getting married so young, but they seemed to understand what Jake and I did. What we had was real and lasting.

"You look beautiful," Lauren said.

She'd had helped me pick out my dress and sandals, another day of shopping and lunch, something we did often after that first time. "Thank you, Mom."

"I have something old." She reached into her purse for the black velvet box that held a silver hair clip with blue stones.

"They're sapphires, so it's something old and blue. I wore it when I got married, I'd like for you to have it now."

Touched by not just the gift but also the meaning behind it, when I was able to speak all that came out was, "Could you help me with it?"

Her eyes were bright too. "I'd love to."

The door opened and a man called our names. "Jake Stephens and Sidney Ellis."

Jake's hand closed around mine. "Ready?"

"More than ready."

"To the beginning of the rest of our lives," He said before he eagerly led me toward the open door.

Our reception was a backyard affair at Jake's house catered by his mom's catering company. We didn't have an actual wedding ceremony because Jake and I had wanted to get married sooner rather than later, but his parents wanted to throw us a reception. They wanted to officially introduce Mr. and Mrs. Jake Stephens to their friends and family.

They hired a band; a dance floor was setup on the grass. Tables and chairs were arranged around the lawn, waiters carrying trays of appetizers walked around. It was elegant and yet simple and exactly what Jake and I wanted.

Jake had lost the tie and jacket and I had stepped out of my sandals. Walking around the backyard hand-in-hand, we both had the biggest, silliest smiles on our faces.

"We did it, wife."

"Yes we did, husband."

"This is the happiest day of my life. And tonight, when I make you mine, I will be the luckiest man alive."

I was a virgin and though Jake and I had been together for four years and we had reached third base often, we both wanted to wait until we were married. And how crazy was it that we knew we'd have this day?

"How do you think Tigger and Stuart will adjust to our new place?" We were taking them with us to New York. Jake insisted. We made sure to get an apartment off campus that allowed pets. How wonderful was he?

"I think they'll be happy—fat and happy and warm all the time."

The band started playing 'The Luckiest' from Ben Folds and Jake immediately pulled me to the dance floor. He wrapped me in his arms and buried his face in my neck. Jake had selected this song and when I listened to the lyrics they etched themselves on my heart. To know this man loved me like he did, the intensity and beauty of that love was humbling.

A commotion started at one of the tables. Jake and I turned in time to see as Connor stumbled into a waiter sending the glasses he carried flying. I tried to pull from Jake, to get to Connor before he made a bigger scene, but Jake wouldn't release me.

"It's our wedding day. We'll handle him tomorrow."

"But your parents…"

"Tomorrow, Sidney. Nothing is going to spoil this day."

"You're right. Tomorrow is soon enough."

That day was the happiest day of my life, but with the sweet comes the sour.

"Sidney, are you ready?" Jake called from the living room of our small apartment off campus. Two years into marriage and it all still felt so new. We had our routines, like grabbing breakfast together at the pancake place right down the street from our apartment, but every day I discovered something new about him. And every new discovery only made me love him more. I never thought I'd ever be this happy, never really believed that my life could be this sweet.

"We're going to be late for class if we don't get a move on," he said as he entered our room.

"I'm coming."

He moved in, his strong arms wrapping around my waist, his lips pressing a kiss on my neck. "It's not really fair that I'm giving you grief for running late when I'm the reason you're running late."

My body warmed at the memory of how Jake woke me that morning. "You can wake me like that every morning."

"Maybe I will."

"Keep talking like that and we will definitely be missing class."

He growled deep in his throat, kissed my shoulder then stepped back. "Too tempting. Have you heard from Connor?"

My happy glow faded thinking about Connor. He hadn't grown out of partying; he had embraced it as a way of life. Drugs and alcohol were like his new best friends. He couldn't hold down a job, his circle of friends was growing smaller and smaller. He didn't even have his own place. He slept in his car. And remembering how happy he had been when he got that car, how he believed the world had opened up to us, broke my heart because that hadn't happened for him. His world had gotten very small.

"No, but I think maybe I need to go home this weekend. Not hearing from him is never a good thing."

"We'll go home this weekend."

Without fail he always had my back. "You are always exactly what I need when I need it. How did I get so lucky?"

He touched my chin. "I'm the lucky one, Sid."

The smile I offered in reply was shaky because of the emotions his words stirred, the wonder of having someone love me as much as I loved him.

He pressed his lips to mine. "I need to feed you."

He already had. I was no longer that lonely girl hungry for love. And I had a lifetime with him. I was a very lucky girl.

"Are you going to fucking cry? God you're such a fucking girl," Connor slurred as he slumped in the corner of a drug den. It was a scene that I'd grown used to in the past two years, since that first trip home during our sophomore year. No longer were the drugs recreational; Connor was an addict. My one-time beautiful brother sat in a puddle of his own urine and was too high to realize it.

"Leave me. I want to be here."

"No one wants to be here."

"Go with your perfect husband, live your perfectly boring life and leave me the fuck alone."

"How can you ask me to do that? You're my brother. I love you."

"Well, I don't fucking love you. So fuck off."

Jake pulled Connor to his feet and slammed him against the wall. "You don't ever talk to your sister that way, fuck head. You hear me? High or not, I'll fucking push your teeth down your throat."

"Whatever."

Jake dropped him; he landed in a heap. "We can't help him if he won't help himself."

He was right, as much as it pained me to admit it. "I know."

"Leave him. Let him wallow a bit at rock bottom and then maybe he'll accept our help." Jake turned those dark eyes on me. "I don't like you in this pisshole, sweetheart. Can I please get you out of here?"

I nodded my head, couldn't put into words my agreement because I hated that I was giving up on my brother. But the definition of insanity was doing the same thing over and over and hoping for a different outcome. I'd fallen into that pattern.

"I'm here for you, Connor, whenever you need me."

"I don't need you."

Jake reached for my hand and tugged me closer. "One day you'll apologize to her."

"The hell I will."

"Let's go," I whispered.

Reaching Jake's car, he pulled me to him and held me close. "I'm sorry, Sidney."

"Me too. I'm sorry we spent our break from school hunting down Connor, again, especially since he doesn't want our help."

"You needed to know how he was. I'm just sorry it wasn't better news."

"We should get back to school. Finals are coming."

"We need to look for a house as well."

"Our first house."

"Big enough to start a family."

"Children with you, I love that idea."

He touched my cheek as he studied my face. "Are you happy?"

"Four years married to you. Yes, deliriously."

"Good."

"Are you?"

“I have you, Sid, absolutely.”

Six months after graduating Cornell, Jake and I moved into our first house. Just outside of Princeton, it was a beautiful little Cape Cod. Jake had taken a job at his father’s firm working as an investment banker and Rylee and I, now that we had completed our undergraduate work, were enrolled in veterinary school.

It was a beautiful autumn day as I sat out back contemplating the potential of our backyard.

Jake appeared with two glasses of wine. He placed one of the glasses in front of me at the same time I tilted my head back for his kiss. His lips tasted like wine. He settled across from me.

“You looked deep in thought just now. What are you thinking about?”

“We should add some gardens. There’s so much space back here and with the fence, gardens would soften the lines. We could even add a vegetable garden. Mom would love that, fresh vegetables to cook with when she pops over.” Lauren and Jasper popped over often. They were respectful and didn’t overdo their visits, but I liked the four of us preparing and eating a meal together.

“Sounds like a plan. I think we should add a hot tub.

“A hot tub? I don’t really see that working into the plans I’ve got rolling around in my head.”

He leaned forward a bit, but it was the devilish look in his eyes that had lust whipping through me. “A hot tub, concealed by large bushes so I can get my wife naked and have some fun.”

That lust settled between my legs. “I’m seeing the merit in this idea.”

Leaning back, he reached for his glass and grinned. “I knew you would.” He took a sip, his expression changing slightly. “Maybe we should put in a swing set, forward thinking and all.”

Desire shifted to love at the thought of children with him—a little boy with that same dark hair and eyes.

"I like that idea."

"We can start whenever you're ready. Now works for me, but I understand if you'd rather wait until you finish school."

"It might be easier with our schedules if I was done with school, but we'll figure it out if we get pregnant before that. Besides, your parents are so close and you know they would love to help."

He put his glass down and pushed his chair back. "So you're giving me the green light to ravish you as often as I want."

My whole body throbbed. "Yeah, I guess I am."

"Then I'll give you to the count of three."

It only took to the count of one since I ran…but not away from him.

"No, your eyes on me. I want to see you come." Jake's body pushed deeper into me as my knees lifted and my hips moved. "God, I love watching you lose control. Come on sweetheart, reach for it."

And I did and each time it felt like the first time; the intense pleasure that burned through me, the weakening of my limbs, the pounding of my heart and the delicious friction between my legs as Jake moved deeper and faster.

Curling his fingers around my thighs, he lifted my hips and sated himself. I understood why he loved watching me come; his expression was beautiful.

We'd been trying to have a baby. I suspected it was stress and overwork that kept that from happening. Jake was now a vice president at the firm and though he could have worked eighty-hour weeks, he wouldn't. He was determined to find the balance between work and home, but maintaining that balance was stressful at times. Rylee and I had a year left in school and after we graduated we wanted to open a practice together, but first we had to put in the time at other places, to learn the ropes and cultivate some clients. I loved every second, but it was exhausting.

And I was sure worrying over Connor wasn't helping on the baby front. He hadn't changed. He seemed perfectly happy to kill himself slowly. We had tried to get him into counseling, had tried everything, but he liked being an addict. Jake, Rylee and I were told by the counselors we were doing it right; we had to practice tough love. No feeding the addict and we had been. Too many times he'd come to us, telling us what we wanted to hear, convincing us he was finally ready to change his ways, to get clean. We'd give him money that he immediately put into his veins. It broke my heart, but nothing we did seemed to get through to him. And still, when he called needing help, we went because we loved him and couldn't turn our backs on him.

"What's put that look on your face?" Jake's soft voice pulled me back to him.

"Nothing."

"You look really pissed, not the look a man wants to see on his woman's face after he's just made love to her."

"I'm sorry. I was thinking…never mind."

"You were thinking about Conner."

"Yeah. I just…we're so happy and he's—"

"When he's ready, Sidney, we'll be there for him."

"I know, but seeing him, what he's been reduced to is really hard. And I hate how that ugliness has touched you and your family. You had no idea what you were getting yourself into."

He brushed the hair from my cheek, his thumb stroking the line of my jaw. "Best day of my life, the day I met you."

Loving the way his touch still seared me even after all this time, I hadn't heard his words. "I'm sorry?"

"I saw this beautiful girl and I knew, with just one look, that you would be in my life forever. I'd put up with a lifetime or two of his bullshit if it means I get to wake to your face every day for the rest of my life."

My heart melted. "I love you."

"I love you." He shifted his hips, a moan pulled from the back of my throat. "I think it's time for round two."

Lifting my hips, and taking him deeper, I grinned. "Good idea."

The phone rang. Glancing at my watch on the bedside table, it was only three in the morning. My heart slammed into my ribs; late night calls were never good when you had an addict for a brother.

"Yeah. Okay. I'm coming."

Jake dropped the phone on the table and threw his legs over the side of the bed. "Connor needs a ride. He's tripping pretty badly."

"Who was that?"

"One of his crack-head friends."

"I'm coming with you."

Jake grabbed for his jeans. "No, you're staying here."

"He's my brother. Why should you be forced to deal with this shit?"

He turned, his expression one I knew well. Love, but determination. "Sweetheart, let me scope it out and see how bad it is. I'll call you."

"But—"

"Let me look after you, Sidney. Please."

"I hate this."

He yanked on his tee before leaning over the bed and kissing me, long and hard. "Keep the bed warm."

"Love you. And thank you."

He touched my cheek as he had a habit of doing. "I'll be back."

I couldn't fall back to sleep, lay in bed wondering just how fucked up my brother was because it was taking Jake an awfully long time getting him home. The doorbell had my heart jumping into my throat. Shit. He was so bad that Jake couldn't even get him into the house on his own. Climbing from bed, anger warring with worry, I yanked open the door prepared to verbally slap my brother. But it wasn't Jake at the door. Two cops stood there, their expressions grave.

What had Connor done now? "Yes?"

"Sidney Stephens?"

"Yes."

"Do you know a Connor Reid?"

"My brother. What has he done? Where's Jake?" I asked as I tried to look around them.

"Maybe we should step inside." One of the cops suggested.

"I'm sorry, yes please come in. I'll make some coffee."

They silently followed me to the kitchen as I busied myself with the coffee. Jake loved his coffee and after whatever Connor had pulled him into, he was going to need some.

"Mrs. Stephens?"

Looking at them from over my shoulder, my heart dropped. Whatever happened, it wasn't good. Turning to them, the bag of coffee I held was completely forgotten.

"I'm sorry to have to tell you this, but there was an accident earlier."

In response to those words, a chill moved through me and my heart pounded so hard it hurt. "With my brother?"

Officer Zane, that was his name, looked down at the floor for a second like he was drawing strength from something before his blue gaze returned to me. "Mr. Stephens' car was struck in a head-on by a tractor trailer. I'm so sorry to tell you this, but both Mr. Stephens and Mr. Reid were killed on impact."

My brain vehemently denied his words. There was no way Jake was dead, my brother, to lose both of them. No way. "That can't be. Jake was just running out to get my brother. I'm expecting them to walk through that door any minute now."

Sorrow and pity filled his expression and even trying to deny his words, my heart acknowledged the truth of them and the reality that my whole world had changed in a blink of an eye. My legs went weak and I reached out for the counter to keep myself standing as a pain exploded in my chest making it so hard to breathe. People often say their lives flash before their eyes when they're facing down death and it did for me. My life with Jake flashed through my mind: the day he pulled up beside me and changed my life, his tall, strong body leaning against my locker, our first kiss, our first dance, the look of absolute love on his face when he pledged himself to me for as long as we both shall live, his smile that even being so slight still managed to brighten every aspect of his beautiful face. And his voice, it rang so clearly in my mind, that soothing tenor that softened to a husky whisper when he told me he loved me. Jake was dead. The sob ripped from my throat.

"Mrs. Stephens, is there someone we can call?"

That someone was Jake; had been Jake since I was fifteen years old. He was the whole of my world. Every happy memory, every joy, every kiss, every part of me included him and now he was gone. My beautiful Jake was dead. My knees crumbled, my body sliding to the floor, my hands fisting the bag of coffee. Jake was gone. Only two hours ago he was in our bed, his soft breath tickling my neck and now he was... Curling into myself, the pain moved through me like a cancer. It should have been me. It was my brother; it should have been me in that car. How would I go on without Jake? All the years that spanned out before me, years without him, how was I supposed to continue on without my heart?

A tractor trailer. Oh my God. "Did they feel anything? Did they suffer?" *Please, don't have let them suffer. Let it have happened so fast that they felt no pain; that Jake didn't hurt and call out to me only for that plea to be unanswered. Please don't let my husband's last thought in this life be worry over leaving me behind.*

"No, it happened very quickly."

And in that moment, I felt empty, broken and furious with my brother as it settled over me—a long life without Jake. Lifting my head, the weight of my grief was almost too much to bear. "He's really gone? Are you sure you have the right person?"

Officer Zane, his eyes were bright. A tear rolled down his cheek. "I'm so sorry."

All the pieces I had collected with Jake, the pieces that made me feel whole, shattered as I was dragged back into the abyss—a dark, empty and lonely abyss.

The Stephens' living room was so quiet, the curtains were drawn and the lights were low. They were both on the other side of the room sitting on the sofa, so close their thighs were touching. Lauren held a picture of Jake, her head lowered, a tissue grasped so tightly in her hand that her knuckles were white against the silver frame. Jasper's arm was wrapped protectively around her shoulders. His head too was lowered, his focus also on the picture of Jake. It was one I knew well, he was young in the photo, holding a football that was almost too big for his little hands. As I silently watched their grief, I felt responsible for it. It had been my brother who had pulled Jake from our bed, my brother that had Jake in that car, my brother whose problems put my beautiful husband in the path of that tractor trailer.

"I can't believe he's gone," Lauren whispered; the tightening of his arm around her was Jasper's silent agreement.

"He was always such a beautiful soul." Lauren's voice cracked, her tears fell harder. "Every second, every moment, he brought so much to our lives."

My fingers hurt from twisting them so hard, my own head dropped as my tears fell uncontrollably. "I'm so sorry." I wasn't even sure I'd spoken the words loud enough to be heard.

"Sidney, honey."

It was so hard to lift my head to them, to the pain I knew burned in their eyes. Both now studied me, like they had the picture still grasped so tightly in Lauren's hands. "You have nothing to be sorry for."

I wanted to argue, but this wasn't about easing my guilt, this was about remembering the beautiful man they raised. "I never said it, thought there would be so much more time to do so, but thank you."

Lauren's head tilted slightly because she knew my thoughts had shifted. "For?"

"For raising such a beautiful, strong and wonderful man. He loved you both so much."

Lauren dropped her head on Jasper's shoulder; her eyes closed as the tears rolled down her cheeks. Jasper rested his lips on her head; his own tears streaking down his face. They both reached a hand out to me and I didn't hesitate, dropping to my knees when I reached them and wrapped them both in my arms, Jake's picture lovingly cocooned in the center of our embrace, as we mourned his loss.

The crash jerked me from sleep. It took a minute for me to remember that I was at the Stephens' house, in Jake's old room. Another crash, which was followed by what sounded like an animal's mournful cry, had me jumping out of bed and rushing downstairs. Mom stood just outside Dad's office. She reached for my hand when I approached, holding me back as much as seeking comfort. Dad was in his office, or what was left of it. Shattered glass and splintered wood littered the floor. But it was the sight of him that had me choking back a sob…destroyed.

"My son." Those words ripped from his throat in pain and devastation.

"My son." Rage followed as he reached for a bookend and hurled it at the wall. "My son."

He dropped to his knees, lifted his head to the ceiling and howled in pain. The sight of his despair gutted me.

He curled into himself. His big body shaking from his sobs and all the while he chanted my son. Mom ran to him, dropped to her knees and wrapped him in her arms. I wanted to wrap them both in my arms, to return the love they had so selflessly offered me, but it felt wrong for me to be there because they had brought me into their family, and because of my brother, that family was now broken.

Connor's funeral had been a few days ago. No one came, but Rylee, the Stephenses and me. Our foster parents hadn't come, hadn't acknowledged at all the loss of their foster son. His crack-head friends weren't there, no one came to recognize that he had once lived and died. I hadn't wanted to be there either. Connor took Jake from me. I hated him, hated him with a passion that was surely unhealthy. But I did. I hated him with everything in me. My brother was a selfish bastard. He couldn't even die alone; he had to take my husband with him.

It was the day of Jake's funeral and unlike Connor's, there was standing room only. I sat in the front, Rylee on one side, the Stephenses on the other, my eyes on the casket. I had asked for a closed casket, his parents agreed. And inside that box was the love of my life. How did a person come back from that, from a loss so severe that every part of you felt as if you had died right along with him? I didn't want to get up in the morning, didn't want to find my way without him. I wanted to hear his voice, his laugh. I wanted my Jake back, wanted the life we worked so hard to have. Instead I got to sit and listen to people offer me condolences on how it would get better. Fuck them. How would it ever get better?

"We're heading to the cemetery," Rylee whispered.

"I just need a minute."

Lauren reached for my hand. "How are you holding up?"

After that horrible scene in Jasper's office, the two of them had turned their concern on me, their way of coping, and even mourning as they were, they were the loving parents I needed because I wasn't coping.

Keeping my focus forward since I couldn't bear to see Jake in her face, I tried to keep the tears at bay. "I can't believe he's gone."

"He loved you."

"I loved him."

"I know. Do you want to drive over with us?"

"Thank you, but I'll go with Rylee."

"Okay." She leaned closer. "You have to forgive him."

My head snapped to her. "Connor?"

"Yes."

"I don't think I can."

"Jake wouldn't want you holding onto that."

And he wouldn't and still anger erupted, sharp and vicious. "Jake's dead. Connor killed him."

"Holding onto that anger won't bring Jake back."

"Holding onto the anger will keep me from completely breaking down. I need the anger right now; I need something to keep me grounded. One day, maybe I'll move past the rage and the fury, but right now staring at the coffin that is the final resting place of my husband, I'll keep my anger."

"We're here for you, Sidney."

She stood, and then she rocked me to my core when she ran her hand down my hair. One of my deepest wishes came true during what was the worst moment of my life. Agony and sorrow warred, but I reached for her hand and my voice broke as my pain all but consumed me. "Thank you."

A few months after Jake's death and I still couldn't leave our bed. He had a sweater he wore every winter, it was wool, he rarely had it cleaned. It smelled like him, so I lay in bed with that sweater, holding it to my face, my lungs inhaling his scent deeply as I wished with everything in me that he'd come back. That I'd wake from the nightmare and he'd be there, smiling at me, touching me, loving me. I slept with our wedding picture too. It wasn't a posed picture; it had been a candid shot of the two of us looking at each other. The smiles on our faces saying so much more than words ever could. We'd been happy. We had found true happiness. Going on alone, finding my way without him, I wasn't sure how to do that.

Knew I wasn't yet at a place that I wanted to do that. I just wanted to remember him, wanted to hold on to the memory of him for just a little bit longer. I wanted to remember the beautiful boy who turned into the beautiful man, the man who had loved me, who had given me a home and a family. I wanted to pretend for just a little longer that I was whole again. Happy. And then I'd figure out how to pick up the pieces and move on.

now

Sometimes love is unwanted, raw and untamed. Demanding all from us, but giving back even more. Not the love we thought we wanted, but the love we need; the love we find we're unable to live without.

~Sidney Stephens

chapter seven

sidney

Three years later—Present Day

Brushing my finger over the picture of Jake, my heart hurt and my eyes stung. I still felt his loss in every part of me, still woke up sometimes reaching for him.

Lauren entered the room, Jasper right behind her carrying a silver tray with crystal glasses filled with ice and tea. They looked good, older maybe, but then suffering through the loss of your only child would age anyone. I could see Jake in their faces causing the stinging in my eyes to turn into a burn. God, I missed him.

"Please sit, Sidney, and tell us about this clinic."

Rylee and I were moving. Dr. Livingston knew of a vet who was looking to retire. He had an established practice and with Dr. Livingston's recommendation and a few phone interviews, Doc Cassidy offered us his practice in Sheridan, Wyoming.

"Doc Cassidy has one hundred and twenty-two patients and he works with three local horse farms which between them include about forty additional patients. Sheridan is beautiful and different, and I'm ready for different."

"We think it's wonderful that you're reaching for your dream. I won't lie, I wish the dream was a bit closer, but I think this move will be good for you," Lauren said.

My head lowered, the tears that had been threatening pooled at the corners of my eyes. An ache formed in my chest and the lump in my throat made the words hard to say. "I wouldn't be here if not for Jake." Lifting my head, I wiped the tears away as a smile curved my lips thinking of him. "The way he came into my life, the way he just fit. He filled all the parts of me that were empty. He loved me, but more, he made me love myself. I'd never have had the confidence to reach for my dreams without him. I miss him everyday, but I have to move on. I have to learn to live, really live, without him. I think this move is the first step toward that."

Lauren brushed her fingertips across her cheek to wipe away her own tears. "We agree. There are too many memories here for you. Starting somewhere fresh is exactly what you need."

"I'm going to miss you both so much."

Jasper's voice broke a bit. "We're going to miss you, but you're only a phone call away."

"And I will be calling. Once we're settled, maybe you can come for a visit."

Jasper's lips turned up into a smile before he said, "Try keeping us away."

"I love you…Mom and Dad."

I had called them that before, but not since Jake died. They lost the battle with their tears. I joined them, dropped to my knees and wrapped them both in my arms.

"Believe me, this is for the best." Rylee stood at my side as I stared at the home that Jake and I had shared. It wasn't our home any more. I had just been to settlement. Newlyweds bought it, ready to start their lives together...a family. Jake and I had wanted a baby, had continued in our efforts and after his death, I had hoped that I was pregnant. I wanted so badly to have a piece of him still. The day my period came had been like losing him all over again. It'd been three years since his death. Three years didn't seem that long, but it was over a thousand missed goodnight kisses and waking in the morning to his beautiful face. Morning coffee in the kitchen where he had always snuck a kiss or two and countless *I love you's*. I had stopped pretending he was alive, had worked to find where I fit in the world without him, but being here where he lived was too painful. Everything reminded me of him. I couldn't move forward if I kept finding myself being pulled into the past. And I wanted to lose myself in the past. It was because of how badly I wanted to escape into the past that I knew I needed a change.

Yesterday with the Stephenses had been hard for them and me, but they were happy I was making the move. They hadn't come right out and said it, but I knew they were worried about me. In the three years since we lost Jake, we still shared every holiday. I loved that I had parents. I loved being a part of a family, but it hurt to know that the one who had brought us together was gone. I treasured those moments with the Stephenses but it hurt like hell too. And even with the pain, I was going to miss them terribly.

Rylee was giving me the look, one I'd seen too many times. "I'm fine. I was just thinking about yesterday with the Stephenses."

Understanding moved over her face. "That had to be hard on all of you, but they should come for a visit once we get settled."

"I offered that to them."

"Good."

"Are you sure you want to move to Wyoming?" I wasn't even sure I wanted to move to Wyoming.

"I think it's perfect for us, Sid. Doc Cassidy has a good mix of clients and with you focusing on larger animals in veterinary school, you know the idea of tending horses is very appealing."

It was true. I loved all animals, but the idea of working with horses excited me and since I had been numb for the past three years, I welcomed anything that made me feel.

"I know this is hard. But Jake would want you to move on. It's been three years, Sidney."

Even with the passing of time, the pain hadn't eased. People say the sorrow eventually fades, the good memories replacing the bad ones. That wasn't the case for me. I had learned to live with the pain, an almost welcomed companion, but I was ready to start somewhere fresh. Somewhere that I wasn't reminded of the man I had loved and lost, wasn't forced to deal with my conflicting feelings for my brother—loving him and yet hating him nearly as much because he had taken Jake from me.

"You're right. It's time. And Wyoming, you couldn't ask for more of a change, but are you sure you want to do this? I need a change, but your life is here."

"Absolutely. Open spaces, bright blue skies and mountains. With Mom and Dad gone, there's nothing holding me here anymore."

It had been a tough couple of years for us. A year after I lost Jake and Connor, Rylee's mom died of a cancer. Six months later, her dad died of a broken heart.

"The memories are hard for you too."

"Yeah."

"Then let's do this."

She didn't react the way I expected, instead she said, "I lost my parents, but they were old and Mom hadn't been well for a while. How you lost Jake and Connor was so unexpected. You're so much stronger than you think. I know what you lost when you lost Jake. It was beautiful, the two of you, but I really want to see you happy again."

Even now, tears burned the back of my eyes. "I don't know if I'll ever be the kind of happy I was with him, but I am ready to try to find some measure of happy again."

"You never know, he could be out there—someone you never see coming. So we're ready to get on the road, to leave all of this in the past?"

"I'm ready." Looking back one last time my heart ached. There were just so many dreams we'd had; so much we had wanted to do. It hurt, not just saying goodbye, but also leaving him and all of those dreams behind. "I love you." I whispered the words I hoped Jake heard and then I climbed into Rylee's car. Tigger and Stuart were in their carriers, a little agitated but not as annoyed as I had feared. They missed Jake, looked for him still, and it broke my heart when I saw them curled up on his pillow. They needed this too and so I looked forward, not back, ready for whatever the future had in store for me.

"Unbelievable." The word whispered, almost reverently, because the sight out the front window of Rylee's car was unbelievable. The Bighorn mountain range loomed in front of us as we drove into downtown Sheridan. "I understand now why they call this God's country."

"You can say that again," Rylee said. "Pictures don't do it justice."

"Not even close."

Coming from New Jersey, the sight of the mountains was definitely outside of our wheelhouse. It took us three days to make the trip, stopping off at motels along the way. I had a litter box setup on the floor of the car and every few hours we pulled over to let the cats stretch their legs, but they were ready for the trip to be over. This last leg of the trip was an easy one; we'd only been on the road for a few hours. "Where's the clinic?"

"That's in town, but the place I found us is just outside of town. Wait until you see it. A log cabin, Sidney! Our new place is a log cabin!" With trying to sell my place and all the emotions that stirred, I let Rylee handle finding us a place. I signed where I needed to sign, but I hadn't given a thought to my new home. I had been too upset about losing my old one.

Tucked in an area dense with spruces that backed up to rolling hills of green, the cabin was a small two-story dwelling with dormer windows and steps up to the front door. A small garden in need of tending wrapped around the structure. A detached barn that acted as the garage sat to the right of the drive.

"Isn't it perfect?"

It was beautiful. "Yes."

"Come on, let me show you the inside."

It was small; two bedrooms, two baths, a living room and a kitchen made up the whole place, but it was roomy, cozy with a huge stone fireplace that took up the whole one wall of the living room. Out back was a deck that overlooked nothing but exquisite Wyoming landscape.

"You nailed this, Rylee."

"I know it's small, but we've a lot of land."

We had both sold our homes and my two cars. We split the mortgage so I had a nice savings, as did Rylee.

Looking at our view, I couldn't help but think of Jake and Connor. They both would have loved this.

Rylee stepped up next to me. "Promise me something, Sidney."

"Sure."

"This is a fresh start and I want you to put in the effort to start fresh with everything. Life is more than a new job and house. There's men, sex, marriage, children."

That pain I'd grown used to, twisted in my gut.

"Look, I know what you're thinking, but you want a family. I know you do. You're not even thirty. You have your whole life ahead of you. Jake will always be apart of you, but there is room in your heart for someone else."

"I'm ready to find happy again. I'm ready to find companionship, but marriage and children, I don't think so."

"That's you being stubborn."

"I'm not trying to be. When I was younger I wanted, no needed, that connection with someone. I'm not that girl anymore and I just don't see myself walking down the aisle again."

She reached for my hand. "Keep yourself open to the possibility. You haven't been. It's been three years and every date, the few there have been, that I've pushed you to go on were over before they started."

She was right. I hadn't even given the men a chance. "They were too much like Jake."

"What do you mean?"

"The same type of job, the same look, the same mannerisms. Every time I was out with one of them all I could think about was Jake. I don't want that. It isn't fair to them or me."

"But you're open to, say…a cowboy?"

I was young, healthy and it had been three years since Jake died. I was ready to find someone to curl up with on the sofa and watch a movie, to hold my hand when we went out to dinner, to have breakfast with the morning after a date. I was open to the idea of companionship, love was another matter. "I'm open to the idea of a cowboy."

"There are certainly enough of them around here. The truck is coming tomorrow, so we can hop into town and visit Doc Cassidy before getting dinner."

"Sounds good. Let me get the cats settled and then we can go."

People were friendly, folks saying hi as we walked along downtown Sheridan toward the clinic. In New Jersey, people pretended not to see you; here they went out of their way to greet you.

Doc was with a patient when we arrived. His receptionist, Ginger—fitting name since her hair was the color of ginger—showed us into the exam room. The woman was pushing eighty, but her cornflower blue eyes sparkled with welcome and her bright pink lips curved in the widest of smiles. "Doc, your guests have arrived."

Doc Cassidy looked like the quintessential small-town veterinary—a full head of white hair, a white lab coat, black glasses, and a slight hunch in his gait. His clinic was small and clean with some equipment that was a bit outdated, but what attracted Rylee and me to his practice was his extensive client list. Sure we had to drive halfway across the country, but this was the kind of practice we had both hoped to open. Taking over for one that was already established was worth uprooting ourselves.

He looked up from the dog he examined. "Welcome. Please come in. This here is Cooper and Mr. Reginald Milburn."

Mr. Milburn dipped his head to us.

"Hello, Mr. Milburn. I'm Sidney Stephens and this is Rylee Doughty."

"Welcome to Sheridan."

Rylee stepped up next to Doc Cassidy. "How old is Cooper?"

"Twelve."

"He has arthritis." Rylee observed.

"Yeah, pretty severe too."

"And yet his tail is wagging." I couldn't help the smile. If only humans bounced back so well.

"Very little gets to Cooper. He's a great companion," Mr. Milburn said. "I got him when I retired from my law practice. He made retirement tolerable."

While Rylee and Doc Cassidy checked over Cooper, I joined Mr. Milburn. "You didn't want to retire?"

Something moved over his expression, regret or maybe pain. "No, but I still consult on a part-time basis."

My eyes moved to his hand and the wedding ring. He added when he noticed, "My Maggie passed twelve years ago. I miss her every day."

My heart twisted because boy did I understand.

"You moved here from New Jersey?" He asked.

Wow, what they said about small towns and everyone knowing everything was true. He seemed to pick up on that when he added, "We're not as gossipy as all that, but you're taking over for Doc here. People were curious. Your names have definitely preceded you."

I wasn't really sure how to reply to that, so I didn't.

He glanced at my hand, a smile touching his lips. "This is a great place to start a family."

The smile died on my lips. He understood. "I'm sorry. I didn't know."

"I lost Jake three years ago. My brother too in the same accident."

"Oh, Jesus. That's news that has not circulated through the rumor mill and it won't now, but I am sorry."

"It's one of the reasons I'm here. It was time to start fresh."

"I understand that."

"Cooper looks good, Reg. No further progression of the arthritis."

"Hear that boy?"

Cooper barked. Rylee lifted him off the table and placed him gently on his feet. Mr. Milburn called for Cooper before he turned back to me.

"It does get easier. If you find you ever want to talk, I'm usually at the tavern at the edge of town. Sometimes it helps to talk to someone who's been there."

It took me a moment before I answered because I was touched and surprised that a stranger would show such kindness. "I'd enjoy that."

"Me too. It was nice meeting you."

"And you. Bye Cooper."

Doc was eyeing me from across the room. "Small town, people talk, but I didn't think they should be talking about that so I didn't mention it."

"Thank you." And I was grateful for that because I wasn't in a big hurry to reveal that I was a widow. I would have to eventually—Jake's absence would get a little hard to explain as would the fact that I was living with Rylee—but just for a little while I liked the idea of having Jake with me as I settled into my new life.

"I have to visit Speckled Egg. Why don't you two come?"

"Speckled Egg?" Rylee asked.

"She's a palomino Appaloosa. She had an abscess on her hoof. I've already drained it and she's on antibiotics. This is just a follow up, but it'd be good for you to meet Jayce Hellar since Hellar Farm is one of my bigger clients."

"Jayce Hellar?" Rylee asked but her focus was on me. I knew what she was thinking; she wasn't very good at concealing her thoughts. She was staking her claim. Sure, this was based solely on his name, but Jayce Hellar was a pretty sexy name. I almost hoped he was sixty, fat and bald just to see her expression.

"He's the owner. He just took over for his old man and it's about time too, because Garrett Hellar is pushing seventy. He's too old to be up on a horse."

Pushing seventy, yeah, there was a good chance Jayce was middle-aged. Rylee did the math too because some of that mischievous sparkle left her expressive eyes.

Doc Cassidy drove us in his old Jeep Cherokee. The Hellar farm was outside of town in the opposite direction of Rylee's and my place. The backdrop of the mountains was exquisite and the serenity of the scene was breathtaking. We drove down a long dirt drive. The house came into view, and damn what a place. The farmhouse was a log cabin, but not like our little log cabin. A deeply pitched roof with windows, large picture windows that I just knew drew the outside in, made up most of the front of the house. Gardens wrapped around the place and were filled with flowers in chaotic wonder. There were two stone fireplaces, that we could see, and just imagining what the inside looked like had me wishing for an invite.

"Beautiful, isn't it? Garrett built the original home. It's been expanded over the years. He'd hoped to have it filled with kids and grandkids, but his two sons, Jayce and Duncan, seem pretty determined to stay unhitched and since he never remarried after the divorce, it's not likely that dream will come true. If it weren't for Marnie—their live-in housekeeper, cook and at one time nanny—the place would look like just what it's become, a bachelor pad. Speckled Egg is in the barn. Got to give it to the Hellar men, they know how to take care of their horses."

He wasn't wrong. The barn was perfectly maintained with working windows, a rubber floor to keep the horses from slipping on the cold and icy concrete, a hot water line and the individual stables were large and meticulously maintained. Speckled Egg was in the far stall. You could hear her whinny, but it wasn't a happy sound.

"Is she in pain?" Rylee asked.

"Probably a little, but Speckled Egg is belligerent. She's a beauty and knows it. She's sixteen hands tall, too tall for trail riding, which is what most of their horses are trained for. Garrett fell in love with her, paid a handsome fee, and she's been living the life of luxury since. Only required to birth the occasional foal. In fact, she's six months pregnant with one now."

A foaling in the future, I couldn't wait! Speckled Egg was gorgeous; the tan of her coat was covered in white spots and it was the shiniest coat I'd ever seen on an animal. And, yes, she had attitude, her long, full tail flicking in annoyance.

"Looking like that, she's entitled to be a prima donna."

Rylee wasn't wrong.

"Her right front hoof had the abscess. Why don't you take point, Sidney?"

I was sure that was why he'd asked us to join him. He wanted to see how I worked with the animals as he had done with Rylee and Cooper. In his shoes, I'd have done the same. "Okay."

Speckled Egg blustered about for a bit when I stepped into her stall. She didn't keep it up for long, not with the cubes of sugar Doc gave me to bribe her. I literally had her eating out of my hand. "Yeah, you're all bark."

Lifting her hoof, there was still a bit of warmth, but the area looked good. "How long does she still have on the antibiotic?"

"Three more days."

"Still a bit warm, but it looks great and she's not favoring it, so that's a good sign. You'll be prancing around soon enough, beautiful girl."

"And she loves prancing." Jerking my head to the newcomer, Speckled Egg wasn't the only beautiful thing on this farm—tall, blond hair, blue eyes and ruggedly handsome. Shifting my eyes to Rylee, the urge to laugh was so strong I lowered my head. She looked seriously thirsty and the newcomer was just what she needed to quench her thirst—a tall, cool glass of water.

"I'm Jayce Hellar and you're the docs taking over Doc Cassidy's practice?"

When seconds of silence followed, I looked up again to see that Rylee was still just staring. Rendered mute by a handsome face.

"Yes. I'm Sidney Stephens and the woman staring mutely at you is my partner in crime, Rylee Doughty."

That snapped Rylee out of it as her eyes jerked to mine. Fire was shooting out of them. In reply, I smiled sweetly.

"How does Speckled Egg look?" Jayce asked.

"The hoof is still a little warm, so three more days on the meds sounds about right, but she looks good."

"Dad will be happy to hear that."

"How many horses do you have here?"

"Twenty-five. My brother has most of them off on a trail right now. There are a few stallions used for siring and a few we use for training." He gestured to the training paddock. "I'm sorry to see Doc Cassidy retiring, but we're growing pretty fast. With two of you taking over, it'll be a comfort to know we've got a doctor on call."

Rylee finally found her voice. "Sidney will be the one on-call, her focus is on larger animals, but I'm available if needed."

There was a small smile pulling on Jayce's lips. Jake's face swam into my vision because he used to give me the same smile. Rarely did his teeth show and somehow his smiles were still breathtaking. Unconsciously I twisted my rings at the memory, an action not lost on Rylee.

"I've got to get back, but maybe you should schedule a time to return and get more familiar with the animals." Doc Cassidy suggested.

"That's a great idea. Why don't I get your number and I'll give you a call." I almost corrected Rylee since I'd be working the clinic as well, but the horse farms would be solely my responsibility. Plus the records were back at the clinic, including Hellar Farm's phone number, but Jayce didn't hesitate to take her phone and punch in his number.

I heard Doc chuckling. His laughing eyes caught mine and he whispered, "Girl moves fast."

chapter eight

sidney

"Did you see that Jayce Hellar. Good God, the man is gorgeous." Rylee was on her third martini and with each one her opinion of Jayce Hellar grew. She leaned closer to me, her cheeks all rosy. "Was I too forward? Taking his number like that?"

"No. He moved pretty fast to give it to you."

"He did, didn't he? I'm wishing I was the one who specialized in horses because spending my days at his farm, I'd be the happiest woman alive."

"No worries, I'll be sure to call you constantly for a second opinion."

"Oh, that's a good idea. I want to see inside their house. Did you see that place?"

"Incredible and with how pretty it looked on the outside, I imagine Marnie keeps the inside just as lovely."

"You have to assume that Garrett and Duncan are like Jayce, so what kind of woman can keep those three in line? And clearly she is because though it's mostly men on the farm, the place definitely had a feminine touch." Rylee finished off her martini and signaled for another. "Last one."

I'd been nursing one beer; I'd get us home.

"What do you say about taking those off?" She asked as her focus moved to my wedding rings. "Fresh start, right? Those are like a huge stop sign, a do not enter. They're your security blanket."

I liked that they were a stop sign, plus I was just used to wearing them.

"It's been three years," Rylee added.

"I know I need to take them off, but I like that they act as a filter. I've been out enough with you and all those drunken guys propositioning you. You can't tell me you enjoy that."

"Of course not, but for every ten idiots, there's one good guy. You'll never meet the good guy if he thinks you're married. Those will keep him from approaching."

"If I find someone that interests me enough, I'll take them off."

"Fair enough."

My back ached. The moving truck arrived at six in the morning. Rylee was dead to the world, curled up in her sleeping bag in her room. I didn't rush to wake her. Sleep was what she needed to help battle the hangover she'd earned last night. We had opted to sell our furniture with the plan of buying new stuff after we'd been in the house and got a feel for what we wanted, so there wasn't much to unpack. After filling the linen closet with our towels and sheets, stocking the kitchen with our pots, pans and other kitchen items, I headed to my room. There was one box I wanted to take my time unpacking, the box with the few mementos of Jake's I couldn't let go. I had lovingly wrapped our wedding picture in bubble wrap. And seeing his smiling face had the tightness in my chest easing. I placed it on the floor next to my sleeping bag. I still wanted his face to be the first sight I saw when I woke in the morning. His sweater, I couldn't bear to part with it. It no longer carried his scent, but remembering him wearing it, seeing him so clearly in my mind,

I just couldn't donate it like I had his other clothes. His football jersey, the first birthday gift I had ever received, was my favorite nightshirt. I felt closer to him when I wore it. It probably wasn't healthy, my holding on to his memory, but I just didn't want to let him go. I didn't see a reason why I had to.

Leaving Rylee sleeping, I headed into town to check out the furniture store we'd passed yesterday on our way to the clinic. I wouldn't buy anything without her, but I could scope the place out. I drove her car, knew I was going to need to buy my own since I'd be spending most of my time traveling to the various farms. I hadn't kept my old car because it was a small hatchback and not big enough for the equipment I'd be carrying. I'd get to the car, but first we needed furniture.

Town was a bit more hopping; the door of the bakery was like a revolving door. I understood the activity because the scents of cinnamon and vanilla were so enticing I found myself heading in that direction—a quick detour, one that ended with a warm, cinnamon goodie was never a bad idea.

Pulling the door open, I had to stifle a moan because damn it smelled good. If the pastries tasted half as good as they smelled I was in for a treat. The place was packed; the line went to the door and every single person seemed perfectly fine with waiting for his or her turn. I'd bring something back for Rylee. Sweet, doughy goodness would do wonders for her hangover.

As I stood there, I studied the people. In New Jersey everyone was eager to get somewhere, moving so fast they tended not to take notice of the moment they were in. But here, it was like every moment was one to savor. And I liked that, especially knowing how quickly life could change. It was important to appreciate what you had while you had it.

It was while my thoughts drifted to Jake that I felt a prickling sensation that lifted the hair on my arms, a charge that had my breath catch. At first, I thought it was just the memory of Jake that caused the moment. But then, quite unconsciously, my eyes moved down the line to the man up front. A tingle skipped down my spine. My reaction to him shocked me because he wasn't at all my type. Hell, he didn't seem the type for Sheridan, dressed in his faded jeans and leather jacket with his hair pulled up in a messy kind of bun and the full beard and mustache. His focus was on his phone, but as I watched, tension stiffened his shoulders; an awareness that had his head lifting and his focus shifting. He didn't scan the crowd, his gaze moved down the line to settle on me as if he knew I was there. Pale blue eyes looked back at me but there was nothing icy about them. I wanted to look away, but I couldn't. As quickly as his attention fixed on me, I lost it as he stepped up to the counter. My heart pounded in my chest and after three years of feeling nothing, I was so freaked out I left. I walked right out of the bakery without my cinnamon goodie and went straight to the car. I didn't immediately drive away, too rattled to operate it, and so I saw as he exited the bakery. He looked up the street then down before he headed in the direction of the parked motorcycle. He was a big guy, tall—several inches over six feet—and muscular, yet he walked with a controlled and deliberate grace. He threw a leg over his bike, the faded denim at his thighs and ass stretching and I actually felt a heat ignite in my gut. The bun shouldn't have worked, not with someone so clearly masculine, and yet it was wickedly sexy when combined with the full beard. The engine roared to life a second before he took off down the street. And for a fleeting moment I found myself wishing I were on the back of that bike.

"The grill was a great idea. Nothing like grilling up burgers with this view." Rylee's feet were up on the deck, a glass of wine in her hand. We had stopped at the hardware store on our way home from work and bought a small charcoal grill. I had thought to get a gas grill, but Jake swore by charcoal. Said it wasn't really grilling if you weren't using charcoal. He was right; the flavor was amazing.

"And that bakery. What a find. I'm going to gain sixty pounds, but those sticky buns are worth it."

I'd taken Rylee to the bakery the day after I left it so abruptly. We'd met the owner, Stella, who was also the baker and the one who worked the counter. She must have figured out a way to clone herself to accomplish all of that and not die of exhaustion. We bought six donuts and six sticky buns and ate all of them in the same day. Rylee was right, we'd definitely be putting on weight eating like that, but it *was* so worth it. I hadn't mentioned the guy, the encounter that had me running away, because I chalked up the moment to exhaustion, missing Jake—because I had unpacked his things only an hour before—and intrigue having never seen anyone like *him* before. A movement off the deck caught my attention. An animal moved through the wildflowers in the distance. Black fur and a sleek body that was too thin. A dog of some kind, an obvious stray, and still he was beautiful even being malnourished.

"Look at him."

Rylee followed the direction I was staring. "Oh God. Is that a wolf?"

"Maybe part, but he's definitely got canine in him."

"Poor thing looks hungry."

"I'll leave him a hamburger."

"Do you think that's wise?"

"You know me and strays. He's hungry; I'm going to feed him. We've only got Tigger and Stuart here and they never leave the house."

"And we're here."

I could sympathize with the poor animal, likely given up because he got too big or ate too much. "It's more than likely the people who took him in didn't realize what they were getting into. He's so thin, clearly not a hunter but an animal used to being fed. And yes, a hungry animal is unpredictable, but I'll be careful and smart in how I feed him."

"You've always been like that, collecting other lost souls. That's one of the things I love most about you."

"Having been there, I get it."

"I know." She reached for her wine. "Are you glad we made the move?"

"I am. I like Doc Cassidy and Ginger, Mr. Milburn and Jayce. I love the town and how everyone isn't in a hurry to get somewhere, that they're fine being right where they are. And look at that view."

"Good. I'm really happy to hear that." She took a sip of her wine, there was more on her mind. She shared when she added, "I saw Jake's sweater in your room. I thought you donated that."

"I couldn't."

"I don't pretend to understand what you're going through, but do you think it's healthy to hold on to his things?"

"I think it's different for everyone, how you grieve over losing a loved one. I've done the stages, I've come out on the other side and I'm even willing to date again. But Jake wasn't just my husband. He was my best friend and a part of my past. Remembering him can't be unhealthy."

"Well, when you put it that way."

My traitorous thoughts turned to the man at the bakery. Rylee knew me too well.

"What?" She leaned up, like a predator catching the scent of its prey. "What's that look for? What aren't you telling me?"

"Nothing."

"No, that look was not nothing. Spill."

"Last week I saw a guy."

"What guy?"

"I don't know. He stood out, I looked."

"Stood out how?"

"Leather jacket, man bun, beard."

"Here? Seriously?"

"Yeah. Like I said, he stood out, I looked."

"Did he look back?"

"What?" I tried for nonchalance, but didn't pull it off. Rylee pounced.

"He did. What happened?"

"Nothing. I was looking, he must have sensed someone staring and he looked back."

"Did the air sizzle?"

"No."

"But something happened otherwise you would have mentioned this before now. What happened?"

"You're like a dog with a bone."

"This is the first sign of interest you've had in man since Jake died. I am a dog with a bone. What happened?"

"I felt like I got the wind knocked out of me."

"Hot damn!"

"Before you start planning the wedding, it was nothing."

"Bullshit."

"I knew I shouldn't have told you."

"Oh, you so should have told me. You had a physical reaction to someone who wasn't Jake. Whoever he is, you shouldn't dismiss him out of hand. A raw reaction like that doesn't happen every day."

The gardens around the house were in desperate need of work and Rylee's idea of fixing them was to plant grass seed. She wasn't a gardener and so while she chilled out inside, I spent a few hours weeding and trimming. It looked a thousand times better but now we needed color. A few pots on the stoop would be pretty too.

Calling Rylee from the front step, I asked, "Do you want to come with me to town? I need plants."

"No, if that's okay. I'm binge-watching Psych."

I loved that show; Shawn Spencer was hysterical. "All right, I'm taking your car."

"Have fun."

The mom and pop hardware store in town had a pretty extensive garden center. Grabbing a cart, I moved up and down the aisles of plants admiring all the colors and varieties. I had had a really nice garden back in New Jersey. It had taken years to get it how we wanted, but in the end it had been spectacular, including the cleverly concealed hot tub. The couple that bought the house also loved gardening, which thrilled me that all the work Jake and I had put into the yard wouldn't be lost on the new owners.

As I put a few trays of hot pink impatiens in my cart, the sound of a motorcycle caught my attention. My eyes moved of their own volition to the source of the sound. He pulled up across the street from me, stopping in front of a woman who stood at the curb. He was so effortlessly appealing that even being prepared for the look of him, I still felt that stir in my belly. He smiled and a shiver of heat danced along my nerve endings, though I doubted there was a soul alive who wouldn't have felt the effect of that sexy grin. He fascinated me, as did my reaction to him. He was sexy, sure, but I'd seen sexy in the years since Jake. Never had I felt such an elemental attraction. Raw enough that curled up on the sofa watching a movie didn't interest me, but naked and sweaty in front of a fire? Absolutely. And having spent the past three years feeling nothing, I had to say it was nice to feel the blood rushing through my veins again and the slight increase in speed of my heart as it pumped that blood.

My focus shifted to the woman and even from my distance, I recognized the look of her; it was one Connor had shared. She liked to party, maybe not as hard as Connor, but she was no stranger to drugs and alcohol. It was obvious she knew *him* well; there was a comfortable easiness about them. I hoped his friend didn't put him through what Connor had put Jake and me through. And it was while I shamelessly stared that his head shifted and his focus moved across the street to zero in on me. In response, I actually felt breathless and, if I were being honest, edgy.

A commotion behind me pulled my attention, but the sight that greeted me just seemed wrong. Mr. Milburn, the lovely older man I had met at Doc Cassidy's office, was having heated words with a creepy younger man, the kind of creepy where I wouldn't turn my back on the guy since he looked more than capable of putting a knife between my shoulder blades. I didn't want to exacerbate the situation, but I did want the man to move on because I didn't like how he was pressing threateningly into Mr. Milburn. I feigned cluelessness and called a friendly greeting.

"Mr. Milburn, so lovely to see a familiar face."

Both men turned in my direction; Mr. Milburn's expression before he smiled was a bit scary. The other guy barely acknowledged me before he walked off.

"Sidney, hello." How he sounded so jovial when he'd been livid only seconds before surprised me.

"Are you okay?"

"Oh, that. Yeah. That's Sammie Chase, a former client of mine. So you're doing a bit of gardening." He seemed undisturbed by the encounter; were all his relationships with former clients so contentious that he'd grown accustomed to that level of conflict? It wasn't my business.

"The beds were already there, but they were in need of some tender loving care."

"Nice. How are you finding Sheridan? I imagine we move at a slower pace than what you're used to."

"Yes, but it's nice. I needed a slower pace."

Understanding moved across his expression, but he didn't reply. Instead he asked, "Do you need help carrying your purchases?"

What a gentleman. "No, I'm still shopping, but thank you."

"I need to get home, it's time for Cooper's lunch. It was nice seeing you again."

"And you."

He strolled away, but stopped and looked back at me from over his shoulder. "Thank you for the rescue."

"Sometimes the damsel needs to save the prince."

He laughed before he said, "Agreed."

I returned to my shopping cart, my eyes moving across the street but the sexy man and his friend were gone.

After the garden center, I came home and planted the trays of annuals I had purchased. It looked pretty, but was far from finished.

While I gardened, my thoughts had turned to the sexy man a few times and the slow burn those thoughts triggered felt really nice. It was encouraging that my grief and three years of abstinence hadn't permanently damaged my libido.

"Trust me, Sidney, you have to meet them in person. I would not do them justice if I attempted to explain."

"Why?"

"Because they're a riot."

"In what way?"

"You just need to go. Spike's medicine arrived with the morning deliveries and you're dropping it off."

"And they won't guess that I'm there to check them out?"

"They probably will, but you aren't going to care. Neither will they. Trust me."

"All right, I'll go."

"Come back here after, I want your thoughts."

"You're weird."

"Maybe, still come back."

"Fine, I'll come back."

The Thompson brothers owned the gas station on the other end of Historic Main Street from where the clinic was located. Spike was their Rottweiler, whom Rylee had seen earlier in the week for his annual check up. I couldn't lie; Rylee's odd behavior piqued my interest.

As I walked down Main Street, I thought about the stray dog. He'd eaten the hamburger I had left for him and the one I left the following morning. My hope was he'd grow comfortable enough around me that I could check him over, but he was semi-wild so I needed to take baby steps.

The Thompson brothers' gas station was on the wrong side of weathered and worn, made even more noticeable since Historic Main Street was a tourist attraction so most of the other business owners kept their establishments in pristine condition. Spike greeted me first; a three-year-old, hundred and twenty pound Rottweiler who was as friendly as he was big. Ichabod and Jeshaiah appeared, a study of opposites. Rylee's descriptions had been spot on. Ichabod's hair, what was left of it, was blond and he was reed thin. Jeshaiah was as dark as Ichabod was light and he was round, like Mr. Miller, with a belly that would make Santa proud. They were a blending of *Beverly Hillbillies* and *The Waltons* and despite their less than clean appearance, as they approached they didn't put me off. In fact, I felt almost comforted because they were what they were. No pretense.

"Who is this pretty lady?" Ichabod asked as he stopped just in front of me, invading my personal space.

"I'm Sidney Stephens. I work with Rylee and she asked that I drop off Spike's medicine."

"You hear that, Jeshaiah, she's dropping off the medicine." He was chewing on a toothpick that he pulled from his mouth and pointed at me. "We could have picked it up."

"Rylee wanted me to meet you."

His lips curled up exposing very yellow teeth. "She took a shine to me."

I didn't mean to laugh, but when I saw the self-deprecating smile spread over Ichabod's face I couldn't stop it.

"She did, didn't she? Sent you here to check me out. Maybe probe me with questions to see if I'm available. A guy like me there's lots of interest."

"Yeah, interest in when you're going to take your next bath," Jeshaiah chimed in.

"You should talk. Why the hell do you think I don't stand down wind from you."

Rylee was right; these two were a hoot. "How long have you lived here?"

"Are you asking for you or your friend?" Ichabod asked.

"Me. Your tanks are vintage, so I'm guessing this was probably the original station in town. Did your family own it even then?"

"Yeah. Pa owned it, his pa before him and now we do. Pa died a decade back. God rest his soul."

"Amen," Jeshaiah added. True affection heard in his soft whisper. I hurt for them but I also felt envious that they had the kind of father who warranted such reverence a decade after his death.

"I'm sorry."

Ichabod waved that off. "Do you have family?"

"Foster kid, so generations of family is lost on me, but something I'd have liked."

Ichabod's expression changed, one that looked even more sorrowful because I hadn't had family. He wasn't wrong. "I'm sorry to hear that."

"I found a family with my husband."

"Good man."

The roar of an engine came from down the street, which had my heart tripping in my chest just as *he* pulled into the station. I never really gave motorcycles a thought, but the way he sat on one I liked…a lot. And I couldn't believe I just had that thought. For three years none of the men Rylee paraded in front of me warranted a second look and this guy I couldn't not look. But getting caught staring again was not going to happen; it was time to go. "If you have any questions about the medicine for Spike, please don't hesitate to call the clinic. It was nice meeting you both."

"How about you give me your number and I'll call you direct," Ichabod said as he winked, then added, "You ever go to the Brass Bull?"

"Frequently, since we moved here."

"Maybe we'll see you and the doc that has the hots for me there sometime."

"I'll buy the first round."

"Ah, you are my kind of woman. Nice meeting ya, Sidney." He then turned and joined his brother who was already filling the tank for the sexy man.

I glanced at *him*, it was hard not to. He spoke, he wasn't talking to me—he was addressing Jeshaiah—but that voice. Good God, I could listen to him read the phonebook and be perfectly content to do so. I should have walked away. The Thompson brothers were otherwise engaged and I was just standing there staring again, but I couldn't get my feet to move. And as he had done before, his shoulders tensed right before he glanced in my direction. He recognized me, and like our last encounter, he didn't look away either. He leaned up against the vintage pump, pushed his hands into the front pockets of his jeans and just stared back. A stare that turned into a blatant once over as his eyes moved down my body, lingering a moment longer on my breasts. When his eyes found mine again, he grinned. It was just the slightest curving of his lips and yet my body throbbed. That was enough to get my feet moving. I tried to convince myself my reaction was due to three years of abstinence, but I was pretty sure even if I were a lady of the night that look still would have gotten me hot. It was just that good.

Doc Cassidy had stopped by earlier for Rylee, an emergency home visit. He was retiring at the end of the summer, so we'd have the whole summer to get up to speed on his patients and it would give them time to get used to us.

Since I was home, I decided to tackle the grocery store. It had been three weeks since we moved here and outside of the burgers I had grilled up, we'd been grabbing dinner out. That wasn't healthy and the house came with a fairly new refrigerator, one that was currently empty. It was time to stock up.

As I drove through town, I wondered if the sight of the mountain right there would ever grow old for me. I hoped not. The beauty, the majesty and how humbling it was to be reminded that we were just Mother Nature's guests.

Sometimes it felt like New Jersey, my life there—the group home, Mrs. Crane, the Millers—was a different lifetime…all but Jake. I still felt him, took comfort in that. The Stephenses were taking a vacation to Greece, an extended several month vacation; I'd called them last night and wished them a safe trip. They promised to send lots of pictures.

It was early evening on a Saturday and the parking lot for the market was packed. Note to self; don't shop on Saturday. I drove around for a while, finding a spot down one of the side streets near the store. Maybe it was like one of those dating while shopping events the store in New Jersey used to have every month. Otherwise, this much activity at the grocery on a Saturday night did not bode well for the social life in Sheridan. Poor Rylee. I was just passing a little side alley when I felt the hair on my arms stand on end. Since the only person to ever cause a physical response in me like that was the sexy man, it was a pretty good guess he was down that alley. I had no business going down there and when I did bump into him, and I knew I would, what would I say? On the other hand, he was down an alley so maybe he was in trouble. I didn't have to argue too hard with myself to check it out. I had only gone a few yards when I saw him leaning over his motorcycle. His back was to me, but even in that position I could tell he was in pain. There were a few drops of what looked like blood near his bike's tire.

"Are you okay?"

"Go away."

His response jarred me since everyone we'd met in Sheridan had been very friendly and, to be honest, kind of pissed me off. "You're bleeding."

"No shit."

To say I was disappointed would be fair. The man was hot, first man since Jake to make me hot, so to learn he was also a dick was a definite disappointment. I contemplated leaving him, but I was a doctor and he needed one; sure, my patients walked around on four legs, but anatomy was anatomy.

"I'm a doctor. Can I take a look?"

He turned then, so suddenly I jerked and almost fell back on my ass. Even being a dick, my body responded to him—the full beard, the dark hair pulled up into a bun, the most piercing pale blue eyes I'd ever seen and full lips, framed by whiskers, that were sneering at me.

"You're a doctor?"

He practically snarled that. His words were more an accusation than a question. "I'm a vet."

If possible, his sneer grew even nastier. "Not a real doctor."

Physically the man was very appealing, but I wanted to kick him in the balls every time he opened his mouth. "I'm a VMD and since I work with animals, you're in luck."

The sneer shifted, but whether he stared in anger or humor I couldn't say.

"Are you going to continue to bleed all over your bike or will you let me take a look?"

Heat and something more primal flashed in his eyes before he moved them down my body again not at all hiding his lascivious leer. Being this close to him I felt exposed, as if he could see through the layers of fabric to my body beneath.

"You talk to your old man like that?"

Like I would discuss Jake with this clown. "What I do with my old man is none of your business. Do you want my help or not?"

"Take a look."

He said that as he lifted his white T-shirt, a motion I suspected he did often in front of women. One he was hoping would get a rise from me and honestly it did. He was built like a freaking god, but the blood marring his eight-pack kept me from actually drooling.

Hunching down in front of him, I heard the chuckle that resonated deep in his throat. "Got to say, I like you kneeling in front of me babe."

Charming.

It was a gunshot wound. Not one he received today, but definitely within the past week. Sometime very close to when I had last seen him at Ichabod's. What I found even more surprising than the fact that he had a gun shot wound, was that he only had one. With his delightful personality, he should be riddled with them… like human Swiss cheese. The thought nearly had me giggling. "You were shot? How did you reopen this?"

"You can tell that?" There was that disbelief again.

There was an exit wound; it didn't take a genius to deduce what caused it. I didn't say that to him. "Yeah. How did you reopen it?"

"That fucking matters why?"

Why me? As if fate hadn't done enough to me, now the fickle bitch put me in the path of this cantankerous asshole. An asshole I actually felt a physical response to. The words rolled off my tongue without thought. "A little lower and to the right and no one would be kneeling in front of you again. Pity."

Something shifted in the air and it was then that I realized this man was dangerous. There was a note of curiosity in his tone when he said, "You've got some spunk. You look like a kindergarten teacher, but you've got a spine."

I ground my teeth, a retort on my tongue, but there was no point in engaging this asshole in a sparring of words. Instead I said, "You're lucky. It's a clean shot, missed the major stuff. It must hurt like a bitch though, right through the muscles. You need a hospital. It should be cleaned and restitched."

"No hospital."

I did look at him then. His expression changed into something sinister. "And no cops."

It registered then that this man was likely a criminal and here I stood in what could be described as a secluded alley staring at his gunshot wound. How the hell had I ended up here? I just wanted groceries, and yet when I spoke, instead of making my leave I said, "Fine. No cops, but you need to be restitched. The clinic isn't far, but I suspect Doc will insist on calling the cops."

"Doc Cassidy?"

"Yeah."

"You're the one taking over the clinic?"

I wish I hadn't shared that. But I didn't beat myself up for long because why was it such a surprise to him that I was taking over the clinic? I was done; he'd live. I didn't even bother acknowledging him when I turned and walked away.

"What the fuck?" He bellowed at me. At me!

I stopped and looked back at him from over my shoulder. I had the feeling, in general, that people didn't walk away from him and I could admit fear skirted down my spine at the scowl on his face. And even still, the next words just tumbled out. "I understand why you were shot. I've been in your company for less than ten minutes and I'd like to shoot you. Get it cleaned and restitched or don't. Either way, you'll live."

"You're a doctor. What about the Hippocratic oath? To tend the ill to the best of your abilities?"

"Like you so eloquently pointed out, I'm just a vet."

He laughed, the smug ass actually laughed. "What's your name?"

There was no way I was giving him that information. He could figure it out since I had let it slip about the clinic, but he wouldn't be getting the information from me. "I'd rather it remain a mystery, one that stays unsolved."

I moved away from him again, but I heard his parting words because he shouted them at me. "I love mysteries."

Tempting, really fucking tempting to chase down the doc, though there was an equal chance I'd wring her neck as there was I'd kiss her. There was no denying that the few times I'd seen her in town she'd gained my attention because she was fucking hot as hell, but she could throw out attitude while looking like a prim librarian and that combination was a real fucking turn on.

My side was burning. Jesus, what the hell was I thinking? I knew better than to ride when I was still healing, but I ached for the road and the wind in my face. A part of me wanted to keep on riding, right back to Cheyenne, but I was needed here. She needed me. The sound of pipes echoed down the alley a few seconds before Tiny appeared, all six foot eight of him. Thank Christ.

He pulled up next to me as his stupid face split into a grin. "Told you not to ride."

"Fuck you."

His expression changed into his usual scowl. "How's she doing?"

"About the same."

"She needs professional help."

"You think if I could get her in somewhere I wouldn't? Fuck, man, I've had to put everything on hold to do this shit. But I made a promise."

"It's a fucking stupid promise. She made her choice, the wrong one. Something she's been doing for a long time."

Even I felt the phantom pain in my one-time beating heart. "Do you remember her as a kid? So fucking sweet."

Tiny's ugly mug looked even uglier when he frowned. "Yeah, she was a good kid. She ain't been that kid in a long time."

He wasn't wrong about that. Fucking drugs and alcohol didn't just destroy the user, but everyone within reaching distance. Carly was one of the gang and even if our lives took us in different directions, even if our bonds were stretched thin, we still looked out for each other. That was the promise we had all made.

"How's Pipes?" Pipes was my and Tiny's custom motorcycle shop that we'd opened a decade ago. We were one of the top custom shops on the west coast now. Growing too fast in my opinion. I wanted to slow it down, take fewer clients and focus on the work. Biased, because I hated the paperwork and expansion meant more paperwork. Luckily for me, Tiny loved all that shit.

"It's good. We've a few new custom orders. D.J. has come up with some sweet ideas. The team can handle it for now, but you may want to make an appearance."

"Yeah, when this heals I will."

"You know it's a bit fucked up that you're caring for the same person who shot you."

"She was high. I can't hold it against her when her judgment was seriously impaired."

"I think your judgment is seriously impaired, but I get it. I respect what you're doing."

It meant a lot coming from him. He grew up with shit, abused, kicked out of his house and yet he landed on his feet. And for all the shit he was giving me about this, he'd do the same. Shit, he'd done it for me. Gave me a place to stay when I'd been kicked out of my house. My dad was a serious piece of work, a con man. Used me in his cons when I was younger until I got wise to what he was doing then he had no use for me. It didn't keep him away though, fucker popped up from time to time when his cash was low looking to play me. He had nothing on me so he couldn't force me to help him like he did with so many others. Last I heard he was on the east coast. He'd come back though, he always did.

Tiny knew how I felt about what he'd done for me, so instead I asked, "We going to hug now?"

"You're a fucking dick."

I flashed him my shit-eating smile. "Yeah, I am. Speaking of which, I just met the new doc taking over for Cassidy."

"No shit. What's he like?"

"*She* is about thirty, fine body, killer face and brown hair the color of mink, the kind of hair you want on your pillow or running down your chest. And the bitch gave as good as she got."

"And did you charm her?"

"No. She wouldn't give me her name, told me she'd rather that stay an unsolved mystery."

Tiny threw his massive bald head back and howled with laughter. "I like her already."

I knew the fucker would, my own mouth splitting into a grin. "Now who's the dick?"

"Where do you think you learned it?"

Returning to the house, Carly was lying on the sofa watching television. Her one-time blond hair was dark and brittle. Her complexion was shit and she was about forty pounds soaking wet. And even though she was killing herself slowly, she'd get high or drunk in a heartbeat. It was a losing battle, only a matter of time before her body cried uncle. But when I looked at her I didn't see what she'd become, I saw the sweet-faced kid she'd been.

She spared me a look, took in Tiny, before her focus shifted back to the television. "I'm hungry."

"There's food in the refrigerator."

She tried to pout, something she had perfected at the age of eleven, but her yellow teeth and cheekbones so pronounced you could cut yourself on them ruined the effect. "Can't you make me something?"

"No. You're supposed to be learning to be self-sufficient. I'm paying rent on this place and I'm keeping you stocked with food. Your friends are coming around the clock to help you get your feet back under you, but if you keep fucking around I'm going to wipe my hands of all this shit."

I knew what came next and had it been feigned I'd be out the door, but it wasn't. Underneath the addict existed a terrified little girl. "I'll be alone."

"You aren't alone, you never have been, so stop fucking around. Pull your shit together or I'm having you committed against your will."

"You wouldn't."

"The fuck I wouldn't. You think I'm going to watch you slowly kill yourself? You shot me last week. Sneaking out, heading into town to get your hands on anything that would make you feel good. It's just like you to find the shit dealer who cut your shit with worse shit and when I came for my shift babysitting you, you fucking shot me. You're lucky I didn't press charges."

"I apologized for that."

"I have a fucking hole in my abdomen. Your sorry doesn't mean shit."

And then the tears came. They always came and this was why I stayed. Because this was Carly, one of the few people I considered a friend, and she was hurting. She needed help and though Jayce, Duncan, Garrett and Marnie all chipped in time to give her that help, we weren't professionals and it was growing more and more clear that Carly needed a fucking professional.

sidney

I dropped Rylee at the clinic and took her car to visit one of the other horse farms that Doc Cassidy had as clients. He had offered to come with me but at the end of the summer I would be solely responsible for these farms, so I declined his very tempting offer. I needed to do this on my own, needed to get comfortable with my clients without the crutch that was Doc Cassidy. I wished Jake could see me, see how far I'd come and how close to the dream Rylee and I were. He'd been our loudest cheerleader, wanted to be our first client when we opened our own practice. I missed him.

Pulling up the drive, I immediately saw how different McNealy's farm was to Jayce's place. The Hellars' farm was a well-oiled machine. Every building and every acre of land was perfectly maintained. McNealy's farm seemed to be struggling. The main farmhouse was in desperate need of a paint job. The fences were down in spots and the field was untended. I was happy to see that the horses I saw grazing looked healthy. Their coats were shiny and they didn't appear malnourished. Whatever struggles the farm battled, at least the horses didn't seem to feel it.

An older man, in his sixties, greeted me as I climbed from the car. And by greeting, he glared and asked in a voice clearly altered from years of smoking. "Who are you and what the hell do you want?"

Lovely.

"I'm Sidney Stephens. I'm taking over Doc Cassidy's practice."

"Ah, the girl from the east coast."

"Yes."

"I guess you want to see the horses."

I hadn't just popped over. I had called and made an appointment with his wife, but since we'd have years of business together I put on my diplomatic hat. "If now is a good time for you, yes, I'd like to get familiar with your horses."

"Never any time for nothing, but being as you're here. Come on."

He led me to the barn, one that had seen better days as he radioed for the groom to bring the grazing horses in; the stalls had all recently been mucked out, fresh water glistened in the wooden troughs and buckets of oats hung from the doors.

"It's feeding time."

Having reviewed the file, I knew the McNealy's had twelve horses. All used for trail rides.

"The names are on the door. You need me?"

"No, but I'll come find you if I have questions."

"Yeah." But he was already halfway out the door.

Reviewing the file, the horses grazed in the pasture for part of the day as I had seen when I arrived. I wanted to get a better look at the kind of grass they were eating. Each received a small ration of grain twice a day. Their feeding schedule looked good based on how active they were.

I took time with each of the horses; most were female and named after flowers. I checked their legs and hoofs; listened to their gastrointestinal tract, checked their eyes, teeth and gums. Felt for lumps and bumps, checked their hips. They looked good, healthy and strong. After the examinations, I walked outside to check out where they grazed. The grass was overgrown, but it was green and lush. Some of the fences were in dire need of repair. The horses could get out, but more disturbing other predators could get in.

Mr. McNealy approached. "You done?"

"Yes, but I wondered about the fences. Aren't you concerned about predators getting in?"

"It's on my list. It's only two others and me. We'll get to it."

He should push that up on his list, but I wasn't about to alienate the man. "Your horses look great. I'll update their files. If you need me, here's my cell."

He took my card and studied it a minute. "I'm glad Doc Cassidy picked a good replacement."

And with those words, he walked away and I couldn't help but grin. For a miserly man, I had just been given a compliment.

The roads leading back to town were terrible with potholes large enough to consume a small car. As I navigated around a hole the size of a hubcap, I ran right into another. The tire immediately went flat.

"Shit."

Inspecting the tire, there was no saving it. I went to the trunk for the jack, wrench and spare; Jake had insisted I learn how to change a tire and being out in the middle of nowhere, I was really grateful for the lesson. Getting the car up on the jack wasn't a problem, but removing the lug nuts was another matter. Who the hell put these on? I struggled, but managed to get two of the four off before I lost my hold on the wrench as my arm slipped and sliced across something under the tire well sharp enough that blood immediately started pooling from the wound.

"Damn it." Rylee had a first aid kit in the trunk and as I worked on unwrapping the gauze, while trying to apply pressure to stop the bleeding, I heard the sound of someone approaching. Glancing around the car, I caught only the sight of a black boot and jean-clad leg.

"Could you…" I started to ask but was immediately interrupted.

"What the fuck have you done?"

My eyes collided with a pair of pale blue ones. Of all the people I could have run into. It was like I was fodder for the gods, entertainment for them as they moved me around their board of life.

"Give me that." He took the rag from me and pressed hard on my cut, hard enough that it started to throb.

"Ouch." I tried to yank my arm away, his fingers tightened. "It hurts enough without your vise grip."

He ignored me. "Why didn't you call for help?"

"I was managing just fine before the wrench slipped."

"You've a gash on your arm deep enough to need stitches. You should have called your fucking husband."

If only I could have. "Can you help me wrap it?"

He grinned, the ass actually grinned at me. "Looks like the tables have turned. You're the one who needs stitches now."

"And I'll get them, but first I need to fix the car."

"I'll wrap your arm and change your tire."

"I can do it."

"I'm here. You're wounded. I'll fix your fucking car."

"Thank you." Offered reluctantly because despite being a dick and high-handed, he was helping me.

"What are you doing out here? Are you on the prowl looking for other animals you can dazzle with your bedside manner?"

I wanted to laugh because he had just called himself an animal. Instead I said, "I see you didn't bleed out."

"No thanks to you."

"I was the one to offer aid."

"You walked away."

"As I recall, you had some concerns regarding my credentials."

"As a doctor, maybe, but as a woman you can kneel in front of me any fucking time."

Of all the…where was that wrench?

He wrapped my arm, was very gentle while doing so, which surprised me. What was an even bigger surprise was the simple fact that while I contemplated rendering him unconscious, I couldn't deny his touch set me on fire. As soon as he finished, he moved to the tire. It didn't take him any effort at all to remove the remaining lug nuts. "You didn't answer me. What are you doing out here?"

"I was visiting McNealy's farm. Giving his horses their annual check-up."

"McNealy, he's a piece of work. Good with his animals, people not so much."

"He has fences down. I'd hate to think of anything happening to those horses."

Pale eyes focused on me. "There are mountain lions around here."

My heart raced in response to that. The idea of seeing an actual mountain lion was exciting and at the same time terrifying. It would be a disaster if a mountain lion got onto McNealy's farm.

"They usually keep to themselves, but if they're hungry there's no telling what they'll do."

And on those dire words he moved around me dropping the jack, wrench and tire into the trunk.

"You know where the medical clinic is?"

"Yes."

"Get that arm looked at."

"I will. Thanks for your help."

He said nothing, just stared at me for a minute before he strolled to his bike. As soon as it roared to life, he was gone with only the trail of dust kicked up in his wake remaining. He was rude and arrogant, but he'd also wrapped my arm and fixed my tire so I wasn't about to complain. My arm hurt like a bitch. I needed stitches and a drink.

Rylee went to get the car. I had had more than a few drinks so it was a good thing she'd agreed to be designated driver. I rarely drank to the point of wasted, had Connor to thank for that, but my arm hurt like hell and I didn't want to take the pain meds. They made me feel loopy.

Enjoying the feel of the alcohol in my blood, I rested my head on my hand and just took in my surroundings. Most of the male patrons were dressed in flannel shirts, jeans and cowboy boots. I thought it was just for pictures, the cowboy look of the west, but it really was how they dressed around here. I liked it. There was something very sexy about a man in jeans and cowboy boots, especially with the body many of them had. Muscles toned not from the gym, but hard labor. I realized I had been out of the game for a while and I didn't put out the 'I'm available' vibe, but I liked to believe I was still observant. And it appeared a few of the men in the place were looking in my direction with interest, but none of them approached. Rylee had been right about my wedding rings. Maybe it was time to put them away.

"Hey, Doc."

A shiver of awareness moved through me hearing that voice and then he came into view when he settled on the stool next to me. My rings clearly had no effect on him. What had Rylee said? The good guys wouldn't approach because of my rings. She was right again because this guy, so not good. My stomach felt all funny looking at him and since my brain was soaked in alcohol none of my mental roadblocks went up. The man really was something else even being rude and cocky. My fingers itched to touch his beard and to trace his lips.

"How's the arm?"

"Ten stitches."

"Jesus Christ." That quickly his demeanor changed to one of incredulity and, I'm pretty sure, disgust. "You're drunk."

"Tipsy."

"What the fuck? You're a doctor and you're mixing pain meds and alcohol?"

I snorted, an unattractive sound yes, but it couldn't be helped. "You're an ass. You know that, right?"

Surprise, it was quick, but I definitely saw it rolling over his face. "And you're an idiot. What kind of VMD are you?"

Even drunk, my blood boiled. Prick. "What makes you think I'm mixing drugs and alcohol?"

He glanced at my arm. "Ten stitches."

"Not that it is any of your business, but I'm not on pain meds. Thank you so much for your concern though. It's nice to know someone cares and vocalizes that concern in such a constructive and compassionate way."

It wasn't surprise this time, but something else flashed in those unusual eyes before he asked, "Are you here alone?"

"No. My friend is getting the car."

"Stag again. Your poor husband."

"You have an unnatural interest in my husband."

He had a reaction to that, but I was too drunk to figure it out or really to care.

"I'm just trying to figure you out."

"You don't need to do that, figure me out. Every time I'm near you I want to run away screaming." *Or jump you and kiss that damn smirk off your face.* "I irritate you just as much, so focus your energies on the countless women in town who actually want your company."

"See, now that just sounds like a challenge."

"Seriously. Did you bang your head recently? You might be suffering from brain trauma."

He had the oddest expression on his face and then that head dipped back and he roared with laughter. "You have a sense of humor too."

"I wasn't joking."

This only made him laugh harder.

My phone buzzed. Rylee was out front. "I've got to go."

"See you around, Doc."

"Is that a threat?"

"No, babe, a promise."

"Fabulous."

He was still laughing when the door closed behind me.

The Roberts' farm was very small. They had six horses out to stud, along with four others for riding. Both Mr. and Mrs. Roberts were pushing seventy and still they maintained much of the farm on their own. Their house was a white farmhouse that was meticulously maintained with the mountains rising up behind it and lush landscape surrounding it for as far as the eye could see.

"This is beautiful. Is this all yours?"

"Yeah. The farm has been in my family a long time. We've about two hundred acres. Just in those woods where that footpath is are the old out buildings of the original farm. They're in disrepair now, in need of being torn down. We had hoped to expand, removing some of the trees and those buildings to accommodate that growth, but it didn't work out. I like our size, but I know my son, Keith, had hoped for more. He's here somewhere, so hopefully you'll meet him before you leave. The horses are in the barn."

A large red barn with an attached silver silo completed the picture perfect scene.

Mr. Roberts stayed with me as I examined his horses.

"They're all very healthy and beautiful."

"They have champion Thoroughbred sire lines, which is why they're so sought after to stud."

"Have any of them run the circuit?"

"Little Prince before we owned him. He won the Preakness twice."

Little Prince was eighteen hands, not little at all, a pitch black Thoroughbred. He was magnificent.

"When I get back to the clinic, I'll update their records." Doc Cassidy's files were all hardcopy, so I couldn't update the records online. It was going to take days to convert the files to electronic, but once done it would make maintaining the records so much easier.

"How are you finding Wyoming?"

"The landscape is breathtaking, the people are extremely friendly and I adore the work."

"That's what we want to hear. The Mrs. has lemonade for us."

It was hot; a cold glass of lemonade would hit the spot. "Sounds great."

While walking to the house, a man appeared on horseback coming in the direction of the mountains. He was attractive—light brown hair, dark eyes and dressed in flannel, jeans, cowboy boots and hat. For just a moment, I took in the scene because I was staring at an honest to God cowboy on horseback and I had to say it was a really nice sight.

"There's Keith. He's the one who manages the place now, keeping the schedules and training the few grooms we have."

Keith's focus was on me and stayed on me as he dismounted. He was obviously trying to figure out who I was. Confirmed when he asked, "Who's this?"

"Sidney Stephens. She's taking over for Doc Cassidy. Came all the way from New Jersey."

"I heard he was retiring. Nice to meet you, Sidney."

"And you." We shook hands, his focus shifting to my ring-less finger since I didn't wear them when I did examinations. I'd seen that same move on countless television shows and movies, but I had never had it done to me. It felt kind of nice being on the receiving end of that subtle show of interest.

"Are you settling in? I imagine Sheridan is a bit different from what you're used to."

"It is, but a good change and the landscape couldn't be more beautiful."

"You're not wrong about that. I need to rub down Solomon, but we should set something up so I can go over the farm and animals with you."

"I'll call you."

"We could even make it a dinner meeting if you're so inclined."

It had been a while since a handsome man flirted with me; it felt nice. Sure, on first meeting he didn't make my blood burn, but he also didn't make me want to strangle the life from him either. "I'd like that."

"Me too," he said with a smile before he led Solomon to the barn. Mr. Roberts watched him for a beat or two before saying, "He's a good boy. Come, let's get that lemonade."

We stepped up onto the covered porch; the pitcher of lemonade dripped with condensation. "That looks delicious."

Mrs. Roberts smiled before looking over at her husband. "Why don't you take Sidney inside so she can clean up and I'll pour us a glass?"

After two glasses of lemonade and several homemade cookies, I was pulling down their drive being careful to avoid the potholes since I really had no desire to get another flat. Halfway back to town, I came upon a woman walking along the side of the road... the same one I had seen with *him*. It was the manner in which she was walking that brought on the wicked flashback of Connor because I'd seen that stagger from my brother more times than I could count. She was clearly on something and I had firsthand knowledge that people under the influence could be very unpredictable, but I couldn't get myself to drive past her. Maybe if someone had stopped to offer help to Connor it would have turned out differently for him. And there was a small part of me—a very small part—that took into consideration *him* in my decision to offer aid. Pulling over, I climbed from the car. She was entirely too thin and had the complexion of a drug user. Her stringy hair was in dire need of a good washing. She didn't notice me until she was practically on top of me.

"Who the hell are you?"

"Sidney. I'm the new vet taking over for Doc Cassidy."

"And you're here now why?"

"It's awfully hot today, would you like a ride?"

"Why?"

"It's kind of new to me, the whole small town everyone knows everyone thing, but offering you a ride on a hot day seems like the Sheridan thing to do."

"Where are you from?"

"New Jersey, Princeton area. It's a different world there. People would step over your dehydrated body, but when in Rome."

She turned, her gaze shifting to something behind her though I suspected she wanted the ride but was having trouble accepting it. She surprised me when she said, "Okay."

Once in the car I asked, "Where am I going?"

"Just keep following this road."

We drove for a few miles before she had me pulling off the main road to a little dirt one. A cabin appeared, very similar to Rylee's and my place.

I had followed her out of the car, but I didn't follow her to the door. I was worried about leaving her alone because she was clearly coming down from something, but then the door opened and *he* filled the space. I could admit I had hoped to see him. What that said about me was not something I really wanted to spend a lot of time figuring out. He hadn't seen me, his glower was directed solely on the woman.

"Where the fuck have you been?" There was comfort in the knowledge that he was an ass to everyone.

"Out."

I wasn't needed here; she was in good, if not pissed, hands so I made my retreat. I didn't get far.

"You."

Accusation dripped from that single word. My shoulders slumped as I turned to face him. He'd taken a few steps from the house, closer to me. Not good.

"How is it you're here?"

The other night he'd been a dick, but he had been flirting too and now he treated me like an unwanted solicitor. I had thought he might be bipolar, with his drastic mood swings. Maybe he wasn't bipolar, maybe he suffered from multiple personalities. I was tempted to ask him which of his personalities I was talking to now. This was definitely the angry one.

"I found your friend walking along the side of the road. I offered her a ride."

His hands balled into fists, but he managed through his clenched teeth, "Thanks."

"Do you have any idea what she's on?"

"No."

"Would you like help? I've a bit of experience with people in her condition."

"No." He practically spat that as he turned his back on me and headed inside.

I prided myself on being both tolerant and patient, but around this man I was neither of those things. "Are you a dick to everyone or is it just me?"

He stopped, his head twisting and those pale eyes froze me where I stood. "This ain't me being a dick. When I'm a dick, you'll know it."

Reasoning with a lunatic was a lesson in futility. I turned away from him because it was either that or wait for my head to spin off my neck like Linda Blair. I had actually wanted to see him. I needed my head examined.

"Doc?"

Now what?

"I get where your head was at offering Carly a ride, but putting yourself in danger to offer that aid is fucking stupid."

"Danger?"

"She's high."

It had been a risk, but one I'd do again. I didn't say as much to him. "You're right."

I'd surprised him again. His head shaking was proof of that. "I don't fucking get you."

"And you don't have to." I climbed into the car before he could comment. And as I drove off, I caught sight of him in the rearview mirror. He hadn't moved; he was still staring after me.

ABEL

The woman had a death wish. Honest to God, I was tempted to hunt down her husband and beat some sense into him. She just ran around the countryside without a care in the world. Offering a ride to a drug addict? Was she insane? Carly could have overpowered her, taken her purse, her ride. Carly fucking shot me and she's known me since we were kids. And why the fuck I cared about the new doc I hadn't a fucking clue. She was married. Maybe I was suffering from blood poisoning from the gunshot wound.

Slamming into the house, I went in search of Carly. She was in her room eating chips and watching television.

"Why am I here?"

Her eyes moved from the set to me. "Cause you love me."

"Seriously, I'm wasting my fucking time. I have a life. You aren't trying. You aren't making any effort at all to get better and frankly I'm done with this."

Her face paled, her hand stopped midway to her mouth. "Don't say that."

"I'm not doing this anymore. I'm going home."

"No."

"If you aren't willing to help yourself then why the hell am I trying so hard? Jayce only left here fifteen minutes before I showed up and I get here and you're gone—off to get high."

Panic entered her expression. "I'll try harder."

"You've said that before. If you don't want to talk to me, okay. But you need to talk to someone."

Her lower lip started to quiver and I hated seeing her look so broken, but she needed to do something to break the cycle.

"Okay," she whispered.

"Okay, what?"

"I'll talk to someone."

We'd been here before too. "If I go to the trouble of finding you someone to talk to, you aren't going to change your mind?"

"No. I'll talk to them."

"You fuck this up, I'm gone."

"I won't."

I climbed onto the bed and reached for the bowl of chips. "What are we watching?"

"Sleepy Hollow."

"Fucking Christ."

She giggled and rested her head on my shoulder and for that moment I let myself believe she was finally ready to accept the help being offered.

Pulling up the drive to the Hellars' farm, I took a minute to appreciate how well the family was doing. As a kid, this place had been like home to me. Back then they were doing well, but now they were dominating. They were good people and hard workers, so their success wasn't a surprise. Climbing from my bike, I headed to the front door. I'd called earlier, knew Marnie wasn't a fan of people just stopping over. The reason for that was she liked to have refreshments for her guests. Giving her a heads up meant she'd been baking. Her cookies were the fucking bomb.

I hadn't even knocked and she was there pulling the door open.

"Abel. It's so good to see you. Come in."

As soon as I stepped into the house, she wrapped me in a hug. She'd been the only mother figure I'd ever known.

"You look well. How's the business?" She asked as she stepped back and gestured for me to take a seat.

"Busy, growing a little too fast."

"Growing too fast is better than too slow."

That was true enough. Garrett walked in at that moment and like when I was a kid, I stood just a little bit taller. Garrett Hellar was a no nonsense man, a shrewd businessman and good father. I envied Jayce and Duncan that they had a father like him, since my own was a worthless piece of shit.

"Abel, son, so good to see you."

"And you, sir."

Jayce and Duncan walked into the room, joking about something, but as soon as they saw their dad they both quieted. Jayce settled on the sofa opposite me, reached for a cookie and grinned but Duncan stayed on the far side of the room. He and his dad had been tight growing up, but there was definitely some kind of odd dynamic going on between them now. What the hell was that all about?

Garrett leaned up against the fireplace, his arms crossing over his chest. "So you're here about Carly?"

"Yeah. She's ready to talk to someone."

Marnie stopped pouring the lemonade, her eyes zeroing in on me. "She is?"

"We talked last night, she's ready."

"Are you sure? She's done this before?" Garrett asked.

"I'm not sure, but she needs more than any of us can give her."

"I agree. My sister knows some wonderful therapists," Marnie said.

"I have to get back to my job, my life, but I'm really hoping I can do that knowing she's getting the help she needs."

"Whatever she needs, therapy, rehab, we'll do it," Garrett said then added, "She's a good kid, she'll find her way and we'll be there to help."

sidney

"I've got this. Why don't you get us some lunch? There's that sandwich place down the street." Rylee asked as she felt Sandbar's stomach, a large orange tabby that looked as if he was contemplating shredding her to pieces.

"Are you sure you've got him?"

"Yeah, he's all bluster."

"Where's his owner?"

That question was directed at Doc Cassidy. He looked up from the chart he studied. "Don't know, found him sniffing around the back door one day. He didn't have a collar, so I took him in. I can't take him to the kennel since he's not very friendly. They'd likely put him down."

Not very friendly was an understatement, but maybe he just needed a home. "We should take him, Rylee."

"What about Tigger and Stuart?"

"They're old and sleep all day and this little guy needs a family. If his presence upsets the others, then I'll work to find him another place. I think even a few days in a real home would work wonders on him."

Rylee looked past me to Doc Cassidy. "Would you mind?"

"No. Take him."

"You do realize that we now have three cats," Rylee said, and though she was joking, I had the sense she wasn't entirely joking.

"Don't forget the dog." Since I was still feeding the stray.

"How could I forget him?"

"The more the merrier."

"I was afraid you were going to say that."

"What do you want for lunch?"

"Surprise me."

"Doc?"

"You're going to Roberto's?" he asked.

"Yeah."

"The grilled chicken and broccoli rabe sub. Let me get you some money."

"No, my treat."

He stopped mid-motion of reaching for his wallet, accurately summing up that I wouldn't budge on the point. "I'll buy next time."

"Deal. I'll be back."

Stepping outside, it was mild even though it was summer. At home, it could get so blistering hot in the summer and frigid in the winter, but here the temperatures weren't as drastic. And seeing that mountain? The landscape in general? I loved the farmlands back home, but here I felt as if I should be charged every time I looked around.

Halfway to my destination, my skin tingled and my body hummed just as I heard the sound of a motorcycle coming up behind me. I wasn't sure I was ready to go another round with him. The man drove me insane.

"Are you stalking me?"

What an arrogant…I ignored him. He jogged up to join me. "Are you deaf?"

"I was ignoring you."

"Why? When you go to the trouble of seeking me out."

I stopped walking, felt the need to put my hands on my hips, but I managed to resist that urge. "How exactly am I stalking you when I was here first?"

He grinned. "You think about me. Don't you? It's okay to admit it."

"Don't you have someone else to bother?"

"But I like bothering you."

"Okay." I started away from him; he easily kept pace with me.

"You must keep your old man on his toes."

Had I? I never acted this way with Jake. "Are you the welcoming committee? Because I got to tell ya, you kind of suck at the job."

"Suck, interesting choice of words, Doc."

Why did I bother? "You might have the luxury of not needing to work, but I have a job. So, if you'll excuse me." He didn't take the hint.

"That's what makes this so perfect. I'm only here for a few weeks, maybe a month or two."

"Makes what perfect?"

"You and me."

"I'm seriously not following you."

"Come on, you feel it. You don't want a ride?"

"Ride what?"

"Me."

Speechless, well, I was almost speechless. "Does this tact work in general for you?"

"Usually I just need to bend a finger but being you're a doctor, I'm willing to put in a little effort."

"And if I were to take you up on your offer, what happens in a month or two?"

"I go back to Cheyenne. No strings."

"So you're offering..."

"Me."

Despite myself, I felt a quiver between my legs. It was lust, pure and simple.

"And my old man?"

I continued walking, he stopped, but he did call after me. "What he doesn't know can't hurt him."

That had me stopping, my head twisting back to look at him. "You really believe that?"

"No."

"Then why did you say it?"

The cocky expression changed; he looked almost serious. "You feel it too. I'm curious."

"Enough to condone cheating?"

He moved closer and his voice dropped. "If you were mine, you'd be so exhausted from all the fucking this conversation would never happen with another man."

Did he just say that to me?

Before I could put him in his place, he headed back to his bike calling from over his shoulder, "Think about that, Doc." And then he was gone.

I was working, but damn it, I *was* thinking about him. I didn't even know his name. He was vulgar, rude and arrogant and yet thinking about what he said, how he'd said it, my body ached. I intended to fight my baser needs because for three years I felt nothing for a man and to feel the sparks I felt for this man, no. He was wrong for me. Not at all my type and he wasn't even from around here. How was it possible that I found myself daydreaming on more than one occasion about him? Imagining how soft his lips were, the feel of his beard on my skin, between my legs. I had to shut that down. It was simple biology. I should call Keith, setup that dinner meeting and why I hadn't done so yet was not something I wanted to ponder.

Mr. McNealy had called earlier. One of his horses, Lily, came down with a case of colic. Upon examination, I had to give Lily a nasogastric tube and administered some analgesics to relieve the pain in her abdomen. There didn't appear to be an impaction nor was her colon twisted. Mr. McNealy had been with me for the examination, but he left a few minutes ago after one of his grooms came running into the barn. I finished up with Lily. She wasn't pawing the ground or making uncomfortable sounds, the medicine was working.

"I'll be back tomorrow to check on you."

She nudged my hand and gave a soft whinny. She was thanking me. And people said animals were dumb.

I stepped from the barn and didn't see Mr. McNealy, so I closed it up, securing the doors, and headed to my car. I'd call him when I returned to the clinic to let him know I'd be back in the morning.

I loved the drive to McNealy's farm; the scenery was just breathtaking. A movement out of the side window pulled my attention, a flash of black. Pulling the car over, I caught sight of the stray dog I'd been feeding. What was he doing out this way when he had a regular food source at my house? I had hoped he was plumping up, but he was still so thin so he had to have been near death before I started feeding him. He was limping, favoring his front left paw. I took mental stock of what supplies I had in the car. There was a tranquilizer gun in the back. If I could sedate the dog, I could get him to the clinic. Whatever was wrong with his leg, it needed to be tended or he'd die out here and while I had him I could treat the mange. He stumbled, falling on his belly. It was now or never. Grabbing the gun as I climbed from the car, I was mindful not to startle him as I moved closer and had just aimed the gun at his thigh when he jumped to his feet. I made a few startling discoveries in the seconds that followed. My stray dog that I thought was only slightly wolf was seriously more wolf than I thought and bigger than any wolf I'd ever seen. And he was growling, but not at me. Turning slowly around, my heart dropped into my stomach. About a hundred yards from me stood a mountain lion. He was spectacular, though also a little too thin, which meant he was hungry and I stood in between him and dinner. I thought to shoot him, but I only had one dart. It was fast acting and would take out the cat before he reached my jugular, but if my aim was off I was in trouble. Retreat was my only option and maybe if he got close enough I could make the shot and save the wolf and myself. I slowly backed up, the mountain lion stalked closer but not to the wolf, to me. Walking low, his focus unwavering, I felt true fear that there was a really good chance I wouldn't be getting out of this alive. And all those times that I wished I had died with Jake, I proved myself a liar because I wasn't ready to die. My hands shook as I lifted the gun and took aim.

I heard the motorcycle at the same time the cat did, his head jerked in the direction of the approaching sound. He stopped moving, gauging the new threat. As the sound grew louder, the cat turned and fled. My legs gave out as I fell to my knees. Bile rushed up my throat as I worked to keep it down. I felt lightheaded so put my head between my legs. I heard him, before I saw him.

"Are you fucking insane?"

Likely.

The dark energy pouring off him was frightening. He hunched down in front of me, lifting my face to his hard stare. "Did you seriously just try to go toe-to-toe with a fucking mountain lion?"

"I didn't know the mountain lion was there. I was going for the dog."

"What dog?"

Looking past him, the wolf—he really was more wolf than dog—was right where he'd been. "I need to get him back to the clinic."

He twisted his head, spotted the wolf. "It looks half dead. Better you put the thing out of his misery."

"No!" I stood and pushed past him. "He just needs food and some medicine."

"It's a wild animal."

"It's a dog." Partly.

"That thing is mostly wolf and it's been out here on its own. It's wild."

"I don't care. I'm taking him to the clinic."

"And how the hell are you going to do that?"

"I'm going to sedate him, put him in the cage in the back of my car and take him to the clinic."

"You're going to do this anyway. Aren't you?"

"Yes."

"Again I have to wonder what the fuck your husband would think."

"He would help me."

"Fucking Christ. Do you know how to shoot that thing?"

"I've never done it, but I know the mechanics."

"Give it to me. How long before it knocks him out?"

"Five minutes, maybe a little less."

"Where do I aim?"

"His thigh."

He lifted the gun, aimed and fired. The wolf jerked, the dart hitting him right in the thigh. The man handed me the gun. "Why don't you put that away and get the cage open."

"Thank you."

"Save it. When the wolf takes a bite out of you, you can explain your irrational behavior to your husband so he doesn't come after me."

It was on my tongue to tell him about Jake, but he was already walking toward the wolf.

Even for all his grumbling, he was very gentle with the wolf when he placed him in the cage. "He's really thin."

"Malnourished, weak from it. I hope it isn't too late." I couldn't imagine what he looked like before he started eating what I had been leaving for him. Poor baby.

"Are you okay with getting him into the clinic?"

"Yeah. How did you happen by?"

"McNealy called, told me one of his groom's spotted a mountain lion, said you had just left."

"You came looking for me?"

By the expression that rolled over his face, he thought I was slow. "Obviously."

"Why?"

"Because I knew I'd find you in a situation like the one I found you in."

I wasn't sure what to make of that. For all of his irritating ways, he had come looking for me and had he not, there was a very good chance that mountain lion—he saved my life. "Thank you."

He heard me and yet he ignored me. "Right to the clinic. Load up that gun in case you need to hit him again."

The warm fuzzy cooled. The man really was irritating and now I was indebted to him. "Can I get your name?"

"We'll save that for the next time."

And then he was gone. My legs were a bit weak, the situation with the mountain lion sinking in on how very close I had come. This wasn't New Jersey; I needed to remember that. I reloaded the gun before I headed to the clinic. It was late by the time I got there. The clinic was closed, as I knew it would be. Pulling around the back, I ran in for the hand truck Doc had for medicine and food deliveries. It took effort and I banged the shit out of Rylee's car, but I got the wolf into the clinic and in an exam room. Rylee must have gotten a ride home with Doc. I checked my phone and saw her message. Before I called her, I examined the wolf. His left leg was fractured, which explained why he'd been favoring it and why he hadn't run from the mountain lion. Working on the wolf was going to take longer than I thought. I called Rylee.

"Hey, I'm sorry I didn't come back. I ran into a little trouble."

"Is everything okay?"

"Yeah. I saw my stray dog on the way back from McNealy's farm. He was limping and he's still so thin and then he collapsed. I was going to tranquilize him so I could get him to the clinic."

"I'm sensing a but."

"I wasn't the only one eyeing the dog. There was a mountain lion."

"What! Oh my God. Are you okay? Where are you? Do you need me?"

"I'm fine, Rylee. I'm at the clinic. Someone came by at just the right time."

"Someone who?"

"No one, just…"

"Sidney, who?"

"The guy from the bakery."

"The one who made you catch your breath?"

"He doesn't make me catch my breath any more. It's more I want to gather my breath so I can scream at him until he's deaf."

"You've clearly had more encounters with him than you've shared."

"Encounters not worthy of repeating." That wasn't entirely true.

"Really and yet he arrived just in the nick of time. How did that happen?"

"You're enjoying this."

"Of course I am. So how did he know?"

"McNealy called to give him a heads up on the mountain lion since he isn't far from McNealy's farm."

"Wait, how do you know where he lives?" She answered her own question. "Ah, the encounters you have yet to share."

"Anyway, all is well. I have the wolf here, I'm going to be a while."

"Wait, you said it was a stray dog now you're calling it a wolf."

"He's part dog." Very little dog, but what Rylee didn't know couldn't hurt her. "He has a fractured leg, so we can't let him go until his leg heals but with the mange, he can't be here."

"You want to foster the wolf."

I did. I really did, but I appreciated he was a wild animal. Any domestication he may have had was rusty or lost, which was why I was thinking of building a pen with a shelter in our backyard. In our profession, there was a good chance we'd be fostering a lot of animals. I shared my thoughts with Rylee.

"There are rules about exotic animals."

"Like I said, he's part dog, but I'll take a sample of his blood to confirm."

"Well there's that. We have to be smart and careful since we're talking about a wild animal, but we can't throw him back out there either. Maybe we could get Jayce and Duncan to help us build the pen and shelter."

"That would be awesome. I'm going to clean him up and set his leg while he's out. I'll be home later."

"I'll call Jayce and see about getting started on that pen."

"I'll move him to the quarantine kennel when I'm done so long as we don't have an outbreak of something, he's okay for a few days."

"I'll see you soon. Oh and Sidney, I want to know the full story about bakery man." She hung up before I could reply.

Dropping my phone on the table, I washed up and keeping the

sedative close, I worked on the wolf. The skin on his leg was torn, the bone broken. I cleaned and treated it with antibiotics before I set it. Then came the task of washing the poor animal and injecting him to kill the mites. I took some blood to confirm that he wasn't pure wolf since Rylee had been right. Wyoming was one of twenty states that banned the private ownership of exotic animals. Not that I wanted to own this animal, but keeping him while he healed could be a gray area and I didn't want any legal issues dropped on us. After I got him food and water, I moved him to the quarantine kennel before sanitizing the exam room.

I pulled up a chair and waited for him to come out of the sedative, since I hadn't a clue how he would react. I must have fallen asleep because it was dark when I finally stirred. The wolf was awake, standing at the bars staring at me. His food bowl was empty as was one of the water bowls.

"You look better. You'll be staying with me for a while until that leg heals."

I was exhausted so I stood and put the chair back. I checked that I locked everything, including my guest. "I'm leaving you for the night. I'll be back tomorrow."

He'd moved; he was sprawled on the floor. His head was up as if on guard, but he looked exhausted and I suspected he'd be fast asleep as soon as the threat of me was out of sight.

"Night, handsome."

As I drove home, I couldn't help but compare the wolf to my rescuer. Both were beautiful, wild and dangerous and under that, a bit lost.

chapter eleven

sidney

A week after his rescue, the wolf was set up in a shelter at the house. He looked good, bulking up from the steady meals, and growing stronger every day. His fur was still matted, but the mites were gone. I had borrowed Rylee's car again, seriously needed to get my own, and made my way across town. My destination, the little cabin in the woods. I was determined to learn his name, to thank him again because I owed him my life and I didn't even know what to call him.

His bike was parked out front, which immediately had my stomach twisting with nerves. I reached for the tin of cookies I had baked. It wasn't much, but I wanted to offer him something as a thank you. Jake had always loved my cookies. My hands were damp as I reached for the doorbell and everything in me went tight as I waited for the door to open. And when it did, seeing him standing there filling the space had my body responding in a very confusing, but not unpleasant, way.

"Doc. What are you doing here?" To say he was surprised to find me on his doorstep would be fair.

"I came to give you these and to thank you again for your help last week."

"How's the wolf?"

"He's good. He's gained a few pounds. His leg was fractured, so we're keeping him until it heals."

"No more run-ins with the mountain lion?"

"No."

He gestured to the tin I held. "What's that?"

I handed it to him. "Cookies."

Those pale eyes found mine. "Homemade?"

"Yes."

"Sweet. Want to come in?"

I did. I was surprised at how much I did, but I suspected his girlfriend would have a problem with that. "That's okay. I don't want to intrude. I just wanted to say thank you. And I'd like to know what I can call you."

"You want to call me, Doc?"

I really thought it was possible that he had multiple personalities because this personality was charming in a rakish way.

"It's Abel Madden."

Abel, yeah he looked like an Abel.

"Thank you, Abel."

"Any time, Doc."

"My name's actually..."

"Next time."

My pulse jumped from excitement. There was going to be a next time. And because I was thrown off-balance at how very much I wanted there to be a next time, I retreated. "I'll see you around. Enjoy the cookies."

"See ya, Doc."

My hands were actually shaking as I drove away from him. I tried to deny the attraction, but every time I was near him it only grew stronger. And for a man who drove me out of my mind. It was because I felt so conflicted, that I pulled into the quiet cemetery. After I lost Jake, I spent a lot of time at his grave. At first, it tore me up but eventually I found solace visiting him. I could use a little of that now.

It wasn't a large cemetery and some of the stones were rather old. People visited, the flowers and flags, pictures and mementos left on the graves were proof that though gone, these loved ones were not forgotten. I had left flowers for Jake every week; a small picture of us was buried at his grave. Even after all this time, it hurt thinking of him there. Not forgotten, but gone from me forever.

Wiping at my eyes, I noticed Mr. Milburn standing at a grave. His head was lowered and his back was hunched. I could feel his grief from my distance and understood all too well how he felt.

His head lifted, his eyes catching mine before a smile touched his lips. I took that as an invitation and joined him.

"I'm sorry to intrude."

"Not at all. I was just visiting Maggie."

My eyes moved to her stone and the lasting tribute to the woman she had been.

Margaret Pearl Milburn
Born:July 14, 1943
Died: April 28, 2004
Beloved Wife

It was just a few months past the anniversary of her death. Those days were the hardest; the memories that you managed to battle back into the deepest recesses of your mind came back with startling clarity on the anniversary. Understanding, I reached for Mr. Milburn's hand and offered him silent comfort as he remembered and mourned his wife.

I needed a car. I didn't want anything new, but I needed something big enough to carry my supplies and it had to have four-wheel drive so I didn't get stuck in muddy farmland. In the past, Jake would have done a bunch of research on reliability and safety. He'd have a whole spreadsheet on the cars I was pondering. He wouldn't have discouraged my picks, but he'd have made certain I had all the facts before I purchased. It had been an endearing if not overwhelming trait.

For this purchase, I asked Doc Cassidy how he felt about his Cherokee. He raved and told me where he'd purchased it. I was to drop his name to the proprietor, Jimmy Dean, and he'd be sure to give me a good deal and would refrain from his customary practice of pulling fast ones. The man was named after a brand of breakfast meat and he owned a used car dealership, pulling fast ones seemed inevitable.

There were several four-wheel drive Cherokees available. Jimmy had even offered to personally show them to me, but he ate chew and kept spitting it out. And not just spitting, but somehow creating an arc with the brown saliva. It was really nasty, in fact so nasty that I might swear off sausage for the rest of my life since Jimmy Dean and arcing saliva would forever be synonymous. Which was a damn shame because I loved Jimmy Dean sausage.

So there I stood looking at four Cherokees that looked remarkably the same, even the mileage was similar. I wondered if you could doctor that like the dad from *Matilda* had. What did one do when looking at a used car? New cars were one thing, you knew what you were getting, but a used car I imagine there were things you should check. Like looking under the hood—what I'd be looking for though escaped me—and kicking the tires. I hadn't a clue. Maybe I should have Googled how to shop for a used car. I then remembered Ichabod and Jeshaiah were right down the street. They owned a garage. They could probably tell me what I should look for. Jimmy Dean hadn't gone far. He loitered a few aisles over from me, pretending to wipe away nonexistent dirt from a windshield. He turned as I approached, spat an arc of brown saliva and smiled.

"Have you decided?"

"Not yet. I'm definitely interested and will be back later today to make my purchase."

"Anything I can do to help you with your decision?"

It wasn't likely he'd answer me honestly, he had that look and I had already been warned that he pulled fast ones. "No, I'm good. I'll be back."

He didn't believe I'd be back, which probably worked in my favor. When I came back, he might be more eager to make the sale.

Ichabod was working the pumps when I arrived. Spike saw me first, barking before running over in welcome.

"Hey, Sidney. What brings you here?"

"I was just over at Jimmy Dean's for a used car and I realized I haven't a clue what I should be looking at."

A look passed over Ichabod's face, so fast I almost missed it, but what fed that look I didn't know. "What kind of car?"

"A Cherokee. Doc Cassidy recommended Jimmy Dean."

"You go out to the area farms, right?"

"Yeah."

"So you want to make sure the engine and transmission are solid or you'll be spending more money fixing them than you did on the car, but you wouldn't know what to check for. Jeshaiah is doing a tow and I'm needed here." He scratched his head; he actually scratched his head as if it helped him think. And apparently it did. "Wait, I've an idea. I'll be right back."

"I'll man the pumps."

He grinned back at me before hurrying inside, which for Ichabod meant he walked at normal speed instead of his usual slow swagger.

An old blue car pulled into the station. A little old lady, who barely saw over the steering wheel, smiled as she parked and shut off her engine. "I haven't seen you here before. Are you new?"

"No, I'm just covering for Ichabod. He ran into the office for a minute. I'm Sidney..."

"Oh, I know you. You're the young girl taking over for Doc Cassidy."

Small towns had very efficient rumor mills. "Yes, with my partner Rylee."

"That's wonderful for you, and Doc, he needs to retire. The man works too hard. I'm Millie Wells. I don't do much anymore but read my romance books and tend my gardens."

"Sounds like a wonderful way to pass the time to me."

"Would you mind filling my tank with regular? I don't know how."

"Sure."

"It takes a lot," Millie warned and she wasn't wrong, so while we waited I washed her front and back windows and checked the air in her tires. When she pulled away, I waved as I clutched the sixty dollars in cash she had handed me, some of which was my tip. I didn't notice Ichabod until I turned to see what was keeping him.

"You're good at that. She has never tipped Jeshaiah or me. If you get tired of caring for animals, you've got a job here."

An unfamiliar, but pleasant sensation moved through me hearing Ichabod's praise. The moment was cut short though by the sound of a familiar engine growing closer.

"What's he doing here?" Seriously we ran into each other an awful lot.

"I called him."

My neck should have snapped in two with how fast I jerked my head to Ichabod. "Why?"

"You need help picking out your car."

"But why him?"

"Because Abel knows his shit."

There was no time to express my feelings on Ichabod's solution because Abel was pulling into the station, stopping just in front of us—so close he almost ran over my toes. He cut the engine, but he didn't climb off his bike. He just sat there straddling it. I couldn't help it; my eyes took it upon themselves to inspect, in detail, the man before me. His thigh muscles in his jeans were spectacular, made even more so in that position. I was blatantly giving the man the once over while he watched me do it.

"I see you missed me, Doc. You know, you didn't have to ask

Ichabod to call me. You could have done that yourself."

My focus snapped to his face to see humor burning in his blue gaze. I would rather scoop my eyes out of their sockets before giving in to the urge to look lower again and even with the threat of blindness in the most brutal way, I still wanted to look lower. I went on the defensive; if I got him to piss me off I would be less likely to gawk.

"I didn't know he was calling you. The thought never occurred to me." And that was true in regards to the used car situation.

He leaned into me, his whiskered chin so close I swear I felt it lightly brushing the sensitive skin under my jaw. And even if the contact was just in my head, the phantom tingles it stirred were strong enough that I nearly moaned in pleasure. "I didn't think you were a liar."

A liar? Where the hell did that come from? "Excuse me?"

"The thought of me never occurred to you is a lie. You think about me all the time."

The man was insufferable, made even more so because the cocky bastard was right. "This was clearly a mistake. I'm sorry to have bothered you, Ichabod. I'll just wing it. Thanks anyway." I started away, but strong fingers wrapped around my wrist that applied very little pressure but still managed to halt my forward motion. I felt both a thrill and irritation looking down at the hand holding me. "Could you please unhand me?"

"I'll take a look at your trucks."

"I appreciate that but surely you have better things to do than look at used cars."

I was surprised at the anger I heard in his tone when he spoke next. "Someone should. I'm here, I'll look at them for you."

What was the point in arguing? I didn't know what I should look for, he did, and he was willing to help. "Thank you. I'd appreciate your help."

"Climb on."

My entire body reacted to those two words, a burning that I hadn't felt in a long time. The truth of it was, I'd been envisioning riding on the back of his bike since that first day at the bakery. Now that the opportunity was here I feared the experience would be so fantastic that I'd fall right off in a boneless mess. "Maybe I should walk."

"I have other things to do. Waiting for you to walk when we're going to the same place makes no fucking sense."

He didn't have to be so curt about it, even if he did have a point. On the other hand, I imagined it would be far more time consuming shoveling the splattered mess of me off the pavement, though I suspected Ichabod had mastered that technique since he and his brother seemed the type to not have a problem with roadkill for dinner.

"Fine. Have you ever been tested for multiple personalities?"

His expression in response was priceless. He thought I was a nut. "Multiple personalities?"

"Yeah, I've met Cocky, Flirty and Angry. You have at least three, but I'm guessing there are more in there."

He didn't know what to make of that; he looked conflicted. Like he wanted to laugh at the same time wanting to turn his bike around and seeing the last of me. "No, I was never tested for multiple personalities."

I almost encouraged him to make the appointment, since knowing was half of the battle, but I wisely held my tongue. I climbed on, feeling awkward since I had never ridden on the back of a motorcycle.

"I'm your first?"

He was referring to riding on a motorcycle, but added the sexual innuendo because he was Abel.

"Flirty is back. I prefer him to Angry."

That earned me a chuckle. "Hold on to me."

I curled my fingers at the waist of his jeans because what I wanted to do was wrap my arms around his stomach and press in close. Abel was of a similar mindset when he grabbed my hands and pulled them in front of him, linking them at his stomach.

"Don't be shy, Doc."

Before I could counter, we were speeding away and honest to God it was the most amazing three minutes of my life. I wanted a motorcycle; one that preferably came with Flirty or Cocky Abel. I didn't think Angry Abel would be nearly as fun. He obviously knew Jimmy's lot because he took us right to the Cherokees. He cut the engine.

"You climb off first."

So I did, my legs hummed and felt a bit unsteady and yet I wanted to climb right back on. Abel didn't immediately climb off, his focus on me. "You liked that."

"Loved it."

Another hesitation before he climbed from his bike and spent close to an hour checking over my four options. I gave in a little, though I'd ogled him enough at Ichabod's, and checked out his ass in those jeans since it was a very fine ass. I waited for the guilt to come—the pain that I was somehow stepping out on Jake—but it never came. For some reason this man didn't bring those feelings. He brought a fresh wave of new feelings, but not those.

"You should get this one. It's in the best shape of the four."

Even I couldn't pick fault with his kindness and it was a kindness to drop whatever he was doing to help me pick out my car. Sure it was sandwiched between inappropriate comments, but it was still kindness. "Thank you."

"You can thank me by climbing into the back and christening it with me." He offered that with a grin and wink. His mood radically changed, his tone tainted with anger. "Should have been your husband doing this. Man has a woman like you he should be standing here looking over your car. He doesn't take care of what's his, someone else will. And you should want more." He looked genuinely pissed.

Again I wanted to set him straight about Jake, but him believing there was an old man at home kept the boundaries firmly established. And with him, I needed those boundaries because he would eat me alive. I was kind of curious about what the running theories were around Jake since no one had seen him, obviously, so where did they think he was? Not that any of it mattered because Abel had a girlfriend.

"Thanks for your help." He started away from me, I touched his arm and he reacted like I'd burned him. "Seriously, thank you for taking the time out of your day to help me."

For a fraction of a second, I thought he was going to kiss me because those pale eyes lingered on my lips for longer than was polite. Instead he jerked his gaze to my face. "Yeah, you're welcome." He climbed back onto his bike and rode off and I didn't know which was worse, that he hadn't kissed me or that I had really wanted him to.

I woke to find Sandbar standing on the floor right by my head. I had a terrible suspicion that he was contemplating slitting my throat. He really wasn't friendly, and considering most cats merely tolerated humans because they fed them, for Sandbar to stand out in that group was saying a lot. Tigger and Stuart were curled together sleeping on part of my pillow. Sandbar kept a wide berth from them. They may be old, but they were strays at heart and he was smart enough to know to keep his distance. I wasn't giving up on him, though. I was determined to learn if there was a sweetie under all that nasty.

"Good morning, Sandbar. Did you sleep well?" I'd set up a bed for him in my room and the living room. He didn't use either. He usually curled up under the sofa.

"I understand your anger. Stranded, alone…I've been there, but you're not alone any more."

The cat didn't blink.

"I'd like to be your friend." Reaching my hand out just a little so he could smell me, he hissed before turning with a flick of his tail and walked out.

"We'll try that again tomorrow," I called after him.

Glancing at my watch, I had to get to work but first I headed outside. I had named the wolf Cain. It seemed fitting, he reminded me so much of Abel.

"Hey, handsome."

He waited at the gate for me. My heart moved into my throat every time I opened the door to give him his food. But the thrill was exhilarating, especially when he didn't lunge at me but stood stoically watching.

"I'll see you later. Maybe we can try for a walk tonight." His leg wasn't yet healed but we walked. Him in the pen, me outside, but he followed me. I think more out of curiosity, but it was a rush seeing such a magnificent animal keeping pace with me. I could spend all day with him, but I had to get to work.

Hellar Farm was a different sight today than it had been on my first visit. It'd been six weeks since the last time I paid a call and after visiting the McNealy farm, the Hellar place really was spectacular.

Most of the horses were stabled; it was a good chance for me to meet them. Unlike last time, Duncan Hellar would be the one showing me around. Doc had given me the lowdown. Duncan was three years younger than his brother. He'd been a bit of a wild kid in his youth, but he'd been shipped off to military school and came back a different person. Unlike his brother's rugged cowboy look, Duncan had a buzz cut, wore fatigues and preferred combat boots to cowboy boots. Unless he was leading a trail in which case he dressed the part of a Wyoming cowboy.

"Caramel Apple is training today, so you'll have to wait to see her."

"You have a beautiful stable of horses."

Duncan's focus shifted to just past my shoulder. "Dad has an eye for horse flesh."

I had yet to meet Garrett Hellar. I found the man to be a contradiction. He surrounded himself with beautiful things—his home and his horses—and yet I sensed more fear than love coming from Duncan. The same couldn't be said of Jayce but of the two, Jayce was definitely more laid back.

"How are you settling in?" Duncan's question pulled me from my pondering. It was an interesting turn of phrase, settling in, and one I'd heard countless times here.

"Our house is slowly coming together. Everyone has been so welcoming."

"There's Dad now," Duncan said just as I heard a car coming up the drive. It was one of those ridiculous SUVs that were so big you could fit an entire NFL team in it. Why? For one person, why so much space?

The car pulled up to the garage and when Garrett Hellar stepped down, I was completely taken by surprise. He was older, in his sixties, and still a handsome devil. Walking toward us in faded jeans and a denim shirt, he was a man who obviously took care of himself. A smile, one that exposed his perfectly white teeth, greeted me first.

"You must be Sidney Stephens. It's nice to finally meet you."

Reaching for the hand he offered, I smiled back. "Nice to meet you."

"Is Duncan being a good guide?"

"Yes. Your horses are beautiful."

"Thank you. We're very proud of our stable. It's hot. Can I entice you with some sweet tea?"

"Please, that would be great."

We walked toward the house, Duncan taking up the rear. "So, you came from New Jersey, is that right?"

"Yes, around the Princeton area."

"And how are you finding Sheridan?"

"It's lovely and the landscape is very different from home. Seeing the mountain while walking through downtown still awes me every time."

"I've lived here all of my life and it still awes me."

"I'm happy to hear that. I worried the sight would grow common. I can't imagine that could ever be common."

He turned his bright blue eyes on me, a smile showing there first before reaching his lips. "I agree completely, Mrs. Stephens."

Stepping into the house, my breath caught. The whole back wall of the living room was nothing but windows that framed the magnificent landscape beyond. A stone fireplace took up the wall to the right, stone up to the ceiling, the opening large enough to walk in. A baby grand piano sat in the one corner, lost in the space, looking more like doll furniture. The sofas were exquisite taupe suede, armchairs in bright jeweled tones flanked the sofas and area rugs dotted the timber floors. "Wow, this is incredible."

"Thank you. Please come in and have a seat. I'll hunt us down something cold to drink."

Settling on one of the chairs, I noticed that Duncan hadn't moved from the door. "Are you joining us?"

"I have work to do, but I'll see you before you leave."

A woman breezed into the room, her American Indian heritage very clear. Her long black hair was twisted into a bun; her dark eyes landed on Duncan first before drifting to me. "You must be the new vet. I'm Marnie."

I started to rise; she stopped me. "Don't get up. Did Garrett go for drinks?"

"Yes."

"I'll go help him." She hurried out as fast as she'd hurried in.

"I'll be outside, I'll see you later," Duncan said before disappearing. He was definitely giving off an odd vibe, one he hadn't had before his dad arrived, but I didn't try to pinpoint the cause because the view held me mesmerized.

On my way to meet Rylee for dinner, I made a mental note to check on Caramel Apple first the next time I visited Hellar Farm. Garrett and Marnie clearly enjoyed entertaining, between the two of them there was never a lull in the conversation. Both were very easy-going and friendly. Duncan hadn't returned to the house, but when I left, as promised, he saw mc to my car. Jayce called a hello as he brushed down Midnight Moon after their ride.

Pulling into a favorite nightspot, the Brass Bull, I noticed Rylee hadn't arrived yet. She had texted earlier saying she had a few files to update and that I should get a table and order us some drinks. Inside the music was loud, the place was packed and the scents coming from the kitchen made my mouth water. I scanned the bar looking for Ichabod and Jeshaiah, something I found myself doing whenever I came here, but they weren't there.

Lorelei, the hostess, asked, "One honey?" She had a beehive hairdo, no lie, a freaking beehive the color of honey.

"Two, please."

"Sure thing, this way."

For a larger woman, she moved with ease through the tables until we reached one along the wall. "Is this okay?"

"It's great. Thanks."

"Can I get you a drink?"

"Draft beer for me, whatever is on tap, and a martini, dirty with three olives."

"You got it. Special tonight is the house blended burger—short ribs, ground sirloin and chuck—with onion rings, Swiss cheese and Bobby's homemade barbeque sauce."

"Two of those, medium. Thanks, Lorelei."

"Sure thing, honey, and welcome to Sheridan. Glad Doc Cassidy is finally retiring. The man works too hard." I must have passed some kind of Lorelei test to earn the welcome because Rylee and I had been dining there frequently but this was the first time Lorelei had offered the words.

"You're not wrong. Between Rylee and myself, we're overwhelmed and he's been doing it solo. I don't know how the man did it."

"I hear that. I'll be back with your drinks."

Notwithstanding the fact that the entire population of Sheridan shopped for groceries on the same day, it had a very active nightlife. This place was hopping; there was a band setting up and an electric bull. I'd never been on one of those, but I think I could be tempted to try it. The energy that moved through the bar was addictive—the familiarity and consistency. Would Rylee and I become one of the regulars, one of the locals who added to the familiar and consistent? For the first time in three years, I was hopeful for the future. And then that bitch fate stepped in when 'Yours' from Ella Henderson started pumping through the place. My eyes jerked to the jukebox and the couple who was swaying to the song, his face pressed against her neck. My heart twisted, my lungs exhaled on a gasp as the memory settled over me. I had first heard the song almost a year after Jake died, the lyrics ripping me apart because of how accurately they expressed how I had felt being with him. I continued to listen to it to torture myself, mourning the loss of something so beautiful. He had loved me unconditionally and I missed feeling that connected to someone. And even missing him, I wondered what he would think of the man who I thought about far more than I should. Would he be disappointed that the first man to stir something in me was someone so very different from him? I was so lost in the memory I didn't realize I was no longer alone. Looking up, my eyes collided with a pair of pale blue ones. Speak of the devil. My attention shifted to the giant behind him. Holy shit, the man was huge, scary as hell and staring at me like I'd just killed his dog.

"Doc."

Dragging my eyes back to Abel, I held his stare and yet, for the life of me, I hadn't a clue what he was thinking because he eyed me in the most unusual way.

"Is your old man running late?"

A tear slipped from my already overly bright eyes because for this man, whom I hardly knew and found irritating more than appealing, I was ready to let go of Jake and that left me feeling both tender and a touch sad. I tried to nonchalantly brush the tear away as I responded with sarcasm, the safest option feeling as I did. "Are you hoping for a quick go in the men's room before he arrives?"

"What'd I tell you, Tiny? Doc here has some serious attitude."

My jaw may have dropped because what a ludicrous name for the giant. "Tiny? Your name is Tiny?"

In response, Tiny's mouth split into a grin. One so wicked I couldn't help but grin back.

"I heard you tried to help Abel. He's not a great patient."

Turning my focus to the man that had caused more than one sleepless night, I tried again to understand what it was about him that interested me. Sure he was sexy as sin, but that wasn't what stirred me. Why him? A man whom I shared nothing in common with, but like all the other times I pondered that dilemma I came up empty. Realizing I hadn't answered Tiny I said, "Being a shitty patient is the least of his problems."

This earned me a full-out laugh from Tiny and a glare from Abel that had both alarm and awareness sliding through me. As I watched, his glare eased, his eyes lit with mischief as his lips turned up into a grin. The man was just too damn sexy for a woman's well being. He seriously needed to go away and tag one of the women that were just waiting to drop to their knees and worship him before I succumb to the urge.

"You've got a fan club that looks to be getting antsy over there," I said, with the hope that he'd take the hint. Instead he pulled out the chair opposite me.

"We'll wait with you."

Tiny was of a similar mindset when he took a chair from another table and dragged it over.

Lorelei appeared. "You want your usual, Abel?"

"Yeah."

"And you, Tiny?"

"Yep."

"So what's keeping your old man?"

Abel was like a dog with a bone and a part of me wondered if all the careless flirting would stop if I told him about Jake. Was he coming on so strong because he thought I wasn't a real option? I was tempted to put that theory to the test. "I'm waiting for my friend. She's just finishing at the clinic."

"Your partner Rylee?"

"Yes."

"What's your name?"

"I suspect you already know the answer to that."

"Maybe, but I'd like to hear it from you."

"Why now? I tried to offer it before."

He leaned closer, so close his breath teased the sensitive skin under my jaw that stirred a hunger in me even as I tried to deny its existence. His next words jarred me out of my haze of lust. "When a woman kneels down in front of me, I'm old-fashioned because I want to know her name."

"You're still on that? I wasn't kneeling, I was hunching."

He moved even closer. "Your name?"

Oh for Christ's sake. "Sidney."

"Where's your husband, Sidney?"

"Why are you so interested in my husband?" Stupid question; it seemed pretty clear why he was interested, but apparently my IQ was inversely related to the level of pheromones in my body.

His eyes were on my lips, that same craving I'd seen at the car dealership burned in them. Sweat broke out on my skin that felt hot and chilled all at once. Those eyes were looking right into mine. "Cause when just the sight of a woman has all my blood going south, I want to know why her old man lets her kneel down in front of another guy, lets another guy pick out her car."

"Her husband died three years ago in the same accident that took her brother. What else do you want to know?"

My head snapped to Rylee. Oh damn, the cat was out of the bag.

His warm fingers on my chin gently turned my gaze back on him. I saw a glimmer of something deeper when I looked into those pale eyes. He studied me for a good minute before he whispered, "Sorry, Doc."

Lorelei appeared.

"We'll take our drinks over there," Abel said as he stood, holding the chair out for Rylee, before he turned and walked away. Tiny followed after him.

Lorelei studied me as she placed our drinks down. I hadn't a clue what she was thinking; she didn't share, before she followed after Abel and Tiny. I guess that answered my question about whether he'd continue to flirt if he knew I didn't have a husband at home. I was disappointed, but what surprised me was just how disappointed I felt at his retreat.

"Who the hell was that?"

"Abel and Tiny."

"And how the hell do you know them?"

"The guy from the bakery, that's him."

"The one that caused a stir, the one who you've been having clandestine meetings with and failing to mention them to your best friend?"

"Clandestine, hardly, but yeah. We've had a few run-ins. He even helped me pick out my car."

"He helped pick out your car? Seriously, you have some explaining to do. How did that happen?"

"I went to Ichabod for help, Ichabod called Abel and he came. Spent an hour looking them over."

"I'm sensing a but."

"He didn't know about Jake."

Rylee looked equal parts confused and outraged. "Why not?"

"Boundaries, felt I needed them."

A slow smile spread over her face. "He gets that far under your skin? That's good."

"Not good. He just hightailed it out of here. I swear I can see tire marks on the floor."

"Likely just caught him off guard." She wasn't at all subtle when she leaned to the side and stared. "He's fucking hot."

"Every woman in the place agrees with you."

"And yet he was sitting here." Rylee's gaze shifted to me, her lips turning down. "I get it. You're beautiful, but you've also got that wounded look too. Any man with a pulse would want to be the one who made that hurt go away."

Jake had, the memory bringing a smile instead of pain. Rylee continued without needing any prompts from me; she was getting into her matchmaker mode. There was nothing to do, but let her have her say.

"I had hoped to hook you up with a cowboy, but I'm thinking the bad boy biker works too."

The idea appealed, I argued against it—self-preservation and all. "Rylee, seriously. I'm not jumping back into the dating scene with a man like that. He'd shred me up and spit out the pieces before I even knew what happened." Besides I was pretty sure the dust that had yet to settle from his speedy departure was a good indication that that ship had sailed.

"Um." She had more to say, but thank God she changed the subject. "So, Jayce called me earlier. I told him we'd be here. He's going to stop by with his brother."

"Nice. I met Garrett and Marnie today."

"Did you see the inside of their house?"

"It's as beautiful as you'd expect and the view out back was award-winning."

"So what's Garrett like?"

"I can definitely see where his sons get their looks. He's even hotter than them and very friendly."

"But?"

"There was just an odd dynamic. For as friendly as they all seem to be, they don't seem particularly friendly to each other. In fairness, it's the dynamic between Duncan and his dad, it's strange."

"Huh. Maybe it was just an off day."

"Yeah, maybe. I got you the burger special."

"Thank God. I can feel my ribs."

I loved Rylee, but she had the metabolism of a fifteen-year-old boy. She ate whatever she wanted, whenever she wanted and as much as she wanted and never gained a pound. She didn't even work out. It wasn't natural. And yes, I was envious since I only needed to look at food and I felt my hips getting bigger.

"He's looked over here three times." Rylee reached for her martini as she wiggled her brows at me.

The thought of those pale eyes fixed on me, eyes that showed a hint of compassion when learning about Jake and Connor, my heart did one long slow roll in my chest. Instead of commenting, I took a long drink from my beer. I was spared answering at all when the door opened and Jayce and Duncan entered.

"The Hellars just showed up."

Rylee started fluffing her hair, unnecessary because she was gorgeous; as she grew older, her wild, curly hair had tamed. It still had a curl, but it was long and wavy and combined with her green eyes, heads turned when she passed.

"Evening. Mind if we join you?" Jayce drawled, his brother just behind him grinning at Jayce's exaggerated cowboy greeting.

Rylee gestured to the vacant chairs. "Please."

"I'll grab us some beers," Duncan said before he headed off to the bar.

"How are you finding our town?"

Rylee tipped her chin down and smiled. "It's wonderful. Everyone has been very friendly."

"How's Doc Cassidy with letting go of his practice? He's been the vet around here for a long time."

"I think he's ready, looking forward to doing other things. I've asked him if he'd like to be a sort of consultant, someone whose brain I could pick, to keep him involved. He liked that idea."

That was so Rylee; she had a kind heart. Jayce clearly agreed. The way he studied her was making me slightly warm.

Duncan returned and settled next to me. "Is there a reason Abel is staring over here?"

Rylee, who was only partially paying attention because she was staring at Jayce in much the way he was staring at her, said, "Sidney met him when we first arrived. He was just here saying hello."

Knowing that Abel was staring caused those butterflies I hadn't felt since I was a kid as well as another emotion I hadn't felt in a long time. Longing.

Duncan grinned into his beer. "You met Abel. How'd that go?"

I can't decide if I want to smack him or kiss him. He drives me crazy, he makes me hot and he's continually looking out for me, going out of his way to do so, which makes it virtually impossible for me, a novice in the world of men, to get a read on him since I'm pretty sure he has a girlfriend. Plus I think he shares his body with at least three other people. Instead of saying all of that I said, "I'm guessing by that look, you know very well how that went."

He laughed now. "Boy doesn't change."

"You know him?" Rylee asked.

"Yeah, we all hung out as kids. Still do sometimes. He moved to Cheyenne, owns a custom motorcycle place."

So he wasn't a criminal, he was a businessman. Then how did he get the gunshot wound? Curious. "Why's he back?"

Duncan's smile faded, his head lowered. "Just some personal stuff."

More curious than I was polite, I asked, "What was he like as a kid?"

Two sets of blue eyes turned to me. Jayce asked, "You interested?"

Yes, and intrigued and confused and curious. I lowered my voice and lied. "No. I just can't imagine him as a child."

"He was always a bit hard, but then growing up as he did I can't really blame him. His dad was a dick, kicked him out of the house when he was fourteen and hightailed it out of town. Weird too that someone who couldn't move fast enough to see Sheridan in his rearview mirror, he comes back frequently enough."

"Why?"

"No idea, especially since Abel doesn't live here any more."

I had to agree with Jayce, Abel's dad sounded like a real jackass. "He was only fourteen when he was kicked out?"

"Yeah. Tiny took him in. After a few years, they moved to Cheyenne and started the business."

So he'd found his way too, survived despite the odds being stacked against him. I admired that; hell, I even respected it. And those feelings were dangerous. Lusting after a man was one thing, liking the kind of man he was, particularly that man, spelled trouble. Time to change the subject. "What about you?"

"What do you mean?" Duncan asked.

"I can't help but get the sense that running trails isn't really what you want to do." It was like I'd hit an exposed nerve. He jerked. "I'm sorry. It's none of my business."

His voice was flat, much like how it sounded earlier at his dad's house. "I'm a Hellar, that farm is our heritage."

Wow, that sounded like it was something that had been drilled into his head.

"You can leave. You should leave." Jayce's comment was also one that clearly had been said before.

"Right, just like that." Pained was how he sounded, like an old wound that never healed, one that still ached. I understood that, boy, did I understand that. Duncan seemed lost in that pain for a minute before remembering Rylee and I were there. An easy smile spread over his face, the ease in which he offered it was proof that he had mastered faking it. "Sorry. We don't need to air Hellar dirty laundry."

My heart went out to Duncan, his struggle to do right by his family at the risk of what he wanted. Life was too short though to agonize over the little stuff; sometimes you had to do what was best for you and if your family loved you they would be happy regardless. I had learned that lesson from the Stephenses, the family I had been lucky enough to marry into. "My husband died. He left our bed in the middle of the night to pick up my brother. An addict. They were hit head-on by a tractor trailer. The driver had fallen asleep at the wheel. In an instant they were both gone. And I have spent the past three years afraid to move forward and unable to go back. But what I have learned, staying stationary isn't living. I don't know your story, but I do know that you have to live your life for you."

I hadn't realized my eyes had teared up until Duncan handed me a napkin. "I'm sorry," he whispered.

"What the fuck?" Abel stood over me seething. "What the fuck did you say to her?"

"Calm down," Duncan said. I thought he was remarkably brave

considering Abel looked about ready to level the place.

Abel hunched down so that Duncan and he were eye level. "What the fuck did you say to her?"

"He didn't say anything."

Abel's head twisted to me, his eyes moving over my face. I noticed his jaw was clenched. "So why the fuck did you start crying after these two assholes showed up?"

Despite his interruption, he was here because of concern for me. And there it was again, coming to my aid even though not a half an hour ago he'd fled. Finding balance around him was clearly not going to happen. "I made myself cry."

He looked confused and on that face it was oddly adorable. "Why the fuck would you do that?"

"Have you ever said a full sentence without the word fuck?"

In reply, I was gifted with a smile—a genuine smile that was not laced with sarcasm or sexual innuendo and honest to God, it was breathtaking. Belatedly it dawned on me that I was staring at his mouth and when I lifted my gaze to his, he looked hungry again.

"Why did you make yourself cry?" He did a face, a 'see I can speak a full sentence without fuck' and again I found his sarcasm charming.

"A bad memory."

Understanding moved over his expression and though I sensed he wanted to ask something, he didn't. Instead he asked, "How's the ride?"

"It's good. Thanks again for your help."

"Yeah."

He seemed to remember there were others at the table at the same time I did. He spared them a glance before his pale gaze came back to me. "See you around, Doc."

He was halfway to the door before I could reply.

"Be careful," Duncan said, his words sounding almost dire.

"Excuse me."

"Abel is really good at roping a woman in, but he isn't one for long-term. I'd hate to see you get hurt."

I'd already come to that conclusion, but it hit a nerve hearing a friend of Abel's saying it. Yes, Abel probably had many notches on his bedpost and Duncan knew of my past, but for some reason that comment from him rubbed me the wrong way. I nodded at him, so he knew I'd heard him, but I couldn't help but think with friends like that who needed enemies.

That night while trying for sleep, something that was becoming more and more elusive thanks to the sexy and deeply confusing Abel, I felt my bed move. Lifting my tired lids, I saw Sandbar standing midway down the bed staring at me. I tried not to move, didn't want him to jump down. Every morning since he came here I woke to him staring at me. This was the first time he'd jumped on the bed. It'd only been a little over a month and already he was on my bed. Progress.

I waited to see what he'd do and when he walked around in a circle before curling up into a ball at my stomach, I wanted to shout with glee. Touchdown. He'd be letting me rub his head soon enough. I slept the stillest I ever had, not wanting to disturb him. And when I woke in the morning, he was still there.

chapter twelve

sidney

Rylee and I were checking out the town's block sale. The alley behind the clinic that ran down to the bakery had been cordoned off so that local businesses could set up tables to offer their goods in a fair-like setting. The area restaurants served up food and drinks as tourists and locals alike moved along the alley for a day of outdoor shopping.

"I love this," Rylee said as we strolled down the alley eating funnel cakes—one of the many treats being sold by the talented Stella.

I did too. It was a wonderful way to sample what the shopping district had to offer. "Doc Cassidy said they do this three times a year."

"It's brilliant. Same products, different atmosphere and from the number of bags I'm seeing, it works."

The stirring of the hair at the nape of my neck turned my attention farther down the alley to where Abel stood with Jayce drinking beer, but Abel's attention was on me. He'd kept his distance since learning of Jake, but I was still the recipient of his mind-numb-ing, body-heating stares. I could admit to myself, that despite the reality that he would chew me up and spit me out, there was an ever-growing part of me that wanted to take that reckless ride with him because I suspected it'd be worth the pain that followed. And acknowledging that I wanted him—accepting that sex with him was inevitable—felt like when I dieted and got a hankering for a spoonful or two of ice cream only to cave into my craving by devouring the whole damn pint. I craved Abel and I wanted to devour him, every last inch.

In true Abel fashion, he blatantly slid his gaze over me and the corresponding aches he set off in my body were as delicious as they were vexing. By the time those baby blues returned to my face, I was in imminent danger of spontaneously combusting. The sexy bastard winked and like lighting a match to a fuse, my entire body went up in flames. He lifted his beer in a sort of salute and flashed me a crooked grin. Yep, I'd never survive Abel and what a way to go.

"Oh look, there's Jayce and Abel. Damn, Jayce looks hot. The man should seriously come with a warning."

Rylee's comment was so strange, it earned my attention but hers was on Jayce and she looked how I felt. "A warning?"

"Yeah, use at your own risk. I want to take the risk."

My eyes caught hers and she grinned. "Let's go say hi." She didn't wait for my answer. She dropped our empty plates in the trash can before grabbing my arm and dragging me down the alley. And she *was* dragging me because I wanted to take the risk with Abel and that scared me because feeling as I did there was a seventy, eighty...eighty-five percent chance I was going to jump him. That would not be a good idea. Unfortunately for me those odds went up even higher when Rylee and Jayce got lost in the crowd leaving me alone with him.

"Doc."

"Abel."

"Do you want a beer?"

Beer? No. You naked? Yes. On second thought a nice cold beer to cool the heat burning through me sounded like a good idea. "Yeah, that'd be great."

He twisted his head to address the young woman manning the beer station; her eyes were glued to him, her expression one of supreme worship. I understood completely because my focus was on the thick column of his neck and how it flowed into his wide shoulders. My hands itched to follow the muscled line of his back, down his spine to the curve of his ass, over his thigh, around and up to...

"Doc?"

It was only then that I realized my gaze had been on his fly, a fact not lost on him if the carnal stare was any indication. I was mortified and seriously turned on.

"Looks like you need to cool off."

What an understatement. I didn't want to cool off, I wanted to get overheated and sweaty with him. And again he read me perfectly by the growl that rumbled deep in his throat. Taking the beer, I drank the entire cup in one long swallow.

"You might want to take it easy. That'll go right to your head, especially in this heat." It wasn't his words but the look he gave me that was nearly my undoing and by that I mean I really almost jumped him. Instead I fought for control over my baser instincts but unlike him, I wasn't as skilled in communicating while burning up with lust, as evident by how abruptly I changed the topic.

"You said you were only here for a couple of months. Can I ask why?"

"Just helping a friend." His playfulness turned somber, answered by a wicked ache in my chest because the seriousness of his expression suggested not just concern for this friend, but a connection that ran deep. I couldn't help but think of the woman I had given a ride to. Was she his girlfriend? And it was the reality that I was sliding down a slope I had no business being on and for a man I knew really nothing about that had me retreating. Mr. Milburn and Cooper were walking toward us. Perfect timing.

I waved enthusiastically until I got Mr. Milburn's attention. Before he reached us, Abel moved closer so his chest brushed up against my back. His soft breath teased my ear. "Too hot for you, Doc?"

I had never felt the level of sexual tension I did then. I nearly wept from the sweet torture. Being coy wasn't happening, so I answered with candor. "Hell, yeah." I managed breathlessly.

Before Abel could reply, Mr. Milner joined us. "Sidney, how are you?"

How was I? Horny, since I apparently had the sexual appetite of a teenage boy. To Mr. Milburn, I lied. "I'm wonderful. Would you like some company?"

"That would be lovely."

Chancing a glance at Abel, a twisted sort of satisfaction and confusion moved through me because he appeared to be battling the same feelings I was. Was it possible he was single? The idea of that had me feeling reckless. I needed to put some distance between us before I threw caution to the wind. "Thanks for the beer."

Abel was looking at my mouth when he replied, "Anytime, Doc."

The man was too tempting.

"Are you enjoying the block sale?" Mr. Milburn asked.

Luckily, I was able to hold a normal conversation, because the farther from Abel we walked, the more in control I felt. "I am and the weather couldn't be more perfect."

"And how are you adjusting?"

"With surprising ease. We've only been here a short while and I already feel like this is home."

"It's a great town."

"Have you lived here your whole life?"

"Maggie and I moved here in the fifties. If you can believe it, the town was even smaller then. I was the only lawyer."

"Do you have any children in the area?"

Pain swept his face and my heart dropped. "Maggie and I had hoped to have children, but it wasn't to be."

I ached for him because I understood all too well how that felt. "I'm so sorry."

Somehow he smiled, despite the pain I saw buried in his expression. "You know better than most, but Maggie and I did okay. We had a wonderful life together; I'll admit the lack of children left a hole in both of us and I think that's why we became so active in the community. The town became our family in a sense." There was a note of something in his voice, but I couldn't discern what fueled it.

"Was she a lawyer too?"

"A behavioral therapist, who offered her services for free to those who needed it—visiting local shelters and halfway houses. She believed that people deserved second chances and that some traveled down a road because of circumstances rather than desire. Our work filled the hole and brought a sense of continuity and connection that we both longed for."

"That's why you continue to work on a part-time basis."

He smiled, pleased that I understood. "Exactly."

Slipping my arm through his, I smiled back. "I think this town and its people are very lucky to have you, to have had Maggie."

"That is very sweet of you to say."

"Have you had a funnel cake yet?"

"No."

"Would you like to split one?"

"I would, very much."

"Are you sure you want to do this?" Rylee stood outside the shelter with the tranquillizer gun. I was heading inside the pen. It had been five weeks since Cain came to stay with us and I had been right. He was part dog and how calm he was in the presence of humans made it clear to me that he had been around them before.

Even for as gentle as Cain was—not snapping or growling or showing aggression—he had been living in the wild for some time and so I had to be mindful of that. I wanted to try to brush his fur, to clean up his coat since he was magnificent and would be even more so when his fur was shiny and smooth. I wouldn't do that today; today I'd just get in his space and see how he responded. Hopefully we could work up to a brushing.

"I do. I think it's going to be fine, but you've got the sedative just in case."

"I don't know about this."

"You said it yourself, he hasn't shown any aggressive behavior."

"I know. Just no sudden moves."

Unlatching the gate, I opened it a crack but I didn't immediately enter so Cain could get used to the idea of me in his space. He walked from the far side of the shelter, right up to the gate and then he dropped onto his butt and just stared at me. Now that he had put on weight, he looked more wolf than dog. He was big too. If that mountain lion came around again, he'd have a run for his money.

I stepped closer; Cain tilted his head and studied me. I sat down next to him. He shifted back a bit, his eyes never leaving mine, and then he dropped on to his belly.

"Holy shit. He likes you. That must feel incredible." Rylee sounded as awed as I felt.

"You have no idea."

"Come on. Come with me. It's going to be fun. We'll be like real cowgirls."

Rylee was joining Jayce on a trail ride. I loved horses but not riding them. I intended to do my own sightseeing, but my feet would be staying firmly on the ground.

"I'm sure. You go, have fun."

"I hate leaving you alone."

"Rylee, we live together and we work together. I realize I'm fabulous company, but you see me all the time."

"I really do want to go."

"Then go."

"Okay."

"Could you do one thing for me though?"

"Sure, what?"

"Just be smart. I get a weird vibe from the Hellar clan. I can't exactly put my finger on it, but just be smart."

Rylee settled in next to me at our small kitchen table. "What kind of weird vibe?"

"I don't know. The dynamic between Duncan and the dad seems strained, like the loving family is a show and Duncan's comment about Abel that night at the Brass Bull struck me as wrong."

"But you were already thinking the same about him."

"Yes, but Duncan and he have known each other for years and for him to so easily paint a negative picture of his childhood friend to a stranger isn't right."

Rylee leaned back in her chair. "Yeah, I can see that. I think he warned you only because he had just learned about Jake and Connor."

"And that could be all it is, but I wanted to mention it or it would have bothered me."

"I get it. We've been doing that since we were kids, watching out for each other and so I will heed your warning."

"And don't fall off the horse."

"I rode when I was little. Not well, but I think I'll be okay."

"I'm going on a trail. I'll leave the details on the counter just in case."

"Make sure to bring your cell and plenty of water."

"I will."

A horn sounded. Jayce was here. "That's for me. I'll see you later." Rylee jumped up and pulled me in for a hug. "I'm happy to see you taking so well to this place. I think it was good that we did this."

"I think so too. And thanks for the nudge."

"It was more a kick." She grabbed her pack. "See you later."

An hour later, I was heading off for my own adventure. As promised, I left the name of the trail I was taking on the counter. The number to the office where the trail trips were coordinated and the time I intended to start. My phone was charged, I had three canteens of water and my car had gas. I stopped at a sandwich shop for lunch and while I waited in line at the deli to place my sandwich order, the door opened and Abel strolled in. He was looking for someone with the way he scanned the place and then his eyes connected with mine. And like a moth to flame, I felt that pull for him.

"Hey, Doc."

"Abel."

"What are you doing?"

"Like at this immediate moment, or this year, or my goals for life?"

"Smart ass. Right now?"

"I'm going on a trail."

"By yourself?"

"Yeah."

"Where's your roommate?"

"She's off with friends."

"And you didn't go."

"Horses were involved, I don't ride horses, just tend them."

"What trail are you taking?"

"Tongue River Canyon."

"Are you getting lunch?"

"As much as I'm enjoying the twenty questions, is there something you want?"

"I'm coming with you."

To say those words didn't excite me would be a lie. "Why?"

"You don't know the area and, as a rule, you never hike alone."

"I was going to join up with a group."

"I grew up here, I know it better than any of the trail guides.

I'll take you."

"Why?"

"Why do you keep asking me that?"

"I just don't understand why you'd want to..." *even if it was the best idea ever.*

"Baby, you're asking me why I want to spend the day alone with you in the wilderness?"

Baby, I never cared for that endearment but hearing that word roll off his tongue in regards to me, I freakin' loved it. To hide just how much, I rolled my eyes. "I walked right into that one."

"Yeah, you did. Get me an Italian hoagie?" He had already walked away, in search of junk food no doubt. Instead of putting up a protest, I placed an order for two Italian hoagies.

The man had a metabolism much like Rylee's by the amount of junk he piled on the checkout counter. "We're only going for a few hours."

"If I have my way, it'll be more like a few days."

If only. "A dreamer, that's sweet."

His response was a head back howl of laughter. He pulled out his wallet; I tried to pay for my stuff, he wouldn't let me.

"Follow me home. I'll drop my bike and we'll go in your car. But I'll drive."

"Why?"

He looked at me out of the corner of his eye, because I had once again asked why. "First, no woman rides on my bike unless she's mine. And I don't ride passenger in any car."

"I rode on your bike."

"Extenuating circumstances."

"Why don't you ride passenger?"

"Because I'm a man."

"Well, I'm glad you know the difference between male and female, but so what?"

"I have a dick between my legs, I fucking drive."

"And if you're in the car with another man?"

"I still drive."

"What do you do, whip them out and compare. The manlier man gets to drive?"

"Whip it out? Talking dirty, I like it Doc."

"You never grew out of puberty, did you?"

"I did. I'd be happy to show you just how far from puberty I've come. Play on words intended."

"Nothing about you makes sense."

The teasing abruptly stopped, his tone almost confrontational. "What the fuck does that mean?"

"You should piss me off every time you open your mouth."

"And I don't?"

"You did, but you're growing on me because now I find you oddly charming."

He was right back to teasing. "Charming? Me? I can work with that. Now get your ass in the car. We're burning daylight."

Opening my door, I didn't climb in but instead called to him. "Hey, Abel."

His head turned, "What?"

"You got through that entire exchange and only said fuck twice."

He flashed me that smile before he climbed onto his bike. Following behind him, we were heading to the other side of town, but not the cabin I had been to. We traveled to an area so remote I'd be perpetually lost if I lived here. We pulled down a long drive and tucked within balsams was a cabin. Abel pulled up to the small garage, parking his bike inside before locking it up. He walked to the driver's side.

"Scoot your ass over."

"What is this?"

"What do you mean?"

"This is your house too?"

"This is my place. I come back to Sheridan at least once a year so I decided to invest in one. The other place I'm renting for Carly."

I wanted to ask why. I really wanted to know why if she was his girlfriend he rented her a place. I was beginning to think I'd been wrong about the whole girlfriend thing, but I so didn't want to get into that now. Instead, I scooted over.

We started back the way we came. "This thing needs a tune-up. Fucking Jimmy. Next time you're off, Doc, I'll take a look at it and don't ask me why."

I had been about to ask him just that. Instead I said, "Okay."

That earned me his attention. "No arguing?"

"I'm learning there isn't a point with you."

"Quick study."

"I heard you build custom motorcycles."

"Are you asking around about me?"

"Maybe."

The noise that came from him could only be called a growl. His hands tightened on the steering wheel.

"Is something wrong?"

"Why did you walk down that alley?"

I wasn't expecting that question. "You were hurt."

"You couldn't see me, not until you moved into the alley. What made you move into the alley?"

How did I answer that? Did I tell him I could physically feel when he was near?

"Answer me."

The force of those two words had the truth rolling off my tongue. "I felt a charge in the air, like electricity. I'd never felt that before and I was curious." And I hadn't. As much as I loved Jake, felt all kinds of wonderful sensations in his presence, I never felt him before I saw him. That was uniquely Abel's.

I'd been looking out the window; at the light, he touched my chin to bring my gaze to his. "Never?"

"Well, that day at the bakery when I saw you for the first time. I felt it then, knew it was you in that alley."

He pulled the car over to the side of the road, slammed it into park before rubbing his hands over his face.

"What am I missing?" I asked because the man looked conflicted.

"How long were you married?"

The mood in the car had taken a radical turn and it was because it had that I found myself answering him. "Jake and I married right out of high school."

"And he died three years ago?"

"Yeah."

"Why didn't you tell me you were a widow?"

It seemed I was unable to hedge with him, my mouth opened and the truth came out, again. "At first I didn't think it was any of your business and later I needed the boundary between us that Jake created."

"Why?"

It was like he slipped me truth serum. "Because what you make me feel scares me."

His inhale in response sounded painful. "Have you taken a man to your bed since him?"

That was really none of his business.

"I can tell from that look that you haven't. Fuck."

"Abel?"

He pulled the car back onto the road, but instead of the comfortable conversation we'd been enjoying, it felt as if a wall had gone up. We pulled into the recreational center and Abel helped me gather my things. He led me into the building and inquired after the tour times. Odd since he had boasted about knowing the trails better than any guide, which meant he wasn't joining me.

"You're not coming."

"No."

"Can I ask why the change of heart?"

He lowered his head, his voice a soft whisper. "I want to fuck you. I've never wanted to fuck a woman as badly as I want to fuck you." He moved even closer, his big body surrounding me as he seduced me with his words. "I want to push you up against that wall, drop to my knees and run my tongue along your sweet heat. I want to slide my hand down your spine and over your ass as I'm settled between your legs, driving into you from behind. I want you on your back, legs spread, and your eyes on me when I'm buried so deep inside you that I become a part of you. I want you on your knees in front of me for real, but I won't offer you a ring or my name. Hell, I'm going home in a few weeks. And a woman like you, I think you need the ring and the name or at least the expectation of them to come. You walked down that fucking alley and offered to help a stranger for no other reason than because you're you. I'd be an even bigger dick than I already fucking am if I returned that kindness with a no-strings fuck no matter how fucking fantastic that fuck would be."

No one had ever spoken to me with such raw candor and never in my life had I been as turned on as I was in that moment. I felt my pulse pounding in places I hadn't felt much of anything in three, long years. Knowing that he felt it too, that it was mutual the overwhelming need to taste and touch, thrilled me, but I also felt a staggering sense of relief that he was pulling back because I was in way over my head with him. Trying to form a reply was impossible so I asked, "How will you get home."

"I'll walk."

I felt the tears so I tried for levity. "You made up for the lack of using fuck earlier."

In answer, he gifted me one of those smiles. "Enjoy the trail."

I wanted to call to him; my throat ached from the effort of holding the words back. Instead I just stood and watched as he walked away and knew he would become my greatest and most profound regret.

Walking along the trail I tried to lose myself in the scenery, in the sheer majesty around me, but all I could think about was the scene earlier with Abel. I didn't know the man; we'd had a few chance meetings so why did I feel so…sad? The images he painted with his words…Jake and I had had a very active sex life, but thinking about Abel doing those things to me. I ached.

He said he thought I needed the ring and the name. I didn't, not any more. I had the ring and the name, loved it and wouldn't have traded it for anything. I didn't want to go back down that road. But I also feared I wouldn't be able to separate sex from love, not when dealing with such a big personality like Abel. Sex with him would turn into love for me, the two becoming synonymous, but I didn't want love again; I didn't want the pain that followed when love faded or worse. So even regretting I'd never explore the feelings he stirred, Abel was right to step back.

The blood-curdling scream yanked me from my thoughts.

"What's happening?" Someone asked behind me, but my focus was on our tour guide, bent in half puking in the bushes.

"Call 911." Someone else screamed.

Moving closer to see what was causing all of the trouble, my eyes landed on the body. It'd been there for a while, the bones were exposed, the eyeless skull staring eerily back at us. "Holy shit."

The trail was swarming with police a half an hour after the call was made and it wasn't just Sheridan officers, but those from the surrounding towns too. The victim was a woman from the bits and pieces I had overheard. It was believed she'd been murdered in these woods, but her body appearing on the trail was likely the result of animals feeding on her. It felt surreal as I sat on a rock watching as the police gathered evidence. Our entire group had been detained. In a place like Sheridan, a scene like this seemed so very wrong. Was she a local? How had she died? Did she know her killer? Was he too a local?

The man next to me was snapping pictures of the body with his phone. He looked familiar, but I couldn't remember where I'd seen him. "Should you be doing that?"

"I have a blog and this is news."

"Her family should be notified before you post her body on the Internet."

"Freedom of speech."

I thought about Jake and Connor and how I would have felt seeing the pictures of their accident before I knew they'd been killed. Fuck freedom of speech, what about compassion? "Officer, should this man be taking pictures?"

"Bitch," he hissed at me, but the cop was already bagging up his phone.

"Could have been your mom or sister or girlfriend. Would you want to see them displayed so heartlessly, all for the headline?"

"It isn't my mom or sister or girlfriend."

"So that makes it okay."

"Yeah, it fucking does."

I walked away before the cops had another dead body on their hands. Dickhead.

They kept us for a few hours and took our statements and boot prints. The body had been removed, taken back to the coroner. Her family would be notified; they'd have the cops coming to their door to shatter their world. My heart went out to them and the struggle they had ahead—coming to terms with their loss, particularly the violent nature of her death.

By the time I returned home, I was dead on my feet. Rylee had been home to change and was out again, grabbing a bite with Jayce. She left where they were so I could join them, but I didn't want to. I wasn't in the mood for company. Instead, I wanted a shower and then I'd spend some time with Cain. Tigger and Stuart were having a rare moment of activity, wrestling like they used to as kittens. Sandbar was on the sofa watching them, but he jumped from his spot as soon as he saw me and walked over. And after the shitty day I had had, that little act of affection from him felt really good.

"Hey you."

I made my way upstairs and he followed. Stayed with me while I showered and changed and even followed me back downstairs. When I started for the door, he was right on my heels.

"You aren't coming outside with me. I know you were an outdoor cat before, but not any more."

He just stood there, expectantly. "Will you let me hold you?

That's the only way you're going outside."

Hunching down, I reached for him; he darted back into the living room. I didn't think it'd be that easy.

Cain was lying down in his pen, but as soon as he sensed me he stood and watched my approach.

"Hey, handsome."

I didn't have food, it wasn't quite dinner time, and still he moved closer. And when I settled near his cage, he joined me and together we watched as the day turned into night.

"You saw the dead body? Why the hell didn't you call me?" Rylee and I were at the clinic working. Doc Cassidy had taken the day off. Every channel and paper was reporting the news of the body found in the woods. Rylee freaked when she learned I'd been there.

"We were detained and I was exhausted by the time I got home. Besides, what was there to tell? The poor woman had been left to the elements and animals. It was heartbreaking."

"That must have been hard seeing a dead body, especially in that condition. I can't imagine how your tour guide felt being the one to find her."

"You see it on television all the time, but actually seeing a real dead body? There aren't words."

Rylee's body shook; I actually saw the shiver that moved through her before she confirmed what I had heard that day on the trail. "She was a local. People thought she'd left town since she tended to drift from place to place. But she died three months ago and the cops think she was likely killed in those woods. That's when the animals got to her."

It was me who felt that shiver now thinking about who could have done that. "Do the cops have any ideas?"

"None. I want them to catch him, but there's a part of me that hopes he's moved on and is far away from here."

"I hear that. I've got to go. I'm due at the Roberts' farm."

"Keep your doors locked."

Another shiver worked through me, but Rylee was right. As beautiful as Sheridan was, I could drive for miles and not see another person. Exquisite, yes, but it also made me easy pickings for someone with malice intent. "I will."

Cain and I sat out back and watched as the blue sky became washed with orange before fading to purple. It was my favorite time of day and yet my thoughts were far away as I thought about Jake; how he'd come into my life, how perfectly we'd fit together. I had found what many never do and even more unbelievable was that I was falling again and for someone who was the complete opposite of Jake.

Rylee settled in the chair next to me. "What's going on? You look upset."

"I've just been thinking."

"About?"

I rested my head on the seat back and took comfort in the view as I tried to put my disjointed thoughts into words. "It's just interesting how things work out. I grew up alone, found Connor at ten and right when Connor started to lose himself to his addiction, Jake walked into my life. He was exactly what I needed, someone solid and strong who loved me. From the very beginning we worked, fitting together perfectly and sliding easily into being a couple. Every day was a gift. The exact kind of love I had always dreamed of having. I always thought his death shattered me, but that's not true. I had already been broken, just pieces of a person before I met him. He healed me, he made me whole, and his death was devastating but I'm still that healed and whole person because he had loved me."

"That's beautiful."

I saw the tears in her eyes; my own were bright.

"I'm sensing there's more."

"And then there's Abel. I don't know him and much of what I do know about him irritates the shit out of me. He challenges me all the time. He's domineering and opinionated. Sex with him wouldn't be lovemaking like I had with Jake. It would be raw, rough and dirty. And I want to smack him on more occasions than I want to kiss him."

"But you want to kiss him."

"I can't explain it Rylee, because I don't get it. I physically feel when he's around. And as much as he drives me crazy, I crave his company. I feel alive, every part of me responds to him. And I'm not that damaged person any more, lacking in love and looking so desperately for it. My heart hurts, but it's whole and more, I don't need to find love again. I have love and family, you and the friends we're making here. Sidney Stephens is a different person than Sidney Ellis. And yet, even not wanting to want it, I want him. He's completely wrong for me, but something in me is drawn to him."

And that's why I was grateful for Abel pulling back, because for me to want him as badly as I did, I needed to like him. And I did; I really, truly liked him. And like could so easily slip into love.

"How is that a bad thing?"

"Because going down that road will lead only to heartache. I've had enough of that."

"You don't know that."

But I did and it scared the shit out of me.

All anyone was talking about was the body found on the trail, the trail I had offered to take Doc on. I should have checked up on her, but I didn't. I needed to put space between us because it wasn't just a flirtation any more. I wasn't sure when causal interest shifted to hunger, but I wasn't good for her…wasn't the kind of man to settle down. Her first experience with a man after the loss of her husband shouldn't be someone with one foot already out the door.

Just thinking about her though put a smile on my face. I couldn't remember the last time I felt genuine admiration for a person. Seeing her that day facing down the mountain lion was the fucking stupidest thing I'd ever seen, but there she was putting herself in harm's way to save that half-dead wolf.

It was the day of the block sale when I realized her hunger rivaled my own, and it was a heady fucking feeling having a woman like her into me. I wanted her. I wanted to lock her away with me for days, weeks, as I sated the burning in my gut she caused. I almost did that day we were heading for the trail. It had been so fucking tempting to pull her into my cabin and fuck her senseless. Nothing could come of it though, so it was best to leave her alone. Especially since I suspected she could become my addiction…just one taste and I'd be hooked.

Marnie was taking Carly to her first therapist appointment. The fact that Carly went was progress. I hoped this worked. I hoped Carly was finally ready to face her own demons because I had a business, employees and a life to get back to, even if lately I wasn't feeling the same urgency to return to that life.

Jayce's truck pulled up my drive. I moved from my spot to join him. "What are you doing here?"

"Just thought I'd stop by and say hi."

"I've been back for over two months and you've never just stopped by to say hi."

He leaned up against his truck and pushed his hands into his pockets. "What happened with us?"

"What do you mean?"

"We used to be tight. What happened?"

"I moved."

"It's more than that."

"I don't know. Have you ever asked Duncan since it all seemed to go to hell after he was sent to military school?"

"Yeah, I guess it kind of did."

"Why was he sent to military school?"

"He'd been acting out, just typical teenager stuff, but you know Dad. He wasn't about to sit back and watch Duncan ruin his future."

"Doesn't seem like working the farm is the future Duncan was hoping for."

"It's not. Or maybe it's not so much that it isn't what he wants to do, but that he hadn't been given a choice in the matter. I get where Dad was coming from though. Duncan was floundering and Dad forced him to find a purpose. It's on Duncan that he's still doing something he doesn't want to, but at this point I think he's afraid of disappointing Dad if he tries something else and fails."

"He's a grown ass man."

"I know."

"Has he ever acknowledged that he's in love with Carly?"

"You saw it too?"

"Fuck, yeah. The kid couldn't speak in a full sentence around her. I don't know why he never acted on that, but he's still pining."

"True. But in fairness to Duncan, Carly isn't really in a place right now for a boyfriend."

"That's fair."

"How are things with you? How's Pipes?"

"I love the work, but I hired an assistant manager and the dude is like a cheerleader on crack. He keeps bringing in new business, forcing us to grow faster than I want. The work suffers when you're committed to so many jobs. He's a good kid, a hell of a mechanic, but we have different visions for the place."

"It's your place."

"I know. I think opening a second location isn't out of the question with the amount of business we're doing. One where the customer base is smaller."

"You're seriously thinking about opening another Pipes?"

"Yeah, but I'm not there yet. I've got to go through the financials with Tiny and we'll want to incorporate. Removing liability from our shoulders, especially when we won't be overseeing one of the locations, is worth the added work. There are so many steps from where I am to where I want to be, but it's definitely something I'm mulling over."

"I'm happy to hear that. Maybe you'll pick a location that's not so far away because it's been nice having you home."

"I never really thought of here as home. I always equated Sheridan with my dad, but as much as you can all be pains in my ass, it has been good being home. And maybe when Carly gets better, Duncan will stop dragging his feet and ask her out and put us all out of our fucking misery."

Jayce grinned. "And if not, we'll give him a little nudge."

sidney

Being present when a body was found would be news anywhere, but in a small town like Sheridan it was doubly so. I think the entire town had introduced themselves to me before breaking into their theories on what happened. Belinda Kramer, the victim, had been a local. She had lived in Sheridan her whole life and from all the accounts I had heard, she was not a very nice person. In fact, "bitch" was used often when addressing her, even now that she was dead. She had a rap sheet as long as my arm, apparently, and never had a kind word to say to anyone. Most weren't surprised to find she ended up dead and yet her death still rocked the town. The consensus was she had been a bitch, but she didn't deserve what had happened to her. Many theorized on who had killed her; the popular opinion was that her killer had been another local. The theory that this quiet and unassuming town was home to a killer disturbed me.

Another fact that made this case so talked about was never had the town experienced something so gruesome. And it was gruesome, every part of it.

I was at the Brass Bull grabbing a bite to eat before I made my way back to the clinic. Rylee had intended to join me, but was detained by an emergency. Lulu, a spirited Pomeranian, was in labor.

I hadn't seen Abel since the day he left me to walk the trail alone and unlike the rest of Sheridan, he had kept his distance. Not even my run-in with a dead body swayed him to seek me out. That pissed me off. Sure, we both had concerns about a physical relationship, but I had thought we were working in the direction of becoming friends. But a friend would have checked in to see how I was holding up. Whatever.

Someone settled next to me. I glanced over to see a smiling Mr. Milburn. And it was then that I realized where I'd seen that asshole from the crime scene, the one who had been taking pictures of the body. He was the same clown who had gotten up into Mr. Milburn's face that day at the hardware store. The guy was a major loser.

"Hi. How's Cooper?"

"He's good. Resting up at home. I never did ask you about your wolf and your encounter with the mountain lion."

"How do you know about that?"

"Everyone knows about that. It's a small town, remember?"

"Right. Well, Cain is doing really well. I'm getting ready to set him free."

"You aren't going to keep him?"

"I would love to, but if he wants to be free I won't stop him."

"And if he doesn't?"

"Then I'll work to make him comfortable again around people."

"How is he with you?"

"We sit together and we walk together. He lets me in his domain."

"No aggression?"

"No."

"Sounds to me like he's right where he wants to be."

I couldn't help the smile because I thought that too. "I hope so."

His expression turned solemn. "You were there when they found Belinda."

"You knew her?"

"Everyone in town did. I'm sure you've heard she wasn't a nice person."

"Yeah, everyone seems to be in agreement on that. Do you agree with everyone in that her killer is a local?"

"No, I don't think so. Belinda, despite Maggie's and my best efforts, was a bad egg. She broke the law to break it. She didn't want help, not mine, not Maggie's, not anyone's. She did what she wanted because she wanted to and didn't care if she hurt people in the process. A person like that makes associations with some very unsavory characters. It's more than likely one of them killed her. I think the theory of a local is based solely on the fact that Belinda liked to push people's buttons to the extreme."

An edge of anger came into his tone, which prompted me to ask, "Did she push your buttons?"

"She was a client, so, yes, frequently."

I understood his anger because it was a lot like my situation with Connor. Mr. Milburn had tried to help Belinda, but she was unwilling to help herself. Seeing someone you care about losing themselves was heartbreaking and infuriating.

"If it was a local, it was likely a good person pushed to their breaking point."

And as callous as Mr. Milburn's take on the situation sounded, he wasn't the only one I had spoken to who felt that way.

"It's still terrible business." He shook off the gloomy mood and turned a bit more in my direction. "So tell me about these horses you get to tend."

And for the next hour I did just that.

Chris Dearly was the barn manager of Hellar Farm. He'd held the position for twenty years. He knew everything about the horses in the Hellar stables. He managed a team of ten grooms and was the main reason Hellar Farm operated as smoothly as it did.

Chris had requested that we meet bimonthly not long after I had started. The meetings usually only lasted about fifteen minutes, but I liked being kept in the loop. The horses worked the trails, injuries happened and often. Not to mention births and deaths. The former always took my breath away, the latter heartbreaking.

"I will see you in two weeks. If anything comes up, you have my cell."

"Thanks, Sidney." He leaned back in his chair. "How are you enjoying Wyoming?"

"I love how different it is from home, the people and the landscape. I love that I can drive down a country road and see buffalo."

"That still turns my head and I've been treated to that sight most of my life."

I glanced at my watch as Chris said, "You're going riding now, right?"

"Yeah, my first time."

Surprise moved over his face. "You've never been on a horse?"

"No." And I had hoped not to be climbing on one now, but Rylee, Duncan and Jayce made a great tag team.

"You don't know what you're missing. Jayce is a show off, but he's a great guide and he'll put you on someone easy. Crème Brûlée or Angel Food Cake would be good."

"Actually Duncan's getting me on the horse."

"Even better."

"I still can't get over that all the females are named after desserts."

"That was Jayce and Duncan. They started the tradition when they were little and Garrett kept it up."

"Except Speckled Egg."

"She's a princess, so her name doesn't quite follow the others."

"Well, the others make me hungry."

Chris laughed as he rubbed his belly. "How do you think I got this?"

"Good to know. I need to take up running."

"Ha. Run for me too. Enjoy your ride."

"Thanks. See ya later."

Stepping outside, it was hot today but the sky was so blue with not one cloud. I started toward the training paddock; Duncan, Jayce and Rylee would be meeting me there. I couldn't believe I had let Rylee talk me into this, but she'd been so excited to show me spots only accessible by horseback. I hadn't gone very far when I heard the sound of voices and followed it to see as Abel and Carly came from around the side of the house. My body tensed in awareness and a bit of jealousy seeing the two of them together. Bitterness was there too since I didn't understand why he made any overtures to me when he was involved with her—opening me up to the possibility of him only to shut down so thoroughly. And it stung all the more because I had begun to believe they were just friends, but seeing them together I wasn't so sure. It was moot anyway. I turned to find Duncan waiting for me, standing by the fence looking past me to Abel and Carly. I saw a bit of what I felt in his expression. Did he like Carly? That certainly would explain a lot. As I grew closer, he shifted his focus to me.

"Hey. Are you ready for your ride?"

"No. Where are Jayce and Rylee?"

"In the barn. You're going to love it. In fact, you'll be begging us to take you out more often."

"I seriously don't see that happening."

"Trust me."

"Trust is not the issue here. Falling and breaking my neck is."

"That won't happen." His gaze moved to behind me again. "I'm happy she's here."

"Carly?"

"Yeah. She stopped coming around and then she moved away. It always felt weird not seeing her."

"You've all been friends for a long time, huh?"

"Yeah, those two were always the closest. On and off since we were kids. I never really understood it since he never sticks around, but whenever he comes back it's like he never left. Thick as thieves those two."

Bitterness, raw and exposed, weaved through his words but watching your friend with the woman you loved had to be hard. His comment that night at the Brass Bull about Abel hooking women but not keeping them made perfect sense now.

He turned from them, his attention completely on me. "Angel Food Cake is very gentle. If something should happen and you get separated, she'll find her way back here. Not that that is going to happen. Can I give you a hand up?"

I knew Angel Food Cake, all her stats, but standing next to her she suddenly looked so much bigger.

Duncan saw my hesitation and moved closer. "I won't let anything happen to you."

"Okay."

"Step into my hand. I'll lift you up and you swing your leg over her back. Ready?"

I took a deep breath; let it out slowly. "Yes."

He lifted me effortlessly and before I knew it I was sitting on the back of Angel Food Cake. Jayce called from the barn. "Ready, Sidney?"

I really wasn't.

Duncan flashed me a grin. "Now for the fun part."

Rylee rode next to me and Jayce was just in front of us checking the terrain, since it had rained the other night. He was looking for muddy and loose soil that could have the horses losing their balance and risking injury. I held on to the reins like I was holding on for dear life; the jarring my body took and the pain radiating from my ass didn't hold a candle to the view. Rylee had been right. It was incredible out here. We had taken a pretty steep trail and even now the one side of it was far enough down that if you were afraid of heights you wouldn't want to look, but the view was unbelievable.

"Exquisite, right?"

"There aren't words. It's like we've stepped back in time to the days on the frontier. No cars, electricity or cell phones. Just nature in its purest sense."

"You can say that again. I'd almost love a little cabin right in the middle of it—rustic, no electricity and just living off the land."

As romantic a picture as she painted Rylee wouldn't last a week in those conditions. My eyes found hers, she knew that too.

"Why didn't Duncan come?"

"He's getting ready for a tour."

"Ah. So Jayce, what's up with him?"

Her face went soft, her eyes seeking and finding the man in question. "I really like him."

"I can tell and it seems the feeling is mutual."

Her head turned, the sweetest smile touched her lips. "I can't stop thinking about him. Is that crazy? It's only been a few months and yet I'm crazy about him."

"I fell for Jake on the car ride home that first day, so no, I don't think it's crazy." Especially since I'd known Abel for as long as she'd known Jayce and I couldn't stop thinking about him either. Maybe there was something in the air.

Jayce was just ahead waiting for us to join him. The look that passed between Jayce and Rylee had me suddenly feeling like the third wheel. I'd give the lovebirds some alone time.

"You guys go on ahead. I'm going to climb off and stretch my legs."

"We'll wait," Jayce said.

"And I appreciate that, but um…I kind of have to…"

He caught on immediately. "Right. Okay we won't be far."

"I'll follow right along."

"Sidney, follow right along. It's not safe to be out here alone. Understood?" I had never heard Jayce sound so stern.

"Yes."

They were adorable together. He reached for her hand to hold as their horses moved slowly along. I didn't have to pee, but I did want them to have that moment. Climbing from Angel Food Cake, because my butt was killing me, I almost fell to my knees with how badly my legs shook.

"I need to walk this off, Angel Food Cake. You graze there, sweet girl. I won't be long."

Rylee was onto something with her cabin. I needed electricity too, but I could get used to opening my eyes to this view every morning. Keith had called to set up our dinner to discuss his farm. I hadn't returned his call, but since he was mixing business with personal I'd have to. Ignoring his wish to meet was unprofessional; avoiding answering about dinner was personal. Keith seemed very nice; he wasn't hard to look at and it was just dinner. The trouble was I felt nothing around him. I wasn't looking for a soul mate, not even close, but I wanted the man to stir me in some way. Maybe it had just been an off day. I'd call him when I got back.

For as fun loving as Jayce was he was also an excellent guide and very responsible. I would guess he was uncomfortable with the idea of me on my own, even with getting some alone time with his lady-love. It was time to catch up to the others. I turned to head back to Angel Food Cake when my foot hit a patch of loose earth and before I could even scream, I was sliding down. I tried to grab onto something without success before lifting my hands to keep the branches that I flew past from getting me in the eyes. I came to a jarring stop and just lay there staring up at the sky mortified and afraid to move and learn I'd broken something. My head hurt, possible concussion from the few rough hits it had taken on the way down—rocks in my path that got my back too because it burned. Sore and with shock setting in, I managed to sit up as my muscles protested and took stock. Nothing felt broken but my back was on fire. I reached around to touch the sorest spots and my fingers came away with blood.

Only me. My first trail ride and I slide down an embankment. Staring up at where I'd come from, it wasn't all that high but steep enough to hurt like hell coming down it. This was why I avoided riding horses. Angel Food Cake. I hadn't tied her up and Duncan had said she'd find her way home if we got separated. Jayce and Rylee were between her and home; they'd find me. I just needed to stay put.

I wouldn't be living this down. Once Rylee got over her worry and concern, she would be having some fun at my expense. Honestly, had the shoe been on the other foot I'd do the same. I stood, since my poor muscles were growing stiff, and paced wondering what was taking them so long. I wasn't being fair; I had only myself to blame for the pickle I was in, but I was in the middle of nowhere. I hadn't a clue how to get back and there were wild animals out here like that mountain lion. That had fear prickling my skin and it was then that I noticed how very quiet it had become. The birds were no longer singing and it was likely they never had been, but the idea that even now the mountain lion was moving toward me, especially since I was bleeding—a scent he'd catch—had my feet moving. I tried to find a way back up the trail, but as far as I could see it was steep enough that I'd never be able to climb it. I would likely just slip back down again and I'd rather forego round two. Would I eventually find my way back if I continued heading in the direction we'd been going? A noise, the rustling of underbrush too close for comfort, had me running. I hoped like hell I was going in the right direction because it would be dark soon.

ABEL

"You look good, Carly."

"I feel good. Thanks for coming with me today."

"I was surprised you wanted to come here. You've stayed away for so long."

"I always loved it here, maybe too much, but I've missed it. It was like home for me growing up. Mom was always working. Garrett and Marnie became like surrogate parents to me."

"So why did you stay away?"

We had just reached the front of the house when she gasped. It wasn't a gasp triggered in me at the sight; I wanted to hit something…namely Duncan. He was standing too close to Sidney, his body practically crowding her. It didn't matter that she didn't seem to have a problem with it because I sure as fuck did.

Carly's reaction penetrated my jealousy. She lowered her head but not before I saw the tears brimming her eyes.

"Carly, why didn't you ever tell him you were into him?"

"I almost did once."

"So what happened?"

"I overheard him and his dad talking. Actually it was more an argument."

"They did that a lot. Why would that stop you from telling him how you felt?"

"My name came up. Duncan didn't have nice things to say."

"That's bullshit."

Fire stared back at me and I liked seeing a bit of the spunk she had had as a kid. "Why is that bullshit?"

"He's been in love with you since we were kids."

Whatever she had to say died. "That's not true."

"Yeah, it fucking is."

"But he said I was low class and not worthy of the Hellar name."

My hands balled into fists thinking about Carly overhearing something like that, but I was downright furious with Duncan because whatever he had said had been a lie. Duncan loved Carly; that was a fact of life. "Is that why you left?"

"Yeah, well mostly."

"Mostly?"

"I don't want to talk about it."

She'd have to eventually, but I moved on. "Duncan has feelings for you. I don't know what you heard and I damn well intend to get to the bottom of that, but Duncan's feelings for you are one of the absolutes in life."

A true smile, one that came from way down deep, spread over her face. "Really?"

"Yeah, really."

"I didn't know."

"Well Duncan is a bit slow."

"No he's not."

"The woman he loves has been pining for him for as long as he's been for her and he never caught on. Yeah, the boy is really fucking slow but I'll knock some sense into him."

Her smile was blinding.

"I really like seeing you smile."

"I'm happy."

"Good. Progress."

"What about you? What happened with Sidney?"

"Nothing."

"Why?"

I'd forgotten her tenacity. I liked she was showing some spunk, but the reason for that spunk not so much.

"We've known each other since we were kids. You like her and from what I've seen, she likes you too. What happened?"

"Bad timing."

"I think it's more than that."

She wasn't wrong, but I didn't want to get into it. "When did you get so fucking smart?"

She grinned because she understood I was conceding the point. "I've always been. I just lost myself for a while."

Happy that Carly was back, I draped my arm over her shoulders. "Glad you found yourself."

"Me too."

I tried to watch the game, but all I could see was Duncan touching Sidney. I knew how Duncan felt about Carly and yet seeing him touch Sidney, how close he stood to her, I wanted to fucking kill him. I wanted to drive right back to the farm and punch the fucker in the face just so he'd know to step back if he were entertaining ideas about her. Which was completely insane because I'd removed myself from the picture. Maybe Doc was right; maybe I did have multiple personalities. My phone buzzed.

"Yeah."

"We need you at the farm."

"What's going on?"

"Sidney's missing."

Fear hit, hard and fast, like taking a kick to the gut, and yet I was already moving to my bike. "I'm on my way."

Twenty minutes later, I was on horseback—something I hadn't done since I was a kid—following Jayce, Duncan, Garrett and Chris. Thinking of the trouble Sidney could have gotten herself into, especially witnessing her showdown with the mountain lion, inched my fear up closer to panic.

"Sidney needed to make a stop. When she didn't come back, I

went looking for her and found Angel Food Cake. Studying the ground where she'd stopped, I…"

"You what?" Jayce's hesitation wasn't helping the situation.

"She caught a loose patch and slid down the embankment."

"Fucking shit." The thought of her lying at the bottom of an embankment broken, bloodied or worse caused a reaction in me I had never in my life experienced. Devastation.

"I'll call Marnie. We'll get a doctor to the house. She'll be hurt, just how badly is anyone's guess," Garrett said as he reached for his phone.

Jayce continued, "It looked as if she stayed put pacing based on the tracks I found."

Hearing she had been moving around, eased the knot in my chest and pulled a grin because it was something I could see her doing. Likely talking to herself too.

"But for whatever reason she left. Something must have spooked her."

And now night was falling and she was alone, hurt and scared.

"Let's split up, we'll cover more ground," Garrett said. "You find her, radio it in."

I went with Jayce; he looked like shit and there was a part of me that thought he should. He had been responsible for her and he fucked up, but then this was Sidney. The woman had a mind of her own. "We'll find her."

"I shouldn't have left her."

No, he shouldn't have. "She's a grown woman, Jayce."

Something moved over his face before he said, "I was distracted with Rylee and lost track of time. That was careless."

Yeah, it fucking was, but rubbing that in wasn't going to find Sidney. "You're human."

"She's never been out here. It was her first time and I fuck up like that."

"Seriously, dude, I know. You fucked up, you know you fucked up, now let's just find her."

"I was surprised you came so fast."

"Don't."

"I'm just saying—"

My hand curled around his shirt as I jerked him toward me. "You seriously don't want to piss me off any more than I already am. Leave it."

Instead of reacting, he looked thoughtful for a minute before he said. "I didn't know. Sorry, man."

"Didn't know what?"

"You really like her."

Oh for Christ's sake. "We're going to talk about our feelings, seriously?"

"No." We rode in silence for a bit but Jayce apparently still had more on his mind. "You're leaving. Is that why you're not making your move?"

I seriously didn't want to talk about this, but Jayce wouldn't let it drop until I gave him something. "Yeah." He had a thought on that, but luckily for me he kept it to himself.

We hadn't gone far when he stopped and jumped from his horse before squatting down to study the ground. "Someone's been through here."

He climbed back up on his horse. "She can't be that far."

I was already moving.

sidney

I couldn't continue. Not only did I hurt everywhere, but I was exhausted, thirsty and hungry. I was going to have to sleep out here. I should have paid better attention to Jake when we'd gone camping that one and only time. He'd been a Boy Scout and could start a fire with just a stick and a rock. It was impressive, but I wasn't having any luck as I hunched there trying to do the same over my little pile of pine needles and twigs.

I no longer thought I was being followed. I probably never had been. The rustling from earlier was likely a rabbit or squirrel and not a man-eating mountain lion. Had I stayed where I was, I'd be back at the Hellars' home in that lovely room in front of the fire drinking something warm. Instead, I was cold, tired and unable to create fire. I yelled up at the heavens. "Suck it."

My back had long ago gone numb; infection was setting in. Maybe that's how I'd go out, not from thirst or hunger or being mauled, but a deadly infection from the worst ever rug burn. Sleep was creeping up on me and I wondered if I should sleep under the tree or crawl up into it. Mountain lions could climb, couldn't they? So it seemed smarter to be on the ground or else I'd suffer a fall before I was eaten alive. Of course the fall might paralyze me so I wouldn't feel anything as I was being eaten. I wondered what that felt like? I was delirious, sure signs of a concussion. Knowing my luck I'd die of a hematoma.

A sound startled me as I turned toward it, but what I saw couldn't be what I was seeing, which brought fear that I'd hit my head even harder than I'd thought. Abel was riding toward me on a horse. Bad boy biker Abel with that beard and man bun was sitting atop a horse like he'd been born doing it. Of all the hallucinations I could have had of the man—I don't know let me name a few: seeing him naked, seeing him naked over me, seeing him naked under me—I see him on horseback? The giggle just kind of bubbled up my throat.

ABEL

I heard her before I saw her. She didn't look scared; she looked pissed. The last vestiges of fear slid from me as a grin twisted my lips. Somehow I didn't find her odd behavior all that surprising. As I grew closer, her reaction was not the one I expected. She started to giggle.

Jumping down, I walked to her just as she said, "I would have rather seen you naked."

Those were her opening words to me. My cock twitched, but

she was clearly in shock.

"You looked good though, on horseback. I like you on your bike better. Sexy as hell."

"I need to get you back to the farm."

"Um. I wish."

"Sidney?"

Looking into her eyes, her pupils were funny. She must have knocked her head. "You hit your head?"

"I think so, but it's my back that's going to kill me."

Every part of me reacted to that. No fucking way. "Can I see?"

"Sure."

Jayce rode up just as I lifted her shirt and bit down on the curse because she had to be in pain. Her delicate skin was raw and red with some of the scratches still oozing with blood.

"I'm so sorry, Sidney."

She hadn't realized Jayce was there. Her eyes slowly followed the sound of his voice. "When did you get here? I wouldn't have thought I'd hallucinate about you. You're Rylee's. I'm going to sleep."

I took her face in my hands. She smiled. "You have beautiful eyes. I've never seen eyes that color before."

"Jayce needs to lift you to me. It's going to hurt."

"Okay."

I mounted my horse. Jayce lifted her and she cried out in pain, the sound ripping through me. I settled her on my lap and wrapped my arms around her being careful of her back as her head came to rest on my chest.

"This is nice," she whispered. It would have been a hell of a lot nicer if she hadn't been hurt.

Jayce swung up on his horse. "I'll radio we found her."

"Tell them she has a concussion on top of the damage to her back."

"Got it."

I rode us home while taking great care to protect the wounded beauty in my arms.

sidney

I woke in an unfamiliar bed, but the sheets were divine. I gave myself a moment to appreciate the softness against my cheek. I was on my stomach, a position I never slept in, so I rolled and immediately howled in pain. The door flew open as Abel charged in. He looked like shit. It didn't take long for it all to come flooding back: my romp in the wilderness including Abel riding to the rescue on horseback.

"Were you on a horse?"

"Yes."

"Um." It was all a bit fuzzy, but when the memories came back into focus I wished I had developed amnesia.

"Oh my God." Mortified, I pulled the sheet over my head.

And Abel, he laughed. "I see you remember all of it."

"If by all of it you mean me telling you I would have rather seen you naked, yes."

I peeked out from the sheet; he was leaning against the wall with his arms crossed over his chest. He was smiling. "You think I have beautiful eyes too."

"I hit my head, hard. You can't take seriously the ravings of someone with head trauma."

"You like me on my bike. I'm sexy as hell, your words."

I dropped the sheet and narrowed my eyes at him. "You're enjoying this."

"Oh, I really fucking am." He turned serious then. "How's your back?"

"Hurts like a bitch. Which I don't get that expression, hurts like a bitch. It makes no sense."

He grinned, the sight causing warmth to pool in my belly. He'd come for me, saved me again. Abel, even with his 180, he was still looking out for me. "Thank you."

"Why didn't you stay where you landed?"

"I freaked myself out, thought the mountain lion was closing in."

"Ah." I actually witnessed as Flirty Abel morphed into another personality I hadn't yet met. The vehement scrutiny he leveled on me was different from the heated gazes I was usually on the receiving end of and was felt in every nerve in my body. Whichever personality this was, I liked it.

The sexual tension that zapped the air around us fizzled when he abruptly said, "A very worried Rylee is outside. I'll get her."

I waited for more, what more I didn't know, but I wanted more from him. He didn't give me more. Without even saying goodbye, he pulled open the door and walked out. That hurt, a lot, but he was making it clear. I'd never get more, not from him. Rylee came running into the room.

"Thank God you're okay."

And I was. Alive, in one piece and, yeah, my heart may have taken another hit, it'd taken far worse. I'd get through this too.

ABEL

Walking right out the door, I climbed onto my bike and rode—straight back to Cheyenne. I'd come back in a few weeks, check on Carly, but I had to get away because everything in me wanted to pull Sidney into my arms and keep her there. And never having felt that for another living being, I was man enough to admit it scared the shit out of me.

chapter fourteen

sidney

Rylee and I were sitting out back; Cain was lying next to me as my fingers brushed through the soft fur of his head. His leg had healed and I had started leaving his cage open during the day so he could leave if he wanted to. He didn't seem to want to leave. I was working with him, domesticating him to a degree, so he could live in the house if the felines accepted him.

It had been two weeks since my accident. My back had healed and my concussion had been very mild. I'd been lucky. Abel had left, went home without so much as a goodbye to anyone. At least it hadn't just been me.

As if she was reading my mind, Rylee asked, "Hey, Sid, what happened with Abel? And don't say nothing because that's bullshit."

"He took a huge step back."

"When?"

"The day they found Belinda. He was coming with me on the trail, insinuated himself into my plans for the day. We were talking in the car on the way to the trail and he asked me why I went down the alley that day."

"I don't understand."

"The first time we exchanged words was down an alley near the grocery store. I felt him, can't explain it, but I felt him. When I told him that he grew really quiet. Asked me if I'd taken anyone to my bed since Jake and then he took a huge step back, but not before telling me all the things he wanted to do to me but how he wouldn't because I was the kind of woman who needed the ring and the name or the promise of them to come."

"And yet he was there that day at the farm. He wouldn't leave your side. Stayed when the doctor examined you, stayed while you slept for two days straight. He'd only just left your room to shower when you woke."

"I can't explain his behavior, Rylee. He acted like Abel that morning, teasing me like he does, and then he walked out without a word and headed home. And the really twisted part, I'm not sure if I'm upset that he left or relieved. I like him, genuinely like him. Under his arrogance, there's a really good guy. But he's so dynamic, such a big personality. He fascinates me almost as much as he scares me."

"Why does he scare you?"

"Because I know if I gave myself the chance, I could really fall for him and that's terrifying."

"You can't be afraid to live, Sid."

"I know. I tell myself that often and still it's a knee-jerk reaction because I know how much living can hurt. Anyway, it doesn't matter since he's with Carly."

"He's not with Carly."

It was a moot point now and still I felt the impact of those words right down to my bones. "How do you know?"

"Jayce. Duncan's in love with her, she's in love with him."

"Ah...that actually makes a lot of sense."

"It doesn't though. Why's the boy dragging his feet? It drives Jayce crazy."

"Because Duncan thinks Abel and Carly are an item and have

been since they were kids."

"He told you that?"

"Yeah, but he didn't have to say anything. His expression when he saw Abel and Carly together said it all. He was tormented watching them."

"Men can be such fools. Abel is included in that statement."

"You won't get any arguments from me."

"Yes, I'll get steak."

"And something sweet for dessert. Chocolate cake or strawberry shortcake," Rylee added.

It was grocery day and Rylee had to work hence the phone call with all her cravings.

"And Nutella."

"It's all on the list, Rylee."

"Okay. I'll grill up the steaks when I get home."

"Deal."

"I've got to go. Mrs. O'Reilly's here and Salem is hissing like no one's business."

"Don't forget to wear gloves."

"Yeah, I learned that lesson the last time. See you later."

Dropping my phone in my purse, I moved down the vegetable aisle and was bagging some tomatoes when someone crowded up next to me. It took a minute to place the face and annoyance moved through me when I did.

"Remember me?"

He was the dick that day on the trail taking pictures on his phone, the one who harassed the elderly. "Yeah, unfortunately."

"I just got my phone back."

"You shouldn't have been taking pictures of her."

He moved even closer, which alarmed me because the man was unhinged. "I can do whatever I want."

"Step back."

"You should learn to mind your own business."

It was on my tongue to rebuff him, but I was fairly certain the man was insane and it was unwise to engage a crazy person. I tried to make my leave. "Excuse me."

He blocked my exit. "I'll be seeing you again."

"Back the fuck off, Sammie, now."

My eyes sought my rescuer, Keith Roberts.

"This doesn't involve you, Keith."

"Yeah, it does. You're in her space. She doesn't want you there. Back the fuck off."

Keith would be dead if looks could kill, but Sammie scurried off, thankfully.

"You okay, Sidney?"

"I am now. Thanks for stepping in."

"You're welcome. Sammie's a pain in the ass. He always has been."

I thought he was a bit more than that, but I kept it to myself.

He glanced in my cart. "Steak for dinner?"

"It is. My roommate has been having a hankering." I had intended to call him, to take him up on his offer of dinner, so I offered it now. "Would you like to join us? I'd really like to thank you properly for making Sammie go away."

"You don't have to."

"I'd really like to."

"Okay, yeah that'd be great."

"I'll text you my address."

"I'll stop for beer."

"Perfect."

"Is this a date?" Rylee asked as she sat on the counter eating the vegetables Jayce was chopping for the salad.

"Yeah, I guess it is."

She almost choked on the carrot she munched on. "Are you

serious?"

"It's time."

She jumped off the counter and pulled me into a tight hug. "I never thought this day would come." She held me at arm's length; her expression full of understanding on just how big a step this was for me. "He'd want this for you. You know that right?"

"I do."

"Does this mean the rings are coming off?"

"Yes, but I'm keeping his sweater and jersey."

Her smile took up her whole face. "That sounds like a good compromise."

"That was delicious. Thank you." Keith looked a bit wary and I completely understood. Though Cain didn't bare his teeth or growl, he didn't appear to be a big fan of Keith's. I had to put Cain in the shelter because I didn't want to take the chance. He was the first person that Cain had a negative reaction to.

"How are your parents?" Jayce asked Keith as he reached for his beer.

"They're good. I think they're finally ready to retire. They love the farm, but they're getting too old to keep up with it."

"I get that. I'm surprised you stayed on. I thought you were eager to leave Sheridan in search of some big city where you could make a go of your music."

"Sometimes life has different plans for us. Maybe one day I'll get there."

"You're a musician?" I asked.

"Yeah. Guitar and piano."

"He writes his own stuff too. His band, Gray Matter, had quite the following growing up."

"Do you still play?" Rylee asked.

"We catch a few gigs during the year."

"When you have your next one, let us know. Right, Sidney?"

"Yeah, that sounds like fun."

Rylee stood and reached for her and Jayce's dishes. "We're having strawberry shortcake for dessert. I can't wait another minute."

I watched as Keith drove off. It had been a nice evening, very comfortable and also clear that there was absolutely no chemistry between us. I wasn't alone in that observation. Keith felt it too and I knew this because sometime during the evening it went from awkward first date to just friends hanging out having a good time. Keith hadn't even sat with me; he'd been across the room by Jayce. Something I was completely fine with. I had convinced myself I was ready to move on, and I was. Unfortunately for me, my sudden wish to move on wasn't so much in general, like I had hoped, but specific to one individual.

Jayce had left earlier. I hadn't missed the way he stared at me all night. He looked a bit smug, but what he was thinking I hadn't a clue. Rylee was head over heels for him. I liked them together; the easiness of them reminded me of how it had always been with me and Jake.

My thoughts turned to the scene at the grocery store more often than I liked, but I got a bad vibe from Sammie. And maybe I had watched one too many crime shows, but the fact that he was there when Belinda had been found, was the only person snapping pictures…he could just be a morbid bastard or his interest could be something altogether more sinister.

Walking around back, I headed to Cain. I hated that I had to lock him up. He didn't seem to hold it against me though. He came right up to me as soon as I approached.

"Maybe next week you'll come inside."

Those pale eyes looked right into mine like he knew what I was saying. He really was magnificent; the similarity between him and Abel was not lost on me, both with that inky black hair and those pale blue eyes. And both were dangerous and wild. Just thinking about Abel stirred more in me than the entire evening with Keith.

"Night, handsome. I'll see you in the morning."

It wasn't a surprise when I finally found sleep that I dreamt of Abel.

We were at the Brass Bull, Keith, Ichabod and Jeshaiah. Jayce and Rylee. Even Chris and Mr. Milburn were there. Everyone had come out but Duncan who was visiting Carly later. I rarely overdrank, but sometimes it felt nice to let your hair down and lose yourself for a bit. I wasn't drunk, tipsy, but Lorelei found my altered state amusing.

Ichabod and I had turned our stools around and were watching the people on the bull.

"You ever do that?" I asked him.

"Yeah, it's not so hard."

"I think I want to try it."

His head turned, his teeth showing from the smile that cracked over his face. "Seriously?"

"Yeah."

"The big guy, that's Bo. Couldn't ask for a better teacher. Go for it."

"I think I will."

Jumping from my stool, I made my way through the tables to the bull just as Bo finished his ride. Green eyes landed on me as a grin tugged at his mouth. "Are you interested in trying this?"

"I am."

"All right." He climbed down and was rather graceful about it considering his size. "I'm Bo."

"Sidney."

"Have you ever done this, Sidney?"

"No, but Ichabod said you were a good teacher."

"He's not wrong. How about I help you up and we'll go from there."

"Sounds like a plan."

ABEL

Stepping into the Brass Bull, I was surprised to see the actual bar empty; it was usually teaming with people at this hour. I settled on a stool and flagged Lorelei for a drink. She was laughing, her focus across the room, but she headed over with my beer as soon as she saw me.

"Hey, Abel. You're back."

"Yeah, I came to check on Carly." And that was true, but really it was a certain doc that drew me home. I didn't understand what I felt for her, but I'd be a fool not to explore it despite living clear across the state.

"You came back just in time." There was a twinkle in her eyes when she said that but she didn't linger long enough for me to ask what the hell she meant by it. She moved back down the bar, her focus across the room again.

Jayce joined me. Where the hell had he come from? "Abel, what's up?"

"Came back to check on Carly."

"Oh yeah. How's she doing?"

"I haven't seen her yet."

The fucker looked smug, suspected he knew I was lying as to why I came back. Confirmed when he said, "Have you heard about Sidney and Keith Roberts?"

My fingers tightened so hard on the mug I was surprised it didn't shatter in my grasp. "What the fuck are you talking about?"

"I had dinner at their place the other night. Rylee was ecstatic that Sidney was finally dating. And it was a date. Sidney confirmed it. She's ready, even said she was taking off her rings. That is some seriously good timing for Keith."

The urge to hurl my mug across the room was strong. I managed to battle that shit back.

"I'm kidding, she's not with him. It took all of an hour for them both to realize it would never happen. Which is good since I kind of thought you and she were heading somewhere."

The asshole didn't need me in this conversation since he just kept running his mouth. "Her wolf wasn't really thrilled with Keith. She had to lock him up because he looked as if he wanted to rip out Keith's jugular."

Smart fucking wolf. "Wait, she still has the wolf?"

"She's keeping the damn thing. It follows her, the sound of her voice, her scent. Never seen anything like it."

"She's adopted the wolf?"

"Half wolf, she ran its DNA because of some state law. She's gotten a license for it and everything. She's like the collector of lost causes. Those two old cats, that new one she adopted, he's like her sidekick now."

Collector of lost causes, sounded about right. Somehow that was fitting, the idea of Sidney taming wild animals. If anyone could tame me, it would be her.

"You haven't heard the best part. Guess what she's calling the wolf?"

"What?"

"Cain."

Fuck me.

"Yeah, so Keith isn't competition, but Bo is another story."

I swear to God, Jayce wasn't making any fucking sense "What?"

He jerked his head; my attention followed his gesture and now I understood why the bar was empty because everyone was around the bull. And there was Sidney sitting atop the mechanical bull. Her face was tilted up as she laughed causing her hair to cascade down her back. And standing so fucking close to her they could have been conjoined was Bo. He had his one hand on her hip and the other at the small of her back. I swear to God I felt like her wolf because I wanted to rip out Bo's jugular and I liked Bo.

"She's got some skill on that bull. They make a handsome couple don't you think?"

"You're a fucking ass."

"I'm the ass?" He turned serious then. "Do you realize what you walked away from?"

Turning my back on Sidney before I gave in to what my body demanded—killing Bo and throwing her over my shoulder—I instead glared at Jayce since he was closer. "What the fuck are you talking about now?"

"Three years man. Three years and not one person could penetrate her sorrow until you. And I know you felt something because it is out of character for you to be noble. You want something and you take it and to hell with the consequences. But you didn't take her. You let her go."

"Jesus, are you seriously trying to get into my head?"

"I just think it's interesting that you would act so chivalrously."

"I'm heading back to Cheyenne, remember? Starting something up with her when I'm leaving makes no sense." Even though I had every intention of starting something up with her. I stood and reached for my wallet.

"I've got this," Jayce said, but he wasn't being smug. If I had detected even a little arrogance, I'd have knocked his fucking head off. "I didn't mean to piss you off, but I thought you should know. She just met Bo tonight. There's nothing going on there."

Heat burned in my gut causing my focus to shift to find Sidney's gaze on me. And it was there in those big brown eyes, so easy for me to read. She wanted me as much I wanted her.

Too worked up to act in any way but a caveman, I turned and walked out. Climbing onto my bike, I needed the wind; needed the freedom that came with riding. I drove around for a while, but before long I found myself pulling up Sidney's drive. Her Cherokee was the only car in the drive, but I suspected she was still at the bar. I told myself I was there because I wanted to see her wolf; a part of me was curious to see how he'd react to me. And that was true, but I wasn't leaving here without her. Suspected I might have my work cut out for me, I'd walked away from her twice, but I could be persuasive when needed. The pen was a decent size, the shelter nice and sturdy. And standing right in the middle of the space was a black wolf. He might be half dog but he looked all wolf. He was big, bigger than your typical wolf. He was fucking regal. And she'd named him Cain.

"Hey handsome. I've got dinner."

My entire body turned hard. She was home already. I fucking loved knowing that. I'd forgotten that husky-edge to her voice, hearing it had my balls tightening. She hadn't seen me yet, her focus on the food in the bowl. A large, fat, orange cat walked beside her, rubbing up against her leg, and fuck me, I wanted to rub up against her leg. As I watched, her body became aware of me before she even saw me. It was likely the same heat I had felt just an hour ago, something I felt whenever she was near. Her head turned, surprise and joy in those soulful brown eyes before she shut it down.

"Abel. What are you doing here?"

"Home so soon."

Anger replaced joy and just under that was hurt.

"Are you dating Bo?" Knew she wasn't, still wanted to be a dick about it.

"How is that any of your business?"

I moved in, not too close, but close enough that she'd feel me all around her. "Are you dating Bo?"

"No, I only just met him."

With that confession, she blushed and the sight was nearly as good as her husky voice. "You're keeping the wolf?"

"I think he's keeping me."

Again, smart fucking wolf. "What's his name?" It was fucking rude of me to ask, I knew his name so knew I was putting her on the spot, but I so enjoyed the expressions that moved across her face.

She squared her shoulders and her chin took on a defiant tilt before she looked me right in the eyes. "His name is Cain."

Taking a play from her book I asked, "Why?"

Her lips turned up on the one side at my question. "He reminds me of you."

"Why?"

Her focus shifted to the wolf. "Look at him. Dark, dangerous and beautiful."

I had never wanted a woman as badly as I wanted her. I wanted to feel her skin against mine, her taste on my tongue. The cat was glaring at me, as if he'd staked his claim and didn't like me looking. Tough shit. "Who's your guardian?"

She bent down and picked him up with one hand, easy since he all but crawled up her arm and I swear to fucking God that animal grinned at me.

"Sandbar."

Watching her stroke the cat under the chin was making me hard because I wanted her stroking me. "Do you have any idea how badly I want you?"

Her smile dimmed as anger sparked again. "You're the one who took a step back."

"I was trying to be noble."

"And now?"

"Fuck noble."

"Maybe I'm not interested."

I moved in, the pulse at her throat went spastic. "There you go lying again."

"You really are unbelievable, you know that? Two times you walked away from me, three if you count your speedy departure earlier this evening, and now you've changed your mind and I'm just supposed to come when you call?"

She wasn't wrong, didn't change a fucking thing. "You feel it every bit as much as I do."

"Maybe I do, but I'm not really interested in heading down a road with you only for you to have another attack of whatever the hell it is that keeps overcoming you and seeing nothing but your taillights."

"Do you really think you have a choice?"

"I do, yes."

I moved even closer, so close I felt her breath. "Your pulse is pounding, your nipples are hard and I bet if I touched you, you'd be wet. For me."

"Of all the—"

"My pulse is pounding and I'm so fucking hard it hurts, but I'm tired of jacking off to the idea of you. I want to feel you, all of you. Tell me you don't feel it, tell me you haven't touched yourself and thought of me."

Her eyes lowered, all the answer I needed. She fucking had. "Send me away, Sidney, or else I'm going to take you—every single inch."

The hand that held the bowl shook, her throat worked and yet nothing came out.

"Your silence is a green light for me."

Something moved over her face, like a memory being remembered, and the beauty of her expression nearly brought me to my knees. Her voice was no louder than a whisper, "I need to feed Cain first."

And somehow I knew that she had just made a huge decision, one bigger than consenting to fuck me. And being the dick I was, I pounced. "You just sealed your fate, baby. I ain't letting you change your mind."

"I don't want to change my mind."

Fuck. "My place."

"Okay."

"Feed Cain and then you're on the back of my bike."

Her eyes went wide. "But you said you didn't let women ride on your bike."

"Unless they're mine. I'm taking you to my bed. You ride on my bike."

If I weren't so fucking hard, I'd actually be enjoying the show. She was going boneless right in front of me.

"Sidney?"

"Yeah."

"You okay with that?"

"Riding on your bike or going to your bed?"

"Both."

"If you're asking me if I'm ready to move on, I am. It's been three years and I've never wanted to move on, never met anyone who made me want to move on, but I've wanted to move on *with you* since that moment in the bakery."

"Fucking feed that animal."

She smiled shyly, but it grew warmer as she looked and really saw. "You feel it too." She wasn't asking.

"Yeah."

"I'll feed Cain."

It took her fucking forever to feed him and even wanting to toss her on my bike so I could get her home and naked, it was fascinating to watch her with him. Jayce had been right. The animal adored her. Sandbar wasn't stupid. He kept his distance, but he didn't leave her. She said goodnight and even petted the animal's head.

She locked up the pen while saying, "We've been working on not so much training, but boundaries."

"Are you planning to bring him inside?"

"Yeah."

"Is that smart?"

"He hasn't shown any violent tendencies, not to strangers or the cats."

"Cats?"

"When I was younger I found two strays. My foster parents wouldn't let me keep them, so Jake adopted them."

"Jake's your husband."

"Yeah."

"What are their names?"

"Tigger and Stuart."

"How old are they?"

"Sixteen."

"And that one gets along with them?"

"They tolerate him. Sandbar is smart enough to know he's unevenly matched."

"And Cain?"

"We'll see how they respond to him, but I suspect they'll recognize a kindred spirit." She scooped up Sandbar; he curled in her arms, but his eyes were on me and the fucker was gloating. She said, "I think Cain is like Sandbar. He belonged to someone once and they turned him out. I won't bring him inside until I'm certain he's ready. In fact, I've started leaving his pen open during the day to give him a chance to leave. He doesn't leave."

She really cared about these animals, needed to give them a home, and knowing she was a foster child I suspected she was looking to find something she hadn't had. That was until her husband. He took in her cats. Dude was either kindhearted or really fucking smart, knowing just what that act would mean to her. I respected him—the kind of man who sought to make her happy. And even knowing just what I was walking into, the shadow still cast by her dead husband, I still wanted to walk into it. "Bring a bag, you're sleeping over."

"Are you asking me or telling me?"

"Whatever the fuck gets you on my bike with an overnight bag."

"So you're asking nicely. Okay, I'll bring a bag."

"I see you still have attitude."

"And you still use fuck in every sentence."

"Nice that some things stay the same."

Her laugh was infectious. "Come inside. I'll only be a minute."

Stepping inside, it surprised me how homey it felt, especially since she and Rylee hadn't lived there long. It wasn't girlie either, just comfortable and welcoming. She disappeared upstairs as I waited in the kitchen. Impatiently waited in the kitchen. I felt like an adolescent about to lose his virginity. And I knew what this was. What we were doing wasn't just a fuck. I didn't want it to be. I was thirty-three years old and for the first time, I wasn't planning my exit strategy, and for a woman I had known for a little over four months with limited contact during that time. And because that was so fucked up, I was intrigued.

Two cats strolled in, one orange tabby and one black and white, moving around the room like raptors. Both sets of eyes were fixed on me and then they jumped on the counter and rubbed up against my arm.

She came down the stairs with a bag over her shoulder but stopped at the sight of her cats. There was surprise in her voice when she said, "They like you." Her eyes moved to me. "Outside of me, the only other person they've ever showed affection to was Jake." That meant something to her; the subtle change that came over her was undeniable. "I'm ready."

I had been about to ask if she was having second thoughts, but I knew after whatever had just happened, she wasn't.

She turned toward the stairs where the other cat sat. His tail was flicking and his narrowed eyes were on me. Unlike the two still rubbing up against me, Sandbar didn't like me at all. "Good night, Sandbar."

It was a cat, but I found myself doing a bit of my own gloating. I grinned at him. He hissed.

"He's usually so friendly."

"Competition."

"What?"

"I'm competition."

"He's a cat."

"He got a dick?"

"Yeah."

"I'm competition."

"That's the most ridiculous thing I've ever heard. Tigger and Stuart don't have a problem with you." She shook her head. "You're teasing me."

I wasn't going to get into the dynamic of the alpha in the animal kingdom, so I said, "Yeah."

But as soon as her back turned, I gave the cat the bird. Taking her bag, I walked out first so she could lock up. By the time I got her stuff in the saddlebag, she had joined me. Excitement burned in her eyes and remembering her reaction when she first rode with me, I fucking loved that she liked riding as much as I did. I reached for the helmet and secured it under her chin before I settled on the bike. She didn't hesitate to climb on and unlike the first time, she wrapped her arms around my waist and linked them just above my cock. I peeled out and she held on tighter—the fucking sweetest torture.

sidney

We reached his house and immediately my heart started pounding, which was likely not lost on Abel since my chest was pressed to his back. He rolled us into the garage and waited for me to climb off before he followed. He took my bag then my hand, and feeling his calloused hand enveloping mine, I'd missed that. We were going to have sex and even feeling self-conscious since I'd only ever had one partner, I wanted him. And the fact that he came to me and confessed his feelings—got downright possessive—stirred my hunger. It could be argued that I was acting irrationally because I wasn't even sure I liked him and was terrified of the depth of my attraction to him, but none of that mattered. There was only one thing going through my head, the intensity of the need staggering, and that was to find fulfillment with him.

The inside of his house was a surprise. I expected a bachelor pad, but it was neat and clean. The furniture was masculine but the leather sofa and chair, and oak coffee and end tables were lovely. His kitchen was about the size of mine, but it had fancier appliances and concrete countertops.

He dropped my bag on the floor before he turned into me. His fingers slid into my hair and his palms came to rest at my jaw. His eyes moved over my face as he took his time looking. The thorough perusal caused that hunger in my gut to spike. The tip of his tongue appeared as he ran it along the seam of his lips, like he was already licking my taste off. His head lowered, my eyes closed and his phone rang.

"Fucking fuckers."

I giggled because honestly the man really liked that word.

"Don't move."

He grabbed his phone and snarled. "There better be blood."

His faced changed instantly as frustration was replaced with concern. "Fuck. Yeah, I'll be right there." He hung up, but his expression was grim. "I have to go. Do you want to stay here or should I take you home?"

"What's wrong?"

"Carly. She was doing so well, but Duncan went to see her and she's coming down from a wicked high."

"Do you know what she took?"

"He thinks heroin, which is a first for her. She usually smokes weed or pops pills, ecstasy or pain meds. I don't even know where the hell she got heroin."

"Maybe we should get her to the hospital."

"She's already coming down. He doesn't want to move her. Jayce is on his way too."

"Heroin was my brother's drug of choice, maybe I could help."

"Are you sure you want to—"

"Have you ever been around someone on heroin?"

"No."

"I can help."

"All right, if you're sure."

"Heroin is not a road she wants to go down."

"I know."

When we arrived, Jayce had already arrived. Cut his night short with Rylee to help. I had to admire these men that they cared so much. I wish Connor had had friends like this.

"Since she's only used once, when the drug starts to leave her system she shouldn't experience any withdrawal symptoms. She will, however, likely vomit and she'll definitely be irritable as the effect of the drug fades. She'll need lots of water, which might be hard to get her to take. And then it's just watching and waiting."

"You've done this before?" Jayce asked knowingly.

"My brother was a heroin addict. I've been through cold turkey with him and withdrawal for an addict is horrific…one of the reasons they stay high so they don't experience the agony of it. This won't be like that, but she is on a dangerously slippery slope if she liked the high."

"I really thought she was past this. Fuck. You were right, Abel. Therapy is not enough. She needs rehab," Duncan said.

"Rehab only works if the person wants to get clean." I cautioned.

"Let's hope this scares some sense into her. Thanks, Sidney, for coming." The worry etched in Duncan's face was proof of how much she meant to him.

The state of her brought back so many memories, but I pushed them out of my head and allowed instinct to take over—dormant knowledge stirring back to life as I fell into doing what I had done for years for my brother. She kept throwing up the water, but she did eventually take some and it stayed down. She even had pockets of sleep, but they weren't long lived. Jayce and Duncan went home—stopping first at my place to help Rylee feed Cain—since we'd be taking shifts; Abel and I took the first one. During one of her naps, I was outside getting some air.

I felt when Abel joined me on the porch. He asked, "How many times did you go through that with your brother?"

Turning to him, I leaned up against the railing. "Connor started heroin at twenty-four and became completely hooked by twenty-five. For five years, Jake and I dragged him from countless drug dens and forced him to go cold turkey. A few times he stayed sober for a few weeks, once a couple of months, but he always went back because he needed the high. We tried to get him counseling, tried to get him into a program, but he always left. He didn't want to be saved. I always thought he started using as a way to cope. Our home life wasn't great, but I think he just loved the high."

He moved closer; the pad of his thumb going to the tender spot where my cheek met with Carly's knuckles earlier when we were trying to get her to take the water. "We should put some ice on that."

"It's okay." But that was said breathlessly because I wanted to close the distance between us so I could touch and taste him.

He felt the need too when his hand moved to my neck, his fingers applying pressure as he pulled me to him. His whiskers brushed across my face as his lips descended, a light brushing like a sampling of fine wine—just a taste to savor. I had worried I would compare Abel with Jake, since he was my only point of reference and the love of my life, but those worries evaporated as soon as Abel's lips touched mine. This was so different from what Jake and I had shared. I wasn't sure if the moan came from him or me since we both wanted more. His arm wrapped around my waist at the same time his mouth opened for a kiss that left nothing to the imagination. My blood was on fire as it raced through my veins; I felt light-headed and my legs were having trouble holding me up. His taste was like him—dark and dangerous—and even tasting him, the hunger he stirred wasn't appeased. I pressed in closer, wrapped my arms around his neck, lifted up on my tiptoes and kissed him back. My tongue exploring his mouth, running along his lips, tangling with his as my body came alive and ached with need.

Turning us, he pressed me up against the wall. My body molded to his like he was consuming me. He was hard, pressed tight against my stomach, my hips moving of their own volition as I sought to ease the ache his touch stirred. His hands moved down my body, brushing along the sides of my breasts, and lower to my hips before moving under my shirt to bare skin. When he swiped my nipple with his thumb, the ache between my legs turned into a spasm as I pressed my legs together and rode it. His fingers moved down my stomach to my waist. He flipped the button on my jeans and immediately his hand filled the space as one of his fingers ran along the edge of my panties before slipping under the silk, so close to where I wanted to feel him. And then his hand was gone. My eyes opened to find his head bent and his hands pressed to the wall near my ears.

"What happened?"

Lifting his gaze to mine, his eyes were no longer the color of an aquamarine, but darker, like a royal blue. "Not here. Your first time shouldn't be on some porch." His mouth moved closer. "You came."

Three years of abstinence and one incredibly sexy man had the power to pull complete honesty from me because I didn't even hesitate in answering. "Yeah."

His jaw clenched, his eyes closed and he seemed to be debating with himself. "Fuck it." His fingers dove into my jeans and under my panties. He separated me and ran his middle finger right along my core before he brought his finger to his lips and staring me right in the eyes, he licked my taste off. What was even more erotic, he enjoyed it.

"Holy shit." The words were out; just fell off my tongue because…holy shit.

"We finish here and then you're in my bed. I plan on spending a good long time tasting you here." He cupped my sex with his palm. "Move your hips. Come for me again."

Hedonistic, absolutely, but my body demanded release so I did. I rubbed myself against his palm as his fingers pressed against me mimicking what his cock would be doing later. I was so aroused it didn't take long. His eyes never left mine as my body crested then went tumbling over the side and I happily gave myself over to it.

"Fucking beautiful," he whispered.

Abel's words stirred a memory of Jake causing my chest to hurt because I didn't feel guilty, didn't feel like I was cheating on Jake. I wanted this man. Wanted everything the look of him promised.

A shout came from the house; Abel touched his forehead to mine. "Round two."

Abel and I were heading back to his place. Jayce, Marnie and her sister Patricia, a nurse, came to relieve us. Marnie had paperwork for a rehab place that was close to Sheridan; Carly was being admitted. She was terrified, she had never done heroin, got talked into trying it, and now she was finally willing to admit she had a problem.

Abel pulled his bike into the garage. I climbed off and his gaze hit mine before he said, "At least she didn't argue about rehab."

"No, she actually pushed for it. That's the first step. Connor never made that step. He didn't want to get better."

"I'm sorry, Doc."

"I'm happy she does."

"And she does want to get better. I had my doubts, but I think she'll find her way."

"She's lucky she has all of you."

He swung his leg over his bike, reached for my hand as he closed the garage door. Once inside, he led me right to the shower. As the water warmed, he peeled my clothes off. It was the only way to describe how he removed each layer. His fingertips touching and exploring every part of me he discovered. When he had me down to only my bra and panties, he took a step back and just looked his fill. His gaze moved up my body before settling on mine. Grabbing the back of his tee, he pulled it forward and dropped it on the pile of my clothes. I'd seen his chest before, the defined muscles and the flawless tan skin, but my focus lingered on the scar of his gunshot wound.

"How did you get that?"

"Carly."

My eyes jerked to his face. "She was high?"

"Yeah."

"That's why you didn't want the hospital or the cops."

"She has enough problems, she doesn't need to get hauled into jail on top of it."

For as cocky and smug as he was, there was so much more to him. And I liked the combination, the smug dick and the gentleman. It worked.

His hands moved to his jeans and taking his time, he worked the button and lowered the zipper. I felt his focus on me, but I couldn't look anywhere but his fly. Then those jeans dropped, his boxer briefs followed. My mouth went dry, a thirst that demanded be quenched. He moved, like a big cat, slow and graceful. His thigh muscles drawing my attention, his abs and chest, those arms with biceps that would take at least four of my hands to span. As he grew closer, my gaze moved to his cock, the tip ending almost at his waist. His fingers brushed along my shoulder before he pulled one bra strap down. His lips followed his fingers, down my arm, across the swell of my breast. With a flick, my bra opened and he moved the silk away from his target—the material completely forgotten as his tongue traced my nipple, first one then the other. Reaching for him, I stroked him, lingering on the tip before slowing moving down the shaft. He was wide, my fingers came nowhere near touching, and I wanted every inch of him between my legs. I wanted to feel him moving inside me. His mouth closed over my nipple, sucking me deep as his hands moved to my hips to work my panties off. Remembering all that he wanted to do to me, the images he so vividly detailed that day at the trail, I wrapped my hand around the base of his cock and dropped to my knees. He growled, long and deep.

"Are you sure?" he asked.

"Yes."

My eyes stayed on his as I touched the tip with my tongue. And just that taste had moisture pooling between my legs. I ran my tongue up the length of him, a slow deliberate lick. Squeezing my thighs on the quivers that were growing stronger between my legs, I closed my mouth over him and pulled him deep into my throat. His hands laced through my hair as his hips jerked.

"Touch yourself." he demanded.

And since I was so close, I did. Sinking my fingers in as I sucked him hard.

"Make yourself come."

Every nerve felt electrified as I worked myself, pressing down on my clit while my head bobbed up and down as I worked him. My body spasmed around my fingers and he pulled me to my feet and reached for the hand I'd had between my legs, bringing each finger to his mouth to savor my taste. Then he dropped to his knees, spread me and drove his tongue in deep. I'd just come, but his tongue was relentless, his fingers working my clit and my body responded—writhing under his touch as the next orgasm moved through me.

"Twice and I haven't even gotten my dick into you," he said as he stepped me backward into the shower, reaching for a condom from the box on the counter. I watched him roll it on and felt like a junkie because I needed more, suspected I'd never have enough when it came to him. He learned my body…where I liked being touched, where I *loved* being touched, and when I couldn't bear another second he lifted me and brought me down hard on his cock. Curling my legs around his waist, my hands reached up for something to hold as my back arched to take him deeper. His hips moved faster as he pounded into me until my body was helpless but to give him what he wanted. It felt as if I was splintering apart as my third orgasm of the night ripped through me. My body was still tingling from it when I touched his face, held it and watched as he came. His hips stopped, his eyes closed, his face harsh with pleasure. Glorious was how I felt, not self-conscious or embarrassed by my behavior, or even guilty. I felt wonderfully glorious. I traced his lips with my tongue, his eyes opened.

I reached for the elastic and pulled it out, his hair fell to his shoulders, black like midnight. Running my fingers through it, we spoke no words, just stayed where we were, his body inside mine, mine wrapped around his. He made the position even better when he pressed me tight against the wall so he could cradle my face in his hands to tilt my head for his kiss.

Working at Hellar Farm, my thoughts were divided between the horse I was tending and Abel. For two days, I'd been walking around in a daze as I fantasized about Abel and the night we'd shared. After the shower, he took me to his room where we spent the night discovering each other. I had behaved wantonly, but it felt good to feel again—to have that fluttering in my chest, to feel both anticipation and longing. I'd missed that, missed feeling connected to someone.

Carly had been admitted to rehab; Abel had spent the past two days helping to get her settled. I truly hoped she beat it and having so many rooting for her, she had a good chance of doing just that.

Cain had come into the house. Sandbar objected, but he was smart enough to stay out of his way. As I suspected, Tigger and Stuart stirred from their naps long enough to glance at him before falling back to sleep. Cain spent a few hours inside before he wanted back out. It was progress.

"Hey you."

Looking up from my examination of Chocolate Cake—the

Hellar boys were nuts—I saw Rylee strutting over.

"What are you doing here?"

"We were slow at the clinic, so Doc suggested I check on you. How's Chocolate Cake?"

"I'm pretty sure it's the suspensory ligament. Not bad though, very slight, but there's definitely some heat and it's swollen."

"I knew she was favoring that leg." Chris, the barn manager, said as he joined us in the barn. "Do you want me to ice it?"

"Yeah, a couple times a day and I'll prescribe an anti-inflammatory. Hand walk her, start with ten minutes a day and we'll increase that as the ligament heals."

"You got it, Doc. Thanks for coming out so quickly. I'll let the groom know."

Rylee waited for Chris to leave before she asked, "So, how are you doing?"

She was asking about Abel.

"I'm doing great."

She studied me for a minute. "You aren't upset he hasn't called?"

"He's dealing with Carly."

"Takes a second to call."

I started collecting my things, knew Rylee watched my every move.

I looked around to make sure we were alone. "I know what you're worried about. I've been resistant to dating, but with Abel we completely skipped right over dating and went straight to bed. Out of character for me, absolutely. Jake was my first and only. What we had was beautiful, sweet, and passionate, but being with Abel was exactly what I thought it'd be. It was raw, almost selfish as we used each other to reach fulfillment, and it too was beautiful. Do I hope to have another night like it? Hell yeah, countless nights. But if I don't I wouldn't change one thing about our night together. He made no promises, Rylee, just the opposite."

"And you're okay with that, a one-night stand?"

"It was more than that." Whispering I added, "I gave him a blowjob, well he didn't let me finish, but I so wanted to finish. It took me years to work up to that with Jake. It was an intimacy that I struggled with but with Abel it was more like a craving. I can't describe it. What's between us is primal, elemental. If I only get one night with him, it was a fucking fantastic night."

She studied me before she said, "Well, the sadness behind your eyes is fading and I'm happy about that, I am, but you were being all philosophical not too long ago and now you're jumping in with abandon. What's that all about?"

"I like how I feel when I'm near him, like who I am with him, and I'll take what I can get from him because I'm finally finding happy."

"Well, I like Abel for that alone."

"Me too. Let me call in the prescription and then we can go. I'm hungry."

"I'm not surprised, if I worked here I'd be eating all the time. A horse named Chocolate Cake. What the hell were they thinking?"

As soon as Rylee and I stepped into the Brass Bull, our names were shouted from the direction of the bar where Ichabod and Jeshaiah were bellied up.

"Let's join them, it's my turn to buy the round."

Rylee looked comical. "Are you serious?"

"Yeah. I think they're a hoot."

"I knew you would."

"Hey, gentlemen. Can we join you?"

Ichabod was already pulling a stool out for me. "Hell, yeah. I'm feeling parched."

I signaled to the bartender and ordered the next round; Ichabod was looking around me to Rylee. "You haven't called me."

Rylee rolled her eyes, Jeshaiah howled with laughter.

"I'm not thinking the feeling is mutual, Ichabod. You might want to focus your attention elsewhere." I realized the error of my comment immediately because his eyes zeroed in on me. "All you had to say was you wanted some of this."

"What have you guys been up to?" Rylee asked to change the subject.

"Not much. The cops came around last week, asking questions about suspicious and unfamiliar cars coming in for gas. They're working Belinda's case, but they were grabbing at straws. It was probably some transient who is long gone by now."

"Really? I thought most people held to the belief it was a local," Rylee said.

"I've lived here my whole life and I can not believe anyone I've shared air with is a cold-blooded murderer. Belinda hung with a bad crowd and if she was as nasty to them as she was to everyone else, one of them probably did her in."

I felt bad for Belinda, though had I known her when she was alive I was sure I wouldn't have liked her, but not even in death did people have nice things to say about her. I liked Ichabod's take on the crime, one he shared with Mr. Milburn, because the idea that a murderer lived in our midst was rather unsettling.

"How's Spike?" Rylee asked.

"Feisty. He likes roaming; he's gone most of the day. I haven't a clue what he's getting himself into."

Roaming around, that concerned me. "You do know there's a mountain lion prowling the area."

"Yeah, I heard about it but I don't think Spike's in any danger. He hangs mostly around Main Street. Probably too much noise for the cat."

I hoped so. Spike was a big dog, but against a mountain cat, I wouldn't hold out hope he'd be the winner.

Ichabod bought the next round before he and Jeshaiah called it a night. Rylee and I moved to a table and were in the middle of dinner when the door opened to Jayce, Duncan and Abel. The sight of him physically moved through me—a chill that swept my body like a wave. His hair was down tonight and I wanted my hands in it, wanted to feel those silky strands between my fingers. His eyes collided with mine before the others, as aware of me as I was of him. He moved through the tables and reached my side. He didn't say hi, just reached for my hand and pulled me from the table to the dance floor. I didn't know what song was playing; I couldn't hear anything but the pounding of my heart in my ears. His arms banded around me to hold me close as he buried his face in my neck and breathed me in. His big body was tense, the muscles hard like a rubber band stretched nearly to its limit. Something was wrong.

"Is it Carly?"

"She's okay."

"What's wrong?"

"I think I'm experiencing withdrawal."

My heart rolled in my chest. His head lifted and that pale blue gaze moved to my mouth. Drawing in a breath, he rubbed his hips against mine. His lips parted and his breath tickled my nose. "I haven't used my daily quota of fuck today."

It took me a minute to realize he was teasing me. "You're a tea—"

He silenced me with his mouth; his invading tongue exploring with a hunger that literally left me breathless.

We returned to the table after the song and I tried to eat, but what I hungered for I wouldn't be getting until later. At some point, my lust took a back seat as I watched Abel with Jayce and Duncan. When I first saw them together I had trouble imagining them as friends, but I saw it now. As Carly healed, it seemed that they were too.

Abel had pulled his hair back—I really liked his bun—his focus on his burger as he listened to Duncan and whatever story he was sharing. And it was while I studied them that I realized outside of his entrance Abel seemed to be going to great lengths to avoid me. I wasn't self-absorbed, I didn't need his undivided attention, but every encounter with him his focus had been fixed solely on me. And now it felt as if he was going out of his way to do just the opposite. Realization dawned. He was going home. I guess when he said he wanted me, that want had a time limit. Regret hit first because under that cocky exterior was a man I'd really like to get to know better, but self-preservation followed shortly after because I no longer suspected, I knew unequivocally, that given time I would fall hard for him. And it was the realization that I was okay with falling, taking that risk with my eyes wide open that terrified me.

"Can I talk to you for a minute?"

Abel's head jerked to me, he saw more of me than anyone, maybe even more than Jake. "Yeah."

I stood, tried to pay, but Abel wouldn't let me.

"See you at home, roomie," Rylee said with a wink.

And she would, far sooner than she knew. Abel followed me outside; we reached my car.

"You're going home."

He pushed his hands into the front pockets of his jeans. "Yeah."

"You weren't sure how to tell me that, were you?"

"No. Not after the other night, but Carly's in rehab. I have to get back."

"It was a good night."

"It was a fucking fantastic night."

"There's that word again." And even knowing this was right—his life was in Cheyenne, his job—I felt my heart break in a different way. Not one that left me shattered, but sad over the missed opportunity.

"Are you okay?"

I wasn't. Shying away from my feelings to protect my heart seemed kind of stupid now seeing as the one who had the power to hurt my heart was leaving—walking out of my life. I'd survive, we hadn't grown so close that losing him would cause permanent damage, but would I ever meet someone who made me feel as Abel did? And should I let him walk away without telling him just how affected I was by him? No, I shouldn't. "I knew this day was coming, but I do wish we had more time to explore this because I'm wildly attracted to you..." I needed a second to swallow down the lump that had formed in the back of my throat. "I like who I am and how I feel when I'm around you."

He rubbed his beard, his downcast eyes lifting to mine and there was regret, maybe disappointment, looking back at me. "My life is in Cheyenne, my business. And if it was just me, I'd be so fucking tempted…" He looked down again, just for a second, his struggle very evident before his focus shifted back to me. "But it isn't just me. I have employees, a partner. And maybe what you feel for me isn't so much about me specifically and more to do with me being the first man you let in since your husband died."

Before I could argue, he kissed me. His lips lingered as he struggled with letting go, and then he took a step back and reached for the door. Stunned by not just his kiss but also the longing that fueled it, I absently climbed into my car and keyed the engine. He leaned into the window. "Take it back to Jimmy and tell him to give you a fucking tune-up for free or he'll have to fucking deal with me."

And even feeling blue he could make me grin. "I will fucking tell him."

He smiled, one of those magnificent smiles. "Take care, Sidney."

"You too."

He stepped back, pushed his hands into his pockets again. It was hard to say the words because I was acknowledging out loud something I'd only recently realized. And even being the truth, it hurt to say. "What I feel for you is more than you being the first since my husband. I loved my husband with every fiber in my being, but given the chance I know what could be between us would eclipse even that."

I drove away because the tears were so close and he didn't need that. He was leaving, I knew he was leaving; putting my shit on him wasn't fair. I waited until I reached the house before I dropped my head on the steering wheel and let the tears fall.

I heard his bike, roaring down the street, pulling up behind me. I tried to wipe my eyes before he reached me, but the door opened and he pulled me to my feet to press me up against him. His heart beat hard and fast, his body tense.

"You fucking drop that on me and then drive off."

"I didn't want you to go thinking what you were, but I'm not asking for anything."

"Leaving you feels like I'm ripping out my fucking soul and then you tell me that."

"It does?"

"I feel you. You're inside me, in my blood and bones. Never fucking felt anything like it. I need you, crave you, and now you're telling me you feel it too."

He sounded pissed at me, like it was my fault he cared so much. I couldn't help the smile. "I do feel it. The intensity scares me a bit."

His hold tightened. "Four and a half hours of good road on my bike isn't all that fucking long," he whispered in my ear.

Oh my God. Did he just say that? "Are you serious?"

"In my bones, baby. Yeah, I'm serious."

There weren't words, so I buried my face in his chest and just gave myself a moment to let it penetrate. He felt it too.

"Get your stuff. You're in my bed tonight."

I tried to pull away from him; he touched my chin to study the tears streaking my face before he wiped away the ones still rolling down my cheeks. "You're shedding tears for me?"

I was no longer finding happy, I was happy, deliriously happy, and because of that I teased him. "No, for the loss of hearing fuck used in every sentence and in every form of speech. It's a gift you've got there."

"Smart ass." But he kissed me, deeply, with a hint of something that hadn't been there before.

~ABEL~ CHAPTER SIXTEEN

The fucker didn't even ride it out of the shop. He put his brand new, thirty thousand dollar motorcycle on a fucking trailer. He'd probably ride it around once every month and the rest of the time it'd stay in his garage or under a tarp. Unbelievable.

"Another satisfied customer." Tiny's words were deceiving because he was as disgusted as me with our latest customer.

"Fucker has more money than sense."

"Agreed."

"Where does D.J. find these douche bags?"

"Don't know."

"I got to tell ya, I'm getting really tired of sweating over a build for it to go to assholes like that."

"Yeah, I've noticed you've been more of a dick than usual."

I didn't even bother acknowledging that comment. Carly had been moved about a month back to another rehab closer to me. She was over thirty days in for her sixty-day treatment and she was doing well, responding to treatment.

"Hey, Abel. You've got a visitor," D.J. called.

"You expecting someone?" Tiny asked as we headed to the office.

"No, probably another fucking yuppie with more money than brains."

Reaching the office, I was surprised as fuck to see Duncan Hellar.

"Hey, man. What the hell are you doing here?" I asked while taking the hand he offered.

"You got a minute?"

"Yeah."

"I'll catch up with you later." But Tiny was already pulling the door closed behind him.

"What's up?"

"I wanted to ask you…this sounds so fucking lame now."

"Yeah, well, you're here so spit it out."

"There's someone I want to…I know there was something going on between you and her and I wanted to know if the way was clear."

What the fuck? What happened to his undying love for Carly? It had been a little over a month since I had last seen Sidney, neither of us could get away, but we talked on the phone every night, so the thought that her feelings had shifted was like taking a fucking dagger to the heart.

"Yeah, there's still fucking something going on."

"I knew it. Damn it."

"Is she interested?"

"I haven't approached her, but yeah. It's in the air, it damn near sizzles when we're together."

That was like taking several punches to the gut. I thought that charge was unique to her and me.

"I'm sorry, I'll back off. It's been there since we were kids. I'd hoped it had faded, but I guess not."

Okay now I wasn't following. "What now?"

"Carly. I know you two had a thing when we were younger."

"We're talking about Carly?"

"Yeah, who did you think I was talking about?"

"Sidney."

"Sidney? I've never thought of her like that."

"Fuck me."

Both relief and mischievousness fueled the smile that spread over his face. "You and Sidney?"

I was tempted to smile like an ass too because shit, the idea of Sidney with someone else. I didn't like it. Not one fucking bit.

"She's not just a hook up?"

"No fucking way."

"I think that's great."

It was a whole hell of a lot more than great. "Wait, you said that Carly and I had something as kids. What are you talking about?"

"You know how she always used to come to the farm, almost as much as you. And there was that cabin in the woods that we played in as kids."

"Yeah."

"I saw her coming from the woods one day, the last day she came to the farm actually, and you weren't far behind her."

"You think I fucked Carly?"

"Yeah and you dumped her so she stopped coming around."

"I never fucked her."

He sounded as surprised as I felt. "You didn't?"

"No, I never thought of her like that and I rarely went to that cabin after the age of eight. If I was coming from the woods, I was coming back from smoking a joint with Carlos. You know the dude that got fired for stealing. You brought girls to our hideout?"

"Yeah, I thought you were too."

"Why'd you think that?"

"It was being used and not just by me."

"What about Jayce?"

"He was too busy chasing pussy in that piece of shit car."

I'd forgotten about that car. Duncan wasn't wrong, thing was shit on wheels.

"I kind of wished it were you."

"You wished I fucked the girl you liked?"

"There's only one other person I've seen coming from that cabin. I thought he was just checking up on us, but if it wasn't you using the cabin to entertain it had to be him."

"Who?"

"Chris."

Humor died because what he suggested was disgusting. "Chris Dearly, the barn manager? You think he fucked Carly?" Even liking Chris, if that was true it was going to be hard seeing him and not breaking his fucking neck.

"No. He wouldn't have forced her. But Chris was like a father to Carly. If he came onto her, that would have freaked her out."

"Yeah, but I can't see him doing that to her, breaking her trust in him."

"Honestly, I can't either, but I do know he has a taste for younger women. They've all been legal that I know of, but just barely."

"Speaking of Carly, what's this shit I hear that you told your dad she wasn't Hellar material?"

"Where the fuck did you hear that?"

"Carly overheard it. That's why she stopped coming to the farm, that's why she left town."

Duncan's face completely drained of color. "She heard that?"

"Yeah. What the fuck was that all about?"

"I liked her. I thought she liked you. I was nasty. Dad got pissed hearing me say that about her. I took a swing at him, but I pictured your face."

"You took a swing at Garrett?"

"Yeah."

"Is that why he hauled you off to military school?"

"Yep."

"So the tension between you now, you never apologized."

"No."

"I don't know if I should pat your back for taking a swing at a man like Garrett, that took some serious balls, or kick you in the ass for being a dick and not admitting you were wrong. Speaking of being wrong, what about Carly?"

"I've liked her since we were kids. I want to try."

"Fucking finally. I know from her own mouth that she would be very receptive to that."

"No shit."

"Took you long enough brother, but better late than never."

Walking into the rehab center, I hadn't been able to get out of my head the conversation with Duncan from earlier in the week. Carly left town because of Duncan, but was it possible she started drugs because of Chris? If what Duncan thought was true I wanted to ask Carly about it, but I hesitated because I was unsure if confronting someone in rehab with the event that could have caused her tail-spin was a good idea. So I was checking in with her doctors. They knew me well enough; I'd been coming around a couple times a week since she'd been admitted. Her head doctor, Dr. Eisner, greet-ed me in her office.

"Abel, nice to see you. What can I do for you?"

"You and I had discussed what could have been the catalyst for Carly's addiction during one of our earlier meetings. Recently I've received some insight on what that could have been. I'd like to know if there's any truth to it, but I'm not sure asking Carly is wise at this point."

She leaned forward a bit. "How significant is this information?"

"It's possible that someone she looked up to as a father figure may have made inappropriate passes at her."

"No physical abuse?"

"I can't say for sure, but I don't think so."

"I can't discuss her case with you, but I can work toward that end in our sessions. This is the environment for that, a controlled and safe place where any lingering issues that arise can be addressed before they snowball. Thank you for the insight."

"Yeah, no problem."

"Carly's had quite a few guests today. In fact her last visitor just left."

sidney

I hoped it was okay that I was stopping by unannounced, but I wanted to surprise him. I had wanted to visit before this, but I was needed at the clinic now that Doc Cassidy had officially retired. I'd managed to get all my patients seen before I made the drive. It had been just over a month since Carly had been moved and she looked great—her complexion and hair both looked the healthiest I'd ever seen them and she'd put on a few pounds, but more importantly she looked happy. Patricia's suggestion of moving her had been a good one. Only thirty days into treatment and she looked worlds different.

Climbing from my car, I stood for a minute and took in Abel's garage. You'd never know what it was since there was no sign identifying it. No walk-ins for them, only people serious about custom motorcycles.

And it was while I stood there that I realized I probably should have called first. Just showing up was rude. He could be busy with a client. I turned toward my car with the intent of calling him when I heard that voice.

"Where are you going, Doc?"

The sight of Abel walking toward me with that cocky grin on his face was one I liked a lot. The memory of him doing the same without clothes had my body growing warm.

"Found yourself in my neck of the woods?"

Leaning against my car, partially because I needed it to keep my balance, I replied, "I just saw Carly, but I really wanted to see you."

"So why were you leaving?"

"I realized I should have called first."

He moved right into my personal space as his hands came down on my car's hood, caging me in. "Any time, Doc. You want me, I'm here any time." His head lowered, his nose moved over my shoulder and up my neck. My eyes closed as I locked my knees to keep myself standing. He nipped my earlobe with his teeth; his tongue ran along the shell as he breathed softly. "Same goes for me sneaking into your house and into your bed. All access, babe."

I couldn't answer. I was too overwhelmed by him that all I managed was reaching out to him so I didn't sway.

His head lifted and I was treated to the sight of his grin. "No need to call first, Doc."

I needed to feel him to believe this was real as I touched his beard and ran my fingers over his lips. I'd certainly dreamt about it enough. "I've missed you."

Burying his hands in my hair, he pulled my mouth to his. He tasted and explored with a need I completely understood and had me forgetting where we were. The need to feel him, all of him, was turning me reckless.

"Not here," he whispered against my lips. "Keys."

I couldn't help the giggle with his ridiculous rule about driving, but I still handed them over.

"My place isn't far."

His apartment door had just closed behind us when he lifted me into his arms. He walked us through his apartment, but I didn't see anything. I would take time later to check his place out.

Reaching his room, he lowered me onto his bed and came down right on top of me. For a good while we kissed and petted through the layers of our clothes, but the need to feel his skin against mine had me reaching for his shirt. And when I found bare skin my fingers moved over his chest and trailed down his abs. He wasn't as gentle with removing my shirt and bra, but then I was okay with that because I had his mouth and hands on me again. Kissing down my stomach, he worked my jeans off and then my panties. Ravenous was the only word to describe the look of him as he pulled me to the edge of the bed, dropped to his knees and buried his face between my legs. Fisting his sheets, my hips moved against his invading tongue. God, I missed this. He knew my body, exactly what I liked because he had me coming in a matter of minutes. He didn't wait; he rolled on a condom and filled me in one powerful shift of his hips sending me right back over the edge. He was nearly as out of control as me, moving with a single-minded purpose of finding pleasure. And when he came, I watched as it rolled over his features. Hooking an arm around my waist, he rolled us so I sat astride him.

"We'll go slower next time."

"No complaints here."

"How have you been? Doc Cassidy has officially retired, yeah?"

"Yep, but we've got a really good system. I love the work."

He touched the hair that hung over my shoulder. "And Cain?"

"He's living in the house now."

His brow arched. "Really? And it's all good?"

"Yeah, though if you intend to sneak into my house, we might need to work on that."

"Good idea."

"I don't think it'll take much since he's even fine around the cats. They know who their alpha is."

"Including Sandbar?"

"Yeah." He started to shake and it felt really nice since we were still joined. "Why are you laughing?"

"I love that an animal you named after me is keeping that little shit in line."

"Sandbar is very affectionate."

"To you. To everyone else he'd like to slit our throats while we sleep."

Who would have thought Abel would be jealous of a cat. I couldn't help my own chuckle. It dawned that I was in Abel's bed, he was still inside me and still we could be so natural and comfortable. Even with Jake, it had taken time before we reached this level of comfort and intimacy.

The pad of his thumb swiped over my lower lip. "What's put that look on your face?"

"I thought I'd imagined the easiness of this, but I didn't."

"I'm usually planning my departure before I get the woman into my bed, but with you I can't fucking stop thinking about you. 325 miles isn't all that far, but it's too far for me."

"What are you saying?"

He rolled us again and sunk in deeper, my knees falling to the side as he filled me so completely. "I'm saying I need to think about some things because I want more of this." He pulled out, my body protesting the emptiness as he handled the condoms, and then he slammed back into me. My spine arched, he lifted my hips and I took his cock repeatedly until my body cried for mercy and gave him what he wanted.

I was wrapped in his sheet and sitting on the counter in his kitchen, while Abel made us sandwiches. His place, like his cabin, was sparse but clean. Definitely a bachelor pad because it lacked the touches of pictures or knickknacks a woman would add, but I liked it. It was all very Abel.

"Are you good if you don't leave until the morning?"

"Are you asking me to stay the night, Abel?"

"Yep."

"I'll call Rylee to let her know, though she knew I was stopping by and was hoping she wouldn't hear from me until tomorrow."

That earned me a grin before he said, "Duncan stopped by the other day."

"Yeah? He mentioned he wanted to visit Carly."

"He thought Carly and I were together as kids. I never touched Carly. She was like a sister. But Duncan has a theory."

"A theory about what?"

He handed me a sandwich before leaning back against the counter opposite me. He'd pulled on his jeans, but he hadn't bothered buttoning them and his hair hung loose around his shoulders. The sight of him was very distracting.

"He thinks Chris may have made an inappropriate pass at Carly."

My whole body went numb as my eyes moved from Abel's chest to his face. "Are you serious?"

"Yeah, fucked up if he did."

"Jesus."

"I spoke to her doc, mentioned the possibility, she's going to skirt around the subject during their sessions."

"The farm was like home for Carly and Chris like family."

"Yeah."

"I hope he's wrong."

"Me too, but it might explain why she turned to drugs."

"Poor Carly." Playing with my sandwich, I couldn't help but ask because I was so very curious about Abel.

"I'm guessing your home life wasn't great."

"My dad was a dick, never wanted kids. Got saddled with me, used me for what he could and then ditched me. Tiny took me in."

"Thank God for Tiny."

"Yeah, you've no fucking idea. I was one of the lucky ones." He pushed his hands into jean pockets. "What about you?"

"Let's just say Jake was my Tiny."

"Yeah, I kind of got that."

"We'd known each other a long time. He was a good man."

"Catching a woman like you, he'd have to be."

My heart flipped in my chest, but what a thing to say and from a man like Abel. And because of it, I gave him a small insight into me. "As wonderful as he was and as much as I loved him, will always love him, I never felt the electricity with him as I do with you, nor hungered for someone like I hunger for you."

Abel closed the distance between us and pulled open the sheet as he lowered me back on the counter. He pushed his jeans down enough to pull his cock free and in the next breath he was inside me. It was different, the way he moved, and the way he watched as my body took him in and out in a gentle glide. He pressed his hand flat against my stomach and moved it slowly up my body as his hips set a pace that created that wonderful friction. Relentless, a sweet, deliberate torture and the orgasm that followed was equally sweet. He pulled from me just before he came, his warmth rolling down my stomach as his mouth settled over mine.

Since Doc Cassidy officially retired, I had been solely responsible for three foalings and each time I was in awe. Speckled Egg's water broke ten minutes ago and even now the little one was coming and in perfect form—the front legs first and the head between them. It was incredible and Speckled Egg, for as uncomfortable as she'd been prior to her water breaking, was pushing like a champ. This foaling was particularly special to me since Speckled Egg was the very first horse I had tended.

"Every time it still amazes me," Marnie said as she and Garrett stood behind me. I wasn't doing anything; just there to ensure it all went well.

Jayce and Duncan were there as was Chris, though I could admit I didn't feel quite at ease with him learning what I had from Abel. I liked it though, how the whole farm took a break to watch the birth of new life. And even with the wonder happening before me, my thoughts detoured to Abel. I'd been home for two days and all I wanted was to go back. After that fantastic moment in his kitchen, we got a shower and watched late night television. I'd fallen asleep and woke to Abel kissing my neck. We made love in the morning before I left. And the sex was phenomenal, but had it only been fantastic sex I wouldn't have made the trip. And he felt it too. He was going to try to come up in the next week or two. He'd given me a key to his apartment and had encouraged me to come whenever I wanted, preferably naked and in his bed waiting. Cocky bastard.

Speckled Egg gave a loud whinny as her baby completely

dropped from her. "It's a colt." And he was beautiful, an Appaloosa like his mom, but dark with white spots. "He's a handsome devil."

"Yeah, he is," Garrett said. "Domino."

"Oh, that's his name?"

"Yeah, there will be others for the pedigree but for short we'll call him Domino."

"It's a fitting name. I'll stay, make sure she passes the placenta and that it looks good."

"I'll whip up some sandwiches and coffee." Marnie said as she started from the barn.

"I'll help. Thanks for being here, Sidney." Garrett followed her out.

"I have to finish the schedule. Easiest birth yet. You're good luck, Sidney," Chris said before he followed Marnie and Garrett.

"So, what do you think?" Jayce said as he pulled up a hay bale and joined me.

"Amazing. I realize it's done every day, but it's humbling to witness a creature coming into the world."

Equally humbling watching as they leave it too, but I wouldn't allow sad thoughts to invade this beautiful moment.

"Thanksgiving is in a week. I imagine you must do it big here," I asked, since I'd been tossing around the idea of hosting dinner for anyone who didn't have plans. Ever since that first Thanksgiving at Jake's, I never missed one.

"Usually, but Dad's going to be traveling, checking out some horses. Marnie offered to toss in a turkey, but to have a chance to go to her sister's and let her do all the cooking, we told her not to bother."

"You're welcome to join Rylee and me."

"Yeah?"

"I never miss Thanksgiving."

"That would be great, thanks. How was Carly?"

"She looks fantastic and she seems happy. Don't you agree Duncan?"

"Yeah, she looked more like her old self."

"It's about time you two stopped dancing around each other."

Duncan's head snapped to his brother's. "You knew back then too?"

Jayce rolled his eyes at Duncan. "Yeah and she liked you too." Jayce glanced over at me, "Duncan, despite his military training, is not very observant."

Twenty-four hours after the birth, Speckled Egg and Domino were both doing well. Domino was galloping hours after his entrance into the world. Most horses were only trotting or cantering at that point, but Domino was impatient. I had just come back from the Hellar place, checking up on them, where I had witnessed firsthand his love of running. I was home now, taking my lunch hour outside on the deck. I'd taken to having lunch at home so I could spend time with Cain. We were establishing a bond and the more time we spent together the stronger that bond grew. The view off the deck was not one I would ever grow tired of. The mountains rising up to the sun, the trees and fields that though were brown in sleep, turned so lush and green in the spring and summer.

Wyoming, I never had any interest in moving out west and yet not only had we, but Rylee and I had found a wonderful job and a home. Even more incredible, she was dancing around love, a first for her, and I had found Abel. What were the odds that I'd move here and find him? A man who I not only enjoyed the company of, but someone who I felt bound to especially after the loss I'd lived through and the difficult adjustment that had followed. It was the sentimental part of me, but I believed that Jake had a hand in our good fortune. He was doing what he always did; he was taking care of me.

Cain had been lying next to me, but he stood and moved to the stairs just as Abel appeared. Surprise and pleasure burned through me as a smile curved my lips because what a sight he made. It had only been three days since I saw him and still I missed him like I would a limb. Seeing it was Abel, Cain settled back down but I was on my feet. "What are you doing here?"

He took the steps two at a time and answered by pulling me into his arms, dipping his head and kissing me senseless.

"I missed you," he whispered when he finally broke the kiss.

His words left me feeling a bit lightheaded and giddy and being in his arms again added anticipation and excitement to the mix. Realizing that the man drove across the state on a whim because he missed me had another emotion moving through me. Love.

"That was a long trip to make." Not that I hadn't been battling the urge to climb into my car and make the trip myself.

He grinned but there was no denying his sincerity when he said, "I'd drive across the fucking country to see you."

I'd have slid to the floor in a boneless mess if his arms hadn't been around me. "I think you're sweet on me."

"If you don't know for sure that I'm sweet on you, I'm clearly not doing it right."

"I do know."

He stroked my cheek with his thumb. "I know you know. When do you have to get back to the clinic?"

My disappointment was very evident after glancing at my watch. "Soon, actually."

"I'll drive you back and after work I'll take you to dinner."

"When are you going home?"

"Tomorrow morning."

In response, my entire body hummed because that meant I had him for the night.

"After dinner, you're coming back to my place."

It was like he read my mind. "Yes I am."

Desire moved over his face and his eyes grew dark like a sapphire. "We should go or you might not make it back to the clinic at all today."

I so didn't want to go back to work, but I couldn't leave Rylee in the lurch. I moved closer, getting up on my tip toes and whispered, "Tonight can't come fast enough."

I had thought we'd be dining at the Brass Bull for dinner, but Abel surprised me with dinner at his place. It was cold, but according to Abel it was never too cold to grill up steak and potatoes. We were in the kitchen and as I finished with the salad, Abel poured me a glass of wine and grabbed a beer for himself.

"How's Carly? Have you seen her?"

"Yeah, the other day. She looks great, a lot like her old self. It's been hard for her, but she really wants to kick it," he said as he came to stand at my side, leaning up against the counter next to me.

How I wish I could have said the same about Connor. "I'm so happy she's finding her way."

"Doc?"

I looked up from the tomato I was slicing. Abel brushed my hair from my shoulder. There was concern and tenderness in his expression. "You never talk about your brother."

Even after all these years, anger burned through me thinking about Connor. "What's there to say?"

"What was he like?"

It hurt thinking of Connor as the boy and man he had been before the addict he became because I loved that Connor, but I had lost that Connor long before the accident. "He was wonderful. I'd been alone until the Millers took me in at ten. They were completely uninterested in children, but Connor was everything I always wished a brother could be."

For as cocky as Abel was at times, he studied me now with understanding and what I liked to believe was love in those pale eyes. "What changed that?"

Bitterness burned like acid through my veins, but it wasn't just Connor that stirred it. I had failed him; I hadn't been able to reach him, to help him.

"You blame yourself for Connor's addiction, don't you?" Even feeling the ugly emotions that the thoughts of Connor evoked, love moved through me that this man knew me so well in so short a time. "Not so much his addiction, but for not being able to help him through it."

"That's carrying a burden you have no fucking business carrying."

"A part of me knows that, but then I remember how lonely I had been, and the staggering disappointment I felt after meeting the Millers. I thought I had eight more years of isolation and loneliness to look forward to until Connor walked into my room with a tray of frozen mac and cheese and soda. He became my family. I met Jake and in part Connor was responsible for that too. He forgot me one day allowing for Jake to roll into my life. But as I healed, found the love and belonging I had always longed for, Connor went the other way. Nothing I did reached him and knowing that I wasn't enough to help him like he had me, yeah, I blame myself for that."

"That's fucking bullshit."

I couldn't help the smile because Abel was not one to mince words. "Maybe, but I can't help the way I feel, especially since it was Connor's addiction that took Jake's life. He would never have been in that car on that road with that tractor trailer if not for my brother. And it's so twisted because Jake is gone, but if he weren't, I never would have met you. The idea of that hurts me to my very core and still the world lost a beautiful man, I lost a beautiful man and all because my brother lost himself to his addiction and I wasn't able to save him."

"At some point, Doc, you have to forgive Connor and yourself." He touched my chin to keep my gaze on him. "I could blame myself for Carly's addiction. I knew her the best and I saw her losing her way. I tried to reach her, but she didn't want to be reached. People can't be helped if they don't want to be. I'm not any more responsible for her actions than you were for Connor's."

Deep down I knew he was right and still it was hard for me to accept because had Jake not pulled up beside me that first day, he'd still be alive. "Jake would still be here had he never known me. And even knowing I'm not responsible for his death, I have to live with that."

I honestly couldn't say what fueled the look that passed over his face, but it was the closest to unsure I'd ever seen Abel look. Before I could ask him about it, he brushed a kiss on my cheek. "I need to check the steaks."

"Eyes on me," Abel demanded as his fingers curled into my ass as I moved up and down his cock. "Come on baby, let go."

And I did. My head fell back and my back arched as the orgasm ripped through me. Abel sat up, curled his arms around me and took my breast into his mouth while his hips ground into me to prolong the pleasure. He'd reached the limit of his control when he flipped us, lifted my hips and started pounding into me. And even being in a state of overwhelming lust, I sensed with each shift of his hips he was staking a claim, trying to reach beyond the physical to something deeper. He had to know he owned me…heart and soul, but I wasn't able to focus for long because my body was making that climb again, so I gave myself over to both the moment and the man.

Cain and I walked through the field behind the house. The sun was just peeking out over the horizon and there was a chill in the air. It was Thanksgiving and we had a crew coming. I needed to start cooking, but like I did every Thanksgiving, I gave myself the first hour of the day to remember Jake. He lingered in the back of my mind all the time, but every Thanksgiving I took time out to give thanks to him. He'd saved me. I wouldn't be the person I was now without him. It broke my heart that such a beautiful soul was taken so young, but the more romantic side of me liked to believe he had been an angel from heaven sent to save the lost soul I had been and when his work was done, he had been called home. And even feeling for Abel as I did, Jake would never be forgotten.

"Hey, Sid. We really need to start cooking and by we I mean you if we actually want to eat the food. Plus, Jayce and Abel have offered to do our last minute shopping and since they aren't likely to offer again until next Thanksgiving, we need to take them up on it," Rylee called from the deck.

"Okay. I'll be right there."

Looking up at the heavens, I couldn't help the grin. "She's still a clown." My smile dimmed as my heart ached. "Thank you, Jake. Thank you for seeing me, for taking a chance on me, for filling all the places in me that were empty. And I'm so sorry. I know you'd be mad knowing there was a part of me that blamed myself for what happened to you and even knowing that, I still do. I love you; I'll always love you. And Abel, I think you'd have liked him. He's nothing like you and still he gets me, every part of me. I think maybe you had a hand in sending me here, leading me to the one person you knew would heal the hurt. And he has. I didn't think that was possible, not after losing you, but he did. So I thank you for him too."

I wiped at my eyes as Cain nudged my leg. Turning back in the direction of the house, I whispered, "Happy Thanksgiving, Jake. I miss you."

Maybe I was just being fanciful, but when the wind kicked up and blew gently through the leaves of the trees, I took that as him answering.

Rylee and I were in the kitchen cooking, Abel and Jayce made a run to get more beverages; we were going nonalcoholic since Carly was coming. The Macy's Thanksgiving Day Parade was on, the scents of sautéing onions and celery battled with the scents of the turkeys roasting. With the crew we had coming it was going to be tight in our little house, but the more the merrier. I put the cats in my room, since none of them were particularly fond of people. Cain was lying on the floor in the kitchen. Everyone who was coming was someone he'd met, so I wasn't concerned about his reaction to the crowd.

"Do you think we have enough food?" Rylee asked.

"Two turkeys and double the sides. If they eat all of this food they seriously need to seek help."

"I think the Hellars and Abel alone could eat it all."

Rylee probably wasn't wrong, but we'd manage.

"I'm glad Carly's coming." Duncan had picked her up yesterday; she stayed the night at the farm.

"She looks great and watching as she and Duncan danced around each other was adorable."

"I bet."

The back door opened to Ichabod, Jeshaiah, Mr. Milburn and Doc Cassidy followed in by Abel and Jayce. Tiny had been invited but he had other plans. What those plans were, Abel didn't know. Duncan, with a smiling Carly, arrived a few minutes later. For the next few hours people milled around our small house, talking and laughing. It felt good, like home.

"You okay, babe?" Abel's hands came to rest on my hips as he pulled me back against him.

I was good, still a little tender from earlier, but that was life—the ups, the downs and trying to find happiness in the balance. "Yeah. I love this."

"Everyone packed in your house like sardines."

"Tradition."

He dipped his chin as his thumb turned my face to his. "Didn't have them growing up, did you?"

"Not until Jake. Something so simple, but it's important to take the time out from living and just appreciate what you've got right in front of you." I took time out often because I could still remember how it felt to be alone.

His eyes turned warm as tenderness moved over his features.

"What?"

"Just taking time out to appreciate what I've got right in front of me."

My heart rolled in my chest. Words wouldn't come, so I answered by kissing him.

Somehow we got everyone around the table we'd rented. It was elbows to elbows with not one inch of available space. Abel stood to give the toast, and to say I was surprised would be fair. He lifted his soda, his eyes on me and I saw understanding burning there. His voice was a bit gruff when he said, "To all those here and those gone. To family."

Tears filled my eyes because he really did get me, every single part of me. Overwhelmed by him I could only lift my glass in reply.

It was a few days after Thanksgiving and Abel had left earlier, heading back to Cheyenne. It had been hard watching him drive away.

Lauren and Jasper had returned from their vacation and I was eager to hear all about their trip. I settled at the kitchen table to call them.

"Mom, it's Sidney."

"Sidney, honey, how are you?"

"I'm good, how are you? How was your trip?"

"Incredible. We ate too much, drank too much, got too much sun and I can not wait to go back. How's Sheridan?"

"It's wonderful. Rylee and I hosted Thanksgiving."

Her voice turned soft. "And how was that?"

"It was crowded, noisy and perfect."

"Sounds perfect. And how's work?"

For the next half an hour we talked about the clinic, Rylee, the town, Cain and Sandbar.

"It sounds like you've found your niche."

"I have." It was harder than I thought it would be, but I wanted to share everything with her and so I took a deep breath before I added, "I've met someone."

Silence followed for a few beats before she said, "I'm so happy to hear that."

"You are?"

"Moving on with your life includes love, Sidney. And I know how much you loved my son, but you're still so young. He would want you to find love again. I know you know that."

And I did, could even hear him in my head telling me as much.

"So tell me about this man."

"His name is Abel Madden and he owns a custom motorcycle shop. He's opinionated and crass, sweet and thoughtful, funny and infuriating and he makes me laugh and smile."

"I can tell, just from your voice, that you're happy."

"I am. He's so different from Jake and I often wonder what Jake would think of him, but I have a feeling they would have been friends had they ever met."

"Well, I like him already because I like hearing you like this."

"For the longest time I didn't think I'd find happy again, didn't want to be happy without Jake. And there was a part of me afraid to try to find happy because it hurt like hell when you lost it. But I'm beginning to learn that it's worth the risk."

"I'm so glad you're finally seeing that."

"Are you upset that I'm moving on?"

"I won't lie. The thought of you and Jake, our grandkids…Jasper and I wanted that for you and for us. Losing him so young, all he never got to do, will always hurt. But you didn't die with him and moving on doesn't mean you're forgetting him. You were our son's wife, but you're like a daughter to us and though I really wish the life you were building was with Jake, I want you to have a life. And maybe we can still be a part of it in some measure."

Tears rolled down my cheeks hearing both the sadness and longing in her voice. "Of course you'll be a part of it. You're the only parents I've ever known."

"I hoped you felt that way."

"I'd love for you to visit, to see what Rylee and I are building here. I'd love to introduce you to Abel."

"We'd love that too. I'll talk with Jasper and get some dates and we'll work something out."

"I love you."

"Ah, Sidney, I love you too."

Rylee was off with Jayce. Cain and the cats and I were hanging in the living room watching *Outlander*. Tigger and Stuart were curled up by the fireplace sleeping and Sandbar was on my lap. Cats and dogs didn't generally get along, but my fellas all tolerated each other. I wouldn't call them friends, but they seemed to prefer my company more than they disliked each other's. Cain lay next to me on the sofa, taking up more than half of it. My phone rang and I didn't recognize the number but I was on call for the clinic.

"Hello."

"Sidney, it's Ichabod."

I hardly recognized his voice, he sounded terrified. "Is everything okay?"

"It's Spike. He's in really bad shape. He got into a fight. I think it might have been the mountain lion."

Holy shit. I jumped from the sofa. "Where are you?"

"The house, it's behind the garage."

"I'll be right there."

On the way to my car, I went through the checklist of what supplies I had on hand. Luckily the clinic was close; we'd move Spike to the clinic once I got him stable since I had a terrible feeling I'd be operating. It only took about fifteen minutes to reach their house and Jeshaiah was waiting outside for me when I arrived.

"How's he doing?"

"He looks really bad."

I followed him in and couldn't help the scan I did because though I wouldn't call them hoarders, they were dangerously close. Spike was in the back bathroom, lying on his side. The amount of blood concerned me. Dropping to my knees, I started examining him. "I'll want an x-ray, but his organs feel good. These gashes, they're going to require stitches. I think you're right. I think the mountain lion did this."

"Is Spike going to be okay?"

"I need you to call Rylee."

Ichabod grabbed his cell and punched in her number. "What am I telling her?"

"Put the phone to my ear."

"Ichabod, what—" I cut her off.

"It's Sidney. I need you to get to the Big Horn Animal Clinic. I need canine blood. Spike was attacked, looks like a mountain lion."

"Oh my God. I'm getting in my car right now. How much do you need?"

"As much as you can get. I'm going to sedate Spike before taking him to the clinic."

"I'll meet you there."

I shifted my attention to Ichabod. "Once he's sedated, I'll need your help getting him into my car. Rylee is getting blood. I'll work on his injuries at the clinic."

"But is he going to be okay?"

I didn't know, wasn't sure the extent of the damage until I got an x-ray, but I was going to fight like hell to save him.

"I'm going to do everything in my power."

Spike had been very lucky. Outside of the gashes that required stitches, he had no internal damage and he also didn't require a blood transfusion. I had him on intravenous antibiotics and a mild sedative since he kept trying to lick and bite at his stitches. He was up to date on his rabies and other vaccines, so his prognosis was good.

Jeshaiah had left, back to the garage to man the station, but Ichabod stayed with Spike. He looked as tired as I felt. My back ached, I was starving and yet I wouldn't leave my patient either. I felt a kinship with him since we'd both been targets of the mountain lion. Something needed to be done about it.

"Ichabod?"

Tired eyes moved from a sleeping Spike to me. "Yeah."

"Where did you find Spike?"

"Not far from the station, just inside the patch of woods behind our place."

That was what I was afraid of. The mountain lion was getting bolder.

"Rylee, we need to call animal control. That mountain lion is a problem. And I realize that it's just hungry, but it went after Cain and me and now Spike, who wasn't far from Main Street."

Rylee's face paled. "You're right. I'll call them now."

"What will they do with it once they find it?" Ichabod asked.

"I don't know. But the thought that it might stumble across kids playing, we have to do something."

"You're not wrong." Ichabod looked back at Spike, his hand running down the animal's neck. "Thank you, Doc. You saved his life."

"He was my first emergency. I'm so grateful for the happy ending."

A slight smile touched Ichabod's lips. "Me too."

I sent everyone home and locked up the clinic before I pulled out the cot Doc Cassidy had in the storage closet. Spike's vitals looked good, but I wanted to stay the night. Rylee had called when she got home; the cats were all fed. I had put them in my room before I ran out, just in case. She decided to keep them there and Cain was sleeping in the corner of the living room. She brought him his food and said he lifted his head long enough to see it wasn't me before falling back to sleep.

I wasn't planning on sleeping, wanted to stay awake just in case Spike's condition changed. As luck would have it, the cot was so damn uncomfortable there was no chance I'd be dozing. I had a book at my desk, a romance novel that Rylee insisted I read. And for as often as I teased her about her reading preferences, I soon found myself completely enthralled in the characters. So much so in fact, that I didn't hear as someone entered through the back door until Abel appeared. I nearly jumped out of my skin. My book fell to the tile floor, which gave Abel a perfect view of the cover.

"Looks like I came at the right time."

The cover was very hot, a half naked couple. It was mortifying, especially since I didn't usually read books like that. It dawned on me that Abel stood ten feet from me. Embarrassment dissolved into pleasure.

"You're a welcome sight. How'd you get in?"

"I stopped at your house first. Rylee gave me the key. I heard you had a tough night. How's your patient?"

"He's good. Stable."

His expression turned dark and a bit scary. "It was the mountain lion."

"Yeah and with how close he came to a populated area, he's getting bolder. We called animal control."

"Good idea." He leaned against the doorjamb, a grin curving his lips. "So, are you going to greet me properly?"

Physically I was exhausted, but seeing him had a surge of energy, and excitement, burning through me. "What's considered properly?"

"Your mouth on mine."

Attempting to stand when all the blood drained from my head was probably not advised and still I managed. The man was not patient since he didn't wait for me to reach him. He came to me and had me in his arms and his mouth on mine in a blink of an eye.

It had been a week since I last saw him and still that was too long. "I so needed this…you."

"Any time, Doc. You know that."

"When are you going back?"

"Not until Monday."

"You're staying the whole weekend?"

"Yeah, preferably in bed with you."

"I like this plan, but I'm staying here tonight."

"Then I will too. Maybe you could read me that book you were so engrossed in when I arrived."

I knew I went beet red, I felt it. "For the record, it's Rylee's book that she insisted I read."

"She didn't insist you enjoy it."

He always had an answer.

"You're right, she didn't. It's good, maybe I will read it to you."

"You can sit on my lap. I'll keep my hands between my legs."

And just thinking about his fingers on me had heat pooling between *my* legs.

"Grab the book."

"Seriously?"

"Is it hot?"

"Yes."

He pulled me to the chair, stopping to pick up the book I had dropped, before he sat and settled me on his lap.

"I'm all ears." But really he should have said all hands because as I read they moved over my body with a deliberate and methodical purpose. I should be embarrassed doing this in the office, but

I was so turned on I didn't care. When I reached a part that was super sexy, I felt him growing hard as he worked my zipper. His fingers slipped under my panties. And as I read out loud the scene of the hero and heroine engaged in hot lovemaking, Abel worked my body—thumbing my clit, pushing his fingers into me, his cock pressing against my ass as he brought me to the brink of orgasm. He shifted us, lifting me to my feet and pulling my jeans and panties down my legs. I stood half-naked in my office. Guilt tried to penetrate the haze of lust he had me in. He buried his nose between my legs and breathed me in; his whiskers added a whole other layer of erotic to the moment.

"You smell so fucking good."

Lust prevailed. His tongue did one long, slow lick as he pulled his cock free. The man had a condom in his pocket, thank God. He rolled it on but his focus never left me.

"Climb on."

I was shameless because I did; I straddled Abel on my office chair, impaling myself on him.

"Fuck, yeah." His fingers tightened on my thighs, his hips pumping as I ground myself into him. Lifting my shirt, he pulled my bra down and sucked my breast into his mouth. I went off like a firecracker. He followed shortly after, but it was several minutes before either of us could speak.

"You'll never look at romance novels the same way again."

Smug bastard, but he wasn't wrong.

The early morning sun was breaking the horizon when I took Spike outside for a small walk. He had slept through the night, had no reaction to the medicines, and this morning woke eager to move around. These were all good signs. We didn't go far, just to the small grassy area near the front of the clinic. He was hungry, though he really only nosed the food I put out for him. He did drink water, which was another good sign.

Pulling over a large doggie bed, Spike curled up in the middle of it and went back to sleep. The Thompson brothers would be thrilled to learn how well Spike was bouncing back and that I planned on discharging him today.

From my desk, I watched Abel sleeping. Somehow we managed the cot, his body wrapped around mine. He'd made it most of the night, but he fell asleep about an hour ago. I had never seen him in sleep. The few times I'd slept over he woke before me. He couldn't be that comfortable; his legs hung over the end of the cot. I tried to imagine him as a child, but it was hard staring at the man he had become. Even in sleep there was that hardness to him and still he was absolutely beautiful.

Last night was never far from my thoughts and even behaving in a way I never had before, I wasn't embarrassed. Abel gave me that, always pushing me past my comfort zone.

"Why are you all the way over there?" He asked even though his eyes were closed.

"How do you know where I am?"

"Your body is not up against mine, only other place for you to be is your desk." He opened one eye, a flash of pale blue settled on me with astounding accuracy. "I get why you're sitting there. I'm loving that chair too after last night."

My body warmed, the idea of round two appealed to me in every way, but Rylee would be arriving soon. "You look exhausted. How's work?"

"Changing the subject." He shifted, resting his head on his hand and glanced at the clock. "Probably a good idea. I wouldn't want your clients seeing too much of you. That's for my eyes only." He winked. "I want to open a branch of Pipes here. I've been working to get that setup."

It felt like a wave, the joy that moved through me in response to that news. "Are you serious?"

"Yeah. The Cheyenne location is growing really fast, spearheaded by my assistant manager. He loves it, thrives on the balancing act of builds and sales. Me, I want to focus on building, back to what it was like when we first opened. Tiny running the business end and me creating."

"Have you found a location?"

"I've got a realtor looking. Jayce and Duncan are scouting around for me too."

This wasn't just an idea he was tossing around; he was implementing it. I was probably being foolish, but I was a little hurt he hadn't clued me in to his plans or asked for my help. "It sounds very exciting. I'm happy for you."

"Sidney?" He studied me like he could read my thoughts but I was spared answering whatever probing question he intended when a knock came from the back door. I jumped up from my chair, like it was on fire, and opened it to the Thompson brothers.

"Sorry to show up so early, but we wanted to see Spike," Ichabod said.

"Come in. He's doing beautifully. I took him for a walk this morning. He ate a bit and drank some water. He's sleeping again, but he can go home."

"He can?"

"Yeah, I'll write up his discharge papers that will tell you when to give him the antibiotics and I'll stop by to see him later today."

Abel was putting the cot away when I returned, the brothers following behind me. "Hey, Abel."

"Ichabod. Sorry about Spike, but Doc here has been taking really good care of him."

"Yeah, she's pretty great. There's my boy."

Spike's head lifted hearing his daddy.

"He does look good. Hey, buddy." Jeshaiah joined his brother, kneeling next to a happy Spike. I walked around my desk to retrieve Spike's file when Abel came up behind me.

"Later, I want to know what was going through your head before they showed up," he whispered in my ear, his hands resting lightly on my hips. "You've got things to do here, I'm going to hunt down Jayce. Call me when you're done."

"Okay."

I had the sense there was more he wanted to say, but didn't. His fingers tightened a second before he released me and headed for the door. "I'm glad Spike is doing so well."

"Thanks, man," Ichabod said but his attention was on Spike.

Then Abel was gone, the sound of the back door closing followed a few seconds later.

After visiting Spike at home, I called Abel. I was over my moment from earlier. He didn't include me in his business dealings and why would he? Even for as easy and comfortable as it was between us, we weren't at that point in our relationship. I liked to believe part of why he was making this move was related to me, he had said as much when I had visited him—the distance between us being too much. What mattered was he'd be closer and for now that was enough.

"Hey, babe. Where are you?" I loved the deep timbre of his voice.

"I'm on my way home."

"I'll meet you there."

"I'll stop by the bakery. Is there anything you want?"

"Sticky buns. No one makes them like Stella."

"You got it. I'll see you soon."

"Sidney?"

"Yeah."

"You were upset at the clinic. Why?"

"I'm over it."

"That doesn't answer my question."

"It was really nothing."

"Didn't look like nothing."

It had been a long time since someone could read my moods so easily. "I'm really fine, Abel."

"All right. I'll see you soon."

Tossing my phone on the passenger seat, I headed for the bakery. A day that included Stella's baked goods and Abel was heaven and it was made even more so because I had two more nights with him. Yep, I was definitely over my moment.

It was a bit surreal to be walking with a fucking wolf and yet there he was, strolling along beside Sidney and me. He looked more wolf than dog and now that he was no longer malnourished, he was fucking huge. He stayed right at Sidney's side, alert and watchful, but he clearly was right where he wanted to be. I completely understood that feeling. Thinking about earlier at the clinic, Sidney had grown quiet after I mentioned my plans for Pipes. I got it, I hadn't included her, hadn't even mentioned it. She'd put a wall up, not one that would have required much to knock down; one that she took down on her own, but I didn't like it. And I had myself to blame for that.

"I didn't mention my plans for Pipes because I didn't want to say anything until I knew for sure I could do it."

Her eyes found mine, a slight smile touching her lips. "I like that you can read me so well, but I'm over that. It was a knee-jerk reaction, but you and me we're still figuring it out."

"I've already figured it out, babe. I just didn't want to get your hopes up and then be unable to make the move." And yet her words had doubt rearing its ugly head. I had Sidney; I knew that. I just wasn't so sure I had all of her. And I was a selfish motherfucker because I wanted all of her.

She stopped walking and when I looked back at her, she just stared at me with an expression I could not read. "What?"

"You've already figured it out?"

"Babe, I'm driving four and a half hours one direction to see you, you're doing the same. That is not something I'd be doing if I wasn't serious."

Her expression turned soft as her eyes warmed with tenderness and the sorry son of a bitch that I was wanted to bask in that look before dragging her ass to the forest floor and fucking her senseless.

A coy smile curved her lips. "You like me, you want to kiss me."

Grabbing her, her soft curves molded against me. "I want to fuck you right here and if I knew your wolf wouldn't mistake my intentions and rip out my throat, you'd be naked already."

"You speak in poetry."

I so was not expecting her to say that, my laugh surprised us both. I couldn't fuck her right now but I sure as hell could kiss her. We were pulled from the moment when her cell went off.

"Hello."

All the color drained from her face. "Oh my God. I'm coming. I'll call when I get a flight. Yes, I'll call."

She disconnected the call, her face was still colorless, a sight I did not fucking like. "I have to get home. Jasper's had a heart attack. It doesn't look good."

"Jasper?"

"Jake's dad. They were coming out here. We were just finalizing the plans. He can't die. He's too young. I've got to call Rylee. I don't know how long I'm going to be and I don't know what to do about my patients. It's too much for Rylee to take on herself. Spike still needs to be monitored and Cain. He's here because of me. If I'm not here, he may not want to be. I can't stand the thought of him out there with that mountain lion."

My gut twisted at her words, at the reality that she might stay gone. And as much as I wanted to protest, to chain her to me, these people were her family.

"Don't worry about any of that. I'll get the flight. You pack. Cain is okay for now, you can cross that bridge when and if you need to."

"You're right. Thank you." But there was something different about her, that wall that had been up earlier was back and reinforced. And there it was again, that fucking doubt because I had a really bad feeling the ghost I was competing with held more of her heart than I thought.

I drove us to the airport in Rylee's car. Sidney jumped out before the car had even come to a complete stop, Rylee following right behind her. "Call me as soon as you know something."

"I will. And thank Doc Cassidy again for helping out while I'm gone."

Sidney hugged Rylee before turning to me. There were tears in her eyes. "Thank you for getting me here. I wouldn't have managed without you."

"I'm coming with you."

Surprise flashed over her face before shifting to an emotion I had never had directed at me. One so powerful it felt like I took a hit in the gut by a velvet wrapped fist.

"You are?"

Two small words, but the emotions behind them left me, for the first time in my life, dumbstruck by the intensity coming off Sidney. When I did finally find my voice, it was gruff as I struggled with the unfamiliar response in me it stirred. "Yeah. You've no idea what's waiting for you. I'm not letting you face that alone."

Her reaction eased the knot that hadn't left me since the phone call earlier, honestly the knot I'd felt since realizing just how far under my skin this woman was. She threw her arms around me and held on tight. Her next words not only disintegrated the knot, but also nearly brought me to my knees. "I love you."

I suspected I was squeezing the life out of her with how hard I held her; it was either that or acting completely inappropriately for both the location and the situation, but fuck I liked hearing her say that.

Once we were settled on the plane, I reached for her hand. Her focus shifted from the window to me. "I never had anyone say that to me."

"Never?"

"No."

Tears brightened her eyes as one rolled down her cheek. I wiped it away with my thumb. "I don't know what it's supposed to feel like, but I know being away from you physically hurts and being with you I feel a peace I've never felt."

She moved closer. Her lips were so close I could almost taste them. "Sounds like love to me."

Threading the fingers of my free hand into her hair, I pulled her mouth the rest of the way to mine and inhaling the breath she exhaled I spoke the words I had never spoken before. "I love you."

In response, she climbed into my lap and wrapped her arms around my neck. I didn't know she was crying until I felt her tears on my skin. Before I could ask her why the tears, she turned her head and pressed her mouth to my ear. "My heart is so full right now I think it might burst. Thank you for bringing me back to life."

No words would come and I experienced another first. My eyes burned from the tears that wanted to fall. And even being in uncharted territory, I was never fucking letting her go.

Sidney held my hand so tightly as we stepped off the elevators at the intensive care floor. A woman saw us and immediately hurried over. Even being in her sixties, as I guessed she was, the woman was a knock out. Her hazel eyes were bright with tears. I released Sidney's hand as the two hugged.

"He's okay. They think he's going to pull through."

"Thank God."

"I'm so glad you're here. Thank you for coming."

"As if I'd stay away."

The older woman took a step back as her eyes moved from Sidney to me. "You must be Abel."

I didn't react at first because I wasn't sure I heard her correctly. Sidney had mentioned me to her in-laws? Possession moved through me because she really was mine.

"I'm Lauren Stephens."

"I wish we were meeting under better circumstances, but I'm glad to hear your husband is doing well."

"Thank you."

I stood in the Stephens' living room while Sidney and Lauren went to get drinks. It had been a week, but Jasper Stephens had been moved out of intensive care and would be coming home in two days. I was leaving in the morning; Sidney was staying a few extra days to help get Jasper settled. I hadn't been sure how her late husband's family would receive me, but they had opened their home to me. I was Sidney's boyfriend and that was all they needed to know. On the mantel were pictures of their son Jake—a timeline of his life. Snapshots of him as a baby and a toddler holding a football that was almost too big for him to carry, to grade school and high school dressed in his football gear. Sidney was in many of them, young and happy. Seeing his life on display through pictures really had it hitting home how young he had been when he died. How young they had both been and how much they had lost. There was no question they were in love. And feeling that emotion for the first time in my life, the idea of losing Sidney was staggering. The fact that she picked up the pieces and started a new life was extraordinary, but even more so was hearing her tell me she loved me. That she could open her heart again and that she opened it to me was humbling.

"Here we are. A Corona for you, Abel." Lauren said as she offered me the glass with a slice of lime on the rim. I tried to tell her the bottle was fine, but seeing how they lived I suspected not many people drank beer from a bottle in their home.

"Thank you both for dropping everything and coming here. It means so much to Jasper and me."

"There's nothing to thank. You're family."

Sidney's words were so simple but that was the truth of it. These people were her family and they had welcomed me into it. Fucking unreal considering they lost their son and I was his replacement.

"Good luck with opening the second store for Pipes. When we visit, I suspect you'll have another customer. Jasper has the bug."

"Seriously? Dad's thinking about getting a motorcycle."

"We rode one in Greece and he fell in love. I've got to tell you, I loved it too."

"I look forward to working up some ideas for him."

"He'll love that."

Sidney joined me at the fireplace, her fingers linking through mine as a smile spread over her face. She was older, but this was my own snapshot of her, smiling and in love with me. Yeah, fucking humbling.

sidney

I thought it would feel strange being with Abel in Jake's home, but it felt like how it always felt with him, natural. We were in bed, neither of us was comfortable with the idea of intimacy in Jake's house, but that didn't keep him from pulling me close and holding me while we watched the news. He was leaving in the morning, and even knowing I would be following him in a few days, I was going to miss him. He wouldn't be in Sheridan when I returned; he'd been away from Pipes for a week.

"Thank you for coming with me."

"Nothing to thank me for. You were needed here, I got you here."

"And have been away from your business for a week."

"Priorities."

I turned, wanted to see those pale eyes. "You've not cursed nearly as much here."

"A challenge."

"So it is a conscious effort."

"Yeah."

"You're a good man."

If possible he pulled me closer, close enough that I felt him growing hard. "I am using every ounce of willpower to keep from fucking you. Don't make that any harder."

"Telling you you're a good man makes it harder."

"Play on words intended?"

"Yes." And the fact that I could flirt with him, here, was a testament to just how much he meant to me. "I love you."

"Fucking Christ."

"Not helping?"

"Fuck no."

"I'll go to sleep."

"Good idea."

"Good night."

I didn't go to sleep though; I just lay there staring. A fact not lost on him. "You're not closing your eyes."

"I like looking at you."

"I'm seriously going to drag you down to the car in a minute."

"Okay, I'll behave."

"Good, go to sleep."

I closed my eyes. "I'm going to sleep."

Silence followed for a minute before Abel said, "I fucking love when you tell me you love me, but don't say it again or I won't be held responsible for my actions."

I didn't say it again, but I thought it and I fell asleep in the arms of the man I loved and somehow knew that Jake was smiling down on us.

Jasper was home and settled in his bedroom, something he strongly objected to. Lauren and I had spent the past few days cooking heart healthy meals for him and freezing them so Lauren wouldn't be stuck in the kitchen. He was walking around, something his cardiologist encouraged as long as he didn't over do it. Currently we were in his room getting caught up. They shared their trip to Greece, which included Lauren pulling out many of the items they'd purchased including a beautiful gold cuff bracelet adorned with precious stones they had bought for me.

Jasper had been listening as Lauren shared story after story, but during a lull in the conversation he surprised me when he said quite unexpectedly, "I like your Abel."

Abel and Jasper met while Jasper was in the hospital. They had even shared a few private conversations when Lauren and I were off getting food. Abel hadn't shared with me what they discussed—I was encouraged that they had those chats—but I hadn't realized how much I needed Jasper's approval until that moment.

"You were needed home and he dropped everything to get you here. It had to be awkward for him to bring you home knowing who we were, but he didn't hesitate did he?"

"No."

"I wouldn't have picked him for you. He's as far from Jake as a man can be. He's rough around the edges, hardened and not at all diplomatic—says whatever he thinks and doesn't give a damn how it's taken. I thought about that in the hospital. God knows I had lots of time to think. When you were younger, you needed Jake. He was solid and centered. He gave you the foundation of love and family you lacked at home. He made you feel safe, loved, protected and did so in his easygoing way. But you're not the same girl you were. You've been through so much, lost so much. Had you found a man like Jake now he wouldn't be what you needed. You needed someone to shake it up, to snap you out of your pain. Abel brought you back, so I approve and I know Jake would have too."

My eyes burned, but Jasper was right. Jake and I had fit and would have had a wonderful life together, but after his loss, Abel was who I needed now. I had been blessed with loving two men in my lifetime and I loved Abel every bit as much as I had Jake. And getting Jasper and Lauren's approval meant I really would have had Jake's too.

On my way home from the airport, my first stop was Abel's. I wasn't afraid any more, wasn't determined to deny myself love and family for fear of losing it. I was ready to move forward, eager to do so, and I wanted that life with Abel.

He was working on a bike when Tiny showed me to him. He looked so sexy in his jeans and tee with his hair pulled back. Abel's head lifted, his gaze landed on me and as soon as it did, a smile spread over his face.

"Hey, Doc."

He moved from the bike, wiping his hands on the rag he held. "How was your flight?"

"Good."

"Jasper?"

"He's doing really well. Bitching about his new diet, so all is right in the world."

Reaching me, he yanked me close and kissed me—a hungry kiss that proved he'd missed me as much as I had him.

"You're staying the night." He wasn't asking.

"That was the plan."

"It's a good fucking plan. I'm out of here, Tiny. See you tomorrow."

"Yep. Glad your father-in-law is doing better."

Tiny rarely addressed me, so those words surprised and warmed me. "Thank you, Tiny."

"Where are your bags?" Abel asked as he all but dragged me from his shop.

"Your office."

"We'll leave them there."

"But I don't have any clothes besides what I'm wearing."

"And since you're going to be naked as soon as I get you home, it doesn't matter."

The man made a good point.

As soon as he locked his door behind us, Abel had me out of my jeans and panties. Really it was remarkable how fast he undressed me. "We'll go slower the next time, but if I don't get my cock into you I'm going to fucking die."

Since I felt the same, I was already working on his zipper, which earned me a growl from deep in his throat. He rolled on the condom—had to love a man who was prepared   lifted and pressed me against the wall. With a shift of his hips, he buried himself deep. We both moaned.

"Fucking finally."

Curling my legs around his waist, my heels worked on pushing his jeans lower as my hips rocked against him.

"Lose the shirt and bra."

My blood felt like fire burning through my veins and even though he spoke the words, I wanted to lose my shirt and bra. Grabbing the hem of my tee I pulled it over my head and reached for the bra clasp. His eyes were on me, watching every move and I took delight in that, purposely going more slowly as I pulled the straps down my arms. In reply, he stopped moving his hips; the loss of friction nearly had me whimpering.

"Two can play that game," he warned.

"Don't stop."

"Then get rid of that bra and give me what I want."

The ache between my legs intensified as I dropped my bra.

"Offer it."

"I don't..."

"Cup your breast and give it to me."

There was significance to what he was asking me, but I wanted his mouth on me, so I cupped my breast and lifted it to his lips. His tongue appeared, the tip teasing my nipple with a skill that left me breathless. And when he sucked the nipple into his mouth, I nearly begged him to take more. Instead, he bit me. Not hard, but hard enough that my body crested and fell right over the edge. Chills danced over my nerve endings as the orgasm swept through me. And it was only then that he sucked me fully into his mouth as his hips moved faster until he found his own release. He rested his forehead on mine, his breathing as erratic as my own. "Let's move this to my room. I intend to go slowly this time, savoring every inch of you, and then I'll feed you."

It was late, almost two in the morning, but Abel and I were still awake. We were in bed, his large body holding me close. Earlier, he had taken his time savoring me and after we ate, I took my time savoring him. We had just showered and settled in for bed, but neither of us wanted to sleep. His fingers running up and down my back had me feeling a bit like Sandbar as I curled my spine into his caress.

He had been thoughtful while we ate; intense and focused when we made love. Something was on his mind but before I could ask about it, he shared. "I never had a father figure. My own is a piece of shit. Always looking for the next score, the next con. Tiny, he's my brother, stronger than most blood brothers, but I never had a man talk to me the way Jasper Stephens did. Garrett Hellar was the closest I'd ever had to a father, but he was raising two sons and building an empire. Sitting in that hospital room talking to the father of the man whose shoes I'm, for all intent and purposes, filling. I understand better the kind of man your Jake was."

An ache formed in my chest, not just from his words but the glimpse into the beautiful man beside me.

"Seeing those pictures of Jake and you, the life you had, the life you lost and now here you are in my bed. Giving me all of you when I've never had anything. Having Jake's father talk to me like I was good enough to fill his son's shoes."

Touching his chin, I turned his face to me. "Jake was a wonderful man, the finest I've ever known, and you are every bit as fine a man, Abel. Jasper and I had a heart-to-heart before I left. He told me that you were the last person he would have picked for me, so different from Jake in every way."

"Yeah, I am very fucking different." Abel moved so fast, throwing his legs over the side of the bed.

Gathering the sheet, I scurried off the bed and blocked him from leaving. "I'm not done. Please look at me."

There was a storm of emotion brewing behind his eyes.

"Jasper also said that had I met Jake as the woman I was now, with all I'd been through and lost, he wouldn't have been the man for me. I needed someone to snap me out of it, to wake me up. And so though he never would have put us together, he approved of you because you brought me back."

Abel's next words were no louder than a rough whisper. "I never had a family, never thought I needed one." His fingers curled around my hips, pulling me to him. "Until you." I wanted to weep, not from pain or sorrow, but profound happiness. Instead, I threaded my fingers through his hair and held him while speaking the words I never thought I'd ever say.

"I loved Jake. When I met him I was hungry for love, starved for it, and he gave it to me unconditionally. Life with him would have been beautiful. But he died and I can't tell you what that feels like. I didn't want what I had with him again, not the beauty of it because the pain of losing it was unbearable. But I did find it again and Abel, in a lot of ways the love I feel for you is even stronger than what I felt for Jake because I didn't want it, fought against it, and still it found me. You found me. Jake will always be a part of me, but my heart belongs to you now."

He moved so fast, pulling me down onto the bed as his body moved over mine. Cradling my face in his hands, bright eyes stared down at me, before he kissed me—the sweetest and most poignant kiss of my life.

"You have a few papers to sign and the LLC is setup. D.J. is on board, taking over as branch manager for this location, but he was pretty adamant that he still wants to run all the builds by you. The boy is starting to realize that he takes too much on. I think he's in for a rocky road in the beginning, but he's smart so he'll get there."

"And the spaces the realtor called you about? When can we check those out?"

"Whenever we want." Tiny leaned back in his chair. "For what it's worth, I'm glad you're doing this and not just because I like seeing Pipes growing and expanding. I think it'll be nice to slow things down and..."

I had known Tiny for a long time and the amount of times I'd seen him tongue-tied was never. "What's going on with you?"

"Nothing, I just think this is a good thing."

"Bullshit. Are you blushing?"

"What the fuck, no."

"You're blushing, you are fucking blushing. What the hell?"

One of his meaty paws rubbed his bald head, resigned to sharing since he knew I wouldn't let up until he did. "Fine. You're not the only one with a woman waiting in Sheridan."

"You're shitting me." Instead of rising to the challenge, Tiny remained silent. A clear sign that this lady was more than a bed warmer. "Who?"

"Right, so you can fucking annoy me with your bullshit."

"Seriously man, who?"

"Stella."

No fucking way. "Stella, the baking goddess? I didn't know you even knew her."

"I lived there too, remember. We had a thing once, it was rekindled."

"Does she bake for you?"

"Why the fuck would I tell you that?"

"She does, doesn't she?"

"You're an ass."

"I'm happy for you, brother. She's a good woman. It's about time you settled your ugly ass down."

"Coming from you, I'll take that advice with a grain of salt."

He wasn't wrong; my past history was not good when it came to women. "It's different with Sidney."

"Is it?"

"Yeah. When we make the move back, I want her ass in my house."

"Even if she doesn't want that?"

"I'll be persuasive."

"From what I've seen, you won't have much to do."

He was right about that.

Tiny stood. "I liked her from day one. She didn't take your shit. A special kind of woman to stand toe-to-toe with you and end up the victor."

"Victor? I think that's stretching the truth a bit."

"Not from where I'm standing."

Fucker walked out before I could reply, not that I had one since he was right, and I could think of far worse things than having a woman like Sidney claiming my heart. Plus her ass would be warming my bed permanently when I moved back to Sheridan. Life was fucking good.

Leaning against my kitchen counter, eating my dinner of Ramen noodles, I eyed the counter across from me and couldn't help the grin seeing Sidney spread out naked on it like some offering. Just another example of how I needed to make this move because here I was standing in my kitchen eating a shit dinner and thinking about fucking my woman instead of actually fucking her. I needed to check out those locations sooner than later.

I wasn't expecting anyone so when I heard the door I immediately thought of Sidney surprising me again with a visit.

Pulling the door open, "Hey, babe," was as far as I got because standing at my door wasn't Sidney but my fucking father, Owen Madden.

"What the hell do you want?"

"I was driving through, thought I'd stop by and say hi."

"You should have thought again." His foot stopped the door from closing. "You'll want to move that. Now."

"How's your girlfriend?"

My entire body went tight, primed to protect what was mine.

"Sidney Stephens isn't it? Small world. I was reading the morning paper a couple of weeks ago and right there in the social pages was a picture of one half of Princeton's most influential couples, Lauren Stephens and her daughter-in-law, Sidney, heading into the hospital to see Jasper who had just suffered a heart attack. You can imagine my surprise to see my own son holding the hand of the young, beautiful widow. I didn't know you knew such established people."

It wasn't just rage that had my hands balling into fists, but a sickening sense of dread. My father had no morality, the score was all that mattered, and to get what he wanted he'd do anything. And from that gleam in his eyes, he'd found his new mark.

"Stay the fuck away from them."

"Come on. We should have a family dinner."

Instinct demanded I slam the fucker's head into the wall—repeatedly, but my father was the master of the underhanded. If I slammed his head into the wall, I had better be certain I killed him and going to prison because of him was not on my bucket list.

"You do know I'll warn them about you."

"I'd expect nothing less, but it just ups the stakes, which will make the payoff that much sweeter."

He moved his foot; I closed the door in his face, but I heard the fucker whistling as he walked away.

Grabbing my phone, I called Tiny. "Owen was just here."

"What the fuck did he want?"

"He saw me with Sidney and her mother-in-law. He's found his next target."

"Goddamn it. That fucker needs to be put down."

"I've got to take a few days, give the Stephenses a heads up."

"And Sidney?"

"I'll tell her, but this is my shit spilling onto them. I need to handle it personally."

"You think that's a good idea? Going behind her back to her in-laws?"

"I don't know, but I'm still doing it."

"In your place, I would too. Don't worry about things here."

"Thanks, man."

"I won't lie, I was surprised by your call. What can we do for you?" Jasper Stephens gestured to a chair in his office. He looked good, healthier and stronger and it hadn't even been a week since I'd last seen him. From the way they were both studying me, they thought this was a shakedown. And in some sense it was.

"My father's name is Owen Madden and he's a con man. I haven't seen him in over a year. To be fair, he kicked me out of the house at fourteen when I realized I was a part of his cons and he no longer had a use for me. He comes back from time to time when his money is running low. I don't acknowledge him, he moves on. He came to see me the other day. Apparently he's been living out here and saw a picture in the paper of us entering the hospital and now he's seeing payday. I don't know what he's up to and what he has planned, but I do know he's capable of anything. Everything in me says I should take a step back, remove myself from the equation, but my life has been influenced enough by that fucker. I'm not about to give up the best thing that's ever happened to me because of him. I know you may feel differently, may even encourage Sidney not to associate with me because of my father. If that's the case, I'll fight you too. I just hope it doesn't come to that."

"She means that much to you?" Jasper would make an excellent poker player; I couldn't read him at all.

"Yeah, the fucking air I breathe."

"That's all I needed to hear. I've got some investigators on retainer. Give me what you can about Owen and I'll put them on the trail. I don't care how good he is, these guys are better."

"Won't you stay for dinner?" Lauren asked then changed her mind and stated. "You'll stay for dinner." She surprised me when she leaned over and kissed my cheek. "It wasn't easy coming here and sharing this, but the fact that you're willing to fight for Sidney, even us, I already liked you, but after today I adore you." She hurried away, I suspected because she was about to cry. She called from the door, "I still have some Corona." Her head turned, her eyes bright, but there was a smile curving her lips. "I'll bring one… in the bottle."

And why I felt the tightness in my chest, I didn't know but it wasn't a bad feeling.

"Okay, son. Tell me what you know."

That tightness intensified hearing Jasper call me son and then I told him everything I knew about my dad.

sidney

I had just been to see Spike; he greeted me at the door with a wagging tail. His stitches had been removed and there was some tenderness but his recovery had been remarkable. Ichabod and Jeshaiah were so overcome seeing their baby back to his old ways that they tried to give me stuff from their house. I politely turned down the butter churn and the old telephone that didn't work. They had an obscene amount of milk glass, not something I would have pictured those two hording, but I turned that down too. When Ichabod pressed the gold necklace into my palm with the enameled magnolia charm, he wasn't taking no again for an answer so I accepted.

I was on my way back to the clinic before my appointment at McNealy Farm, following up on Lily who since her bout of colic a few months back hadn't had a reoccurrence. Abel had called earlier. He was coming up this weekend, asked if I would come with him to check out the possible locations for Pipes. I was thrilled he asked. There was something else he wanted to discuss, but preferred doing so in person. He left it wide open and though my thoughts jumped to a few topics that I would love to discuss, I wasn't so sure that was the kind of conversation he wanted to have.

"Sidney Stephens."

Sammie Chase stepped from the doorway of the bakery. Annoying and creepy, but there was something else about him that stirred fear. This guy was not right.

"Keith isn't here to save you this time."

Despite the fact that this guy was seriously unhinged, he grated. "From what? You? I don't need Keith to do that."

Like a child throwing a temper, his face turned red and blotchy. "You should be careful about how you talk to me."

"Or?"

I didn't know what he intended to say, his hands curling into fists was not a good sign, but someone else approached interrupting our disturbing conversation.

"Is everything okay here?" Mr. Milburn and Cooper.

"Yes. Sammie was just leaving."

His glare should have left me bleeding before he stormed away.

"Are you okay?"

"Yeah, but he's not right."

"No, he's not. You're shaking, are you sure you're okay?"

I *was* shaking because that encounter rattled me.

"Has he done that before?"

"Once."

"Maybe you should report him to the sheriff. I didn't like the way he was looking at you."

That earned my full attention. "Do you think he'd hurt me?"

"I don't know."

And since I couldn't answer that question either, it couldn't hurt to have the sheriff made aware. "I have an appointment at McNealy's farm in an hour. "I'll go see the sheriff now."

"I'll come with you."

The sheriff's office was like a throwback to the days of cowboys and Indians. In fact, I was almost disappointed not to see the tin star pinned to their shirts. Four wooden desks arranged two by two took up most of the space. A few folding chairs acted as the waiting room and an old scarred table, tucked up against one wall, held the coffeemaker that looked nearly as old as the rest of the place. Sheriff Dawson Lenin was middle-aged with thinning gray hair and a belly that stuck out a bit from his belt. Stress lines creased the area between his eyes and around his mouth, but I understood having a murderer on the loose in town.

He came from the back of the station where I imagined his office was located. "Reginald. I think I might take you up on that fishing trip. My doctor says I need to unwind because the stress is going to kill me."

"Anytime, Dawson."

Sharp brown eyes shifted to me. "And you're Sidney Stephens. How are you finding Sheridan?"

"It's a beautiful town."

"Yeah, it's seen better days though. Please sit."

"Are you making any headway?" Mr. Milburn asked as we settled at one of the desks.

"No. Most think he's gone, left right after poor Belinda, but my gut is telling me something different." He rubbed the back of his neck, frustration clear in that motion. "I know this is personal for you. Maggie had tried so hard to help Belinda, to get her to change her ways. I promise you, Reginald, I will find out what happened to her."

How sad for Mr. Milburn, not just the tragedy of Belinda but also the daily reminder of her link to his wife. Turning my thoughts to what else the sheriff had shared I asked, "So you think he's local too?"

"Yeah, I do even though I can't think of anyone in this town capable of such atrocities. Anyway, you wanted to see me?"

This man had enough to deal with; he didn't need me dumping on him too. Though I thought he was wrong in that Sammie Chase was definitely capable of the horrors Belinda had suffered. "I realize you've a lot on your plate, but this sort of falls into that. I was there the day they found Belinda."

"I'm aware."

"Sammie Chase was also there, snapping pictures of the body for his blog. I reported him to one of the cops. He didn't like that. Since, he's approached me twice in a threatening manner, in fact he did so just now."

"Cooper and I were taking our walk, but Sammie's body language was enough to have me stepping in."

"Sammie Chase has his issues, but he's harmless." Before I could object, the sheriff held up his hand to stop me. "I understand, I do. I've seen Sammie in action, but I've known the kid all of his life. He's harmless. He pushes until someone pushes back. I'll push back. He won't bother you again."

Outside the sheriff's office, Mr. Milburn voiced my thoughts. "I was surprised to hear Dawson defending Sammie, but the man reads people better than anyone I know. If he says Sammie's harmless, I'm inclined to believe him."

"I just hope him pushing back doesn't anger Sammie more since he's doing all of this because I got his phone taken away. Having the sheriff showing up on his front step is a far greater offense."

"It can't hurt to be careful, but if Sheriff Lenin's looking into it, you can be sure he'll handle it. There's a reason he's held the position for the past twenty-five years."

"I imagine you worked with him when you were practicing."

"All the time, which is why I know how good he is at his job."

"Well then I will take comfort in that and allow the sheriff to handle Sammie."

"Good idea. I'd suggest we do lunch, but you have an appointment now."

"I do, but I'd like a rain check."

"Absolutely."

"Thanks for the rescue."

"I'm a sucker for a damsel."

Returning home after visiting Lily, I was surprised to see Rylee already home. "What are you doing here?"

"I closed up early. We haven't had a chance to talk since you returned from New Jersey, so I got wine and pizza and we're sitting out back and catching up."

Sometimes we get lost in the day to day, but reminders to appreciate the people around you were always good. "I love you, Rylee."

"I know you do. And Cain, he wants some of this pizza."

"A slice won't hurt him."

"That's a pretty necklace. Where did you get that? Abel?"

Absently I touched the enameled magnolia. "No, Ichabod gave it to me as a thank you for Spike. They're hoarders, this was the last of a long list of offerings. He wouldn't let me say no."

"Those two crack me up."

We settled outside even with the weather turning colder.

"So spill, I know Jasper is doing well, thank God, but what happened with Abel? That had to be strange for all of you."

"Jasper gave me his approval and Lauren couldn't dote over him enough. Abel took it all in stride, but he hardly cursed while there. A conscious effort."

"No way."

"I brought the man who has claimed my heart to the home of the man who claimed it first and yet, it felt right. I love him."

Rylee's expression went soft. "I know you do."

"He loves me too. Said he never had anyone tell him that before and didn't know how it was supposed to feel."

Tears filled Rylee's eyes. "He never had anyone tell him they loved him?"

"No."

"Sounds familiar."

"I know. It's like this time I'm Jake offering to Abel what he never knew he was missing."

"I love happy endings."

"We're not at the ending, not by a long shot. He asked me to look at the spaces for the new Pipes and there's something else he wants to discuss, but he wouldn't talk about it over the phone."

"What do you think he's got on his mind?"

"I honestly don't know. I couldn't get a read on him."

"Interesting."

"So what's going on with you and Jayce?"

"The man drives me crazy. He's opinionated, a flirt and reckless and I adore him." She leaned up, excitement turning her eyes bright. "I remember watching you with Jake, the beauty of it, and how I secretly wished I could find that. I've found it."

"Oh, Rylee." My own eyes were bright; thrilled that Rylee had found a love like that.

"It's like we're the same person, but different enough to keep things interesting. He knows every part of me. Even the parts that are less than beautiful, but all he sees is beauty."

"Smart man."

She reached for my hand and squeezed, a small smile playing over her lips. "He's still living at home, and with the home he has I get it, but he's been dropping hints about moving in."

"Here?"

"Yeah, but I've been avoiding the subject because this is your home too."

"He can move in. It'll be a little tight, but we're all friends."

"You seriously don't mind?"

"You've found the love of your life, of course I don't mind if he moves in with us."

She unsuccessfully tried to pull off nonchalant; she was practically hopping in her chair. "Do you want to call him?"

"Do you mind? I won't be long."

"Go, but tell him he cleans up after himself or he'll have to deal with the animals and me."

"Will do." She kissed me on the way to the door and then disappeared inside. A few seconds later, her happy voice carried out to me. Cain and I stepped off the deck to give her privacy. I wondered if that was what Abel wanted to discuss, our living arrangements. When he was here, we spent every minute together so it would make sense that I'd stay at his place, but I had Cain and the cats. If I was going to be away that long, I'd want them with me. I wasn't sure how he'd feel about that.

"Keith's band is playing at the Brass Bull tonight, a last minute schedule change. Want to go?" Rylee called from the deck.

A night out with friends, music and drinks. "Sure."

I only had one other amateur band for reference, the garage band down the street from the Millers who had screamed more than sung and in keys that hadn't yet been discovered. Keith's band, Gray Matter, was amazing. So good in fact I was surprised he wasn't doing more with it. Not only was their music good and the lyrics poetic, but the band had a presence and energy on the stage.

"I don't understand why he isn't doing more with his music." Rylee voiced my thoughts exactly.

"There was a time he was hard-charging with the band but that kind of fizzled. I don't know why because clearly they've still got it," Jayce said.

Duncan returned with our drinks, taking the seat at my left. "Did you hear that Carly is coming home?"

"She is?"

"Yeah, she finished the program and has spent time in a halfway house kind of place, but the doctors think she's ready to come home. She's going to stay with Dad and Marnie for a bit until she figures out what she wants to do."

I couldn't help thinking of Connor and how if he had more people pulling for him, would he have been able to kick his addiction? "That's wonderful, really fantastic news." Leaning into Duncan slightly, I asked, "And you? What are your intentions?"

The boyish smile was one I had never seen on his face. "I won't rush her, she's got enough to deal with, but when the time is right."

"I'm happy for you."

And he continued to surprise me when he blushed, just the slightest coloring of his cheeks. "Thanks."

The bellow from the door turned all our heads as Ichabod and Jeshaiah entered. "You need another round?" Ichabod called.

"Get one anyway," Jeshaiah said before he pulled over a chair and joined us. "Evening folks."

"What brings you out?" Jayce asked.

"Heard Keith's band was playing. It's been a while since we heard them last."

"They're only on their first set, so you haven't missed much," Lorelei said as she dropped the plates of loaded fries and nachos on the table.

Ichabod joined us, his eyes landing on the necklace. "You're wearing it."

"Yes, it's beautiful. And thank you again, though it was completely unnecessary."

"Spike is still here because of you. It's the least we could do, besides what the hell are we going to do with it?"

"Maybe if you stopped collecting junk." Lorelei said but her attention was on me, more specifically the necklace, and honest to God it looked as if she had seen a ghost.

"Lorelei?"

"Ichabod, where did you get that?"

"I don't remember. Hey, Lor, you okay? You don't look so good."

"Belinda Kramer had a necklace just like that."

All eyes turned to me, but I was already unfastening the neck lace. The thought that I was wearing the poor dead woman's jewelry was horrifying.

"You need to remember, Ichabod, and tell the sheriff."

But Ichabod was the one who looked ill. "All this time I had that, I didn't even think. It could have helped her, maybe even found her before…fuck."

Lorelei rested her hand on Ichabod's shoulder and gave it a reassuring squeeze. "You didn't know. I only knew because I was surprised to see something so dainty and pretty around her neck."

"I'll call the sheriff now. Can I use the phone in the office?"

"Sure thing, hon."

"What's going on over here? You look like someone just ran over your dog." Keith's band had finished playing their first set and he'd jumped down to join us. He gestured to the necklace. "What's that? Why are you all looking at it like it's going to grow legs and crawl away?"

"It's Belinda's."

Keith's head jerked to Lorelei, his expression suggesting he thought she was teasing him. "Seriously?"

"Yeah."

"How did you get it?"

"Ichabod found it. He gave it to Sidney here as a thank you."

I felt more than saw his attention shifting to me; it was rather intense. "That sucks."

He summed that up perfectly, I had nothing more to add.

Ichabod remembered where he'd found the necklace, it had been on the ground near the dumpster in the alley behind the bakery. The sheriff tracked down what landfill the dumpster's contents were delivered to and had men searching it for possible evidence. He'd lucked out that the fill was a fairly new one, so though there was a lot of trash to comb through, it wasn't a mountain like it could have been.

Back in New Jersey, Ichabod would have been brought in for questioning, but here everyone knew of his propensity to collect things. And being someone who knew him the least, even I couldn't imagine he'd have the stomach for murder.

I was at the clinic working on converting our records to electronic; something that was taking far longer than I'd anticipated since there just wasn't time to dedicate to it, when the door opened and Abel came breezing through. Instinct was to jump up and throw myself at him, but instead I leaned back in my chair and just looked my fill.

"Doc."

"Abel."

"I heard you had some excitement here this week."

"A little. I got to tell ya, I'm growing really tired of having to wait a week between visits."

He leaned against the doorjamb as his hands found the pockets of his jeans. "You don't say."

"Um. Like that, right there. Making a woman wait a week when she has all of that is cruel."

"Wait a week for what?" A wicked grin curved his lips suggesting he knew exactly what it was I didn't want to wait a week for.

We were alone, so I answered honestly. "To touch, to taste, to feel the whiskers of that beard on my skin. To pull my hands through your hair, fisting it when you're doing something I really like."

Devilishness faded into hunger. "Keep talking like that and I'll give you a reason to fist my hair right here."

Lock the door almost escaped my lips and as much as I wanted him to do just that, the clinic was open and there could be an emergency. We'd have to wait until later. "Tempting. Very tempting."

Abel changed gears so quickly I nearly got whiplash. "I need to talk to you."

Unease moved through me. "Okay."

He moved from his spot and paced a lot like how Cain used to in his shelter. "What's going on Abel?"

"My father paid me a visit."

"Your father?"

"He makes a habit of just popping up, but this time he had a purpose. He's been living back east and saw a picture in the paper of Lauren, you and me entering the hospital."

Something ugly twisted in my gut; Abel said the man was a con man and the Stephenses were loaded. "What did he want?"

"By your expression, you know. I went to see the Stephenses earlier in the week to warn them."

My body tensed as chills of foreboding danced down my spine. "You went to see the Stephenses to tell them about your father?"

"Yeah."

"By yourself?"

"They needed to be made aware and since it's my shit bleeding onto them, I had to do it alone. I didn't want to put you in the middle."

The man continually surprised me; like a well of just so much goodness wrapped up in a seriously hot package.

He shifted his feet and though he spoke out of anger, there was concern weaved through his words too. "If you're pissed about me going without you, fucking get over it."

"I am so glad I walked down that alley."

I'd surprised him; his expression was adorable. "You're not mad that I went without you?"

"No. That had to be hard though. I know how much you dislike your father and having to share him with them. What did they say?"

"Just like that."

"What?"

The grin was classic Abel; the lowering of his head and the slight shake that followed wasn't. "I thought you'd be pissed that I went behind your back. I would have anyway, but the idea of losing ground with you did not fucking sit well with me."

"What happened?"

"Jasper has a team of investigators and lawyers on retainer. And as good as I know my dad is, I think he's met his match with Jasper."

"Likely. The man hasn't gotten to where he is without dealing with the likes of your father, but the fact that you were concerned and went to them speaks volumes."

"Lauren said as much, even let me drink my Corona from the bottle."

"You're kidding."

"No."

"She really likes you if she allowed that. That's a first."

"No shit."

"Um. So are you going to kiss me?"

He was already halfway to me and I didn't waste any more time and met him the rest of the way. His fingers slid into my hair, tilting my head for his kiss. His lips lingered when he asked, "Are you still going to check out those properties with me?"

"Yes."

"We need to talk about living arrangements when I move back. I like your place, but three's a crowd."

"Four."

He pulled back slightly. "Four?"

"Jayce is moving in."

"He and Rylee are at the move in stage?"

"Yep."

"Shit. There must be something in the fucking air."

"Why do I have the feeling you're talking about more than them and us?"

"Duncan's finally making his play, fucking Garrett and Marnie have been a thing for years. No one knew."

I had wondered; they acted like peas in a pod. "How were they discovered?"

Abel grinned. "Jayce walked in on them having sex. Serves him right, thirty-something year old man still living at home."

"It's a huge home."

He blew that observation off and added, "And Tiny."

"Tiny?"

"He's been sharing a bed with Stella."

"The Stella. Oh my God, she bakes for him doesn't she?"

Abel's expression went blank for a second before he threw his head back and laughed, the thick muscles of his neck drawing my eyes. I wanted to kiss him there. Later I would.

"What?"

"I asked him the same thing."

"Great minds and all."

He cupped my ass and pressed me tight against him. "Fucking great everything."

God, I loved this man.

"You finish here, I'll swing by for you at closing time and we'll check out those buildings."

"Sounds perfect."

He was halfway to the door when I called to him. "Thanks for warning Jasper and Lauren."

He grinned an Abel grin. "See you soon."

If someone told me six months ago I'd be this happy, I'd have told him or her they were full of shit. Maybe fate wasn't so bad after all.

"You're thinking this one." Abel stood on the other side of the empty building; one that was located a street over from Main Street, but there was still decent foot traffic. What I liked about the space was that it didn't get lost in its location. The other three options were closer to the heart of town but they had no street appeal and looked as if they were tucked in at the last minute. This place felt open even though it wasn't that large a space.

"Yeah. The others were too cramped, lost in all the other stuff going on around them."

"I like this one too." He'd been checking out the small glass enclosed office that would be Tiny's, but now he was walking toward me. I hadn't a clue what he was thinking until he wrapped me in his arms and touched his lips to mine. "Do you know what else I like about this place?"

"What?" That may have come out a bit breathless.

"The room upstairs."

I actually quivered with lust.

"I see you're getting me. It's certainly faster than dragging your ass home. Think of what we could do with all that extra time."

He chuckled, probably because I went a little weak in the knees. "What's the timing for this move?" I asked, since the alternative reply was something altogether different.

Abel dipped his chin, those pale eyes on me. "The LLC is setup and I've contacted my friend, who helped me setup Pipes, and am on his schedule. I'll want to be here when he starts working. I just need to list my apartment and move my shit."

"Do you want my help with packing?"

"Sweet, babe, that you offered, but you saw my place. There's not much. I'll get a couple of guys to help me load the shit into a truck. In two weeks my address will be Sheridan." His chin dipped again, even lower, as he curled his back so we were nearly eye level. "We never did finish the discussion about living arrangements. I want you at my place."

"What about my animals?"

"Are they a part of you?"

"Yeah."

"So what do you think?"

"Even Sandbar?"

"Even that little shit."

"Then yes, I would like to move into your place. And the timing is perfect. You'll be home just in time for Christmas." Really only days to spare but at least he'd be here.

"You'll want a tree."

"Yes."

"Never had one."

A sharp pang twisted in my gut thinking of him as a child, alone and neglected. I understood all too well. "We can pick one out together."

He touched me, a slight brush of his fingertip from my jaw to my chin. "I'd like that. Your bedroom furniture is kick-ass. If you want to bring it over, I'll make arrangements to get rid of mine."

"Yeah, I'm taking you up on that." My bedroom set was kick-ass, a mahogany mission panel bed with matching dresser and TV armoire—rustic and beautiful. Plus, I spent the money on a high-end memory foam mattress that I'd kill to keep. Well, maybe not kill but certainly maim. "As for the rest of the house, I will be adding the missing touches like pictures and stuff."

"Whatever you want as long as I get to wake up with your hair on my pillow."

He wasn't shy about sharing how he felt and still he took my breath away every time he did. Touching his bearded chin, I ran my thumb over his cheek. "And yours on mine."

He made a sound from deep in his throat, but it was the heated look that accompanied that sound which had that quiver of lust moving right down my body to settle between my legs. "Let's wrap this up and get something to eat." He lifted my chin and pressed his mouth to mine. "And later, I'll eat you."

The quiver became an ache. "I like this plan."

The realtor was ecstatic to have made the sale since the property had been on the market for almost a year; understandable because outside of being turned into a garage like Abel needed, it would require a lot of work to make it an inviting retail space.

Dinner was at the Brass Bull, Bobby's take on a pulled pork sandwich with pickles and a spicy mustard sauce. And now Abel and I were at one of the pool tables. I'd never played the game. Abel was teaching me and I had to say he was a fantastic teacher. I hadn't heard a damn word he said because his instructions included bending me over the pool table so his front molded to my back. His whiskered jaw brushed my neck and cheek and his hand covered mine as he explained the shots. He wasn't immune, the hard length of him pressed against my ass, which only further aided in me completely tuning him out.

He gained my attention when he nipped my earlobe, his tongue running over the spot he bit. "You're not listening, Doc."

"I am not listening, Abel."

The cocky bastard pressed his hips into me, his voice a soft purr. "Why's that?"

Why's that? Tease. "Because…" Tilting my head, my eyes found his as I breathlessly stated, "I forgot to balance my checkbook."

It took him a second before his face split into a grin. "Is that what the kids are calling it? Got to tell ya, Doc, I'd balance your fucking checkbook anytime."

I physically felt those words as my clit spasmed and my nipples turned rock hard. I muttered to myself. "That backfired."

He chuckled, his beard tickling my collarbone as he pressed a kiss on my throat. "Are you hot for me?"

"You know that I am."

"You ready to leave?"

I was so ready to leave, would have run right out of the bar and all the way back to his cabin, but our names were shouted from the door as Jayce, Rylee and the Thompson brothers stepped through.

"You okay if we stay a bit longer?" Abel asked as he eased away from me and immediately I wanted to protest the loss of his warm, strong body, but I needed to pull myself together and wouldn't be able to do so having him so close.

"Yeah. What about you?"

"Just storing it away for later," he said, winking at me. God, I couldn't wait for later.

"I heard you bought that place on Gould Street," Jayce said as he and the others joined us at the pool table.

"Yeah."

"So you're really doing it? That's fucking awesome."

"Doing what?" Rylee asked.

"Opening a Pipes here," Jayce said.

Rylee's eyes went wide right before she smiled so big it took up her whole face. "Really? You're moving back?"

Abel dropped his arm round my shoulders and pulled me tight against his side. "Got a reason to."

"Hot damn! First round is on me," Rylee screamed and hurried off to the bar.

"I'll help her," Ichabod said then added, "Good to hear you're coming home."

A chin nod was Abel's reply.

Jeshaiah moved behind us to the table. "Twenty-five bucks says I kick your ass and since you're liquid enough to expand, you can afford that."

"You're on." Abel touched his lips to mine before he turned to Jeshaiah. "Make it fifty."

"Oh yeah."

Neither Abel nor Jeshaiah came out ahead since they were evenly matched, both winning two games and losing two. Rylee and I were sitting at a table, drinking beer, watching the crowd around the electric bull. Jayce and Abel were leaning up against the wall, long necks hanging from their fingers, laughing at Ichabod being thrown here and there on the bull. Wobbling after climbing off, he joined them. Abel handed him his beer so he could have a go on the bull. Someone had hit the jukebox as the first few cymbal clashes of Halestorm's 'American Boys' pumped through the place. Fitting song for what we were watching, especially when Abel strutted up to the bull and saddled it so his faded jeans hugged his ass and thighs; I took a long drink from my beer to cool off. It didn't work though as my focus moved to his flexed right arm, the muscles stretching the sleeve of his tee; his broad shoulders and back on display as the cotton begged for mercy. Combined with his hair pulled back in a bun and that beard, he was hot and he was mine.

"I think you need to pinch me."

Rylee laughed, her eyes warming when she looked over at me. "I told you."

Reluctantly I turned my gaze from all that was Abel to Rylee. "Told me what?"

"That there was someone else out there that you'd never see coming."

"You were right. I never saw him coming and you never saw Jayce coming."

Her hand settled over mine. "I'm so happy we moved here."

"Me too. Abel asked me to move in with him."

"He did?"

"Yeah, so you and Jayce will get our place all to yourselves."

"I'm not going to lie. I love the idea of that, but I'll miss you."

"You'll see me every day."

"True." We both turned back to Abel and unlike Ichabod, he was riding that bull like no one's business. "Wouldn't have thought a biker could ride a bull like that."

With the way he handled that horse when he came riding to my rescue, I wasn't surprised. "I'm beginning to understand there is very little the man can't do. God, he's hot."

"Amen to that, sister."

My head jerked to hers before we both burst out into laughter.

That night, I rode Abel like no one's business and after, he curled his big, muscled body around me as we drifted off to sleep. Yep, I never saw him coming and I was never letting him go.

ABEL

I had so much shit to do; Remy was coming soon to help me plan out the floor plan for Pipes II before he got started on the work. He cost a mint but he knew his shit. I had to finish packing, get D.J. up to speed on his new role as manager since now he'd have the added responsibility of payroll, but my mind never strayed far from thoughts of my father. The prick was up to something and until I knew what, I couldn't really focus. The fact that he had stopped to see me meant there was a fucking good chance he was heading to Sheridan or was already there. Thinking about Sidney being easy pickings, I should have fucking showed her a picture of the bastard. I'd been so caught up in her, I hadn't even thought of it. I reached for my phone.

"Sheriff Lenin."

"Sheriff, it's Abel Madden."

"Hey, son. I hear you're coming home."

"In two weeks."

"Good to hear, so what can I do for ya?"

"My father is on his way to Sheridan."

I completely understood the hiss that came over the line. "What for this time?"

"He's learned about my relationship with Sidney, more specifically that her in-laws are very well off."

"He's making a play."

"Yeah. I'm not there and I don't like that he will be."

"You want me to keep an eye on her."

"Yeah."

"We're stretched thin with investigating Belinda's murder, but I'll get the boys to drive by the house and clinic periodically. Might help if you get the Hellar boys help too, especially since Jayce is seeing the best friend."

"How do you know that?"

"I'm the sheriff, I know all."

That didn't surprise me. "I'll call Jayce now. Thanks, Sheriff."

"You bet."

My phone buzzed as soon as I disconnected with the sheriff.

"Abel, it's Jasper Stephens."

"Mr. Stephens."

"Call me Jasper. Is this a bad time?"

"No, what's up?"

"I've some news on Owen Madden."

I stood and started to pace because I had a feeling I wasn't going to like what I heard. "Okay."

"He's on his way to Sheridan."

"Yeah, I just talked to the sheriff, made him aware."

"Good. I'll be calling him next. Owen Madden has a bank account in Sheridan, one that receives monthly deposits in cash, seven to be exact. The exact same sum every month."

"Shit. Hush money."

"Yeah, he's blackmailing at least seven people in Sheridan or towns close enough to make the trip to that bank. Every deposit has been made through a teller and since they're deposits not withdrawals, no identification was needed."

"Goddamn it."

"Another interesting fact, the woman, Belinda Kramer, he knew her."

My fingers tightened on my phone. "Come again?"

"He knew her, they met outside of town every couple of months. After these visits, the deposits being made into that account increased by one. It's not likely your sheriff has found that connection because he hasn't a reason, until now, to focus on Owen but it's information he'll want."

"She was feeding Owen the dirt."

"That's what my investigators think. Another interesting fact, he was in the area during the time of her death."

"Why would he kill the person who was feeding him the information?"

"He likely didn't, but it is a connection I think warrants further investigation, which is why I'll be turning over what I know to Sheriff Lenin. My concern is Sidney. She's unaware of all of this."

"The sheriff and some boys I know are looking out for Sidney. She'll be covered and I'll be back in Sheridan for good in two weeks."

"Owen seems to favor blackmail, but there isn't anything in my past or Lauren's that would gain him what he seeks and that makes me nervous. We're building a case on him and with luck we'll get to him before he tries for us, but I don't like the ambiguity."

"I don't either."

"If I learn more, I'll call."

"Thank you, Jasper."

"You can thank me by getting your affairs in order and getting back to Sidney."

"Fair enough."

sidney

Abel was back in Cheyenne, but watching him pull away hadn't been as hard this time since in two weeks he would be back for good. I had lots to do in that time. He'd given me his key, his words better than any flowery prose out there. *Do whatever shit you have to, babe, to make it feel like home*. I was ready to move my bedroom furniture over and Ichabod had a truck to help me with that. I also wanted to buy towels and dishes, maybe some throw pillows—little accents to turn his bachelor pad into a home. Plus Christmas was coming, so we needed a tree and garland, ornaments and poinsettias.

I had no appointments at the farms so my plan was to spend the day inputting the rest of our patient records into the computer. Rylee had a pretty full schedule, I only had a few clients scheduled, so if needed I could stop and lend a hand.

Rylee popped out from one of the examination rooms. "Sidney, would you mind getting me a donut? I've been thinking about Stella's Boston creams all morning."

"Sure." I moved from around my desk because honestly I wouldn't mind one of her sticky buns. "You want coffee too?"

"Yeah, please."

"I'll be right back."

Stepping outside, it was definitely cold but nothing like New Jersey in December. Pulling my coat closed, I headed for the bakery pondering what Stella's offerings were for the day when I noticed Sammie Chase across the street. He really was a little weasel. He wasn't alone; an older man was with him, someone I had never seen before. Whatever they were discussing, it didn't look pleasant. Sammie actually looked scared, piquing my curiosity about the man. Specifically what it was he had to say that had the power to rattle a creep like Sammie. They didn't talk for long. The man leaned in, and even from my distance, it was clear the gesture was threatening before he turned and walked away. Sammie didn't move. He just stood staring after the man, his hands twisting nervously in front of him. After a few minutes, he headed in the opposite direction. What had that been about? But the scent of chocolate wafting from the bakery turned me from that thought as I hurried to Stella's to get whatever caused that sinful smell before they were all gone.

Later in the day, the door to the clinic opened and Carly stepped in. The transformation was so astounding, even just from Thanksgiving; I almost didn't recognize her.

"Carly, hey." I moved from around my desk to join her.

"Hi. Sorry to just drop by, but I wanted to thank you for helping when I'd hit rock bottom."

Even as my gut twisted hearing the words I had always hoped to hear from Connor, I was thrilled that she'd found her way to the other side. "I'm just glad you're doing so well."

Her fingers twisted together, she was nervous, but before I could ask her about it she said, "Duncan asked me if there was something specific that triggered my decline. There wasn't. I was lonely and a bit unhappy, but most people experience that. It just happened I had a drink one day and that led to two drinks and then three drinks. Then I took a hit from a joint, started dropping ecstasy and before I knew it I was trying heroin. That scared the shit out of me. That was when I finally realized I had a problem and was ready to accept the help being offered, but before that I didn't think I needed it." She paused for a second, her voice stronger when she continued. "I'm telling you this because if your brother didn't believe he had a problem, if he craved the high, nothing you could have said or done would have mattered. Even if he had a team of people like I was lucky enough to have, it wouldn't have made a difference."

Her words were hard to hear, but the weight I'd carried since Connor lost himself so completely lifted from my shoulders. I had always believed I could have done more for him, that I had failed him. Getting this insight into what Connor was likely thinking was closure I never believed I'd find. My voice broke a bit. "Thank you. You don't know what that means to me."

"I think I do."

A tear rolled down my cheek because along with the weight lifting, the anger and resentment I still felt at times when thinking of Connor slipped away too, allowing for forgiveness to settle in their place. I tried for a smile, wiped the tear away and asked, "So what's next for you?"

"I was just at Mimi's Floral Shop. I'm starting work there in a few weeks. I always wanted to work with flowers and her assistant just had a baby and decided not to come back."

"That's wonderful. And you'll be close so maybe we could grab lunch sometime."

"I'd like that. I heard Abel is moving back."

"In two weeks and I can't wait."

A slight hesitation followed before she added, "I'm glad he found you."

Warmth settled in my belly at her words. "Me too."

"He's a good guy."

"The best. And Duncan?"

The blush that moved up her face was a surprise to see. "We're making up for lost time." Her hands twisted in front of her again. "I ran from here when I was so young. It was stupid; I never should have gone. Back then I just felt lost, alone and afraid but I had what I needed around me and I just didn't see it."

"Love, especially when we're younger, can hurt."

"That's true. Hey, I heard you were there when Belinda was found. That had to be horrible."

"It was."

I didn't get the sense her asking was merely conversational; I had a feeling she had more on her mind, which was confirmed when she asked, "Not to be morbid, but is it true that Sammie Chase was there?"

"Taking pictures, if you can believe that." Her face went pale, but it was the worry that swept her expression that had me asking, "Carly, what's wrong?"

"I was so out of it when they found Belinda, not seeing anything but where I was getting my next hit, but Sammie Chase isn't right. I know people think he's harmless, but I think he's disturbed. I had hoped he wasn't there, but I think I need to talk to the sheriff."

Fear unfurled in my gut because I agreed with her, and he didn't like me. Not even a little. "Why do you say that?"

"I saw him when I was younger, carving up an animal in the woods by Hellar Farm. It was disgusting and after I caught him, he was always watching me."

"Oh my God. I thought he wasn't right, but that's serial killer behavior."

"I agree. Freaked me out enough that even though I'd been planning on leaving town to get away from Duncan, Sammie's unwanted attention sped that up. The sheriff makes excuses for him and I get it because Sammie was awkward and kids teased him growing up, but I think he was awkward because he isn't right."

"I think you're right about both Sammie being disturbed and that you need to tell the sheriff. I've been to see him about Sammie because he's gotten up in my face twice all because I reported him to the cops when he was taking pictures of Belinda. He can seriously hold a grudge. If you want, I can come with you to see the sheriff."

"Thanks, but I'm meeting up with Duncan shortly, he can come with me. I didn't mean to dampen the mood."

"I'm glad you told me. The three encounters I've had with Sammie, including the day they found Belinda, I let him get to me enough that I provoked him back. I won't be doing that again, but enough about him. Congratulations on the job. When you start work, Rylee and I would like to take you out for a celebratory lunch."

"I'd really like that."

"Welcome home, Carly."

Sitting on my bed, I should be packing, Abel was coming home in a week. Instead I sat there, Cain on one side and Sandbar on the other, staring at my wedding picture. I traced Jake's face and the full smile that showed teeth, a sight that was so rare for him. Looking into his face it all came back—every memory, every laugh, and every tear. How it felt when I was in his arms, his soft breath on my cheek, those beautiful dark eyes staring into mine as he moved over me, in me.

"Thank you for pulling up next to me that first day and offering me a ride. One of the smartest things I've ever done was accepting it. I'm okay. I'm happy. I'm in love, so I'm ready to say goodbye but know that a part of me will always belong to you."

I pressed a kiss on his face, wrapped my wedding picture in bubble wrap and laid it on top of Jake's sweater and jersey before sealing up the box that wouldn't be going with me to Abel's, but home to the Stephenses.

"Let's go for a walk, Cain."

It was cold as we walked through the field of wildflowers that had died down for winter. We had only moved here six months ago and yet so much had happened. Cain kept pace at my side; his head up and alert before he stopped walking and looked behind us a few seconds before I heard Rylee calling my name. She was out of breath by the time she reached us. Bending in half, she put her hands on her knees.

"What are you doing home?"

"News…I have some…give me a minute."

"Did you run the whole way from the clinic?"

She straightened. "Cute. You're not going to believe it."

"Believe what?"

"They just found Sammie Chase."

I felt numb and incredulous hearing that alarming news. "What?"

"Dead. They found him a few hours ago."

"Holy shit. Dead?" My brain struggled to catch up. Dead. Another murder. "Where did they find him?"

"His house."

"Oh my God. I was so convinced he was the one who killed Belinda. Carly stopped by last week, told me she had seen him carving up an animal when they were younger."

"That's disgusting."

"Yeah. She went to the police to report him. Him showing up dead, I don't know, it doesn't seem likely that he was Belinda's killer. Just another victim."

"Preliminary report puts time of death yesterday at around two in the afternoon," Rylee said then added, "Doesn't it seem weird that the people being targeted are the not very nice ones in town?"

"Yeah, come to think of it, that is strange. And Sammie had serious problems, but…" My stomach twisted. "The likelihood the killer returned is not high, which means the belief that the killer is a local is probably right."

"Yeah, that's what people are saying."

"Jesus, that's really unnerving."

"You're not kidding. I like it more and more that Jayce is moving in with me and you with Abel. Two women out in the middle of nowhere with a killer on the loose doesn't seem very wise."

"You can say that again. Let's get back to the house and lock it up."

"And open a bottle of wine, maybe two," She added.

"Sounds good."

It wasn't until later that I remembered the man I'd seen talking to Sammie. Had I seen his murderer? First thing tomorrow morning, I'd stop by the sheriff's office. My cell buzzed and reaching for it, I saw it was Abel.

"Hey. I am so glad to hear your voice."

"I just heard about Sammie. Is Jayce there yet?"

"Yeah, he arrived a few hours ago."

"I don't want you going off on your own."

"Believe me, I have no intentions of doing that."

"I'll be back in two days."

"Really?"

"My woman is living in a house in the middle of nowhere with a fucking serial killer walking around. Yeah, I'm fucking coming home."

"I want you here, so you won't get any arguments from me. When you get back we need to get a tree. I've got tons of ornaments and lights and nothing to put them on."

His chuckle eased the knot in my gut. "First thing then."

"Well, not first thing."

The sexy growl that rumbled over the line was answered by a sizzle that moved straight down my body and settled in some very pleasant places. "If Tiny wasn't here, I'd be listening to you come over the phone."

Every cell in my body responded to that. I'd never had phone sex but suddenly was having a hard time thinking about anything else.

"You need to distract me, Doc, or I'm throwing caution to the wind and you'll never be able to look Tiny in the face again."

"On my God. You are such a tease."

"I'm not fucking teasing."

"Okay, subject change. Ichabod and Jeshaiah are helping me move my bedroom furniture tomorrow. I went shopping for things for your house."

"Our house."

My smile was unavoidable, *our house.*

"What did you buy?"

"I found the most adorable pink ruffle comforter with matching heart pillows. I could not resist. And the floral area rug I got for the living room really complements your masculine furniture. There are lace hand towels in the bath and pale blue ones with little pigs in aprons for the kitchen. The pink Kitche nAid mixer will get a lot of use as will the blender, nothing like Margarita Mondays."

Dead silence.

"Abel, are you there?"

"I did say whatever the fuck you needed." That was said in more of a muttered growl.

"You don't like pink?"

"Do I fucking look like a man who likes pink?"

"Come to think of it, no. Oh well, it'll grow on you."

"I've got to go, Tiny and I still have a few more hours getting the files in order. Don't go anywhere alone."

"I won't."

"Love you, Doc."

A happy sigh escaped my lips, a sound not lost on Abel. He chuckled.

"I love you."

"And Doc?"

"Hmm."

"No more fucking pink."

He hung up. He was in for a surprise, but a good one.

Sheriff Lenin was a hard man to track down, understandably so, but I did manage to get him for a few minutes before dinner the day following the news about Sammie. He looked exhausted and stressed. His comment to Mr. Milburn about his doctor demanding he take it easy ran through my head. He definitely looked like a man who needed to do just that.

"Sidney, I've only got a few minutes."

"I heard about Sammie and I saw something I think may be important."

His expression changed, the cop looked back at me now. "Okay."

"About a week ago I saw Sammie on Main Street with a man I've never seen before and they looked to be having a heated discussion. It didn't last long before they parted ways, but it was definitely contentious."

"And have you seen that man again?"

"No."

"Do you think you could describe him to a sketch artist?"

"Yeah."

"All right. Do you have time now?"

"I'll make time."

That earned me a smile. "I appreciate that. I'll call Nicki and get you two in a room together." He reached for his phone, but before he dialed his eyes found mine. "Thanks, this could be the break we've been looking for."

Nicki Butler was in her sixties and her hands were showing signs of arthritis, her fingers curling into her palms and yet the women could draw. Sheriff Lenin stayed with us, eager to see the sketch of the man. It took about an hour, but when she finished it was uncanny how accurately she'd captured his likeness. The sheriff's muttered curse turned my attention to him.

"Do you know him?"

"Yeah." He pulled off his hat and rubbed his head. "That's Owen Madden, Abel's father."

Fear hit first because Owen was targeting Jasper and Lauren and it was possible he'd killed Sammie, but anger followed because Abel was going to flip out when he learned that not only was his father in town, but that he'd had contact with Sammie before he died. And it broke my heart and pissed me off that Abel would have to deal with the potential blowback of Owen's actions, especially when he was never a father to him.

"Owen Madden approached Abel not too long ago, looking to pull a con on my in-laws."

"I know. Abel called me, told me there was a good chance his father would be coming to town and if I could keep an eye on you. I contacted the local hotels. He doesn't have a reservation at any of them and I haven't seen him, but he's been here if you saw him a week ago. So where the hell has he been staying? Not many folks in this town care for his company. I can't imagine any of them putting him up."

I got hung up on the fact that Abel had called the sheriff and asked him to keep an eye on me. Something Abel would so totally do. Inappropriate timing, but I couldn't help the smile as I looked down at my lap. Tomorrow couldn't come fast enough.

"There aren't many places for him to be. I'll get some of the boys on it. Thank you, Sidney."

"Sure."

"Abel is coming home tomorrow, yeah?"

"Yes."

"I'll contact him in a few days, after he's settled in. Maybe he has a better idea of where Owen is holing up. Would you like a ride home?"

"I've got my car. Thanks, Sheriff."

"Keep your doors locked."

"Will do."

I was sitting on Abel's front step. He had called to say he was twenty minutes out. I felt like a little kid on Christmas morning, excitement twisting around in my belly making it hard for me to sit still. Abel was coming home to stay in a house we'd be living in together. I never thought I'd want to see another face first thing in the morning but Jake's and now I could think of nothing else but of opening my eyes to Abel's handsome, bearded one.

I hadn't moved the animals over yet, wanted to wait until the house had familiar scents, including Abel's, but I hoped we could move them in early next week. I heard his motorcycle before I saw him. As he grew closer I saw the smile that spread over his face. I stood as he drove up his drive and kicked the stand down before cutting the engine

"Hey, baby." He'd just barely gotten his helmet off and I was throwing myself at him with a force that almost knocked him clear off his bike. "Happy to see me?"

"You know I am." I buried my face in his neck and breathed in him. Strong arms moved around me, pulling me even closer.

"Doc?"

His mouth descended as soon as I lifted my head. The kiss was long, wet, deep and absolutely perfect.

"Where's your stuff?"

"Tiny is driving it up." He playfully smacked my ass. "I need to stretch my legs."

"Oh, right." I took a step back, but only far enough for him to swing his leg off his bike. He asked, "Are you all settled?"

"I am, but before we go in…" I reached for his hand. "I've got to tell you something."

"Sounds serious."

"Your dad is in town."

His entire body went tight. "Did he approach you?"

"No, nothing like that. I didn't even know it was your dad. I saw

Sammie having an argument with someone last week. I mentioned it to the sheriff. He had a sketch artist work with me. Turns out it was your dad."

Something dark swept his face and he clenched his jaw so hard I was surprised he didn't break something. "Owen and Sammie knew each other?"

"Yeah, but it didn't look like a friendly conversation."

"And now Sammie's dead."

Sure, the thought popped into my head too that Owen killed Sammie, but the fact that Abel went right there was disturbing. "You think he's capable of that?"

"I think he's capable of anything."

"The sheriff has some officers looking for him. He said he'd contact you in a few days to pick your brain on possible locations your dad could be holing up." Tilting my head to study him, I added, "You already knew he was in town."

"After Owen visited me, I knew he was heading here. I called the sheriff and asked him to look out for you. Jasper called too, had some information that only confirmed Owen's intentions."

"Yeah, the sheriff mentioned that. Are you going to fill me in on what Jasper shared?"

"Yeah, but later."

That seemed fair, so I let it drop. "Are you ready to see your house?"

He pulled me close. "Our house."

I liked how that sounded. Grabbing his hand, I pulled him to the front door and wrapped my free one around the knob. "Ready?"

"Not sure."

Pushing the door open, I stood to the side and watched as he took it all in. Ruby, sapphire and emerald suede pillows were artfully tossed on his leather furniture. An area rug, with the same colors in geometric patterns, covered part of the floor. The kitchen had accent pieces in the same colors—a large bowl for fruit, a bucket for utensils and a cookie jar since I'd always wanted one. I replaced his chipped dishes with white dishes, simple and elegant, but I spiced up the table settings with iridescent purple flatware. On the counter was a Depression glass vase I'd found at Ichabod's and fell in love with that I filled with fresh flowers. I did purchase a mixer and blender but I didn't get pink, I got persimmon. Sitting by the fireplace was a basket with silver accents for magazines since I loved looking through magazines on a Sunday morning while having coffee. A cashmere/wool blend afghan in the same bold colors as the throw pillows and rug was draped over the back of the sofa. In the bedroom, I purchased a comforter in navy blue and charcoal gray and added a few throw pillows in plum and ivory to add contrast. But my very favorite addition was what Abel was studying. I'd been shopping online looking for prints because Abel's walls were completely bare. I didn't want to just purchase for the sake of purchasing because I was certain Abel would not be a fan of prints of wildflowers and mountain streams. I focused my search on prints that featured motorcycles. The man rode them and built them, he should have a print of one. I had countless prints of animals, though I wasn't sure I'd be hanging them here since they really didn't fit with his personality. And then I saw it. It was a painting, the scene a parking lot somewhere but your eye was drawn to the subject of the painting from the streetlight that shone down on him—a man, leaning up against his motorcycle, ankles crossed as he looked down as if in thought. But it was how much the man looked like Abel that had me falling instantly in love—faded jeans and white T-shirt. He even had the full beard and messy bun. I hung it on the wall over the television. It was like having Abel home even when he wasn't.

"That's the shit." He twisted his head as those pale eyes slid over me. "No pink?"

"No."

He closed the distance between us. His fingers pulled through my hair on either side of my head as he kissed me, his head angling to take the kiss deeper. It wasn't just a kiss; it was a claiming. My legs were completely useless when he touched his forehead to mine.

"Love what you've done to the place."

Words were not possible at the moment. He seemed to get that.

"We need a tree," he added.

"Um."

"We'll go now, get the tree, decorate it and then I'll unwrap you under it."

My knees buckled. Abel chuckled.

"Sound good? Just nod your head, Doc."

I nodded my head and we went off to find a tree.

The tree was important; it had to be perfect. I was usually a tall, thin kind of tree person but for Abel's cabin I was thinking short and fat. Abel had another idea. He found a tall, fat tree—a Fraser fir from the look of it.

"What do you think of this one?"

"Will that fit?"

"It's eight feet. The cabin ceilings are ten."

"My star topper may not work, but we'll work around it."

"We good?"

"Yeah. Your cabin is going to smell amazing."

He leaned in, his thumb touching my chin. "Our cabin."

I felt gooey inside every time he reminded me of that. "Our cabin."

"I'll cut off the bottom and get it on your car."

"Okay, I'm going to check out the garlands and wreaths."

We returned to the cabin with the tree, white pine rope garland, a big balsam wreath and clippings of pine, holly and winterberry branches. While Abel pulled the tree from the car, I dug from the garage the two wooden crates from the feed store that I'd gotten from Ichabod. I had purchased bags of topsoil, since these could be used as planters in the spring and summer too. Once the crates were filled with soil, I arranged the branches and the combination of pine, holly and the splash of color from the winterberry looked so festive. Abel carried the tree over and leaned it against the railing of the porch.

"Nice, Doc."

"It needs white lights. Do you have an outlet outside?"

"Yeah."

"I have white lights in the garage. Extra for the garland that will be draped along the porch."

He moved behind me, wrapping his arms around my waist. "We need a tree stand."

"I bought one and ribbon that I've already turned into bows."

His whiskered chin touched my cheek. "You've been busy."

"I love decorating for Christmas."

"This is a first for me, so I'll follow your lead."

Some of my Christmas joy faded as I turned into him, my thumbs curling through his belt loops. "No Christmas either."

He didn't answer; he didn't have to.

"There's no denying we're different, but in a lot of ways we're the same. I'm glad I'm the one who gets to share in all of these firsts with you."

In answer he touched his lips to mine. "Where's the tree stand?"

"Garage."

"I'm assuming the tree by the fireplace?"

"That was my thinking."

"All right. Do you need help out here?"

"No, I've got it well in hand. And I have eggnog and cookies for when we're decorating the tree, and Christmas music. We have to listen to Christmas music."

He strolled to the tree, but looked back at me with a grin. "Is that a rule?"

"It is."

"Good to know."

He lifted the tree like it weighed nothing and disappeared into the house. I stood there for a few minutes staring at the place he'd last been, warmth moving through me that he was mine. Then I got to work decorating the outside of our cabin.

Abel stood next to me, hands in his pockets. I didn't get the sense he was as into this as me, but he was being a good sport. We were outside looking at the decorations now that it was dark. The porch was strung with the white pine garland wrapped with white lights and where the garland was fastened to the railing, I'd placed a bow made from the Christmas plaid ribbon I'd purchased. The front door had a big balsam wreath on it, also with a bow and white lights but these were battery operated and had a timer, so no wires showed. And the two crates of branches I arranged, wrapped in white lights, flanked the front door.

"It's perfect. Don't you think?"

Abel didn't respond. Turning my attention to him, his was completely on me.

"What?"

His voice was a bit gruff when he said, "What I think is perfect is seeing how happy this has made you."

Maybe there was part poet in him after all. "And you?"

"I drove up my drive today to see my woman sitting on our porch waiting for me. In the course of little over a week you made us a home and now you're standing outside freezing your ass off to look at the twinkling lights you put up mostly because you want to give me my first Christmas. Yeah, I'm fucking happy. Now could we please go inside? There are a few ways I have in mind to warm us up."

He didn't wait for a response, lifting me into his arms, and started back into the house. Wrapping mine around his shoulders and encircling my legs around his waist, I affectionately whole body squeezed him. "Welcome home, Abel."

He spent the next few hours showing me just how happy he was to be home.

I followed Abel to his shop; his friend would be arriving shortly to start the work on converting the empty building into Pipes II. We talked about his father, what Jasper had learned. Abel wanted someone with me for the visits to the farms, I told him no. I wouldn't say we fought, but we both were quite adamant. I'd be careful, but I wasn't changing my life for his father, no way. But I did bring Cain with me because it eased Abel's worry a bit, not to mention my worry about Owen breaking into the house. If he thought I was there, would he try to kidnap me? I didn't know what the man had planned, but I did know the cats would hide from an intruder; Cain would attack. I wasn't risking him.

Abel climbed from his bike, and I happily watched as he strolled to my driver's side window.

Leaning in a bit, he asked, "What are your plans for today?"

"I'm visiting each of the horse farms. I'm stopping at the Hellar's place first, to check on Speckled Egg and Domino and to meet with Chris. McNealy, just because I enjoy his gruff and almost inhospitable manners, and lastly the Roberts' farm because Keith wants to go over a few things with me."

His jaw clenched; he wanted me in the clinic. "I really don't like you driving around with Owen in town."

"We talked about this. He isn't going to have that kind of power over me."

"Your car is a piece of shit. So what happens when it breaks down on the side of the road?"

"That isn't going to happen."

"How the fuck do you know?"

"What would you suggest?"

"You stay at the clinic with Rylee."

"I can't."

"Then take another truck."

"Whose?"

He pulled his phone from his pocket, scrolled to a number before putting it to his ear. I only heard his side of it. "Jayce, need your truck. Stubborn, yeah. She's stopping there first. Thanks, man."

"Let me guess. Jayce is offering me his truck because I'm being stubborn."

"Yeah, switch out when you get to the farm."

"You're a pain in the ass. You know that right?"

"What I know is my father is a fucking dick, possibly more dangerous than I thought and my woman is being stubborn, putting herself in potential danger. And even though it goes against everything in me, giving you this, I also know I have to give in. So if I'm fucking giving in, you're going to be in a brand new fucking truck that won't break down on the side of the fucking road leaving you fucking vulnerable."

I was grinning and not just because I was crazy about this man, but I'd missed his overuse of the word fuck.

"Why are you grinning?"

"You only used fuck five times in that explanation. You're losing your touch."

His eyes lit with humor, I even got a little grin, but then he was back to all business. "Doors locked, windows up and you stop for no one. At least you've got Cain. He senses anything, you come right here. Understood?"

"Yes. And thank you."

"Just be fucking safe."

I had to say, Jayce's truck rocked, a 2016 Dodge Ram 2500 Limited. I could take down small buildings with this baby. Maybe it was time to upgrade. Speckled Egg looked wonderful and Domino was growing fast and he loved to run. I'd over heard Chris and Garrett talking, they were thinking about putting Domino in some races. Sure, Thoroughbreds ran the races of the Triple Crown, but there were races for Appaloosas popping up all the time. He was young and he liked to run; it might be an interesting fit.

Mr. McNealy didn't disappoint and was as grumpy as usual though I was picking up on the nuances of his grumpy and I swear when I pulled down his drive, I caught him grinning. I reached the Roberts', but their truck was gone, not a surprise since they shopped on Monday. Pulling around the back, I parked next to Keith's truck.

"You stay here. I don't think the horses will like having a wolf in the barn."

Cain's head tilted, like he really understood me. I left the window down; his head immediately filled the space. "I'll be back."

Strolling toward the barn where Keith had an office setup, I heard the horses as I approached; they were making more noise than usual. I suspected they sensed Cain. Keith's office was at the back of the barn. I stopped to soothe each horse, loved that they reacted to my presence and did settle. One of the stables was empty and when I reached Keith's office that too was empty. He was probably out on a ride and just lost track of time.

Pulling my phone out, I called him and heard his phone ringing in the distance. I left the barn and headed around the back of it. Bile rose up my throat at the sight that greeted me even as I ran closer. Morning Star, one of the Roberts' horses, was lying on her side, huge gash marks over her belly. I didn't see Keith, but his phone was in the grass just to my right. It had to have been the mountain lion. My hands ran over Morning Star and even as I inventoried her wounds, I knew she wasn't living through this. Tears collected in my eyes, her death rattle growing weaker with each breath. I rubbed her head and wished I could get the morphine I had in the truck to take the pain away, but she wasn't going to last long enough for me to get it. So I sat with her, stroking her head and watched as she took her last breath. A painful lump formed as the need to cry and scream moved up by throat. I heard the gunshot seconds before a flash of black flew by me. Cain.

"No! Cain, no." I never in my life ran as fast I did in that moment because the thought of Cain going head to head with the mountain lion...and Keith, what condition was he in, especially after seeing poor Morning Star? When I reached the scene, I saw Keith leaning up against a tree, his head down, his arm held at a funny angle. His shotgun on the ground next to him and about fifty yards from him was the mountain lion. Blood smeared its mouth; his front paws tinted red.

"Keith, talk to me."

"Stay back, Sidney."

"I can reach the gun."

"Don't move."

"I have to."

I hadn't even taken two steps when the mountain lion charged me. My hands flew up in a useless defensive gesture, but before the mountain lion reached me Cain lunged, putting himself between the cat and me. I fell back on my ass, scurrying closer to Keith and the gun, my eyes fixed on Cain and the mountain lion in a death match. Tears streamed down my face, my fingers searching for the gun but my focus never left Cain. It happened so fast, but felt like forever. A horrible death wail sounded, birds took flight and the woods silenced, and there was Cain standing over the body of the cat whose throat he'd ripped out. His head turned in my direction, before he limped his way over to me. I dropped to my knees and hugged him, not just hugged him, I buried my face in his neck and hugged him. He was okay, thank God, he was okay.

My focus shifted to Keith and that's when I saw the gashes on him, the blood rapidly pooling from them. "I need to stop that bleeding."

"Morning Star?" His voice was barely over a whisper.

"No, I'm sorry."

"He came out of nowhere, like something spooked him. Jumped us."

"Don't talk. Conserve your energy."

Reaching for my phone, I called 911.

"I need an ambulance at the Roberts' farm. Keith was attacked by the mountain lion. We're about three hundred yards beyond the back of the barn." I let my phone drop from my ear as I helped settled him against the tree.

"Your arm is broken." He obviously knew this, but I was in a bit of shock.

"Fell on it when I was thrown from Morning Star." His voice turned hoarse. "She threw me off her back to protect me."

Tears were streaming down my face, but I couldn't think about Morning Star and her courageous act because I had to stop Keith from bleeding to death. I took off my jacket and used it to staunch the flow. Keith was losing consciousness.

"Stay with me, Keith. I need you to stay with me."

"He saved you." Keith was looking at Cain. "He fucking saved you. I've never seen anything like that."

Sirens came from the distance. "Do you hear that? They're coming. You're going to be okay."

It felt like eternity before I heard the paramedics calling out.

"We're over here," I called back.

I never felt such relief as I did seeing them running toward us. "His right arm is broken and he's got four very deep gashes across his chest."

"We've got it."

I stepped back and turned my focus on Cain. Outside of a few superficial cuts and the impact injury causing the limping, which would work out on its own, he was fine. Cops arrived, Sheriff Lenin among them. He took in the scene, including the mountain lion, before his eyes came back to me.

"Are you okay?"

"Yeah. Keith though."

"They're doing everything they can. Your wolf took out the cat?" There was both incredulity as well as awe in the sheriff's voice.

"Yeah, but not before the cat killed Morning Star."

The sheriff was looking at Cain in wonder. "Unbelievable, he was wild." He seemed to shake it off before he added, "I saw Morning Star, damn shame that."

A cop came up behind me and placed a blanket over my shoulders. Sheriff Lenin's strong but gentle hands steered me to the front of the house. Cain never left my side. A gurney with Keith came around shortly after. They loaded him up into the ambulance, the sirens kicking on as they sped down the drive. It was only minutes later when a motorcycle came barreling up the drive. "You called Abel?"

"I had dispatch call him."

"Oh shit. He's going to be seriously pissed."

That earned me a grin. I personally didn't see anything humorous about the situation. Abel had worried I'd find myself in harm's way, I convinced him I would be fine and yet I arrived on the scene of a wild animal attack. He was going to lock me in the cabin or chain me to him. Though the idea of being chained to Abel was not a bad one. Humor fled when I saw the expression on Abel's face, an expression I never wanted to see again. Tormented pale blue eyes settled on me, the expression that followed caused tears to burn my eyes from the beauty of it. He moved with almost super human speed, cutting the engine, climbing from his bike and moving toward me in quick determined strides. When I was in his arms I could feel his heart pounding even as his hold tightened like he wanted to absorb my body into his. I touched his face, running my fingers over his beard. "I'm fine."

Those pale eyes moved over my face like he was committing to memory all he took in. Even his voice was strained. "What happened?"

"The mountain lion. Keith said it was like it was spooked; he attacked Keith while he was on Morning Star. Morning Star didn't make it and there's a chance Keith won't either. But Cain killed the cat when it came at me."

His entire body went rock hard; the devastation I'd seen when he first pulled up washed over his face again. His focus shifted to Cain as he lowered himself in front of him. Something definitely passed between them, and then Abel was yanking me close—holding me so tight I was having trouble breathing. "Son of a bitch."

"I'm okay, Abel. It's Keith we should be concerned about. And his parents. Oh God, someone has to tell his parents."

"I've got an officer tracking them down," Sheriff Lenin said. "I'll need a statement, Sidney, but it can wait."

"I'll be in tomorrow."

"Good enough for me. You can take her home, Abel. I'll have one of the boys drive your motorcycle back to your house."

"Thanks Sheriff," I replied. Abel said nothing.

He led me to Jayce's truck, held the door for Cain, before he belted me into the passenger seat.

"Keys."

I handed them over. He remained silent during the ride, but the tension in the air was palpable. We arrived home and I didn't hesitate to climb from the truck, Cain following me. I knew the storm was coming; the clouds had been collecting for the entire ride home. I braced myself since I had been a bit reckless, charging ahead knowing there was a dangerous animal in the area, but I wouldn't have done one thing differently. Abel climbed from the truck and put some distance between us. That was not a good sign. Now that the shock had abated, anger replaced it. He was so pissed he had to pull himself together before he could address me. For the first time since I met him, I was scared.

He moved so fast, had me in his arms and in the house before my brain caught up. I was vaguely aware of Cain padding to the living room when Abel pushed me up against the door, his hands working my zipper before he yanked my jeans and panties down my legs. His jeans slipped to his hips as he pulled his cock free and slammed into me, almost painfully. I expected a fast, hard ride but he went completely still as soon as he filled me. He dropped his head on my shoulder. His fingers were digging into my thighs and with the weight of his body pressing against me I was pinned to the door.

"Abel?"

A shiver went through him and feeling his big, strong body shake unnerved me. I could barely hear him. "They only said there'd been an attack, mentioned you were there. I thought it was you. I thought I was driving up the Roberts' drive to identify your body."

"Oh my God."

"When I saw you, standing, alive. I almost fell to my fucking knees."

"I'm sorry. I didn't know. God, I'm—"

His mouth closed over mine, his tongue pushing past my lips tasting me with a thoroughness that left me weak. His hips got into it, slowly at first, a delicate slide in and out, but before long his thrusts turned hard and fast as I rocked my hips into his rhythm. The orgasm nearly tore me in two. Abel came right after me, the thick muscles of his neck rigid as his head tipped back and his eyes closed. After a few minutes, I cradled his face, traced his lips with my tongue, pulling him closer to me by linking my feet at his ass.

"I'm okay."

I didn't like the look I saw in his pale eyes, devastated. "How did you do it?"

"What?"

"Go on after losing Jake."

"I found you."

His hold on me tightened. "I couldn't do it. If I lost you…I couldn't fucking do it."

"I'm not going anywhere." Forcing his gaze on me I said again, "I'm not going anywhere."

Some of the shadows lifted from his expression, he even gave me a half grin, before he shifted his hips. The moan that escaped my lips couldn't be stopped.

"No you're not."

And to prove his point, he carried me to the bedroom and kept me there for the rest of the day. That night when I stirred from sleep, Abel still had me wrapped tightly in his arms with his face buried in my hair.

Abel followed me to the clinic in the morning; kissed me long and deep before he headed to his shop. I stopped at the bakery for coffee and ran into Mr. Milburn and Cooper, but it was the state of Mr. Milburn that stirred concern. He looked worried, but more he looked disheveled when he usually was so tidy in his dress.

"Are you okay?"

"I just heard about Keith. It's terrible."

"It is, but he's going to be fine."

"Yes, thank goodness. To think you were there though, so close to danger."

"That mountain lion won't be hurting anyone anymore."

"That's a relief. I don't want to keep you from work, I just heard and wanted to make sure you were okay."

How sweet. "I'm fine, but thank you. How are you?"

"Good. A little freaked out by current events."

I understood that. "Me too."

"I'll see you later then."

"Maybe you'll come to dinner sometime this week."

"I'd like that."

"I would too." I waited while he and Cooper walked away before I stepped into the bakery. Ichabod hollered from his place at the counter.

"Yo, Sidney. What do you want?"

"Just two coffees."

"How you doing, honey?" Stella called.

"I'm good. Better knowing that Keith is going to pull through."

"Yeah, I heard that. It's wonderful news. I should send him some baked goods."

Baked goods from Stella, Keith would love that.

"I'll get Tiny to drop them off."

Ichabod joined me, handing me a carrier with the coffee. "I don't like hearing about animals dying, but I got to say I'm glad that mountain lion isn't roaming around anymore. And Cain, no one understood why you took him in, thought you were slightly nuts for doing it, but he's a fucking hero."

"Yeah, he is."

"I've got to get Jeshaiah his coffee or his disposition is just shit. My turn to buy the next round at Brass Bull."

"Sounds good to me."

"See ya, Sidney."

I watched Ichabod for a minute as it settled over me that this was home. It had only been six months, but Rylee and I were now considered one of them and I had to say, that felt really great.

Reaching the clinic, I unlocked the door while calling, "I've got coffee."

"Good thing I called out. Jayce stepped in front of Rylee, covering her body with his own; both were in different stages of dress.

"Oh. Sorry."

"No, we are. We lost track of time."

"I'll leave."

"We'll only be a minute."

Rylee peered at me from behind Jayce, she was grinning.

"I'll get donuts to go with the coffee. Take your time."

"Best friend ever," Rylee called after me and then she giggled. I went for donuts, ate two in the bakery to give Rylee and Jayce more time.

Tiny was in the office, setting up the computer. Remy and I were building the worktables and the wallboards for the tools, but all I could think about was that fucking phone call. I thought she was dead and I fucking couldn't breathe, hadn't wanted to. It'd been three days and still just thinking about it caused my gut to twist in agony. Keith was okay; he was going to make it and only because Sidney had been there, had stopped him from bleeding out. Wildlife patrol came and removed the mountain lion. At least that threat had been removed. And Cain. I had told her to put him down that day months ago and yet he'd jumped in front of her, putting himself in harm's way to protect her like she had done for him. If he hadn't been there, she'd be dead. He could have whatever the fuck he wanted for the rest of his life. Sidney had made arrangements for Morning Star's body to be cremated. It had hit her hard, losing her, but from what I had heard there wasn't a thing she could have done.

"Hi Abel."

Carly strolled into the shop, Duncan with her. She looked good and they both looked happy. "Hey. I heard about the job, congratulations."

"Thanks, I can't wait to start."

Sliding my gaze to Duncan I asked, "How are you?"

"Dad and I have been talking and I'm going to start a branch of Hellar Farm that works with racing horses."

"When did that happen?"

"Our newest horse, Domino, he's a runner. I want to see what he can do."

"From the look of you, it sounds like something you really want."

"Yeah. I've come to learn it's not the farm I don't want, I just want to focus on something more than trail rides and training."

"I'm happy for you brother. And you two seem to be making up for lost time."

Duncan's arm went around Carly's shoulders; she leaned into him, the action almost instinctual. "Yeah, we are. We stopped by to see if you wanted to grab lunch?"

"I'd like that, but I'm behind." And I was because I'd been cutting out early to spend time with Sidney. She was having a girl's night with Rylee at her house tonight, which meant I could put in some extra hours. "Jayce and I are meeting up for dinner at the Brass Bull around seven."

"All right, we'll see you there. We'll let you get back to it."

They started away; I called after them. "I'm glad you're back, both of you."

Tiny called it quits at five and Remy left around six. I was meeting Jayce and the others in a half an hour, just enough time to get the last worktable setup. I'd been thinking about Christmas and knew part of it involved presents. I had an idea for Sidney, but I was going to need some help. Rylee was the obvious choice, but I could also call Lauren. Christmas Eve was tomorrow; I needed to get on that. I couldn't help the grin thinking about Sidney on Christmas morning in those pajamas she'd bought. Thank Christ she hadn't gotten me any because I would have hated hurting her feelings but there was no fucking way I was wearing pajamas with cats in Santa hats. Besides I think she preferred my dress for bed, that being naked. I tried to convince her to do the same, but she always dressed after we fucked. I didn't mind, I enjoyed the show, enjoyed even more removing her clothes in the morning.

The sound of the door opening turned my attention to see as Sheriff Lenin entered. "Abel, do you have a few minutes?"

"Yeah."

"I got a call from a Jasper Stephens. He mentioned you knew what he shared with me."

"He's kept me in the loop."

"Got some good direction from his investigators. I've been looking into Owen, not liking what I've been learning."

"The blackmail?"

"That and the fact that he knew both Belinda and Sammie, was in town at the time of both of their deaths."

"You think he's the killer?"

"He had means and opportunity. In Sammie's case, I've done some digging and withdrawals from Sammie's accounts match deposits in that bank account Owen has."

"So Sammie was a mark."

"Yeah, but those deposits stopped in March."

"Giving Owen motive."

"Yeah."

"But why Belinda?"

"Maybe she didn't want to play anymore or maybe she wanted a bigger piece of the pie."

"What do you mean? He was giving her a cut?"

"Yeah."

"Shit."

"It's all circumstantial, but it's enough for me to bring him in for questioning. He's the only person that was linked to both victims, was in the area at the time of their deaths and doesn't have an alibi. I'm telling you as a courtesy because I know he's got his sights set on your girl. He catches wind I'm looking for him, it might cause him to put into action whatever he's got planned."

It wasn't anger but fear for Sidney that burned through me at that warning. Owen was a bit like the mountain lion, wild and backed in a corner. His actions were unpredictable at best.

"Thanks for the heads up."

"You bet."

I really wanted to finish building the worktable, but after hearing the sheriff's news so much for working late. I reached for my phone to dial Sidney to tell her that her girl's night just became co-ed night when Owen stepped from the shadows with a gun trained on me.

"Drop the phone, son."

"What the fuck are you doing?"

"They've got it all wrong and I ain't sticking around to have two murders pinned on me."

"Again, so what the fuck are you doing here?"

"I need cash and I know where I can get a mountain of it."

Sidney.

"The Stephenses will pay whatever I ask and you're my leverage."

"If you think I'm going to help you blackmail them, you are out of your fucking mind."

"There's a car in the back, let's go. And if you think to call for the sheriff when we get out there, I will shoot him."

"Fuck you."

"I'll shoot you too and then find that pretty little lady of yours. Maybe I'll even enjoy her before I put a bullet between her eyes."

Bloodlust came over me as my hands curled into fists.

"There's no way you reach me before I squeeze the trigger and if you think I'd hesitate, you're a fucking fool. Move."

"I'm going to rip your fucking throat out."

"No you're not. See that blue sedan? Walk to the trunk."

Everything in me wanted to attack, take the risk, but if he shot me I knew he'd make good on his threat. I wouldn't risk her. "You fucking put one finger on her and I swear to God you will die slowly."

The trunk opened. "Get in."

"Fuck that."

"I knew you'd be stubborn. I counted on it."

I heard two pops right before pain exploded in my chest and as I doubled over, strong hands pushed me into the trunk. "I'm not ransoming Sidney, I'm ransoming you. She'd pay anything to get you back." A flash blinded me before he added, "Too bad you'll be dead when she does."

sidney

"I'm sorry you walked in on us that day. I thought we'd have more time."

Rylee and I were curled up on her sofa, drinking a glass of wine. I stopped home for Cain. After my rescue he didn't like not being at my side. Currently, he was sprawled out in front of the fireplace. "Don't worry about it."

"Jayce was a bit embarrassed."

"I didn't see anything important."

Rylee's head snapped up before she burst into laughter. "You should have seen your face."

"I can only imagine. I wasn't expecting a show, but I can't hold it against you since Abel and I did the same."

"You did not."

"Yeah, the night I stayed to watch Spike. We had sex on my chair."

"You did?"

"Yeah, while I read him that book you told me to read."

Her smile turned coy. "Kinky."

"Kinky or not it was hot."

"I bet. So what's he doing tonight?"

"Working late. He's been leaving early to get home to me."

Compassion moved over Rylee's face. "He's still rattled."

"I don't think it helps that his dad is in town and since we haven't a clue what he's up to, Abel is on edge."

"I can understand that."

My phone buzzed and I was tempted to let it ring, but it could be Abel. It wasn't, I didn't recognize the number.

"Hello."

"Sidney?"

"Yes."

"Owen Madden."

Everything in me went cold. "What do you want?"

"So you know who I am. That will save us time. I have something you want and I'll give it to you for one million dollars."

At his words, an array of horrifying scenarios flashed in my head. He kept talking. "Before you dismiss me, I'm sending you a text. You'll want to look. One million dollars. I'll give you an hour. Time is of the essence."

The line went dead followed shortly with a text alert. Swiping the screen, I saw a picture of Abel, but it was the red blooming on his shirt that had bile rushing up my throat. My hands shook, tears welled in my eyes and rolled down my cheeks not quite believing what I was seeing. "Oh my God."

I heard Rylee's gasp, but based on where Abel was bleeding time *was* of the essence.

"Call 911, Rylee."

She didn't move. Turning to her, I grabbed her arms. "I need you to call 911. Now."

"Yeah, right. Okay."

She hurried to the house phone; I was already calling the Stephenses.

Jasper answered, thank God. "Sidney?"

"Owen Madden has Abel. Abel's been shot and I don't know how much time he has. Owen wants one million dollars."

"Son of a bitch. I'll transfer it immediately."

My voice broke, "Thank you."

"You've called the cops?"

"Yes."

"I'll contact the National Trust of Sheridan, make arrangements for the transfer. They should have enough money in house to cover it. I'll notify the sheriff."

"Thank you, oh God thank you."

"Hold tight, Sidney. We'll get him back."

I didn't even hear the phone disconnect, my thoughts were on that picture. Abel had been shot at least twice in the chest. There was a really good chance he was already dead. And the thought of losing him, I couldn't go through that again. If Abel died, there would be no coming back from his loss. I folded into myself, the sobs burning up my throat. I couldn't lose him.

"No." I jumped from the sofa. "He's alive."

Rylee watched me and I knew from her expression she wasn't so sure of that.

"He's alive Rylee. We're going to get him back."

She squared her shoulders and even feeling doubt, something I saw clearly in her expression, she said with conviction. "Yes. We're going to get him back."

Over the next half an hour the house filled with people. I continued to pace the kitchen waiting for the sheriff who was getting the money as impatience and fear burned a hole in my gut. I didn't know how it would work? Would the bank give us the money? What did the sheriff intend to do once he had it? What I did know was I was going to Abel; nothing was going to stop me. Mr. Milburn stepped up to me. "Can I get you something?"

"No." Realizing I had been curt, I immediately reached for his hands. "But thank you."

"He's going to be okay."

"I believe that too." And I did because he had to be. I couldn't lose him.

The sheriff came in through the back door, a duffel bag in his hand. "Got it. Sidney, call Owen."

I hit redial.

"You're early. Do you have the money?"

"Yes. I want to talk to Abel."

"Making demands."

"I want to talk to Abel."

Dead air for a few seconds before Abel's weak voice came over the line. "Doc."

"Abel, baby. I'm coming."

"Don't—"

"Only you. Do you understand? I see anyone else and I'll put a bullet in his head."

"Okay."

"On the Roberts property, there are some out buildings. You'll see the car."

"I'm leaving now."

"I mean it. Come alone."

I grabbed the bag from the sheriff and ran out the door.

"You can't go alone." Sheriff Lenin ran after me.

"He'll kill Abel."

He grabbed my arm. "I'm not letting you go alone."

"Abel is dying. I have to get to him. Owen has already shot him twice; he won't hesitate to finish him off if he sees you or your cops. I will call you as soon as I can, but please I have to go to him."

"No. I'm only letting you do this at all because we don't have time to fuck around, but you are a civilian and not trained for this. Where are you meeting? My men are discreet. Owen won't see them."

Tears of frustration rolled down my cheek. "He'll kill him."

"Sidney, trust that I know what I'm doing. He won't know we're there."

There wasn't time for this so I conceded. "The out buildings on the Roberts property." I grabbed the sheriff's arms. "He can not see you. Promise me."

"I promise. Fucking clever of him, probably where he's been

holing up. He was likely what spooked that mountain lion to attack Keith."

I hadn't thought of that, didn't think long on it now. "I have to go."

"We'll be watching, but I'll hold back. If he tries something, we're coming in."

I wasn't sure how Owen drove a car to the out buildings, he clearly knew of another way in. I took the footpath I had seen that day Mr. Roberts showed me around. The buildings came into view, a blue sedan parked in the front of one and Owen Madden standing just next to it.

"Where's the money?"

"Right here."

"Toss it."

"Where's Abel?"

"Inside."

There wasn't time to demand to see Abel; I tossed him the bag. He grabbed for it like a greedy child, a sickening smile spreading over his face at the sight of it.

"You shot your own son."

"He was never a son, just a burden."

"You're a bastard."

"Yeah, a rich one."

"I want to see Abel."

"By all means." He said that, even gestured grandly in the direction of the building. I didn't hesitate, ran up the steps and pushed open the door. I heard the car engine turning over, but my attention was on Abel in the middle of the dirty floor. He was so perfectly still.

"Abel!" I dropped to my knees at his side and my hand shook as I felt for a pulse. Then I nearly wept in joy when I felt one.

"Abel, baby, I'm here. Listen to the sound of my voice. The ambulance is on its way."

His eyes cracked open, a hint of pale blue peeking out. "Doc."

"Don't talk."

"Love you."

Tears ran like rivers down my cheeks. "Don't you say that. Don't you act like it's over. Do you hear me? Stay with me. You better fucking stay with me."

"Took the pieces, made me whole," he whispered.

"And you made me whole. Stay with me, Abel. Help is coming."

But his eyes closed and his breathing grew labored and all I could do was sit and watch him die.

Abel had flatlined on the way to hospital. He'd been in surgery for hours, but it wasn't looking good. I needed to stay positive, he was alive, but the thought of wearing black again, of sitting next to a casket with him in it. The sob burned up my throat as tears flooded my eyes. That emptiness I hadn't felt since I was young, I felt it. Chipping away at the memories I'd filled it with, breaking down all that I was. Determined to leave me in pieces again. Abel was still here with me and as long as he drew breath, I would battle that emptiness back. Wiping at my eyes, I looked around the waiting room where there was standing room only. Abel thought he didn't have a family, but he did. And all of them were here praying and hoping. The doors opened and Mr. Milburn walked in. He wasn't so much walking as he was staggering. I jumped from my spot to go to him, but Sheriff Lenin appeared just behind him with a gun pointed at him.

"Drop it, Reginald." Sheriff Lenin shouted.

It was only then that I saw Mr. Milburn had a gun in his hand. He moved right up to me.

"Mr. Milburn?"

"Owen won't bother you again."

"Reginald, I mean it. Drop the gun."

"They couldn't get away with it. It isn't right. I spent my life defending people like that, my wife dedicated hers and for what? What did our lives work amount to but helping those not worthy of being helped. I couldn't allow it. I had to do something."

"What are you saying?"

"Belinda. Maggie had tried so hard with her, day and night, weekends where Maggie spent hours and hours trying to reach her and that woman comes to me on the anniversary of my wife's death sharing with glee how she'd been manipulating the townsfolk—giving information to that vile man so he could blackmail our neighbors and friends—and wanted me to help her cover her ass in case it all went to hell."

Oh my God.

"And Sammie, he was a sociopath, been killing small animals since he was little. He was just working his way up to murder and with how he'd been harassing you. He had to be stopped."

I felt like I was in some surreal alternate universe listening as the gentle Mr. Milburn confessed to murdering three people. "*You* killed them?"

"I had to. I knew of their dirty deeds and I helped them escape their punishment, time and time again, hoping they'd change their ways. They didn't, had no intention of doing so. I had to make it right."

As horrible as his confession was, for Belinda to approach him on the anniversary of his wife's death, to push his buttons on that day of all days, I understood why he snapped. And he wasn't wrong about Sammie and Owen, I'd have killed the bastard myself if I had had a gun. It was wrong, so very wrong, and yet…

He turned to the sheriff and handed over his gun. "I had to Dawson."

Sheriff Lenin sounded as if he held the weight of the world on his shoulders when he started reading Mr. Milburn his rights.

I held Abel's hand, sitting next to his bed in the critical care unit. He'd survived the surgery, but the doctors said he wasn't out of the woods yet. He was warm, his large palm pressed against mine. Feeling that heat gave me hope.

He was so still and seeing big, strong Abel so still was unnatural. I didn't even know what I said to him, just wanted him to hear my voice, wanted him to know I was close. Owen was dead. What Mr. Milburn did was wrong, absolutely, but no one was going to miss Owen Madden. And still my heart ached for Mr. Milburn because he'd never see the outside of a jail cell again.

My hand tightened on Abel's. "That day in the bakery, I felt you before I saw you. I think you felt it too. When you looked in my direction, I had never in my life seen anyone more beautiful. I think I fell a bit in love with you in that moment, even when the feelings you stirred, the intensity of them, scared the shit out of me. And later in the alley, even with your cocky arrogance, something inside me was drawn to you. Every part of me wants, no needs, every part of you, so I'll sit here as long as you need me to."

I woke and it took me a minute to realize where I was and then I felt Abel's hand move in mine. My eyes flew to his; pale blue stared back.

"Abel."

He squeezed my hand. "Oh my God, Abel. I need to get the doctors."

His words were as soft as a whisper but as lasting as a brand forever etched on my heart. "I felt you too."

The Hellar home was packed; it was the only place large enough to house everyone and it looked as if the entire town was here. It was Christmas Eve, not really it was well into February but my friends decided to hold off Christmas until after I got out of the hospital. It had been two months since I'd been shot. When I thought of that day, my fucking father putting two bullets in me all for money, it sickened me to know I shared DNA with that fuck.

Learning about Mr. Milburn had been a shock, shit I was still trying to digest the news that he was a serial killer. Shooting Owen right in front of the police station when he was being hauled in. What he'd done was wrong, but why he had done it, I understood. Owen was an asshole, an even bigger one than I'd thought because he had set up most of the people he'd been blackmailing, like Chris Dearly. The man liked younger women and Owen orchestrated a meeting with one who was too young and then milked him for money to keep quiet. And now Owen was dead. I'd never have him darkening my doorstep. If it made me a monster to be fucking thrilled that he was dead, I was okay with that. And Cooper, he lived with Rylee and Jayce now.

Sidney never stopped watching me. I found myself periodically throughout the day feeling her eyes on me. After the scare with the mountain lion, thinking she'd been killed, and knowing what she'd been through with me had been so much worse, yeah I got it. She didn't talk about it, what those two days had to have been like for her especially since she'd lost her first husband so violently. A meltdown was coming, I felt it in every part of my being, but all I could do was be there when she broke.

Cain walked over, dropping on his ass right in front of me. Looking into his eyes, ones that were the exact color of my own, was fucking surreal. He hadn't left my side since I returned from the hospital. He still adored Sidney, no doubt about that, but I had been brought into his inner circle—an extension of her. Sidney had her own Cain and Abel, something she enjoyed saying often.

Tiny settled on the sofa next to me. "Hey man. How you doing?"

"Good. A bit sore but not bad."

He looked down at his hand, whatever he had to say weighed heavily on him. "I shouldn't have left that day."

"Don't."

"He wouldn't have gotten the drop on you if I had been there."

"There was no way to know he planned on making that play."

"Still."

"Tiny. Don't. My father was a fuck and now he's dead and I'm not. Let's move on."

"She never left your side. Not once. And even knowing all that had to be going through her head, she held it together. You have to wonder if she's processed it all yet."

"She hasn't."

"So you're waiting on the storm."

"Yeah, but we'll ride it out together."

"You need anything, give a holler."

"Will do."

"Stella needs my help in the kitchen."

"Doing what?"

"Tasting."

Lucky bastard.

The hairs on my arms stood on end; a jolt, like electricity, burned through me, which had my eyes seeking out Sidney. She was on the other side of the room in a group with the Thompson brothers, Rylee and Jayce but her focus was on me. It was a look I'd never had from her, one I'd seen a lot in the past two months. Blessed was the only word that came to mind to describe it. And as beautiful a sight as it was, it was just another indication that a storm was brewing. I bent my finger to her and her expression changed; this one I preferred, humor and incredulity. She headed toward me, and watching her body move was always a really fucking nice sight.

"Do you need something?" She asked.

"You."

Her face went soft as she settled next to me. "You have that."

Yeah, I fucking did. "Is this a big enough Christmas celebration for you?"

"It's wonderful. I love how practically the whole town is here. But honestly, I'm looking forward to tomorrow night when it's just you and me."

"Amen to that."

Jasper and Lauren were leaving early in the morning. Sidney and I had both encouraged them to stay, but they'd been here the whole two months helping Sidney care for me, keeping the house going and the animals fed. They were good people. The fact that Jasper hadn't even hesitated with the ransom money floored me, but during my time in the hospital he had shared that I was Sidney's family and so I was theirs now too. Good people, really fucking good people.

"How are you feeling?"

"I'm fine, Doc."

"You're stiff and sore."

"Yeah, but considering it's only been two months since I was shot, I'm more than fine."

Her body tensed and she shuttered her eyes. “Can I get you anything?”

Taking her by the chin, I forced her eyes back on me. “You have to deal with it, Sidney. Whatever is going on in that head of yours, you need to let it go. Maybe not now, but baby, you have to let it go.”

“I’m fine.”

“You’re not fine. You’re not sleeping, you watch me like a hawk and you avoid the topic of my shooting whenever it comes up. You haven’t dealt with it, you’ve pushed it aside but sooner or later you’re going to have to deal with it.”

She dismissed that; a smile that didn’t reach her eyes curved her lips. “I really am fine, but now I’m going to see if I can help in the kitchen.”

Her lips touched mine and at least in that she was being honest…warm, hungry and sweet. “I’ll be back.”

I didn’t know when the storm was coming, but it was definitely coming.

Jasper joined me. “How’s she doing?”

“Not good.”

“I feared that. One thing I’ve learned about Sidney, she handles things in her own way. All you can do is be there for her.”

“I ain’t going anywhere.”

“She loved my son, deeply, but when I see her with you it’s something more. After what she lost, to give herself over so completely, it takes a remarkable man to bring someone back from the emotional edge she’d been on. Lauren and I both worried if she’d ever allow another man in and I’ve got to tell you son, I’m damn glad you’re the man she did.”

That tightness in my chest was back and a lump in the back of my throat made talking hard. “Thank you.”

“Now I have to continue on with my mission.” He said as he rose.

“What’s that?”

“Lauren wants eggnog, very spiked eggnog.”

The storm came in the most unlikely way. Our delayed Christmas morning and Sidney and I were drinking coffee on the sofa. A fire was burning; the tree was lit, a new tree since the other had long ago died. I was contemplating pulling her onto my lap, my cock getting hard at the thought. We hadn't exchanged gifts, circumstances as they were we didn't get around to it. Normally, Sidney pressed right up against me, but that morning she kept herself at a bit of a distance. She wasn't drinking her coffee, which she usually downed her first cup and was onto cup two before I'd even started mine. The animals were scattered around the room, but she barely acknowledged them. Her focus was on the flames dancing up the chimney, her eyes grew bright and one tear rolled down her cheek.

"I didn't get you a Christmas present."

"Don't need one."

"It's your first Christmas. You should have a present."

"I have you. Only present I want."

Her body jerked, like my words physically hurt her, and then she was up, her mug slamming down hard on the coffee table as she ran from the room.

"Sidney?" I was up after her but she'd already cleared the front door and was running down the drive. She didn't have on shoes, it was fucking cold outside, but she didn't seem to notice. Then she just stopped, dropped to her knees and bent her body in half. Her sobs were loud, pained, as if her very soul wept. I scooped her up and she curled into my body like a child, her face burrowed into my neck as her body convulsed with the force of her tears.

I carried her back to the living room, grabbed the blanket she'd bought and insisted we needed, and wrapped her in it, my hold on her never easing.

"Let it out, baby."

She cried until she physically wore herself out and when she slept, I carried her to bed and stayed with her. All day and into the night, she went from tears to sleep. It was early the following morning when sleep finally claimed me. When I woke, I stretched and reached for Sidney. Her side of the bed was cold. I glanced at the clock and realized I'd only been asleep for two hours. Sitting up, I rubbed my hands over my face. My chest hurt like a bitch and then I grinned. Doc was right. That expression made no fucking sense.

Climbing from bed, I went in search of her. I wondered how she'd be after yesterday. My hope was the cry released it all, that she had finally let it go. Walking into the kitchen, the coffee wasn't on. There were no mugs sitting out. Cain stood by the door and a glance outside showed that Sidney's car was gone. I hunted down my phone and called her, but it went straight to voice mail. I called Rylee.

"Hey Abel. I was going to call you. How's our girl?"

"Is she there?"

"No. What happened?"

Concern churned in my gut, the first pang of fear iced my blood.

"Abel, what happened?"

"She broke down yesterday, cried all day and into the night. She was gone when I woke."

"I'm guessing you tried calling her."

"Yeah."

"Maybe she's at the clinic. I'll run over and give you a call."

"I'll meet you there."

I got dressed, found my keys, but that fear was taking root. For Sidney to leave without a word, after yesterday, we weren't going to find her at the clinic. She left. Just the thought of it hurt worse than the bullets I took to the chest, but I knew it in every part of me. She left me.

I left him. Ran with no destination in mind but to get away. I didn't get far, couldn't because leaving him hurt more than almost losing him. I finally got it, sitting in my car on the side of a country road outside of Sheridan. Life wasn't about longevity; it was about quality. Loss hurt, love hurt more, but even knowing I would lose Jake, I would have done it all the same. And Abel, he was alive; he was here. I hadn't lost him, but seeing him on the floor of that abandoned shack, his blood staining the old wood haunted me. He had come so close and every time I was at the Roberts' farm I was forced to remember him lying there so still, forced to remember every feeling from those two wretched days in vivid detail. I'd never find peace with those demons clawing to get out. Reaching for my phone, I called Keith.

"Sidney, people are looking for you."

My heart twisted, but I had to purge the memory if Abel and I were ever to find peace. "I have a favor to ask."

ABEL

Six hours had passed, the longest fucking six hours of my life. Keith called, told me where to find Sidney. She was at the shack where Owen had dumped me. I pulled my bike next to her car and shut off the engine. She was there and the sight of her actually made my fucking knees weak. Her hair was pulled up, she wore gloves and in her hand was a sledgehammer. So focused on her task she didn't hear me. She was pounding the shit out of the building and every hit I bet was cathartic, releasing the last of the ugly that still haunted her. I fucking got it; I'd be doing the same had the roles been reversed. Keith had stacked a few sledgehammers, so I reached for one. I approached, her head turned, her eyes found me. Tears ran down her face, but she smiled. The sight of it settled in my chest. Without a word, I joined her in beating back her demons.

sidney

He had come. I wasn't sure he would when I asked Keith to call him. He joined me in tearing down the building, giving us back control over a situation we'd had no control over. We hadn't been at it long when the others started showing up. Rylee and Jayce first before the trickle turned into a wave as our friends and family helped us tear down the last link to Owen Madden and the horror he brought into our lives.

I stood there long after the shack had been reduced to splinters, after everyone had left. Abel stood near, but we hadn't spoken a word.

I needed to apologize, opened my mouth to do so when he said, "You left." He sounded so remote, distant.

"I'm sorry. I shouldn't have—"

"Six hours."

"I shouldn't have left."

"Six hours; six fucking hours."

"Forgive me. I panicked, got scared. You were so still in that hospital and the thought of losing you."

He moved so fast, his long strides eating the distance between us until I was pressed tight against his chest. "Six hours I walked around without my fucking heart."

I exhaled on a sob and pressed my face to his chest.

"I get why you left. You've been through this before and you almost had to go through it again."

I looked into his tear filled, pale eyes. "That's just it. I lost Jake and it tore me apart, but the idea of losing you. I can't imagine a world without you, know that there is no way I'd ever come back from it."

"You didn't lose me."

"I know and that's what I realized. I didn't get far, just outside of town, because it hurt more to leave you."

His fingers pulled through my hair. "Even if we only get a month, a year, I'd take that over days like the last six hours. Never needed anyone never wanted anyone and then you walked into my life. And now I can't imagine living without you. We can't know tomorrow, but we can sure as fuck live for now."

"I'm so sorry I left."

"Don't do it again." The seriousness of his tone, the steely determination in his eyes, I knew I'd hurt him.

"Never."

"Whatever happens, we're in this together. You opened this world up to me and now you're stuck. I'm not letting you fucking walk away."

I ran my finger over his whiskered cheek. "Forgive me."

"I already have." He kissed me, sweetly at first before it turned hot, wet and hungry.

I stepped into the bakery, the scents of cinnamon wafting out onto the street. The line was to the door as people happily waited their turn. I felt the air charge as a shiver of awareness moved through me. My eyes moved down the line to the man in the front with the messy bun and beard. His head turned and those pale eyes landed on me. He moved toward me with a graceful, deliberate stride and his focus was unwavering. He moved right up into my personal space. His scent teased my nose and my body ached being so near him. A grin appeared on his mouth, just the slight lifting of his lips on the one side.

"I told you once you could kneel in front of me any time."

I slapped his arm because his words had taken me completely out of the moment. "Abel!"

He laughed, a rich sound that settled over me in the most wonderful way. He dropped to his knee and my heart stopped beating. He pulled something from his pocket, but his intense gaze never left my face. "I love you Sidney, can't imagine living a day without you. Marry me, make a life with me."

My knees went weak, buckled as I dropped to them. I had to touch him, my hands wrapping around his face, my thumb stroking his lip.

"Yes."

His ring was so Abel. An iron band, worked smooth to the touch and resting atop it a brilliant cut diamond. He slipped it on and all those pieces that had made up my life for so long melted together and like that iron were made stronger.

He leaned in, his lips touching mine when he whispered, "Let's climb into the back of your car and celebrate the moment properly."

I couldn't help the eye roll.

"On second thought, let's go back to the cabin since I plan on celebrating all night." All the air left my lungs in a rush as he stood and threw me over his shoulder.

"Abel, I can walk."

"I know, but this is so much more fun. Wanted to do this that day in the alley."

"You did?"

"Yeah, looking like you do and throwing out that attitude, fucking hot as hell."

Enjoying that little insight I hadn't realized we reached his bike until he dropped me gently to my feet. "And now mine."

"I think I was even then."

"I know you were."

"Smug bastard."

"But right."

He reached for my hand, ran his thumb over his ring, before straddling his bike. "Let's go, babe, we're burning daylight."

I climbed on, linked my hands at his waist and rested my chin on his shoulder. "Let's go home."

His head twisted, "I'm already home, baby, but let's get back to the cabin so I can celebrate with my woman properly."

God, I loved him and feeling playful I asked, "What's considered properly?"

"Naked."

His engine drowned out my laugh and his and then we were rolling down the street, me holding him so tightly it was hard to say where I ended and he began and I wouldn't have had it any other way.

"Doc, I'll help you."

"I'm fine, Abel."

"Babe, wait for me."

Her exaggerated exhale started the bout of giggles that came from the back seat. Looking back at our two-year-old daughter, Annie, I grinned. She was the spitting image of Doc right down to the attitude. I wasn't sure about kids, didn't know the kind of father I would be having the kind of father I had, but as soon as she was born it was like a piece of my heart that had been missing had found its way home. "What are you giggling about, baby girl?"

"Help me up." Her hands were raised as she wiggled her fingers.

"Let me get mama out first."

"Poppy kiss mama."

Sidney's head lowered, her shoulders shaking with laughter. Annie had started this about a month ago. Caught Doc and me kissing in the kitchen and now demanded we do it at her beck and call.

"Not now."

Her lower lip turned into a pout, but then a puppy walked by the truck and she forgot all about me not kissing her mama. I hadn't forgotten about it though, intended to sneak a few while we searched for our Christmas tree.

Coming around to Sidney, Cain standing at her side, I couldn't believe she wanted to come. She was due any day now. "Are you sure you don't want to sit in the truck?"

"It's tradition, Abel, all of us looking for the tree together."

She was very big on traditions, ones we shared with our friends and family and ones that were just ours. I gave her shit about it, but I loved the traditions we were creating too. "You get tired, I want to know."

"Okay."

Her hand moved down my cheek, her eyes taking on that softness I'd grown used to seeing in the four years we'd been married. "Love you."

Poppy did kiss mama, long and hard. Annie clapped in approval before I took her from her car seat. Usually she wanted up on my shoulders, a total daddy's girl, but since Doc started showing Annie usually stayed close to her. Like right now, they walked ahead of me with Cain between them. Doc was pointing to trees and Annie rejected them with a shake of her head. Like her mom, Annie loved all things Christmas. At one point, they stopped and stared. I knew they'd found the tree, but it was the sight of Sidney running her hand down Annie's hair that had an ache burning in my chest. She did that a lot, something so simple, and yet the love behind the gesture humbled me. A family of my very own, un-fucking-believable.

Annie was sleeping by the fire. Cain lay next to her. His affection shifted a bit after she was born. Annie didn't make a move without Cain right at her side. It seemed fitting, I had Abel and Annie had Cain. I never thought I'd feel so loved, so complete. All that happened in my life, every bump in the road, every ray of light had all led me here. Standing in a rustic cabin in Wyoming, my baby girl sleeping with her wolf, my son kicking me in the belly and my heart in the kitchen pouring me eggnog. I was blessed and every day I took a moment to appreciate just how much. Sandbar rubbed up against my leg. Even he had settled in, found his place. He walked from me and curled up at Annie's back near where Tigger and Stuart were sleeping.

I reached for an ornament and then froze. My water broke. Abel walked into the room, took one look at me and froze too.

"What's wrong?"

"My water broke."

He didn't hesitate, moving to the phone to call Ichabod. We had a list of people, went down that list when we needed people to watch Annie. Otherwise, they fought about it. "It's time." He hung up and called Jasper. They were staying at Hellar Farm for both Christmas and the birth. "It's time. Ichabod is on his way. We'll see you at the hospital."

He moved to me, his hands coming to rest on my stomach. "I'll get your bag in the truck. As soon as Ichabod gets here, we'll go. You okay? Do you need anything?"

I linked my fingers through his. "Just you."

"You've got that." He pressed his lips to mine and let them linger. "In case I forget to tell you later, thank you."

I smiled because I never tired of seeing the softer side of Abel. "For your son?"

"For my life." And for just a flash, I saw the depth of what that meant to him, before his lips turned up into a grin. He kissed me then strolled to our bedroom. Yep, I was blessed.

Twelve hours of labor and two of pushing and our son entered the world. For the next several hours, my room was a parade of people coming to welcome him. Rylee and Jayce arrived first, their son,

Michael, holding on tightly to his daddy's hand.

"Oh my God, he's so beautiful. Look at his little hands," Rylee cooed while Jayce grinned. Her gaze moved to mine before she whispered, "All the pieces make a life."

I reached for Rylee's hand. She was so right.

Duncan and Carly came in next and seeing Carly's round belly had tears prickling my eyes. She had found her way, she had conquered her addiction, and now they were expecting their first child in a few months. Mimi made her co-owner of the floral shop with the intent of handing it over to her when she retired. And Duncan had the racing branch of Hellar Farm growing at an obscene rate. He too had found his place and Domino, Speckled Egg's colt, was a racing champion.

Jasper and Lauren, who were grandparents to Annie, she even called them grandma and grandpa, followed after. Lauren's face went soft when she held our son, a part of her thinking of Jake I was sure. "What's his name?"

Abel, who hadn't left my side, looked to me. "I named Annie. It's your turn, Abel."

"I'd like to name him after Tiny, his given name, but not for a first name."

"What is Tiny's real name?"

"Percival."

No wonder he went by Tiny. Jasper was more kind in his response. "It's a strong name."

The look Abel shot Jasper had us all laughing.

"And the first name?" I asked.

"Family, I never really understood the concept, not until you, Doc. But it isn't about blood and DNA. It's about the people in your life that mean something, the ones you turn to in times of great joy and pain. It's the ones that lift you up or hold you up, the ones who leave you with more of yourself than you had without them. My son, I'd like to name him Jake because he left Sidney with more of herself than she had without him and she has given me more of myself than I had without her."

The sob burned up my throat, not from pain, but love for this man. "God, I love you."

He touched his lips to mine, but his focus shifted to Jasper and Lauren. Both were very quiet, touching baby Jake as tears streamed down their faces. Lauren's head lifted, her hazel eyes shining in tears. "Thank you."

Baby Jake was asleep in my arms, Annie slept between Abel and me and Abel's head was on my pillow as he touched Jake's toes. "He's beautiful."

"He is. He looks just like you. Those pale eyes and black hair."

"We make good looking kids, babe. We should have at least two more."

"Okay."

"Just like that."

I looked into those pale eyes. "Kids with you, yeah, just like that."

His hand spread over my belly. "How are you feeling?"

"Sore, but okay."

"He's a big boy."

"Just like his daddy."

"You do know what this means, right?"

"No."

"You're going to be healing for a while, so looks like I'll be getting you on your knees quite a bit in the next few months."

And even feeling drained, exhausted, sore from pushing his son out of me, my body sizzled at the thought. Still. "Your children are here."

"Yeah, babe, because you *were* on your knees."

"Parenthood has not matured you at all."

"Nope."

"I'm glad. I like you just the way you are."

Humor shifted to tenderness before he said, "Had someone

told me I'd ever be here, my children pressed close and you looking at me like that, I'd have told them they were fucking nuts. Never been so happy to be wrong. You thanked me once for bringing you back to life. Thank you for giving me a life."

I kissed him, couldn't form a reply even if I wanted to, the emotions were too close to the surface. At ten, I had wondered where I would end up, who would ever want me, who would ever love me. I held Jake tighter, touched Annie's hair and kissed Abel deeper. My answer was all around me.

Sometimes you write a book that just tears you up and this was that book for me. Creating such a wonderful character in Jake and knowing his fate was hard. But the backstory for Sidney and Jake was needed to make the parallel to Abel and Sidney's story. I love Sidney and how she just keeps going even when life is constantly knocking her down. And Abel, he is my very favorite of all the male leads I've written. He's cocky, arrogant and yet an undeniably good person. Sheridan, Wyoming is a real town, one that I have never been to but would really like to visit. I took creative license in how I described it, all but the mountains that really rest up against the town like a magnificent sentry.

Tigger was named after my own Tigger—an orange Maine Coon who died a few years ago. He was my sidekick, always with me, even came when I called him. And when my first-born came home, like Cain and Annie, there are no pictures of her without him standing in the background. Losing him was like losing a little piece of myself.

Stuart was named after my first car that I gave to my sister. For almost twenty-four years he got her where she had to go. It's a car, but me, my kids, my sister and even my husband cried seeing the tow truck driving him away.

And Sandbar, fashioned after our cat Salem—handsome as sin and nasty to the core, unless you're feeding him.

To the Beta Beauties who not only give fantastic feedback on story flow and character development, but who I also consider my friends, even having never personally met most of you. A love of books brought us together, but it's just plain old love that keeps us together. You're the best and I am working on t-shirts... Audrey, Amber, Ana Kristina, Andie, Dawn, Devine, Donna, Kellyanne, Kimmy, Lauren, Markella, Meredith, Michelle, Raj, Sarah, Sue, Trish and Yolanda.

Trish Bacher—the Editor in Heels—my copy editor. Once again your attention to detail astounds me. I love collaborating with you and can't wait for the next project.

Thank you, Amy Giles, for your proofreading expertise. And thanks for reaching out for no other reason than your love of books and Indie authors. I believe this is the start of a fabulous relationship.

Melissa Stevens, the Illustrated Author. I am in awe of you. The typeset you've created is incredible. And the title page art, the painting of Abel you created, it's like you climbed into my brain and captured the exact image I was hoping to bring to life. You are amazing.

Lisa DeSpain, I don't know how you get into the code of the document and bring all the typeset to life for the eBook. I think if I did know the how of it my eyes would roll into the back of my head, but it's a work of art when you're done. Thank you.

Hang Le, the bar was set high because I simply adore your covers and yet you completely blew me away. I freaking love this cover. It so perfectly represents the story and is just visually exquisite. Thank you, thank you, thank you!

To my twin sister, Audrey, and Michelle, my sister from another mother, who read all of my books first—your tireless support means more than I could ever say. And one of these days we'll all be on the same side of the Atlantic. I'll buy the first round.

To my husband and children, love is not strong enough a word.

And Artemis, my precious dog who never leaves my side—my companion and my friend. I love you beautiful girl.

The Beautifully series…

Beautifully Damaged
Beautifully Forgotten
Beautifully Decadent

The Harrington Maine series

Waiting for the One
Just Me

Standalones

His Light in the Dark
A Glimpse of the Dream
Always and Forever
Collecting the Pieces
Devil You Know coming 2017
TBD Title coming 2017

To learn more about what's coming, follow L.A. Fiore...
https://www.facebook.com/l.a.fiore.publishing
https://www.facebook.com/groups/lafemmefabulousreaders
https://twitter.com/lafioreauthor
https://www.instagram.com/lafiore.publishing

Send her an email at: **lafiore.publishing@gmail.com**
Or check out her website: **www.lafiorepublishing.com**